The Fate Weaver

THE FATE WEAVER

A Novel in Two Centuries

by Jill M. Phillips

A BIRCH LANE PRESS BOOK
Published by Carol Publishing Group

A Birch Lane Press Book
Published by Carol Publishing Group
Birch Lane Press is a registered trademark of Carol Communications, Inc.

Editorial Offices: 600 Madison Avenue, New York, N.Y. 10022
Sales & Distribution Offices: 120 Enterprise Avenue, Secaucus,
N.J. 07094

In Canada: Canadian Manda Group, P.O. Box 920, Station U,
Toronto, Ontario M8Z 5P9
Queries regarding rights and permissions should be addressed to
Carol Publishing Group, 600 Madison Avenue, New York, N.Y. 10022

Carol Publishing Group books are available at special discounts
for bulk purchases, for sales promotions, fund raising, or
educational purposes. Special editions can be created to specifications.
For details, contact: Special Sales Department, Carol Publishing
Group, 120 Enterprise Avenue, Secaucus, N.J. 07094

Manufactured in the United States of America
10 9 8 7 6 5 4 3 2 1

Library of Congress Cataloging-in-Publication Data

Phillips, Jill M.
    The fate weaver : a novel in two centuries / by Jill Phillips.
        p.   cm.
    "A Birch Lane Press book."
    ISBN 1-55972-102-2
    I. Title.
PS3566.H47927F37   1992
    813'.54—dc20   92-9354
                                                        CIP

To D. and D.
Who know why, and how much

But thou that art highest of the Gods most high
That art lord if we live, that art lord if we die,
Have heed of the tongues of our terror that cry
For a grace to the children of Earth . . .
                                    —Swinburne
                                    Erechtheus

PROLOGUE

Dies Irae

Europe, 1348–49

As they prepared to land at Dover the dead came out to meet them: a hundred bodies lifting with the tide. England, hag-ridden with plague, had set some of her unfortunate sons adrift. Now they bobbed like wood in water, and no one dared to look at them for very long.

Alicia crossed herself in fear and someone at her elbow muttered "Jesu!" Adelina clutched her sister's hand and pointed to a place far down the shore beyond the citadel. Someone had planted a black silk banner there—the wind rippled it like Adelina's raven hair—and Death's face floated over all.

*   *   *

They called it *Pestis atra,* the plague, the pestilence, the "death," and no one knew where it came from, but everyone knew that it killed. Boils on the body brought death within a week; chills and fever could kill a strong man in a single day. The pagan East had bred it: returning travelers told of strange omens in the year 1346 when fire fell from the sky and mountains crumbled and serpents grew the length of dragons. Millions died in earthquakes and floods and the famines that came after, and lay unburied where they fell. Clouds of contagion gathered and drifted toward the West. Europe convulsed, and waited.

Some said England would be spared because God favored Edward Plantagenet over Philip de Valois in their war. French power was on the wane and Philip seemed powerless to restore it; God pity the luck of any man who followed three hundred years of direct Capetian lineage to the throne. Philip had known minor successes in the early period of his reign: he managed to impress his knights and nobles with lavish entertainments and a general show of luxury, but it could not make up for all his losses in the field. Since the most recent great defeat at Crécy, it had become common to blame each new misfortune on the king, and when the burghers of Calais gave up their keys to Edward and his army, the doomsayers lamented France's fate and said that King Philip was cursed.

In England some men said King Edward had overreached himself invading France, that in so doing he had violated the sacredness of Christendom's most ancient state. Monarchs: some great, some small, all greedy. Claims and counterclaims: what did they matter to the Common Man? Kings alone it seemed could bring down the wrath of God, but when they did, all men suffered equally beneath His hand.

Now this new misery had been set upon them as a judgment. Men prayed for deliverance; then, as all about them perished, they prayed for death. At last, left to fear and wretchedness and the profound neglect of their Creator, they wondered if He listened, or if He even lived at all.

*   *   *

At the end of January in the year 1348 Jacques Daumier, a prosperous draper of Marseilles, made ready for the marriage of his two daughters. They were a highly desirable commodity: modest and beautiful (one black-haired, the other blond), they were also very young; Jacques knew he would have no trouble in finding husbands for them. But when the plans were finally drawn, he had done even better than he hoped. Alicia was betrothed to a Burgundian chevalier, and Adelina to a handsome gentleman of Champagne. Both men had vague yet indisputable collateral lineage links to the new Valois dynasty, something to tickle the pride of any ambitious artisan.

But plague came to Marseilles before the bridegrooms, and in March the Daumier family fled north, toward Paris. Their progress was slow, impeded by danger. Everyone was seeking sanctuary from the infected south in Paris and Rouen; theft and violence were common on the road. Jacques's family traveled only a few hours each day and by unfrequented roads. At night they slept in sheds or abandoned forest huts and took their food where they could find it.

It was July before they reached the outer environs of the capital, but once again the plague had shown its face before them. Soon Jacques and his wife fell afoul of it; a week later both were dead. Poor Alicia and Adelina had to pay a cartman ten *livres* to take away the bodies of their parents. At the Cemetery of the Innocents near Chausée St. Lazare, the king had caused a pit to be dug to receive the bodies of all common victims of the plague. There, without prayer or priestly ceremony, the Daumiers were put in with all the rest.

August brought heat and stench to a city gone mad with panic. King Philip and his kin had removed themselves to Normandy, and most of the city's nobles had gone with him. Those without carts or horses and those too sick to steal them were compelled by circumstance to stay behind in Paris. At the Hôtel-Dieu, a hospital on Ile de la Cité beside the crumbling Roman wall, the sick died by hundreds every day on pallets made of straw and some in beds bequeathed by the canons of Notre Dame, till it seemed no one in the city would survive.

Parentless and therefore unprotected, most of their money gone, the Daumier sisters were forced into a life of degradation. They stole what food they could find and sold worthless amulets against the plague. More often they gave themselves to strangers in return for bits of bread and cheese or a little wine. Their shame was secondary to the fear that these unknown men might infect them, and each night they checked the secret hollows of their bodies for signs of buboes.

By mid-October the plague was at its height. Alicia and Adelina knew they must leave Paris or eventually succumb. So they walked the fifty miles to Amiens; a farmer's heavy cart took them the remaining distance to Boulogne. On the shore, in the shadow of Caligula's ancient lighthouse, a thousand exiles waited passage to the only sanctuary that remained.

When they saw what waited for them, the sisters despaired of where to go. They knew London lay somewhere northwest along the pilgrim road to Canterbury, but it would be folly to go there. If it was not already stricken, it soon would be, with a group of mendicants huddled at the tomb of Thomas à Becket, who, it was said, could work miracles on earth. It was no use to find themselves a city; Paris had been nightmare enough for them.

Hopelessly lost and frightened, they took the southern road along the beach, which led toward Hastings. Hungry, hand in hand, they stumbled down the rugged path in silence. The lilac sky intensified to purple, the craggy outline of the cliffs went black. A wind came up. They slept along the shore.

*   *   *

BOOK ONE

House of the Allfather

Alfriston, East Sussex
August 1349

On a gentle rise just above the downland coast of Sussex can be seen the huge likeness of a man cut into the chalk. Naked, he holds a staff in each hand. He has been called the Long Man of Wilmington, or more cryptically, the Long Man with Staves. He is the largest hill figure in all of England. His genesis is unknown.

* * *

In the anteroom beyond the great hall they were playing ragman's roll. Justine was in Simon's private closet at the opposite end of the manor house, but she could hear them through the open door. There would be explanations to make if the Lady Eleanora came within. Justine had been told to keep to the apartment she had been given. Eleanora called such behavior "probity," but Justine understood that her aunt was merely jealous. She was nothing but a crabbed, bitter woman, peaked with ill health, and old. And what attentions could such a woman—her behavior solidified by a lifetime of exactness to convention—expect from her yet virile lord and husband?

Justine Liré, made a widow at fifteen by Crécy, was waiting to be made a bride once more. Her uncle, lord of Goat's Rue and all Alfriston, had promised to find another man to be her mate. But seven months had passed since she had come to live here at the edge of the great forest, and the promise was as yet unfulfilled.

She had faith in her uncle, though. He was a quite remarkable

9

man, this Simon de Falaise. The surname had long since been corrupted to "Fallas," but Simon, proud of a Norman heritage which included the founder of his line Guy de Falaise (who had crossed with William of Normandy and been given Goat's Rue as his portion), trotted out its French antecedent on occasion. Justine liked that, because she felt her own Angevin blood strongly, and found it impossible to believe the French had killed her husband. It was true that she had hardly known him, but in any case a husband absent was better than no husband at all.

And now she had none; time was growing short. She was only a petty noble after all. Her mother, Simon's sister and the youngest child of nine, had married a justiciar, when lack of a proper dowery had left her little choice. Justine had managed a far better alliance when her turn to marry came: wed at thirteen to one of King Edward's lieutenants, a man with considerable estates. But she was his second wife and had borne him no children, so when he died, his wealth went to the issue of his first conjugation. There was little left for her, save a tiny pension. Her own parents had taken her once more to their hearth. But they could offer no brilliant betrothal contract for a daughter with neither wealth nor virginity to give. They could recommend a few good and honest working gentlemen, but Justine balked at each. One William Brent, a tapissier *who had learned his art in Flanders, was sent away without an interview.*

Justine had set her heart on someone rich. She understood what that would mean and was young enough to regret it. The man her uncle found for her might be old and have not one tooth left inside his head. Yet she would marry him if he had money enough to please her purse. She hated the tawdriness of being poor, the constant need to make do and fix a sleeve because a new gown was an expense beyond her means. She did not wish to live out her life the pensioner of a ghost.

At least here at Goat's Rue there were alternatives to penury and boredom. There was always some bal masque *or feast day celebration, some group of visiting nobles with their households and bachelor knights to entertain. Here at least she had a chance to show herself, to be the tiny center of a swirling universe. In time someone would find her, some rich man eager to make her his wife.*

Till that time came, however, Justine had other hungers to appease. Her husband had taught her to enjoy the bedroom arts, and two and a half years of chastity since his death had made her greedy. It had taken but a few days at Goat's Rue for Justine to make a place for herself in Simon's bed. From their first meeting she had seen the lust shining in his eyes whenever he looked at her, felt his hand always trailing beneath the table at meals, ever searching for a prize.

So now they were lovers, and all things were good within her world—for now. Still there was no bridegroom in sight, and at times Justine felt her nerves failing her. Outside her comfortable existence times were hard. Might not such troubles creep their way into her life in time?

Money was hard sought and harder found since the last great battle with the French. There had been crop failures, and this made for food shortages and riots in the cities. In the country, people kept more to themselves, since fear of the plague had settled on them like miasma. Somewhere across that stretch of sea that separated France and England, a dark, invisible sickness waited. Some said it was the witchwork of Joan, Queen of France, who in a fury at her husband's defeat by Edward Plantagenet had put the curse of death on England.

There was talk it had already settled in the green hills of the West Country, rumors that when London fell to it, there would be lawlessness and murder. But that was talk for fools, surely: if God loved England (as He had shown favor to her above France) no pestilence would come; all would be well. All the same, whenever she heard such talk, Justine, her soul overlaid with guilt for sins too easily accomplished, would cross her breast in show of pious seriousness and breathe a hasty prayer. In times such as these a little care for one's own soul was wise.

At last realizing that Simon was otherwise occupied this morning, Justine left his room and went into her own to bathe and dress her hair. There were guests come to sup this evening, including the abbot of St. Audric, Geoffrey Fitzstephen. Justine had heard much of him; he was apparently a prelate of great fame. Simon called him a man of considerable wisdom and less charity. Presumably this reflected their periodic differences regarding land rents and tithes—they were the two highest-ranking lords in the district.

She stripped off her *cotte* and shift and stood for a long time appraising her image in the silver mirror. Justine loved to see her body naked. She had a tall, slim figure and the kind of small, high breasts favored by the fashions of the day. Her legs and arms were delicate, yet shapely, and her skin the color of ivory. How beautiful she was! How wonderful it was to be young and beautiful with all her life before her. . . .

Justine bent closer to the mirror, a comb clutched in her hand, and began to brush her hair with heavy strokes. At table, or in audience with gentlefolk, she kept her long and glossy brown hair well braided, looping each braid at the ear. But sometimes she left it as it was now, as unbound as a maiden's. It would sway and move as she did, brushing her delicate cheeks ever so lightly as she bent forward, absorbed in some sewing chore or act of reading. Her eyes were brown too, and showed flecks of gold when she was merry. They were well shaped, like almonds from the East.

From her pearwood chest she took the gown that she would wear this evening. She had sewn it herself with panels of gold and purple velvet that Simon had brought back from London for her. She had made it according to French design. Justine had always loved "dressing French," as did most ladies who cared for their appearance, though recently such ways had somewhat disappeared from general favor. It was enough for English women to copy those "damned attenuated sleeves" or "funnels of folly" as the Church was like to judge them. Justine cared nothing for what the dictates of religion had to say about such things. What mattered that? What could God know of dresses?

After her bath Justine smoothed her skin with pumice, then applied a perfume distilled of rosewater and fragrant oils. Simon would want her tonight. He was an ardent lover for a man of fifty; she only hoped whatever man she wed would be as good. She dressed, a smile curving her cherried mouth. How pleasing it would be to flaunt her secret station. But, oh, the consequence of such an act! Public penances for Simon, the nunnery for her. And all because they took a little pleasure from the parts God gave them.

Idle steps carried her through the hall and out onto the little porch above the garden. The tiny gold bells stitched to the toes of her pointed gold silk slippers tinkled merrily as she went. The garden was a fine place, one of the loveliest in the district, in bloom year round, despite the season. Where Justine stood now a ridge of hawthorn cut off her view of the silver fishpond. At her feet was spread an array of flowers as colorful as any Saracen carpet.

Rowan was just beyond: the handsome, fool-faced servitor whose duty it was to feed the dogs and mind the livestock. At times he did a little gardening too, but he was hopeless at it. Today he swung his pruning hook in clumsy arcs at the sweeping branches of the winter-blooming willow. She was lucky to have come upon him in the midst of such a chore. Silent, Justine watched him for a while, waiting for him to take notice of where she stood.

Ho! he'd seen her, she could tell by the way his face suddenly went red. Ever since the first day Justine had come to Goat's Rue and seen him looking at her, she had made it her game to tease him. It was harmless, surely; how many servants (though there were few handsomer than Rowan) were treated to such innocent dalliance with a member of the lord's own household?

"Would you be master here, Rowan?" she called out to him and saw how he hid his face behind his hands. It was what she said to him each day since the time she'd seen him self-crowned with a wreath of shrubbery. He was a silly lout, grinning at her like that, not daring to come close, though her smile dared him. How perverse Nature was to create a poor man with such broad shoulders and eyes the color of blue flowers.

She heaved a little sigh of discontent. And to think the man she got would just as likely have stinking breath and fart at table. Life could be marvelously unfair. She wanted riches at the sacrifice of all else, it was true. But despite it all, there were times when Justine's silly and romantic heart beguiled other wishes, other dreams.

Laughing, she leaned to the railing and cried out, "Here's for you, my timid lover!" Then she pulled a length of violet ribbon from her sleeve and cast it lightly toward him.

In honor of the abbot's visit, Justine had been instructed by her aunt to behave more modestly than usual, to cast her eyes downward when he spoke. Justine thought this was foolish; the abbot was no doubt a man much like other men in all his parts; why must one act as if a churchman were a saint simply because he'd given his life to God? All the same, she would do whatever Eleanora asked. Justine depended too greatly on her favor to disobey. A few ill-timed words in Simon's ear could send her back to a life as pensioner at the hands of her late husband's miserly relations. Simon wanted her, but he would not openly defy his wife.

Jacquelyn, the spindly, simpering daughter of the house, was directing arrangements for the meal and ordering the food placements when Justine came down. Lady Eleanora was often indisposed by poor health, and at such times Jacquelyn acted in her place as *chatelaine,* taking that meagre burden far too seriously, for she was herself only twenty and but two years married, her husband serving as a provost to the mayor of Brighton.

The two young women exchanged malicious smiles and complimented each other falsely on their gowns. Justine passed through on her way to the garden, there to gather up a clutch of flowers for the abbot's table setting. *And what would you think, my dear cousin, if you knew I had dallied with your groom on these very steps?* Justine wondered. But she said nothing, and bent to pull the flowers from their beds.

At supper that evening Eleanora complained about the quality of food and sent her dish back to the kitchen for a second time.

"These cooks are villainous," she grumbled to her husband. "All this fancy French food puts boils on my back. I want plain food without sauces, cooked in salt and drippings the way we English like it best."

Simon, who enjoyed his food cooked any way by anyone, shot a scowl to his wife. "Nonsense, woman, even the King has his French cooks."

"Aye, as he no doubt has his French whores," she answered bitterly. "When men have a taste for food or fucking, they inevitably turn to France. But that's no endorsement of quality, my husband . . ."

Simon winked at Justine, who sat between them. "You like it well enough, aye, girl? Pigeon baked in honeyed apples? Now there's a treat, I'd say."

Justine nodded, dappling her fingers in the water dish. "And plum cosy, that's my favorite." She looked up at him with expectation in her eyes. *Shall I take the place of this shrew in your bed tonight?*

The talk between the men was all of soldiering and politics, the abbot showing himself to be a man of worldly knowledge as well as sacred learning. He was a good table guest, entertaining if not actually witty, though Simon missed being able to tell his usual round of ribald stories during the meal. Even if the abbot was no prude, such talk would not be seemly in his presence. So with grudging good taste the lord of Alfriston held his tongue.

"I saw a curious thing on waking this morning," the abbot confessed to Lady Eleanora as they shared a fingerbowl. "There was a waxwing on my balcony, just at dawn. Some might call that an omen."

"Indeed," she replied, "but London's full of them, I hear. It's all these damn fools bringing them back from the East, as if England hadn't birds enough. The one you saw was probably such as that, escaped."

"Most likely, but it unsettled me all the same," the abbot answered, neatly shelling an egg and rolling it in a dish of crushed herbs. "I do not hearken after superstitions myself, of course. But there are those who would count a waxwing as a messenger of ill intent."

"The plague?" Simon asked, looking up surprised, a bit of beef dangling from the corner of his mouth. He shook his head. "It doesn't bear repeating, Geoffrey. We've all troubles enough and need no more. I'll leave such talk for gray-haired grandmams at their hearths."

"Talk won't bring plague, nor will it keep it away," the abbot answered tersely. "There are stories from the West Country, rumors of whole villages accursed. *And* talk of omens . . ."

Justine looked up, suddenly interested. "I heard such a tale," she boasted. "It was told me at matins just last week by a gentlewoman of Wilmington." She lifted her cup and sipped at it daintily before continuing. "She told how a woman in her own household, a servant, had gone to the river's edge to draw some water for washing. As she approached, she saw another woman already there. Mistaking her for someone she already knew, the servant called out a greeting. At that moment the other woman turned to show herself. But she was no human woman. She had the gaunt white face of a spectre, and a red scarf was twisted round her neck. Is that not the spectre of the Plague Maiden?''

For a moment after she had finished speaking all that could be heard was meat hissing in the fireplace. Justine's tale had shocked them all to silence. Finally it was Eleanor who spoke up. "Hear now, girl: such things are no fit talk for table. You'll have the abbot thinking we're a bunch of fools who put our trust in omens.''

"But he himself said—" she began, protesting.

"Indeed," Geoffrey Fitzstephen answered, "this subject was my doing, I'm afraid. I ask you to pardon me; we'll speak no more of it.'' He turned immediately to Simon. "Have you heard the bad news from Pevensey? They've lost another hundred acres of ditched fields to the flooding. . . .''

So the men talked, as Eleanora picked glumly through her meat, pushing half of it aside. At last, when she had drained her cup a second time, she turned to Simon. "This wine is over-sweet,'' she complained.

He shot her an instantly reproving look. "How unkind you are! Why, the monks of St. Audric made it from their own fruit. It tastes well enough to me.''

"I don't care if Christ Jesus pressed the berries himself,'' she mumbled. "It still tastes like slop and swallows like swill.''

The abbot, shocked, looked up from his *charlette,* and caught the all-too-knowing look that passed between his host and young Justine. *There's something there not right,* he thought unchari-tably, then turned back to his plate and went on eating.

Simon was sweating, and the droplets fell on Justine's upturned face. It was hot in her room, even with the bedcurtains thrown back and the windows gaping. But satisfying this young thing was hot work in any weather.

He loved her body, the way she could wrap herself around him like a coil. Simon had always preferred women who were sapling slim, and Justine was limber as a cat. Her lovely dark hair hung down the whole length of her arms, rippling in waves of silk as he thumped against her. *Beautiful child . . .*

For the sake of their situation, he usually remembered to withdraw from her in time. They would have a lot of trouble explaining to a prospective bridegroom if Simon accidentally got her with child. But there were times she drove him into such a frenzy that he couldn't stop himself from filling her. Even now he felt his conscious thoughts were ebbing, spinning away like a comet in the midnight sky.

But she was the one forgetting now, or like him, beyond caring. She drew her long legs up around his neck and held him to her and would not let go. He felt his muscles, tight as jackstrings. In a moment he would be past imagery, his mind gone black. . . .

Simon held the gasping girl to him for a few moments, then rolled away from her and sat up, reaching for his braies.

Pulling at his arm, she asked, "You aren't leaving yet, are you?"

He turned to answer her, then looked past her to the open door where Tim-Tom, one of the servants, stood. His face was rose-red, and he shuffled his feet nervously. "My lord?"

"Good Christ!" Simon bellowed, stuffing himself inside his braies, "Don't you know better than to enter a bedchamber without knocking?"

He hung his head. "I did, sire."

Justine sat up in the big bed, her breasts still mottled with the marks of Simon's rough caresses. "What is wrong?" she asked.

Tim-Tom looked away. "It's Lady Eleanora calling for his lordship." He turned to Simon. "She's bad sick, sir. Her ladies sent me to fetch you back."

"What's the matter with her?" Simon asked, fastening his jupon. "She was well enough at dinner."

"It's fearsome, sir. Vomiting and sweating—and there's blood coming from her nose."

"Jesus!" Simon's face went white. He turned to go, then remembered Justine and spun to face her. "Close the windows and lock them," he directed her.

"Simon!" she wailed, feeling his hand slip from hers.

He was halfway out when he turned back. "Lock the door, child. And don't come out! Don't come out for anything!"

Wordless, Justine obeyed. All that night she lay alone in her bed, waiting, but Simon did not return. There were noises in the corridor, anxious whispers, and the sound of soft running foot-

steps. Toward morning she heard something that sounded like a
scuffle. A tray dropped, crockery broke, the pieces running along
the floor like splintered ice.

*   *   *

"Shrive him."

The abbot's voice was cold and resolute. In the flickering can-
dlelight his shadow, the color of lead, lay against the wall.

The surgeon listened, but he shook his head. "Don't give him
up to Christ just yet. There are some things still to be done. Eastern ways: I've heard it said an herbal poultice on the chest will
aid the heart and keep it beating. And we'll feed him on cloves
of garlic to bring sweats and clean the blood."

The surgeon knew much of what he spoke. He had already
seen a few cases of the pestilence—cured none, but there was
always hope. Now he was tired and needed sleep after having
traveled all night on foot and over bad roads from Lewes to come
in answer to the abbot's message: *One of his monks was ill, perhaps dying; probably from the plague.* It was possible; there
were many evil rumors afoot these days. Some said the lord of
Alfriston and all his household had taken to their beds. *God pity
them.*

The abbot listened to what the surgeon said but was not
moved. He knew it didn't matter what the surgeon did, the man
would die. He looked to the young priest who stood at his side.
"Shrive him," he said again, and turned away.

Throughout the night the dying man was fed herbal remedies
and kept covered under blankets. The surgeon dozed in a chair
at his side. Candles guttered on the walls. Outside, the wind rustled like thin silk.

Near morning the sick man woke to see Death standing over
him, grinning, face gray as slate, and whispering his name.

Another died, and in the days that followed still another. The
monks knew a few precautions. Each kept to his own cell, and
all communal dining was discontinued. Even prayers were taken
singly. None walked abroad, save for the abbot, whose restless
footfalls echoed to the walls each night. Most often when he

could not sleep, he took himself into the library, and sometimes he was not seen for several days.

Geoffrey Fitzstephen knew what was coming; he'd known for some time. All the omens that he pretended not to believe had pointed toward this: evil and loss and hard retribution. And these days Geoffrey believed in omens more than he believed in God.

It had not always been so. Born to a wealthy and titled family, he had spent his youth in the usual round of fêtes and forays, reveling in all the usual excesses of the *jeunesse dorée*. But soon he had come to wonder what goodly profit there could be in a life of dissipation, asking himself *Where shall I spend Eternity?* And one day he had given himself over to God, freely and full of gladness. That was when he had come to St. Audric, the Benedictine abbey, and it had become his home. Of course, in those years, before Geoffrey gave his energies over to the service of the Church, there had been many women—some of them beauties and all of them jades—but never had there been anyone to love till God.

He might have become a Cistercian; he had fame enough for that and his Angevin bloodline was long. But he was drawn instead to the Benedictine house founded in the seventh decade of the seventh century by a truly unusual man.

Audric the Holy (fl. A.D. 644) was a quasi saint by medieval standards, but there had been no one like him in a thousand years. His beginnings had marked him down for fame. Born the illegitimate son of Sabert, King of the East Saxons, he was conceived in the year his father "washed in the waters of Salvation," allowing himself to be baptized at the hands of Bishop Mellitus.

Audric's mother was Jorth of Mercia, who came to Sabert as a servant and soon became his mistress. She was a strange, elfin woman with white-blond hair and silver eyes, a woman renowned for the working of miracles. It was her influence that helped convince Sabert to renounce his pagan gods for Christianity. When he died, Jorth gave young Audric to Bishop Mellitus, hoping to keep her son safe from any plans of murder by his royal stepbrothers, anxious claimants to their father's throne.

Those same pagan princes, later refused the Host by Mellitus, who believed them to be idolators and unrepentants (though they pretended differently), expelled the bishop and forced him to cross over to Gaul. The boy Audric was taken with him. While the bishop waited for justice and the Holy See to recall him, he taught his young ward the mysteries of Christ. At last when Mellitus was able to return, he brought the boy, now twelve and exceptionally precocious, with him to London as an oblate. There his religious education was continued. As he grew, it became obvious to all he had been born to serve God and Man through service to the Church.

As a man Audric showed his talents well. As Bede would do later, he authored a history of the English Church, but his secular writings chronicled the history and ritual of the pagan Saxons of East Sussex with ill-concealed interest. One such work, the Alfaeder (The Allfather) *was later debated at the Council of Whitby and judged heretical. Written in the old runic Saxon script, the original manuscript still reposed within the library at St. Audric Abbey seven hundred years later, when Geoffrey Fitzstephen came to live there.*

The Allfather *was controversial enough, but there were other books:* a Compendium Magico, *and other books filled with details of potions and elixirs known to the early Saxons. Audric claimed to record these things purely for the sake of history, but there were those who believed that he was a secret convert to the old pagan ways.*

The controversy at Whitby changed Audric's fate and marked him as an outcast for the remainder of his days on earth. It was not until a decade after his death that the personality and fame of this strange, contradictory man knew a rehabilitation.

Because of his heresies, Audric had been buried at the foot of the pagan "Long Man with Staves" on the East Sussex downland. It was a place very near to the religious house he had founded in the last years of his life. For most of Audric's years on earth he was a wealthy man; his royal bloodline had assured him of that. Even when the stench of heresy corrupted his name and drove him from active service in the Church, Audric continued to fund his house of charity.

When Wilfred, bishop of York, came to preach Christ's gospel to the backsliding South Saxons in the year A.D. 680, he heard fascinating stories of how Audric's grave had become a place of pilgrimage. Miracles were accomplished there, so the locals said: lepers cured, women unable to bear children made fertile. Time and time again Wilfrid heard the testimonies and saw the results of Audric's strange and holy power.

This was no heretic! The man buried at the foot of a pagan god was one of Christ's own saints who deserved a public rehabilitation of his legend. Wilfrid himself worked very hard to see this accomplished, and in the year 704 Audric was beatified by order of the Holy See. It was decided, however, that his body should not be taken from its grave but left to rest there as a testament to Christianity in a pagan place.

The coming of the early Middle Ages—that time of great and miraculous faith in mysteries—venerated Audric's fame to its zenith. The religious house he had begun was named for him. But unhappily, with the passing of time, the fame grew faint. Few monastic scholars could read the old runic Saxon script, and all Audric's treatises, including his volumes on spells and magic, pre-Christian England, and The Allfather *had never been rendered into Latin. Few were the scholars who could read Audric's work. Fewer still those who could grasp Audric's strange philosophies, and understand them.*

Geoffrey Fitzstephen understood.

He knew every volume, every line. He venerated Audric's ideas, revered his name. It was the legend of Audric that had brought him here in his youth. Now, more and more during these dreadful days since plague had crossed over into Sussex, Geoffrey Fitzstephen was driven to read the books.

Somewhere within them there was an answer as to why God bade His followers to suffer and die. In all his days on earth the abbot had seen his Church turn its face too surely from the common mysteries of Life. It had forgotten the humble clay of its inception. Once Man and Nature had lived in dumb and glorious accord, all One to whatever god watched from above their heads. Now all bowed before the Chrism and the Host, but their hearts were empty, all their oaths a lie.

And so God had punished them: Man in all his Ignorance and Pride was being punished, and none among his fellows knew how to make things right again. Each evening Geoffrey sat alone with his books, waiting for night to black his window, and wondering.

What did God want? He scarcely knew anymore. . . .

Fraught with fear and driven by hunger, the Daumier sisters plodded on along a coast road carved out so many centuries ago. Afraid of traveling too far inland and losing their way altogether, the young women kept the harsh murmur of the sea in their ears. Whatever lay above the road—hidden from view by trees, black, bare-limbed, oddly twisted—was a mystery.

There were no people here, or very few. Perhaps beyond the dunnish slopes a town or village might await, but they saw only fishermen and vagrants with whom they bartered with their bodies for scraps of food and water. No one they met spoke of the Death—perhaps they had put themselves beyond its reach?—yet all the while fearing the consequences of a gathering, they needed the protection of a kindly farmer or a village almshouse. Winter was coming; it was nearly here.

November, month of fêtes and festivals in pagan times.

In Marseilles the flowers would bloom, the air would still be warm and moist. But in this cheerless place—which seemed to be naught but a barren promontory jutting its rocky jaw into the sea—there was only cold and lack of comfort. Each night as Alicia and Adelina sought shelter in a copse of trees, they clung together for warming and listened to the wind rioting in the dark. Soon, even if the Death did not find them, cold and too little food would kill them all the same.

O Jesu, Mary! Please a little comfort and a little care!

In the refectory, shifting amber light lapped the walls while fitful shadows grew and fell away. Abbot Geoffrey sat at his meal with Matthew, Prior of St. Audric's. The two men ate rye bread with honeyed beans and unshelled eggs. Once there had been meat served at this table (it was forbidden, but the abbot was a liberal man). Now there was only common food, and they were glad for anything at all.

Matthew was as unlike Geoffrey as any man could be. There was no pride in him, only obedience and virtue. He had a smooth face of indifferent features and beatific countenance. If any man alive could be called the abbot's friend, it was he.

"I had a dream last evening," Geoffrey confided, his soft tones echoing away to the walls. "Two people approached me at the north door. One was a man who held in his hand a sword with rich trimmings. The other person was a woman. She carried a basket full of fruit, which she showed to me, and bade me eat."

The prior clucked his tongue. "Aye, as Eve bid Adam . . ."

Geoffrey shook his head. "The meaning was quite different, I think."

"What does it mean then?"

Geoffrey leaned close to the prior and as he spoke his gray eyes flashed dark as storm clouds. "Men bring naught but wars and discord into this world."

The prior arched an eyebrow. "And women?"

The abbot's face lighted with a smile. "Women," he said, "bring *life*."

Early the following morning Geoffrey went to the Long Man.

It had become a ritual with him during these twenty-six days since plague had come into the valley. Few knew of his visits, and those who did made no criticism to his face, though wondering why he should seek solace in a hillside drawing put there centuries ago by men who had never known Christ. Perhaps it was only Matthew who noticed how changed the abbot was whenever he returned from his pilgrimage: a strange and silent look of resolution etched into his face, as if a crucible had been endured and overcome. But for whatever consolation Geoffrey found in traveling to the Long Man with Staves, the prior was immensely grateful. God did, after all, work his miracles mysteriously.

Yet, through it all, their brothers were dying. Five monks in as many weeks; today two more had sickened and been shut away in the *hospitium* (the infirmary now considered too pest-ridden to be usable.) A day of fasting and silent repentance was observed each week, but so far it had made no difference. What anger God must have toward Man if He would punish those who loved Him most! Was *that* the question whose answer the abbot sought at the feet of the Long Man?

But there were enough worries of a temporal sort for all at St. Audric Abbey. Their food stores were down, and there was little chance they would be soon built up again. The growing of vegetables and the cutting of grain needed well and living men, as well as those who cared to pass their time in such a way. Life had suddenly become too uncertain to spend it in harvesting some other man's meal. Once the monks of St. Audric had provided for all their eating needs themselves, but that practice had been done away with half a century ago.

There were riots too. Believing food and safety could be had within the abbey walls, peasants from nearby Alfriston came to raise their fists and call up curses from outside the walls each day when no one came in answer to their shouts. They felt abandoned by both God and His church. *Who cared if a poor man lived or died?*

But it was not for want of charity that St. Audric's gates were closed. They feared outsiders would bring in the plague at first; when plague came through the barred gates they feared a mutiny, or theft of their stores. So long as they had some food, bread would be dropped over the wall each day at sunset. That was enough. The order went out from Abbot Geoffrey. Let the furious peasants shout their evil greetings. If King Death had his way there might soon be none to hear.

*　*　*

Wind in the treetops, gray clouds overhead. *Snow weather.*

There was no way of knowing how far they had traveled, or even for how long, but finally Adelina insisted that they must begin to carve out an inland route for themselves. Neither she nor Alicia had any sense of the land they were traversing. A few names stuck in their minds: London, Canterbury, York. All very far away. But it was important that they find some place of habitation. With hardly more than snatches of unappetizing food taken at long intervals since leaving France, the sisters were near to starving.

Of the two girls, Adelina was the bolder, and now she spoke her mind. "We've got to find a town," she said, "or even a small village. Perhaps in such a place we can find work."

Alicia regarded her with doubting eyes. As daughters in a comfortable bourgeois family they had never worked, except later, to sell their bodies in Paris, or fashion crude implements as talismans against the plague. Who would employ them? Indeed, what were they fit to do?

A few days later they found themselves at the gates of Goat's Rue manorhouse. Someone on the road had pointed them in that direction, saying that if the lord of Alfriston still lived he would most surely give them food and shelter.

As they approached, the sisters saw nothing to indicate that any one of the household still lived. Only a few chickens and pigs cackled and squealed in the courtyard. All else was still.

Alicia clutched at her sister's arm. "It looks deserted," she said, her voice trembling.

"Perhaps he took his family away to some safe place."

"Or the plague has already carried off everyone who lived within these walls." Alicia shivered, looking at the big gate, trying hard not to imagine what lay beyond it.

"Perhaps there's food here somewhere," Adelina said hopefully. She brushed wisps of black hair from her face. "Here, let's tidy ourselves in case there are people in residence. Then they won't send us away as beggars."

A few feet away stood a rain barrel, nearly full. Both of the young women bent to it, using scraps of cloth ripped from their *cottes* to wash themselves. From beyond the cookhouse a man stood watching them.

Eleanora had been the first to die, only a few hours after Simon had been called to her room. By the following midmorning the ladies who had waited upon her showed the same symptoms as their mistress: vomiting, sweats, blood from the nose. Then death. Jacquelyn fell ill that evening and died within hours.

Simon made arrangements to send his two younger daughters, twins Blanche and Bonne, away with Justine into the country, but before they could leave, the twins sickened and died. Terrified for her own safety, Justine sought to escape on one of Simon's horses but Rowan saw her going and stopped her, locking her inside the cookhouse when she tried to get away. He

brought her food and water faithfully each day, and after two
weeks when he let her out again they were the only two left alive
at Goat's Rue.

Alicia's face went pale and she straightened up, nudging her
sister, alarm in her voice. "Look, there's a man coming toward
us!"

Rowan was as surprised as the sisters to see someone; it had
been ten days or more since anyone had passed on the downland
road. He stopped a few hundred feet away. These new arrivals
could be carrying plague, though if truth be told they did look fit
enough.

"We've only come to beg water and a little food," Adelina
explained. "Are you master here?"

Rowan, resplendent in Simon's clothes, lifted himself up,
cocky as a rooster. "I am now. Who would you be?"

Adelina explained, telling of how they had come to England
after their miserable sojourn in Paris and the deaths of their parents; and of how they had wandered since.

"Aye, they're all dead here as well," Rowan answered, ventur-
ing closer, "save for me and my wife. She's lost her wits since all
this happened, the shock of seeing everyone around her dying.
I have to keep her tied to a stump out in the barn or she'd wander
off. Been struck dumb, she has. Can't even say so much as her
name anymore."

"Can you help us?" Alicia asked, "we've no plague, and we
haven't had anything to eat for two days . . ."

He nodded, but his help did not come free, and the sisters realized that at once. In the middle of the dusty vacant road Rowan
pulled out his plump member, offering it to Alicia first. Kneeling
passively in front of him she took it in her mouth.

Adelina turned away as Alicia did her work. When her own
time came she trapped him between her breasts, a trick borrowed from a Paris whore. Because her breasts were big he
didn't mind and came quickly, wetting her flesh with a thin foam.
Afterward he led the sisters out back to a storage barn where the
food was kept hidden among heaps of unthrashed wheat.

On the floor of the barn, squatting on a straw pallet used as a
bed and pulling fleas out of her hair, was Justine. No one who

had known the vain, teasing girl three months ago would recognize her now. It was more than just her filthy clothes and unwashed body. Justine's face was vacant and her eyes expressionless. Fear had rendered her insensible of her surroundings. Perhaps it was a blessing. A girl like Justine would rather lose her mind than live conscious amid such misery.

Rowan gave the sisters unleavened bread that he had baked over an open fire that morning, sliced pig meat, and a jug of milk apiece. They fell upon the food, gorging themselves gladly while Rowan watched, amused. Justine never looked up.

"Why are her hands tied as well?" Adelina wondered, settling back against a pile of straw, her stomach full for the first time in many weeks.

"She tried to hurt herself," Rowan explained. "I caught her with a knife, trying to cut her wrists." He pulled Justine up by the horse's halter that was around her neck. She came with him willingly and sat at his side.

"Is she really your wife?" Alicia asked, not believing it. In Paris she had seen other women wearing that same look of repressed terror, women who had been raped insensible by men and kept as virtual prisoners because they lacked the strength and means to get away. People got worse when times were bad. They would do anything.

"She's my wife well enough," Rowan snapped. "Perhaps not to God's way of thinking, but to my way of thinking God's much to answer for, putting us in the midst of all this . . ."

"Why don't you let her go?" Adelina asked, pitying the poor creature who sat with head hanging on her chest. "Surely anything is better than keeping her tied up like an animal."

"And where would she be now if I hadn't locked her up to keep her safe?" Rowan asked belligerently. "I loved her for a long time, though she was above me. Now the high ones are all dead and she's naught but me. Even if she's only an idiot thing now, I still want her."

Later when it grew cold Rowan built a fire and boiled herbs in water for them to drink as tea. "How did all the others die?" Alicia asked as they sat in a small circle around the fire. "Was it the plague boil that killed them?"

Rowan stirred the brew with his finger and tasted it. "No

plague boil, not for one of them. This was plague, but of a different kind. My lady Eleanora failed first, coughing with blood coming from her nose. Soon the others began to follow: Lady Jacquelyn, the younger daughters . . . death came fast to them. My Lord Simon, fearful for himself, set upon a precaution which he had heard would keep him safe: to drink four cups of milk each hour—milk curdled by the juice of cherries. Then all unknowing he choked himself on a cherrystone and died before he could catch his breath again. Poor sod . . ."

"How did you survive it then?" Adelina asked with trepidation. "And the girl?"

"How did you?" Rowan replied. "It's all a mystery. And I wouldn't wonder if God hadn't left some of us alive to bear witness to this madness."

Alicia looked to the open door where a strip of deep gray announced more than the approach of evening. Soon they would be here, the short dark winter days when wind sang in the chimneys and night was never far away. Where would they all be when that time came? Trembling, she sank down amid the straw.

Alicia woke to the sound of groaning and a shadow flapping on the wall like a bat's wing. Adelina lay on her side breathing softly. Alicia turned to her, pushing at her arm, rousing her to wakefulness, whispering in her ear.

They left before the sun was up, stolen bread stowed in their clothes. Alicia had convinced her sister they must leave. If he could keep the idiot girl tied up to a stump he could do the same with them. They had enough terrors to fear without being made prisoners against their will.

They were far away when morning's weak light shone through the tiny cutout windows of the barn disclosing the unhappy scene. Justine lay on her back convulsed in death, flies buzzing at her open mouth. At her side, his clothes undone, was Rowan, staring sightless at the ceiling. His face was mottled and horrible, blood sticking to his lips like jam.

A rat, boney and bedraggled, nibbled at his ear.

Geoffrey Fitzstephen stood on his balcony and watched the sun disappear into a bed of amethyst and silver clouds. He had spent the day in solitary meditation, yet his heart was heavy, nor was his mind at rest.

A messenger from Hastings had brought evil tidings on the previous day. The monastery of St. Thomas à Becket had been overrun by plague. Its abbot, Philip of Pevensey, was among the newly dead. Geoffrey had known him well: an able and intelligent man, now food for maggots. What was God's plan in all this madness, or was there any plan at all when kings and prelates and God's own elite on earth sickened and died as easily as poor, unlettered farmers? Why had God turned His back upon His own? And since He had, should men not be tempted to turn their backs on Him?

With some distaste he observed the gathering of people just outside the gate. They came every evening at this hour, chanting the few psalms they knew, filthy hands outstretched for bread. Tonight there were fewer and the abbot pondered that. More dead. And tomorrow more ophans and widows crying at his gate. God, but the world was wretched!

At such times there was only one solace known to him, one means to calm his soul. Geoffrey turned quickly on his heels and crossed the worn floor. In the library he would find peace. Once he had been able to soothe himself with prayers, but that no longer worked. Now there was only respite for him in his study of the pagan arts. In the books that no man of his calling was supposed to see.

He kept many forbidden books within these walls. There were rare manuscripts by Chrétien of Bruges, which included vivid drawings of erotic couplings, and love poems from the East. As a youth he'd known his fair share of dalliance, but since taking vows of chastity Geoffrey Fitzstephen had not so much as touched another human being, male or female. Recently he had thought of little else.

It was more than flesh-lust; his mind ached from abstraction and scholarship. The books fed his need for sensation, even if it was only to look at. Abstinence was a sacrifice for any man, but he could bear it—as he bore the hundred other burdens of his office—so long as on some evenings when the wind was up and all was cold about him, he could come alone into this room and know his secret joy.

There were the other books too, and lately he had spent a good few hours with them. Audric's history of the pagan Saxons held him in thrall. Men had been better then, truer to what God had intended when He made them. Could a pagan be a better man than someone who called himself a Christian? What a tangle it all was. . . .

Of all Audric's writings *The Wyrd* was Geoffrey's favorite. It was an odd mixture of history and philosophy, but what attracted his interest most was the way in which it revealed the nature of women to him, truly, and for the first time.

Audric had understood women, understood as no other man of his time had. No Bede, he had possessed many of them, even at the time of his service to the Church. But what stood out in his writings was a fascination and reverence for women unrivaled by anything Geoffrey Fitzstephen had ever read.

There is a Male Law and a Female Law in Nature and all that is Female is Best among them. As the Goddess Frig has two faces, one fair as the morning and the other shaded dark as night, so shall womankind bring life into this world, and in her time she shall bring death, for each is necessary; and for both shall she be blessed.

Geoffrey read the words over and over, struggling to divine the meaning as Audric had intended it. His own dream, the woman offering her basket, seemed to echo Audric's theories. What did it really mean, how far did it go? Bending so close to his candle that the wax splashed upon his knuckles, Geoffrey read till almost morning. Finally with eyes aching and all his sinews gone stiff, he snuffed out the light and took himself to bed. Tomorrow he would go to the Long Man with Staves once more and seek an answer. He was almost certain he had lost his own soul years ago, somewhere in the candlelit secrecy of his room with only a fist for a mistress, or in the blazing light of his own doubts. But he would save his brothers if he could. If God or the Long Man would only answer.

Something in his heart told him that tomorrow there would be found a solution, an answer flying on the wings of hope.

The following afternoon two young women, sisters, came to the west gate at the abbey, begging bread. Geoffrey had spied their approach from his balcony. Immediately he called the prior to him, giving him instructions to go down into the courtyard and fetch them up.

Matthew hesitated for a moment, unsure of where his true allegiance lay: with God or His earthly instrument, the abbot. All the
same he was displeased with Geoffrey's order.

"Are you acquainted with these two young women, sire?" he
asked.

"Of course not!" Geoffrey snapped. "And how should I know
them when my life is spent inside this place?"

"Do you wish me to convey your charity to them?"

"Is it not the business of the abbey to feed mendicants and
clothe them at their will?" Geoffrey asked sharply.

Matthew bowed his head in meekness. "A hundred others
come to our gates every day and we send them away with only a
few bits of bread in their hands. Why should these women be
treated specially?"

Geoffrey's gaze lighted on the prior's face, impatient. "I shall
make decisions regarding such things. Do as I say now and bring
them to the chapter house that I might interview them fully. And
afterwards we shall all take our evening meal together."

"There are vows which have forbidden us to sup in the presence of women," Matthew reminded him.

Geoffrey knew what verbal stones the prior was casting, and
he did not like it. There was a warning note in his voice when he
spoke. "Matthew, there are circumstances which determine if
we should revise our methods according to the times in which
we live. Our Lord Jesus, who supped with tax collectors and harlots, would scarcely be offended at the sight of two wandering
females whom we've brought in against the cold."

Again Matthew bowed his head, unable to look the abbot in
the face. "As you say. But I'll not sit at table with them."

"Doctrine is much, Matthew," Geoffrey said quietly, "but it is
not all. Examine your heart. Christ will not suffer it to stray from
what is right."

Matthew, turning to leave, stopped at the door and turned back
again. "There are many others out there in the courtyard, sire.
Shall I bring them in against the cold, or suffer them to eat the
bread we throw, and then let them find their own shelter in the
dark?"

"I have spoken: bring the women in."

So Matthew went down as he was directed and as he went the

abbot consoled himself that what he had said was true, whatever
his final motive might be. He was there to serve God, but more:
to act and think. God had gifted him with a subtle mind of sur-
passing brilliance. Was he then not capable of decisions without
the Church's hard-won permission on his side?

Forgive me if I do wrong, O Lord, but I must act.

Geoffrey crossed himself piously, then went down into the
chapter house to meet the women, after directing a meal to be
laid for them there as soon as possible, including what little meat
was still left among their stores.

The women were waiting for him, standing side by side in
awed silence as he approached. He noticed at once that their
clothing was good, but worn and dirty. Each wore a heavy cloak
over a soiled velvet gown. They were beautiful too, though very
different from one another. Geoffrey had nearly forgotten what
it was to look a lovely woman in the face. Immediately he felt his
manhood stirring, not only in his loins but in his soul.

He recognized their ancestry and spoke to them in faultless
Provençal.

"I am Geoffrey Fitzstephen, abbot of this place. Come, do sit
with me, and eat. Our meal is waiting."

Both made a curtsy out of reverence for his office. "You are
kind to see us, sire," Adelina said, her dark eyes cast down in
meekness. "We asked only bread."

He bade them rise. "You shall be my guests here for as long a
time as you wish." There was an odd light in his eyes. "I have
reason to believe some Will other than your own has brought you
to my door."

They looked at one another, unsure and hesitating.

"Come," he said again and walked swiftly before them, leading the way to a private sanctuary beyond. "I assure you we have
much to offer one another. Nothing will be spared you if you will
but do your part."

Silent, the sisters followed.

They ate, as he had promised, and though the food was lowly
it tasted good in their mouths. And wine! They hadn't drunk anything to match it since their days in Marseilles. When all had
been consumed he led them down a hallway and through a
secret door where a chamber waited, canopied and candlelit.

The sisters looked at one another. Did he want them both?

In a room beyond a wooden tub had been filled with hot water and oil of almonds; candles burned all around. The sisters bathed and wrapped themselves in muslin sheets, shaking out their wet hair, walking on tiptoe into the abbot's room.

He had removed his *scapular* and habit and lay atop the bed waiting for them. He was a handsome man, his skin pale and smooth except for a many-years-old wound high on his left breast that had faded to near imperceptibility. Alicia felt herself blushing down to her toes. She could never have imagined seeing a churchman naked, least of all one who was endowed with so much manhood.

He did not fall upon them greedily and take them with rough indifference to their own feelings. Instead he caressed them with real tenderness, first one, then the other, his kisses fell upon their upturned faces light as mist. He traveled the landscape of Adelina's voluptuous, big-nippled breasts; of Alicia's delicate, strawberry-tipped breasts. When he took them they knew his pleasure, and their own, and fell asleep on either side of him, satisfied and secure.

As for Geoffrey, for the first time in thirty years he fell asleep with the soft sound of female breathing in his ears.

*   *   *

In the days that followed, Alicia and Adelina were given a large common room opposite the one belonging to the abbot. It was a vain try at discretion, for there could be little doubt as to why they had been lodged there.

Not everyone at the abbey knew of the two female "guests" in residence, but Matthew knew—and that knowledge sat upon him like a stone. All men were sinful, it was true—but the abbot was committing unconscionable Mortal Sin, flaunting his sin in the face of the Creator. Harlots lodged in an abbey, eating the brothers' food, drinking their wine! If God had not already called down His wrath upon St. Audric's Abbey, then surely He would in time.

As distraught as Matthew was, Geoffrey was jubilant to that degree. He loved the Daumier sisters and rejoiced in the pleasure that they gave him. But that was only their temporal function, for they fed his soul as well, and in his new knowledge Geoffrey had come to understand Audric's philosophies in *The Wyrd* better than he ever had before.

The goddess Frig and her two faces, fair and dark. Now he knew the Christian ethos was a lie. It had abandoned women utterly, leaving them nothing to choose for themselves but roles as handmaidens or harlots. Nowhere in Christendom was Woman's full creative power celebrated. In a world of kings and clerics they had no place, save as breeders, and then only when sanctified by marriage.

Now Geoffrey had begun to see the Truth; it both elated and terrified him. Nature, disguised beneath a veil of pestilence, had reasserted Herself, demanding all be made right again. The domination of the Christian world by Men was wrong; it was *sin*. Women were the sovereign sex, their wombs the universe where life began. What Christianity ignored or even punished, the pagan faiths had understood. Audric had understood: his obsession for cataloguing pagan rites and practices proved that.

Did God? If not, why had He sent the sisters?

Across the brilliance of a winter afternoon a curious tarnishing was spreading, dark clouds lapping at the sky like waves upon a beach. Adelina, well-occupied with needlework, watched Nature's daily pantomime from her window, cloistered and content against the harshness of the outside world.

It was a curious life she led now, as alien from the terrible days preceding it as those days had been in comparison to her happy life in Marseilles before the plague came. There were times she felt herself a captive here—as her sister must also feel—but it was a felicitous captivity all the same.

She did not love the abbot; he was too distant from her for that, despite his nightly presence in her bed. He was an odd man, silent as a stone. His passion was relentless, and yet she had never felt dirtied by his touch as she had by other men. It was as if he took her body only as a means of communing with her soul.

But she and Alicia were more than the abbot's whores. Each morning they spent hours nursing ailing monks in the infirmary. Three had recovered and it looked as if there would be more.

The Daumiers had no special skills in healing, only what they had seen the Sisters of Charity perform in Paris. To these ends they soaked strips of linen in vinegar, winding them about the patient's chest. Where the plague boil appeared they covered it with a paste of garlic and crushed pearls. None of the ailing monks exhibited the coughing fits or bleeding from the nose that characterized a certain form of the plague that took its victims swiftly, and often in the midst of their sins. Here there was mild headache followed by nausea, and after a day or two a swelling in the groin and armpits. When the boil appeared they dressed it and when it was enlarged they slit it with a heated knife. However crude their methods may have been, this much was true: since the Daumier sisters had come to St. Audric's Abbey, not one victim of plague had died. The sisters did not realize what significance the abbot found in that.

Stitching carefully, the thread held taut in her other hand, Adelina tried hard to imagine what their life would be like a year from now. They could not remain in this place forever. Either plague would come for them, or God would once more turn a forgiving face to Mankind and lift the curse. When that day came, if it did, she and Alicia would be free to return once more to France, though nothing waited for them there.

She tried to recall the face of her betrothed and could not; she had only seen him once and then in the company of a hundred others at a feast-day celebration two long years ago. *A flower-decorated dais where gleemen plucked their citterns and fair ladies danced.* She could still see that image in her mind, still smell the delicate scent of rose and narcissus. Yet she could not call up the face of Guillaume de Corbay. She said the name aloud, trying to make it hers, but could not, though it had once sounded sweet on her tongue.

But all those plans were only memories now, belonging to another time, another girl named Adelina who did not know what hunger was, or fear, who had never seen Death's dark and freezing face.

Nothing made sense; nothing, not anymore.

It was early April when Alicia first knew that she was pregnant. Strange, for so long after fleeing Marseilles her monthly courses had stopped, but shortly after coming to the abbey they had begun again. Now within her a child was growing daily. Surely this was a God-given miracle, for who but God could have touched her womb with promise in the midst of such great suffering? Outside this sanctuary men were dying, but in her body she carried *life*. Perhaps this little unnamed babe would be more fortunate than the infants she had seen tossed into the pit at St. Lazare. It might be that in times like this God looked with favor on a child sired by a churchman. Each day she made the sign of the cross over her belly and prayed for her baby to be well.

She had been unsure at first how Abbot Geoffrey would respond to her news that she had his child in her. It had not escaped Alicia's notice that the abbot cared more for Adelina than for her. It was true he cosseted them both, but it was Adelina he desired; Alicia had seen it a hundred times in the way he looked at her. She didn't care; their relationship was tenuous at best, and certainly temporary. But she couldn't help but feel he would have been more joyful to learn his favorite was to bear his child instead.

She was right. He was happy for the news when Alicia told him, yet something went out of his eyes, some look of hope, and Alicia knew she would never see it again. On that very day he undertook to redouble his efforts, and for several weeks he filled Adelina faithfully, determined that he give her a child as well. But however he tried (with daily as well as nightly visits) it did not happen.

It was only then that Adelina noticed a carnality in the abbot that had not been there before. All that summer and into early autumn while Alicia was carrying the child he never came near to her, but Adelina saw him more often than she would have liked. He was different now, quite different altogether. All his tenderness had gone; he could not enjoy her body anymore unless he inflicted pain or shame. There were times he forced her to give herself to others in the abbey, including all those whose plague sufferings had been cured by her ministrations.

Adelina did not understand what purpose such things served, save that of lust. She felt degraded, and wished with all her heart that she had been chosen by God to bear the abbot's child. Then she would be allowed to live in perfect isolation from all company, as Alicia did, and would not have to endure the ignominy of a harlot's life.

Plague had gone from this place, and yet some sickness worse than it had come to stay. One day when she was bathing, Matthew came to her begging for her favors, crying that he had never known a woman in all his life. From that time to this he was as single-minded in his lusts as any other of his brothers. It was wickedness indeed if truly holy men like Matthew had fallen victim to its evil. *God help them all.*

What Adelina did not know was that God no longer ruled here. He had been cast out and superseded by His earlier incarnations, the pagan gods who lived in stones and fire and crops that grew out of the ground. For this was God *before* the Son; a god of red anger, a god of blood. No Christian would recognize Him behind the totem mask he wore. But all the same He *was* God, a God they chose to worship. And He was no false God, but the *real* God, as He had been in the beginning, a Pagan Father over all . . .

It was this God who shone his face gladly upon the woman who birthed her child in screams the day of the first frost; upon the black-haired beauty who drowned in her bath that same day and was buried at the Long Man's feet. That night one of the brothers unearthed the shallow grave to violate her body. After he had satisfied his lust he was struck through with shame and knew that this was not what God intended. He ran to the far cliffs to cast himself into the sea, leaving the evidence of his crime uncovered.

For many days the dead woman's body lay, legs spread to the sky, her pointed shoes aloft to heaven.

Long Man with Staves

San Francisco, California
July 1964

This is still a free country, ladies and gentlemen.
Cassie looked down at the tips of her pointy-toed shoes.
For some people. Not for me.
It was late. Soon she would have to go back to the room, but not yet. Not till she had thrown off the fear of being recognized, of being followed, though she knew she was quite alone. It might be paranoia. Somehow one always felt more isolated and afraid among a crowd.

She had thought it would be so easy to avoid him here. No one would notice a pregnant Englishwoman in the midst of all this American fury. Paul and Pru had suggested that. "If he's anywhere in the world in July," they'd told her, almost in tandem, "he won't be *here.*"

So they had whisked her off to the city with them, afraid of leaving her alone at the house after last week when Pru had found evidence of a prowler out back; someone had trampled the bleeding hearts and pink lilies.

Cassie knew who it was was, knew without question. Blood told her that and more; some inner sense. Even now he might be waiting for her close by, behind one of those darkened windows. Waiting to take her back to him.

Quickening her pace, Cassie swung onto the sidewalk outside the Mark Hopkins and raced up the walk beneath the canopy. The coat of arms (a crude Americanized version of a medieval emblem) showed two gold horses rampant; beneath it the legend proclaimed WHERE GOOD FRIENDS GET TOGETHER. The irony made her chuckle.

The lobby was still busy with people though it was already late:

41

well-dressed women in red dresses or blue dresses or white dresses or combinations of the above, all with pointed shoes; men whose exhausted faces contrasted oddly with their stark white shirts. She thought: *I'm one of them: For anyone who notices me, I'm one of them.*

He would know the difference of course, he would pick her out from all the others. She ground her heel into the carpet. Stop it; stop worrying. Go up to your room on the seventh floor. Find Paul and Pru. Shelter there. He isn't here, he couldn't be. It's just your mind gone silly and imaginative.

She was thirsty; all that walking. The bar was busy but she went in anyway and had to stand for a long time against the wall holding a chilly glass of Pepsi-Cola stuffed with ice. By the time she'd inched her way to a tiny vacant table her glass had been refilled three times and she was sleepy. But it was worth sitting here a little before going up. Anything to remain anonymous a while longer.

It was eleven thirty-four when she stepped out of the elevator, turned right, and walked the whole length of the corridor. Mounds of uncovered dishes on trays with bits of food left over sat outside nearly every room. *Messy,* she thought.

The key slid grindingly into the lock, the door flew open. Inside Paul and Pru, ringed with friends unfamiliar to her, sat on the double beds, avidly involved in a dozen separate conversations. Beyond, a television, ignored by all, hummed tonelessly. They didn't see her at first, or, if they did, paid no attention. But as she hurried past, Pru suddenly called out, "Do you want something to eat? Anything? There's lots left . . ." But she shook her head and leaned to the big bureau, fishing for her cigarettes amid the litter. Tissues. Pru's pearls. A placard (JUSTICE FOR HOFFA, INVESTIGATE RFK), today's *Examiner,* an article ripped from the *Sporting News* ("Callison Clubs 3-Run Homer off Radatz in 9th: N.L. wins 7–4"), hotel keys, and finally an open pack of Salem.

She hurried inside her own room through the connecting door. She leaned against it, breathing, an unlit cigarette in her mouth. *God bless Paul, God bless Pru.* Her thoughts revolved in endless whirls of thanksgiving for them that went round and round. They were good people; they had been good to her; they would doubtless go on being good into the future.

And yet they did not understand; could not, could never.

With all their talk of "New South," "New West," "New Direction in American Political Thought" (A *Choice* Not an Echo?) how could they ever understand anything as ancient as her fear? To their way of thinking it was straightforward, so simple. She was in trouble. They were her friends. They would help her. One, two, three. So they had sheltered her in the little house on Seaside Drive since March. She could hide there for as long as was necessary, hide from him. They owed it to her, they said; hadn't they all grown up together? Weren't they practically a family? So she had accepted their help saying, *Only for a few months, just till November's over, then I'll be safe no matter where I choose to go.*

But now November, dreaded November, was four months away and each passing moment brought it closer. *Dear God, keep us safe till then; just till then,* she prayed.

Cassie tugged at the zipper of her dress and let the garment fall away in soft folds to the floor. She wanted a bath, anything to relax her aching muscles, but later. Now sleep, only a nap. She sank to the bed, molding her body to its comfort, then remembered she had forgotten to pull off her shoes. Already half dozing she reached down and slid them off, first one and then the other, and tossed them away into the darkness where they fell.

Twelve miles away he let himself into the house on Seaside Drive, having found a key hidden in the porch flowerpot. Why were people so stupid, putting things in such obvious places? It was hardly sporting, affecting such an easy entry.

She would not be here of course; he knew that, knew where she *really* was. She was with *them* and *they* had taken her into the city to help lose her, but all they had done was make it easier for him to come here and stand for a moment in the place where she had been till only a few days ago.

He had known she would come to them, who did she think she was fooling? Was he stupid, blind? She had no one else, not anymore. They thought they were helping but they weren't. They could never understand because everything was easy for them, and *new*. New and improved. But was it? Was it really?

He and she came from something older. He had accepted it,

even if she could not. That is how he understood why this thing, this admittedly dark and ugly thing had to happen, and when it did there would be a kind of freedom for them both. He did not really want to think what else it meant; something darker and more dreadful, something the color of nightmare, and so old. But it had been before, and would go on after them, long after; an eternal thing.

The passageway was only a black rectangle, but he followed it all the way to the end and on the right where her bedroom waited. He had never seen her there, never been inside this place before, and yet he *knew*. And as he stood just inside, engulfed by shadows, he fancied he could still scent her perfume in the air, hear a faint whisper of French blue taffeta.

She was out there somewhere, very close; his thoughts could almost touch her. But there was time. He could leave here now, go back to England, do what must be done. In time she would come; do what she knew was right. She had no other choice.

Paul, Pru—you can't keep me away.

She awoke feeling his breath upon her cheek. *Cassie . . .*

She sat up and snapped on the bedside lamp. She was alone. There was nothing but a little fluttering of the curtain where the window had been left open. Relieved, she lit a cigarette and lay back against the pillow, blowing smoke rings at the ceiling.

Money. That was her biggest problem. Paul and Pru had been generous when they could, but they hadn't much money to begin with. She had managed to earn a little from the typing jobs Paul had found for her, but that hardly added up to much. If only there was a way to put her hands on several hundred dollars at once. But there wasn't; it was hardly worth thinking about.

She stubbed out the cigarette, lit another, and finally when it had burned down to the filter she got up and trailed into the bathroom. A hot bath would appease her aching muscles.

The fluorescent lights and spotless white tile reminded her of a morgue, or a hospital operating room, not that she'd ever seen either, except in movies. She flicked on the water and reached to the sink for soap. Wrapped in fragrant pastel tissue, it looked like a Christmas gift. Where was the soap she'd used only once the day before? Funny how Americans always liked things to be new, untouched by anyone else.

There was a dish of scented bath cubes by the tub and she tossed two of them in, watching as the rushing water spun them into a tiny whirlpool. A light carnation scent rose on a cloud of steam and filled her nostrils pleasantly. She peeled off the slip, leaning to test the water with her toes.

Fourteen years in England had dimmed the memory of bathtubs big as double beds. Relaxing, she stretched herself full length in the water, sliding down until her hair was wet to the scalp. Her feet made dance steps in slow motion as her eyes closed and her breath grew heavy. A little of the water rose to meet the white porcelain rim and lapped gently over.

BOOK TWO

The Oats Goat

London, England
Yesterday

Silence. Falling. *Sleep.*

Where she was the air was warm and moist, smelling sweetly of coconuts and almonds. She was alone and nowhere all at once, lost within the pale walls of memory and dreams. There was something—a low bubbling at her ear, the sound of sticks falling lightly on grass and being swept away by wind. . . .

Joanna sat bolt upright in the tub and swore. Once again she'd fallen asleep in the bath and let the water overflow on Jayson's pale blue Aubusson. It was the second time this week she'd been so careless. Grabbing a few towels from the airing cupboard, Joanna bent to pat the sopping carpet. She would be sure to hear about this at dinner tonight. Nicely, of course. Jayson rarely raised his voice. But he was a fastidious man who loved all his beautiful things. Sometimes Joanna felt like one of them.

But for the death of an English king they might not have met. Joanna Lynne Latimer was on an extended graduate study program from UCLA, reading medieval history at Oxford, and working on a novel in her spare time. Her book, The Rose Bled White, *was a re-creation of King Richard III's final days, and so she often spent her weekends up at Bosworth, walking the battlefield paths where he had died. One rainy October day she met Jayson in the Buttery and boldly introduced herself.*

He was not unknown to her; his photo adorned a half-dozen books she owned. Professor of Plantagenet studies at a Midlands university and the author of several scholarly texts, Jayson Gardiner had become a popular writer overnight with publication of Incest and Infidelity in Medieval England. *Books on several*

49

other tantalizing subjects followed, including The Love Song of Abelard and Héloise *and* Sweets for a Season: France's Isabel of Hainault and Other Teenage Queens. *Talking over steaming cups of tea, professor and student were caught up in a mutual attraction that led them to a hotel in Leicester that same afternoon.*

The affair with Jayson was interrupted the following spring when she returned to California—interrupted, but not ended. Throughout the next two and a half busy years—Joanna received her masters, published The Rose Bled White *and a second novel,* Thomas of Canterbury, *enjoying a flurry of success when it was bought by television for a Hallmark Hall of Fame Production—the lovers called weekly, wrote monthly, and managed at least two weeks together every summer.*

Eventually the relationship had to be resolved. Joanna didn't really want to leave her comfortable life in Costa Mesa, but she did want to be with Jayson, and in any case her two new novels were set in England, necessitating trips for research. So she sold her condo (its perks included built-in spa and close proximity to the South Coast Plaza), loaned to a friend her '65 Mustang (the only car she'd ever owned, it had been her father's till he passed it to Joanna at her graduation. It boasted the original Pony interior and the remnants of an AuH$_2$O in 1964 bumper-sticker still legible in certain light), put everything she owned except for clothes and books in storage, sent her black-and-white tomcat Mittens up north to live with her stepmother, Sylvia Lynne, and moved (with only a few reservations) into Jayson's Hampstead flat.

They had been living together for several months when Joanna began to wonder if she'd made a mistake. Despite having so much in common (even careers, since Jayson had quit teaching and now worked entirely at his writing; there was even talk of a novel), she and Jayson were really very different people. And, of course, there was, as she'd come to think of it, the Age Thing. *To be honest, he didn't look his age. At fifty-two, there was little gray in his dark hair and no flab at all on his quite marvelous body.*

It was not unusual for Joanna to become involved with men old enough to be her father; it had happened twice before. But

Jayson, in his own dignified way, was demanding and author-
itative and it was always too tempting for Joanna to lean on
him, to let him pay the bills and make decisions for her. In the
beginning she had liked that because it isolated her from petty
difficulties, allowing all her energies to flow into her writing.

But now she wondered. The early things—things that had
seemed spontaneous and liberating in the beginning—had set-
tled in as habit and she was caught in them, more committed to
her present circumstances than she'd first intended. Their rela-
tionship was a fact of life; both treated it as such. There was no
talk of marriage or any plans encompassing arrangements
other than they now enjoyed, yet recently Joanna had begun to
fret abstractly about some future time when they might no
longer be together. Satisfied in their present state of domesticity,
Jayson never noticed her dilemma, never sensed her fears. . . .

In the bedroom she bent to her dressing table, a skin moistur-
izing spritzer in her hand. The mirror gave back the image of a
pale oval face illumined by large hazel eyes and framed with a
mass of shoulder-length dark curly hair. Joanna had the kind of
healthy "California" looks that adapted well to whatever style
she chose, and that usually meant bohemian: dangling earrings,
layered silk skirts and blouses, and rope sandals, even in the winter sometimes. At twenty-seven she occasionally opted for an
even younger and more teenage look ("Madonna Joanna" as Jayson called her when she dressed like that) and she'd even been
known to wear her short-shorts with stiletto heels out on the
street, something that had scandalized Jayson till she managed
to habituate him to it.

She was still busy at the mirror when she heard him outside on
the landing, keys tinkling in his hand. After a lifetime of bache-
lorhood, Jayson still retained many bachelor habits. Even if he
knew she was at home he never called out her name when he
came in the door, but went about his business as if alone. She
could hear him in the kitchen now, setting things out for supper.

They hadn't planned anything special tonight. Lately they took
their meals at home, mostly, with only an occasional night out.
That was their usual custom when one or both of them was
engrossed in a project. Earlier in their live-in togetherness she'd

sometimes been able to coax him out to Spots or Annabel's, but
he loathed both the music and the glitterati, so after a while
Joanna became accustomed to quiet Friday night dinners at
Keats or Frascatti's or even (when she could convince Jayson to
join her) the local Pizza Hut. Now he was involved in translating
a book of twelfth-century French poetry and Joanna had begun
the research for a new novel, *The Scourge,* set in the fictional
fourteenth-century Sussex village of Oatenham during the Black
Death. It was only in the planning stages but kept her occupied
enough that she could appreciate having dinner in, particularly
when Jayson was cooking. Like everything else he did, he did it
well.

Pulling on jeans and a T-shirt, she padded barefoot into the
kitchen to join him. "Hi, lover," she said, stretching for his kiss.

He held her for a moment then broke away, reaching for the
copper kettle, holding it aloft. "Tea?"

Joanna pulled open the refrigerator, scouting for a soft drink.
"I guess," she answered, popping the ring on a Diet cola. Pepsi.
"What are you making us for dinner tonight?"

"Fish and rice pilaf."

She made a face. "No thanks. You know I hate fish. Anyhow, I
had a Big Mac for lunch and scads of fries and a shake." She slid
into a chair. "I don't think I could put another thing in my
stomach."

He worked with his back to her, setting things out on microwave trays, cleaning up after his preparations as he went along.
"I rang earlier," he said, running water in the sink. "You didn't
answer. Were you out, or busy?"

Her bare toes tickled the silk fringe of the table runner. "Both.
I was out for a while, like I said, I went to McDonald's, and then
the bookstore. And I was in the bathtub forever." She remembered the water mess but volunteered nothing. "I thought you'd
be home when I got here. What kept you?"

He had gone to lunch at the Conservative Club with Dr. Jeremy
Fripple, a former colleague of his whom Joanna had met only
once and hadn't liked. A chinless, insignificant little man with a
silly, pompous name. Joanna had marked him down as a closet
gay; his high-strung manner reminded her of a Melrose Avenue

hairdresser she'd gone out with a few times in the middle of a dating funk.

"Jerry made me an interesting proposition," Jayson began, and Joanna bit her tongue to keep from saying *I'll bet.* "There is a series of lectures and round-table discussions planned for next term at UCLA on the subject of the economy in France and England during Plantagenet times. Dr. de Navarre of Mannheim University, who was supposed to chair the discussions, died suddenly last week and they're looking for someone to replace him. Since Jerry is friendly with the head of the department, he suggested me. . . ."

The tea kettle screamed and Joanna, distracted, jumped a little. "But you don't even teach anymore," she protested as he carefully strained out the leaves and set a cup of tea in front of her. The rich scent of Keemun flooded her face. She looked up at him, surprised to see how pale he'd gone, his fine features tense, as if anticipating an argument from her. Jayson hated arguments. *He's already decided to do it,* she thought, *and he doesn't know how to tell me.*

They were both silent for a long time. While she watched with questions in her eyes he put out his supper and sat down to eat it, dabbing the fish with lemon and a sprig of parsley. He tasted it, ate for a moment, then all at once he pushed the plate aside. "It's nothing permanent, Joanna," he explained, confronting her disapproval squarely, his cool gray eyes riveted to her face. "Just a few months in Los Angeles, and you'll be busy anyway with your book."

He was right and she resented it; Jayson knew her better than she cared to admit. While reading galleys for *Tabitha's Claw* (shortly after moving in with Jayson) she'd hardly seen or spoken to him for a week. So far she'd had difficulty getting involved in her new book; some time alone, away from Jayson, might be what she needed. She almost said that she could easily come with him, but didn't. He could have suggested that himself if that was what he wanted. For some reason not immediately obvious to her he wanted this separation. Joanna, always afraid of looking too closely at a situation for fear of what she might find, was afraid to ask why. It was ironic. For two and a half years she'd been in

Southern California, he in England. Now they were about to be separated again, but in opposite places.

Pouting, she asked, "How long will you be gone?"

"As I said: a few months. I'll probably leave here late in August and return by December first."

Immediately she gasped, "But that's ages!"

His stern expression softened. "We'll both be far too busy to be lonely, Joanna."

When he was patient he made her feel childish and silly. More than once he had criticized her emotionalism, especially in regard to their relationship. And she *was* emotional, possessive, even clinging. His authoritarian attitude fostered such reactions, yet whenever she became too demanding he seemed to pull back, resenting her dependence on him. It might be better if she just accepted this new development with grace.

"Okay," she finally said. But all the same she was angry. He had made his decision without talking to her, without caring how she would feel. She got up and kicked her feet into thongs. "I'm going out for ice cream. Wanna come?"

"No," he said and held out his arms to her, "but give us a kiss before you go. . . ."

That night Joanna dreamed. She was back in California, but instead of a condo in Costa Mesa her home was a skinny thing on stilts high above the Hollywood Bowl. She was standing alone in her living room when suddenly from the patio she heard a shrill cry; it sounded like a baby. When she went outside to look she saw that it was Mittens, his little body torn and bleeding, half eaten by coyotes. Jayson stood on the grass, his face shadowed, and then he came forward, and she saw something terrible in his eyes. Pointing at the cat he shook his head and said, "I told you this would happen, I *told* you . . ."

Catapulted into wakefulness by her own sobs, Joanna grabbed up her robe and blundered from bed. Shivering (*damn* these cold floors, even in May, damn these chilly, gas-heated rooms!) and went out into the living room where she buried herself in a wool throw on the sofa and sat for a long while looking miserably out into the night. A jeweled caterpillar was making its way slowly up Finchley Road, its progress slowed by winking rubies.

She wanted a cigarette badly on this, the fourth full day of abstinence in an attempt to quit, cold turkey. It had been her own idea; Jayson, a nonsmoker, never cared whether she quit or not. Still, if she smoked now he would look at her a little oddly in the morning when he washed out the ashtray, as if to say, *Joanna you little fool, can't you do something as minor as keep a promise to yourself?* Oh, well, she'd probably go back to it in time anyway . . .

A thimbleful of peach brandy got her feeling better, and she tried to decode the dream. Like it or not, and she did not, it was tied to something she and Jayson no longer talked about, but which had been very much on both their minds in the months shortly after she'd come to live with him. There had never been any question but that the attraction between them was physical as well as intellectual, intensified by those long periods of forced separation. Joanna, whose résumé of sexual experience was fairly wide though not unusual, was secretly delighted by Jayson's tastes, particularly piquant because he scarcely came near or even touched her unless they were making love. He never talked about what women he had known before, but Joanna imagined there had been many. What surprised her more than anything was the fact that shortly after Christmas of last year he had begun suggesting that they have a baby.

Joanna didn't want a baby, at least not now. What was the point? She was young enough to wait for years. He wasn't, and didn't wish to be an old-age pensioner when his firstborn child went off to college. They argued over it for weeks, reasonably at first, then bitterly, until at last the situation came to an all-out fight with Jayson shouting and Joanna crying. She was on the Pill; one day while she was out he ransacked her things and threw them down the drain. She called him obsessive and he slapped her face; later they made up on the Regency card table in the sitting room.

Finally, about the same time she got tired of resisting he grew tired of insisting, so they simply let the matter drop. Joanna got another prescription, and things went back to what they had been before, or nearly so. No baby, at least not now. But Joanna couldn't help thinking that something vital had been damaged during all those weeks of wrangling. In time she was able to put it from her mind. Until tonight. Until the dream.

Something was wrong; the dream proved it. Something vague and shadowy that she could not define. Jayson felt it, too, that was the scary part; he was going to Los Angeles to escape whatever consequences were the result. Confused, she fumbled for the brandy and spilled it; she began to cry. Softly at first, then sobbing helplessly, till Jayson came and took her back to bed. There under the duvet she fell asleep in his arms, with the tears still wet on her face.

*   *   *

Joanna was feeling moody and ill-humored the following morning as she padded, sock-clad, around the kitchen making up a late breakfast for herself.

Tap tap tap from the other room. She checked the blue numbers on the microwave. 10:14. Jayson began his work every morning at precisely nine o'clock, just like a man going to the office. He had so much discipline. Sometimes it made Joanna feel more than a little jealous.

She should work every day, like he did. She should simply put herself down in front of the typewriter and begin work on *The Scourge*. But it was always so much easier to *think* about working; to shop, cook, read, take walks—all the while thinking about writing but not doing it. Of course that wasn't going to get it written. Sooner or later she'd have to—the Nike ad flashed in her mind like a road sign—JUST DO IT.

She boiled an egg but forgot it while she fussed over tea and bacon. When it was past poaching, she chopped it up into bits for egg salad, mixed in sweet hot mustard and mayonnaise, crumbled the bacon on top, then swept the mixture between slabs of Mother's Pride. With the sandwich and a mug of tea balanced in her hands, she headed for Jayson's workroom.

He didn't notice her as she sank onto the sofa opposite his desk, or, if he did, refused to look up from the page.

"Busy?" she asked, feeling rebuffed.

"You can see I am." *Tap tap tap.*

"Okay if I just sit here and eat?"

"Go ahead." *Tap spacebar click.*

Joanna chewed in silence, brushing crumbs from her lap onto the carpet, thinking she'd have to bring in the vacuum later to clean up the bits. Jayson was dogmatic about neatness. Though he rarely said anything, she knew he cast a wary eye whenever she threw her clothes about or left dishes sitting in the sink. It never occurred to Joanna that he might be oversensitive about such things, that *she* might actually have the prerogative of her own habits, however bad. It wasn't even love that dictated these unspoken rules, for she had loved other men more than she loved him. But Jayson was *Jayson,* unstintingly correct, quietly authoritarian, and she believed unwaveringly—almost like a child—in his power to be *right.*

Still it was difficult sometimes, which made her think the answer was to get a place of her own, perhaps nearby so they'd be able to see each other almost as much as they did now. She didn't have to depend on Jayson for money (though she often did) and she could certainly use some space. But being alone now was not what Joanna wanted, though she often felt it was what she needed most. She didn't want to grow too dependent on Jayson, though with each day that was exactly what was happening.

She had finished the sandwich and was sipping the last of her Lemon Lift by the time Jayson pulled the page from the type-writer and looked up at her. "Good morning," he said crisply.

"Not so far: I can't seem to get my eyes open."

"You're not an early riser."

"I used to be."

He shifted a little in his chair. "You have to learn to relax, Joanna, you've been having a lot of bad nights recently."

"I know." She thumped her heel against the carpet.

"You don't sleep well . . ."

"I *know.*" She didn't need him to remind her, and yet she couldn't quite bring herself to tell him that she didn't want to sleep because sleep meant dreams and dreams were wearing her down. "I'm always a little strung out when I start a new book," she added lamely, sensing his distraction. Jayson never appreciated interruptions to his work, and at the moment she counted as a major interruption.

"Are you going to work on the book today?" he asked, his gray eyes narrowing—his "tutorial expression," as she always thought of it.

"Later," she answered, getting up to go, then pausing in the doorway. "I think I'll take a walk, do some shopping . . ."

His hands found the keys. "It won't write itself, Joanna." His voice was pleasant enough, but she caught the ominous note of disapproval that always made her feel like a delinquent child.

Tap tap tap. In the bedroom she stuffed her wallet full of credit cards and got ready to go out.

*   *   *

It was June and the streets literally crawled with tourists, but Joanna never minded their numbers. After all, that's really what she was, just a tourist on an extended visa. Sometimes she missed California, but she rarely allowed herself to contemplate a move back there because it would only happen (and this Joanna *knew*) when she and Jayson no longer lived together, and she was far from ready to admit that day would probably come.

Some days she walked for miles without stopping, not seeing much; too distracted to see. Often her steps took unexpected turns and Joanna would find herself at a familiar bookstore or a favorite shopping haunt like Miss Selfridge or Whistles. But most of the time her strolls were aimless pilgrimages to nowhere, designed to get her out of the flat and away from Jayson while he was working. That way she wouldn't be tempted to interrupt him and he wouldn't be tempted to scold her for being idle.

Actually she wasn't. Joanna could work out no end of plot problems while keeping herself occupied with other things. It was her way of concentrating, of achieving *focus,* and it almost always worked. But even if her mind was distracted her emotions weren't. There was always a rush of nerves when she began working on a new book, conflicting feelings of total commitment and total vulnerability. But *The Scourge* was making her fairly tingle with anticipation, even though day after day slipped by without her putting so much as a single word on paper.

England decimated by the Plague of 1349. The idea of using her textbook knowledge of the era as a springboard for fiction had been with her for a long time, before she'd even begun work on *The Beggarman King* or *Tabitha's Claw*. Oddly, it was one of Jayson Gardiner's books that had first turned her on to the idea. At sixteen she'd taken a copy of *England Under the Plague* out of the Pacifica library in order to satisfy a history class requirement and ended in reading the 592-page text from cover to cover in a single weekend. Perhaps it was one of the reasons she always saw Jayson as her mentor. His grasp of history had inspired her own, a decade before they first met in a suitably historical setting.

This book would be good, her best. She was anxious, nervous, even thrilled when thinking about it, birthing characters in her imagination, bringing others to life again long after death had consigned them to the urns of history. With every book she got a little better, a little closer to the writer she knew she could be. Perhaps Jayson was right about this impending separation: she could throw herself into the new book and not have to worry about slighting him with an artist's indifference.

Walking slowly along the wharf she kicked a bit of driftwood, picked it up and tossed it into the river, watching as the tide scurried it away. She threw her cigarette into the water after it. A few rebellious sparks flew, blazed for a second, then drowned in the air. The light began to fade; it grew chilly. She went home.

One day after spending the morning browsing in the National Portrait Gallery, she was caught unaware (and without a raincoat) by a sudden downpour. Surefooted in Reeboks, she raced across the Square and ducked inside St. Martin's-in-the-Field. Shivering, she made her way quickly up the center aisle and slipped inconspicuously into one of the pews. A handful of people sat at indistinct points throughout the church. Some, like her, were refugees from the weather. Others were suppliants with heads bent, bargaining for a few minutes' worth of God's time.

Joanna, no suppliant today but pious all the same, closed her eyes and silently repeated the Lord's Prayer. Religion came naturally to her, the way a talent for music or dance does to some. Born a Lutheran—until his death her father had been the Pastor at St. Luke's in Pacifica—she had only recently begun "being

Protestant" again. During her college years Eastern religions had both baffled and sustained her. Later, swept up in a mesmerizing tide of medievalism, she had converted to Rome.

Love and religion had always been curiously linked in Joanna's life. At nineteen she'd been surprisingly virginal until a parapsychologist from Berkeley had remarked that her aura displayed inexhaustible amounts of sexual energy, and wouldn't she like for him to teach her how to tap into such a power? Her affirmative reply had led to a weekend of marathon sex with him in an oddly tilting house on a crooked street in Sausalito. The whole experience was more enervating than enlightening and put Joanna off sex for several months.

The following semester, after transferring to UCLA, she fell in love with her professor of Eastern philosophies. Armed with knowledge gained at the hands (and other anatomical parts) of her parapsychologist, Joanna entered into an intense affair with the professor. It ended when his wife (of whom Joanna knew nothing) showed up one day at the foot of the bed while he and Joanna were trying out positions from the Kama Sutra.

It was shortly after the relationship ended (the erring professor returning to his wife) that Joanna decided to take medieval history as her major. The fervor of the Middle Ages left its mark on her. She fell eagerly into Catholicism; there was even talk of entering a convent. The following summer she traveled to England with a group of students. It was there she met the man who would for all time serve as the metaphor for her Catholic period.

She first met David Lair at Goethe's, a swank coffee bar in Marylebone, just off the Edgeware Road. Goethe's catered to a neophyte bohemian crowd of would-be artists and writers, most of them students looking for a muse. David Lair was no student. He was already a famous West End playwright with his current success, Girls in White Dresses, *slated to open on Broadway in the fall.*

Handsome, green-eyed David was a throwback to the John Osborne type of dramatist/celebrity: angry, intense, magnetic. One of Ireland's "artist exiles" he alternately hated England and courted her favor, like a gigolo eager to please. He had orig-

inally trained as an actor at Dublin's prestigious Abbey, and indeed it was with those talents that he held the crowd of students and casual patrons spellbound each night at Goethe's.

Joanna was there one night with a few of her friends. Like everyone else, she listened enraptured to his recitations. Halfway into the second stanza of Wilde's "Ballad of Reading Gaol" she knew she was in love with him. She was only marginally familiar with his work, but from that night on she undertook to seek out every line he'd ever written.

It took six weeks of nightly visits to the coffeehouse before she was bold enough to introduce herself; she was far too modest to realize he had noticed her long before. That very night, after the crowd at Goethe's had dispersed, David suggested a more private venue: his newly refurbished Edwardian terraced house in Battersea Park. Joanna was so in love and awestruck she only wished she still had her virginity to give. No man deserved the gift of her purity as David did. . . .

For six weeks—the brief span of their affair—she loved him slavishly, a love that she was too mesmerized to notice he did not return. But he fostered her ambitions as a novelist, told her she had the most beautiful breasts in the world, and praised her religious conversion since he was himself a devout (if somewhat lapsed) member of the Catholic faith.

At the end of six weeks he calmly announced to Joanna that his wife (yes, once again there was a wife!) was going to have a baby and he didn't think it "sporting" (a playwright *and he could find no better word!) for him to see other women. As blandly as that the great love affair of Joanna's life was dismissed.*

Humiliated, Joanna begged him to reconsider, but he refused with as little grace as if she were an overzealous fan demanding an autograph at an inopportune time. For weeks Joanna agonized over her Great Loss, starving herself, even contemplating suicide (she was never really serious about that but couldn't resist the scenario). She wrote letters addressed to MR. DAVID LIAR, deliberately transposing the letters of his surname to characterize what she had come to believe was his true self, but she never mailed them. Over and over she telephoned his house, but it was always a woman's voice who answered. Finally (and

*most humiliating of all) she rang up to find the number had
been changed. That she could have been accounted such a nui-
sance shamed her, shocked her back into herself.*

*She would get over him; she would go on living. There would
be no other men in her life: she would give herself up to writing
and religion. A few days later she made a weekend trip to Bosworth field, intent on researching her novel. And there in the
Buttery, almost as if he had been waiting for her all his life, was
Jayson Gardiner.*

She looked up, flushing at the intensity of her memories, as a
priest brushed past her, walking swiftly down the aisle, their eyes
meeting for a moment. It had been a long time since Joanna had
been inside a church and his gaze seemed a silent reprimand.
That was silly, of course; he had no way of knowing. Actually, she
had been to church a few times with Jayson, who went regularly,
but Joanna disliked the Anglican service, and so she preferred to
stay home, sleeping in, or watching "Sports Roundup" on chan-
nel 4.

There was a smell of old wax and wet wool in the church, and a
sense of need, the result of centuries' worth of whispered prayers.
Now she knelt and made a supplication, very general: peace in
the world, an end to hunger, good reviews for *Tabitha's Claw*,
due out in mid-September. When she had finished, Joanna made
an offering of two pounds to the wooden box outside the vestry
door. Then she pulled her damp sweater closer and stepped out
into the grayness of a dying afternoon. It was still raining, and she
ran across the street to Charing Cross. Behind her, dripping and
silent, the stone lions of Trafalgar Square looked on.

*   *   *

The remainder of June and July passed in a stretch of unevent-
ful days. Joanna continued her afternoon rambles through the
city streets and worked intermittently at her book. Jayson completed the final draft of *Witchcraft in Medieval Lincolnshire* and
concentrated on the lecture series upcoming in September.
There was no more talk of babies or separations, and Joanna's
bad dreams faded into memory.

Their schedules were somewhat incompatible. Jayson rose early and worked with only a few breaks till early evening. Joanna stayed up late, and rarely got up before noon. Lately, Jayson had been spending a lot of his days away from the flat, working at the British Museum researching his lectures.

On such a day, foggy with sleep, Joanna strolled out into the hallway for the mail, unmindful of her scant attire: bikini panties and a mini T-shirt. "The people in this building are beginning to wonder just what kind of girl I'm living with," Jayson had told her more than once. But this morning (or afternoon: she vaguely recalled the clock sounding out its dozen chimes as she still languished beneath the duvet) there was no one in the hallway to spy as she sorted through the mail, which one of the building's early birds had deposited on the cherrywood table. It was such a pretty piece; Joanna had been tempted many times to drag it into the flat and plead ignorance or burglary by a masked intruder, but she never did.

Inside she tossed the bills on Jayson's desk, including the one from Harrods, trying to remember what last-month extravagance would rate his usual gentle scolding. In the kitchen she fixed herself a cup of tea, tossed the junk mail into the wastebasket, and carried what remained to the living room. Comfortable in a Bergère chair amid Jayson's faultless decoration, she examined the mail. The Musical Heritage Review. Catalogues from Horchow and Strawbridge & Clothier. A postcard from Aunt Rue, who was touring Canada with a group from church. Joanna smiled affectionately, envisioning her aunt ferreting out the best from every antique store in a shop-till-she-dropped marathon from Edmonton to Montreal. "Returning S.F. Aug. 25" confided the postscript, which Joanna interpreted as a reminder to write.

The other piece of mail was a letter bearing a Queen Elizabeth stamp and a faint Lewes postmark. There was no return address. She was about to discard it as junk mail, too, when her eye caught something and she looked again. *Ms.* Joanna Latimer, read the typed address. That was unusual. Here in England letters or mail of any kind invariably came addressing her as "Miss." Even her subscription to *Best* ignored the MS. that she had handwritten on the order form with an exaggerated sense of rebellion.

Using Jayson's undirtied butter knife, Joanna sliced the top of the envelope and drew out the single folded sheet. A full page of space-and-a-half, neatly typed characters met her eye. At the top, printed in green, were the words EAST SUSSEX COUNTY COUN-CIL. Puzzled, Joanna sipped her tea and read.

Dear Ms. Latimer:

I am happy to tell you that certain research materials relating to the period of the Black Death in England (c1349) have recently come into our hands via a generous personal donation and it would be our pleasure to make them available for your use in researching your current novel The Scourge.

These records include diaries kept by Simon de Falaise, Lord of Alfriston, up to the time of his death in 1349. Being well acquainted with your earlier historical novels, and knowing the depth of your research ability, I assume you have no difficulty in reading Latin.

Certain other documents, some presumed lost for centuries, include the writings of Geoffrey Fitzstephen (the abbot of St. Audric at the time of the Black Death), which attest to the horror of that era. No doubt since your book is set in Sussex at that time you should find these documents fascinating, and they are yours to study at your leisure here in the library reading room for as long as they are needed.

Should you wish to visit St. Audric for this purpose we will be happy to receive you. The village is located in the heart of the Cuckmere valley only two miles east of Alfriston and just off the main road. Mrs. Munro, proprietress of The Sheaves bed and breakfast inn, should be able to arrange accommodations for you at any time after August 25. For myself, I shall be away on holiday the last two weeks of the month, but upon my return shall be pleased to assist you in whatever manner possible.

Sincerely,
Kate Callison
(Librarian, St. Audric)

Joanna read the letter again, and then a third time. Despite the openness of the invitation, there was something faintly cryptic and disturbing about it. Few people (and certainly no strangers) knew the subject of her new book; fewer still knew its title. And yet Kate Callison—whoever she was—had named it. How was this possible?

Early in her career it had been quite common for Joanna to solicit information from every conceivable source, and this usually included the small local libraries within the perimeters of her narrative's setting. Ever since moving to England she had dispensed with that practice, since information was never more than a phone call away. Outside of a few random visits to the British Museum reading room, all her research for *The Scourge* had been confined to Jayson's incredible personal library collection (his "medievabilia" she always called it), and to her own backlog of notes.

Joanna knew Sussex well from many weekend jaunts alone or with Jayson, and yet she had never heard of St. Audric. That was another puzzle. Someone there knew she was writing a novel set in a particular place and time. How could that be, unless this Kate Callison had a nose for information that bordered on prescience? The more she thought about it the more confusing it became.

Joanna, who loved a mystery at the sacrifice of nearly all common-sense explanations, nonetheless scanned the facts with candor. One: She had never heard of the village of St. Audric (though she recognized the name of the saint it had unquestionably been named for). Two: She had never heard of Kate Callison. Three: No one, outside of a few friends and the people at Pendragon Press, knew the subject and title of her book. And four: She most certainly had not inquired of the Sussex County Council, or any library in the East Sussex area.

The tea, gone tepid now, tasted flat and flavorless, so she pushed the cup aside. *How could anyone there know something she had not been told?* It was impossible, eerie. Yet the letter was proof. And unless she was either crazy or still dreaming, it was a tangible fact in her hand.

For the next few hours Joanna went about a series of chores, always returning perplexed in the midst of this task or that to stare down at the letter, a crisp white oblong in the center of the kitchen table where she had left it—and always expecting (however unreasoningly) to find the words had changed or that another reading would render up a clue. But it remained as indecipherable as a code.

Sluicing out the kitchen sink of its grungy waste water, Joanna puzzled over that thought. In a way the letter *was* like a code, revelatory only in a superficial way, and filled with hidden meanings. Its stiff, almost formal prose hid an invitation that was nothing short of a command. She was being commanded, however gently, to go to St. Audric. But *why?* And once again the silent rejoinder in her mind asked *how?*

By the time Jayson came in at five thirty, Joanna had managed to complete a hasty clean-up of the flat. Leaving pasta and sauce boiling on the stove she dashed to the bathroom for a quick shower and shampoo, then dressed herself in her favorite black silk caftan.

Jayson was at the stove frowning (the pasta was no doubt overcooked) when she came out, rubbing her hair with a towel. She tilted her face for his kiss but he had already turned away, the saucepan in his hand.

Joanna slumped in a chair watching silently as he put the finishing touches on their dinner preparations and decanted the wine. It was easy to see he was in one of his silent, self-absorbed moods that discouraged conversation while not actually forbidding it. She had hoped to tell him about the letter and elicit his advice, but now it might be better to wait for a more convenient time.

"You're quiet tonight," she observed as they ate.

Jayson looked up, his expression revealing little. He was always so composed it was difficult to read him. "Just tired," he answered, twisting spaghetti on his fork with a quick, deft movement. "I had one hell of a time getting those books I wanted, and then Kevin didn't show up so I never got a look at those maps he promised to show me." Peevishly he snapped a breadstick in half, mumbling, "Research can be such a pain in the ass. You're lucky you write fiction."

The words hit her like a slap and she answered sharply, "I have to research my books—what do you think I've been doing with *The Scourge* these past few months?"

"Not much," he answered quickly, his guileless tone making the words sound all the more rude. "It seems to me you spend most of your time shopping or sleeping or watching the telly."

"That's not true!" she objected, sounding hurt and female. "Just because my working habits are different doesn't mean that I don't accomplish as much as you do."

"Very well," he said neatly. "May I have the sauce?"

She thought, and not for the first time, that she had misjudged Jayson; that he wasn't really a very nice person after all. In the beginning Joanna had chosen to see the many ways in which they were alike, ignoring their differences, which were considerable. She saw him as her teacher, so it was hard to think he could be wrong. But sometimes when his disposition turned sour, like tonight, she felt a little like a fool for allowing him so great a latitude in her mind.

Pushing her plate aside she reached for her cigarettes, ignoring their tacit agreement that she never smoke during meals. "A letter came today," she announced suddenly.

"Anything interesting?"

"I think so." She slid the folded letter out from beneath the plate where she had hidden it (strange she should think of it in such a way) and handed it over to Jayson, who took it with no great show of interest. She kept silent, watching his face as he read.

"What do you think?" she asked when he had finished.

He handed the letter back to her and went on eating. "I think you should go."

"But it's all so peculiar! I never wrote to that woman; I've never even heard of her! And how could she have known about my book? Nobody knows about it except the people at Pendragon Press, my agent, you . . ."

He shrugged. "So she's got a friend at Pendragon Press! Why do you have to make it such a mystery, Joanna? You have a lot of fans, and word gets out. The publicity for your last book probably mentioned something about researching a novel on the Black Death. And I have heard you mention it in an interview a time or two." He shook his head reprovingly, but now he was smiling.

"You don't really think it's something spooky, do you? What a silly girl you are at times."

She refused to be put off by his words. "Listen: I know this much. I never said the book was to be set in Sussex, because I wasn't even sure of that myself till just a few weeks ago. And what about the title? How can you explain the fact that a woman I have never met and don't know from Adam, has the title right? I don't care what you say, this whole thing is *weird* . . ."

"All right," he agreed amicably, "it's weird. But there's still got to be some explanation." He pushed aside his plate and reached for his sweet. "I always said you had a Sherlock Holmes mentality. Check it out."

"Don't worry, mister," she answered tartly. "I intend to."

She had planned to wash the dishes and then settle down to do some writing, but after finishing his pudding Jayson wanted to make love, and though she wasn't even vaguely in the mood, she agreed readily enough. Recently they had both been so preoccupied that their sex life had taken on the stale drudge of habit. Spontaneous times like this were not to be denied.

They began with Jayson riding her on the Persian carpet in the hall and ended in the bedroom with Joanna face down on the waxed wood *Directoire* settee, panting and satisfied. He was so good: he never came before she was ready, and he could keep her on the brink forever. There were times (like now) when she believed that everything she knew about making love she'd learned from Jayson. Everything else before him had been only *fucking,* nothing more.

Later Jayson retired to his workroom while Joanna spent the entire evening watching television, including a show on BBC 2 that chronicled the disintegration of the ozone layer and destruction of the rain forests with depressing accuracy. When it was over she sat in bleak silence, her happy mood vanished, miserably recalling all the waste and reckless consumption she had generated in her twenty-seven years of life. In the last decade while the earth's atmosphere was being poisoned and the very future of Existence threatened, she had been studying history— researching events and cultures vanished from sight hundreds of years earlier.

What had Joanna Lynne Latimer contributed to the future?

Feeling mortified and a failure, she turned off the lights and went to bed. Jayson was asleep with the night-table lamp still burning and his reading glasses on. She climbed over him, jostling the bed much more than necessary, hoping he would wake up and want her again. But he slept. After a little while she did, too.

In the days that led up to his departure for Los Angeles, Jayson and Joanna knew a resurgence of their love that was reminiscent of their early days together. She was always sweet and compliant; he never criticized or lost patience with her. They made love as they had in the beginning, too, each enraptured by a fantasy that no one but the other had been able to satisfy or understand. It was as though, then as now, they could look deep within the other's eyes and see their own self reflected there—a fragile thing, flawed and afraid, but beautiful.

If an impending separation could work such magic as this, then Joanna was almost grateful for it. She kept telling herself that it was only a short time—three little months—no more than that. They had lived through longer periods of absence and in comparison this would be easy, she knew it; they'd see.

"It's my turn," she squealed, splashing wildly and grabbing for the sponge, "now turn around and let me wash your back . . ."

It was five o'clock Monday morning, August 24, three hours before Jayson's flight was due to leave from Heathrow. They had spent the night eating oysters stuffed with chocolate sauce and making love. Now they romped together in Jayson's bathtub, and even he was too engrossed to notice how the lapping waters cascaded over the side, wetting his expensive rug.

"I'll miss you so much," Joanna crooned, letting the oily droplets run down his back, "what am I supposed to do for fun around here while you're gone, buy a vibrator?"

"Don't you dare," he answered sharply, grabbing her wrist and kissing it. "Do without: I plan to."

"I will if you will." She giggled, pulling her hand away to make a cross-your-heart gesture on her dripping breast.

"It's not such a bad idea, Joanna," he said seriously, turning to face her, "all that libido going into the work. You'll be glad of the results, I promise you."

His penis lolled in the water between them and she reached to fondle it. "I don't know about *that*," she murmured just before her face disappeared into the water, "but I do know that I will miss you. . . ."

Forty-five minutes later he was dry and dressed and standing at the front door, cases in hand, waiting for the taxi. Joanna had begged to drive him to the airport but Jayson had refused the offer. "Remember, we decided: no tearful partings," he reminded her. "And you know how you get."

They had settled all the things that needed settling: she would scout around Sussex at her leisure gathering material and a "feel" for her novel. Since she would probably be away a good deal of September before settling down to write the book in earnest, and Jayson would be likewise occupied with settling into his new environment, they had agreed not to contact one another until October 1, when Jayson would call the flat and give her an address in Los Angeles where she could reach him.

At first Joanna had protested. "But why can't I call you? I know you'll be staying with Professor Hilliard till you find your own place. My God, I was a student in his comparative history class . . ."

"And he'll think I'm a henpecked old fool if you keep calling me up to ask if I've got myself a suntan, or if I'm eating right. And I won't have you sitting around here being broody, with your mind wandering and one ear on alert for the telephone when you should be concentrating on your own work," he had argued. "Now come on, Joanna, let's be adult about this."

So in the end, as usual, she had complied willingly.

They kissed good-bye and parted with a minimum of emotion. By the time Jayson's plane taxied down the runway to await take-off, Joanna had shed her tears and crept back to bed with a handful of cookies, stuffed his pillow between her legs, and fallen asleep.

She spent the day sleeping, and the following morning, which was overcast threatening rain by afternoon, she wheeled the TV into the bedroom and passed the hours watching soap operas, game shows, and a videotape Jayson had recorded of them making love. She consumed several pints of Häagen-Dazs chocolate-

chocolate chip ice cream. She ordered out for a double sausage pizza. She slept.

Joanna awoke around midnight to the sound of armies warring in her room. The square of light just in front of her disclosed the origin of the battle. Afterward a young man wearing a toga, his hair combed like Fabian Forte's, walked back and forth among the dead, calling for his brother.

On Wednesday her period came and so she allowed herself the luxury of yet another day (or two) in bed, feeding herself on Nuprin and Reese's Peanut Butter Cups.

Finally, on Saturday, Joanna took herself in hand. No more lounging about and stuffing herself with high calorie goodies; no more mooning over Jayson's absence. She loved him, and she missed him, but she could do without him for a while.

It was time to shift from sensual overindulgence to mental alertness; time to put things in order. There had been the usual promotional business for her new book, but she'd disposed of that, thank God, in August, so she was free to spend herself in preparations for *The Scourge*. Joanna meant to go "location scouting" in Sussex, looking for the spot whereon to re-create her "vanished" fourteenth-century village. And since she had already been invited, there was no reason not to visit St. Audric first.

The letter from Kate Callison was tucked away somewhere amid her notes; Joanna found it after a fifteen-minute search. Reading it now the letter seemed less mysterious. Perhaps she had misjudged it at the first.

The operator could find no number for a Kate Callison in St. Audric or Alfriston, so Joanna rang up The Sheaves instead.

"Two-four-seven-eight," the voice came back at her.

"Is this The Sheaves?"

"This is Mrs. Munro."

"Not The Sheaves?"

"Mrs. Munro *at* The Sheaves, I can't say it plainer." The woman's voice was sharp and agitated, as if the call had been an interruption.

Hurriedly Joanna began explaining. "Mrs. Munro, I'm a novelist, and I plan to do some research in the East Sussex area. Is it possible for you to put me up for a few weeks, perhaps as long as a month?" The idea came to her even as she spoke the words. Why not make St. Audric her base for exploring Sussex? There was nothing to keep her in the flat, and in any case it only reminded her of Jayson's absence. There were no "must tend tos," no plants or animals to be watered and fed. She was free to travel where she wished and that is what she would do.

"Mind you, it's not a fancy place," the unfriendly voice at her ear warned.

"I'm not asking for something fancy," Joanna snapped back, "just something comfortable where I can work."

"No doubles."

"All right, a single then. But something big enough for me to work in. I don't want to be shut up all day in a room no bigger than a closet. Oh, and I'll need a desk and chair. And perhaps a bookcase, a small one, if you can manage it."

"I can manage a desk and chair" was the terse reply.

"Okay. Just so you know, I use a typewriter and I work at night. Is that going to be a problem?"

"Not so long as you bring your own."

"Well, *of course* I'll bring my own typewriter!" Joanna was fast becoming impatient with this woman's rudeness. "What I meant was I'll be typing at night. Will *that* be a problem?"

There was a grumbled answer that Joanna took for no.

"I'll be arriving the day after tomorrow, Monday."

"Very well: that's twelve pounds per night, with breakfast every morning. Supper's five pounds extra and I must know by noon. Cash only: no checks or credit cards."

Joanna couldn't resist the impulse to beat her down a bit, so she paused as if thinking it over while she mentally computed the cost of a one-month stay. "How about three hundred even for the month?" she asked, adding quickly, "half in advance." She certainly wasn't about to turn the whole three hundred over to this old bitch. If it turned out she didn't like the area and didn't want to stay, she would have one jolly time trying to get her money back. She waited, her long nails tapping out a dance of irritation on the table.

"Just a moment, please."

Joanna waited. Someone was talking in the background; she could hear two female voices arguing quietly. Then Mrs. Munro was saying, "That's all right then; three hundred for the month. And breakfast as I said. And supper still extra."

"And no checks or credit cards," Joanna parroted. "Then I'll see you on Monday." She had nearly hung up when she remembered to say, more pleasantly this time, "Oh, and my name is Joanna. Joanna Latimer."

The phone went down on her words with a heavy click.

"Sweet lady," Joanna cooed and slapped the receiver into place.

She started that evening, sorting and packing her notes and other research data first. There was a lot to take, but she wouldn't need all of it, so she tried to be selective. Clothes were less of a problem. Without Jayson to dress and undress for, her choices were uncomplicated. After a quick her-side-of-the-closet raid, Joanna took out a few layered voile skirts and their matching ribbed turtleneck sweaters, two shirt-dresses, a pale blue terrycloth shorty robe, and a multicolored Ruth Norman caftan. A further appraisal caused her to throw in her black knit sheath and matching trapeze jacket. It wouldn't hurt to have one dressy outfit. For the rest she scavenged through the drawers for underwear, oversize Sleepy-Tees, sweats, and a few pairs of jeans. Except for jeans, Joanna didn't wear pants very often because she was too short to look good in anything with very tailored lines, and a little too big in the behind (her second best feature, Jayson always said).

Working quickly with a great sense of purpose and momentum, she tossed various sundries into a black Victoria Jackson makeup bag: skin spritzer, moisturizer; a bottle each of Shalimar, LouLou, Jontue. Her hand hesitated over the Poison, and moved on. She only wore that for Jayson.

By late afternoon she'd completed her chores. Two cases stood in the hall, flanked on either side by her portable Royal and a banker's box filled with notes and books. Edgy with anticipation now that her plans were under way, she made dinner from the fridge, using up things she'd just have to throw away before leaving anyway. The result was a fruit salad made from kiwi, pineapple, and cherimoya, topped off with a grilled cheese sandwich using the last of the pumpernickle bread. Before going to bed that night she watched the Dirk Bogarde version of *A Tale of Two Cities* and speed-read the new Stephen King in a single sitting.

Joanna awoke at eleven the next morning to the sound of church bells. Sunday: one more day. It seemed silly to delay her trip another twenty-four hours. If The Sheaves could take her for a month beginning tomorrow, they could certainly squeeze her in for a single extra night.

After showering (the bathtub was too big and empty without a playmate) Joanna pulled on a sundress and sandals (it was going to be *hot* today), tied her hair in a ponytail, and collected her toothbrush and a few last-minute items. She gave the milk and leftover produce away to the young Pakistani performance artist on the second floor who was always ogling her in the hallway; set the alarm, locked up, and carried out her luggage.

Jayson had two cars, a black Daimler and a no-nonsense blue Ford Escort. Joanna had permission and keys for both, but the Daimler was too big and difficult for her to handle, so she took the Ford. Never very certain where she was going when driving in the city, she took the Edgeware Road up to Park Lane, skirted Grosvenor Place, cut west at Kings Road, and crossed the bridge at Chelsea. From there it was south to Purley to pick up the A22. She had a vague recollection of the general route from the trip she and Jayson had made once to the Toft, East Dean, to visit playwright Christopher Fry, a friend of Jayson's. If Joanna's sense of geography was any good at all, Alfriston lay only a bit more to the west. Oh well, there was a map in the glovebox.

She stuffed a tape of *Tosca* into the cassette player and began to sing "Vissi d'arte" aloud in a duet with Callas. They didn't sound the same, but who was there to hear and make unflattering comparisons? There had been a time, when she was very young, that Joanna had dreamed of being a singer. . . .

Out of the city the air grew cooler, she could almost scent the sea. A light fog, shot through with sunshine, rolled up from the coast. She sang.

*   *   *

The village of St. Audric was not so old as many of its kind in England. It had grown up around the abandoned abbey of the same name during the late sixteenth century, flourishing briefly as a market town a century later. Bounded by the "Long Man" hill figure on the north, by the Friston Forest and chalk cliffs to the south, it was no less an impressive place for being small.

The High Street, cutting in just below Windover Hill and the South Downs Way, ran half a mile down a gentle slope to the place where it intersected Alfred's Lane. This was little more than a single carriage road just above the churchyard. Its name reflected an era when King Alfred and his men traveled it on the way to their capital at Winchester.

Trespass Lane (corrupted from the original *tréspas* of Norman times) forked out near the top of the High Street into three separate paths. One led past Shepherd's Cot; the other became Abbot's Way and stretched to the very door of Blackmantle (once the Benedictine Abbey named for St. Audric); the third led back over the slope to Windover Hill and the Long Man. In the late nineteenth century an archaeologist had discovered a rich Saxon burial ground just beyond Shepherd's Cot. The remains of that find could be seen on display at the Museum of Local History at Lewes.

For centuries this little piece of land beside the River Cuckmere was a place of this inn or that, with few permanent living accommodations. In the early eighteenth century a developer from London changed all that. King George's Row, a wide street faceted with attractive Georgian homes to the east of Trespass Lane, was the legacy of his plan. Malting Road, once no more than a little path on the other side of the High Street, became a development area in the 1860s when a group of rich bohemian types founded Fiddler's Green, an artist community just below the South Downs Way. Fiddler's Close was a two-angled street just off the Green that knew a modicum of development in the twenties when several "modern" homes were built there. From that time to the present, the village of St. Audric remained, quite remarkably, unchanged.

These days the Georgian Row was occupied by "London types," while the modest Fiddler's Green two-up-one-down bungalows once used as workshops by Pre-Raphaelite artisans were family houses now. Except for scattered rural dwellings near the abandoned Mill, and those just above the Friston Forest, there were no other houses in St. Audric.

What the village had in abundance for its size was shops. Although it was five miles off the main motorway, St. Audric naturally attracted a certain amount of the overflow of tourists from Alfriston. It served its own habitants with a bank, post office, saddle shop, grocery store, and bakery—all standing in the High Street. As Joanna Latimer had learned, there was also a library.

Blackmantle, named for the black capes worn by Benedictine monks who had once lived within its walls, had been a private residence since 1385 when the powerful Mortimer family had taken it over. Later the Percys held it for a time. Then in 1584 it came into the hands of Sir Gerald Latymere by a curious set of circumstances. A penniless knight, he had distinguished himself by uncovering an assassination plot against the Queen. As a reward for his service he was offered his choice of manors and rents. But he asked for the ruined abbey instead, and was given it by a grateful sovereign. He named it Blackmantle, put up the beginnings of a village, and in such a way St. Audric had come to be.

It still flaunted its Jacobean heritage in architecture: cream-colored and timbered buildings tilting crazily at the top lined the High Street. Curious customs dating from that same time could be found here: well-dressing ceremonies at Fiddler's Green each Midsummer's Eve; a *bal masque* every All Hallows'. At Saturnalia there could always be found wreaths of winter greenery left as offerings at the Long Man's feet. In such a place the old beliefs never die.

Some of the buildings predated Jacobean times. These included a pub, The Plague Maiden, which was simply called The Maid by residents of the village. A charity hostelry had stood in its place during the Black Death, when Abbot Geoffrey Fitzstephen had ordered one to be built. Later it had fallen into ruin, its ramshackle remains swept away. An inn was built there in 1364. A few years later, during a return of plague to Sussex, it was named The Plague Maiden. The pub's signboard still proclaimed witness to that terrible time and the origin of its ghastly name: a white-faced woman brandishing a red scarf.

There was another pub set in the High Street. The Hawk and Scarecrow had a curious past that drew many tourists to its doors, particularly Americans. Built at the time Sir Gerald took the land over, The Hawk and Scarecrow bore a reputation for being haunted. It had been featured in several books on the subject of occult phenomena in England, and members of England's prestigious Ghost Club had spent an all-night vigil there in 1971. They had managed to record on film the outline of a vaporous figure, which some chose to believe was the apparition of Maggie Glynne.

Maggie's story was a famous one, and sad; its history well documented. Born to the ranks of the local gentry (she was the granddaughter of Sir Gerald Latymere), Maggie was betrothed at seventeen to the lord of Alfriston's son. It was the time of the Civil War in England, and Maggie, whose family supported the king, unwisely fell in love with one of Cromwell's handsome young lieutenants. Forbidden by their families to marry or to even see one another, the young couple planned a secret elopement with the help of a local justiciar from the neighboring village of Wilmington.

They arranged to meet an hour before midnight on July 14, 1644, at The Hawk and Scarecrow, which Maggie's father owned. Nearly an hour passed as Maggie waited alone in the timbered room, with only the stub of a little wax candle to light the path of her beloved. But he never came.

The following morning the justiciar came to the inn to report the tragic reason for her lover's absence. He had found the body of her intended husband in the Hollow, a lonely stretch of beech trees just beyond the village. He had been clubbed to death. Later some would claim Maggie's jealous brothers and her thwarted betrothed had connived to do the deed.

At the inn the justiciar found Maggie, her body hanging from the center beam by her wedding veil. The tragedy softened the hearts of both families who would have interred the bodies of their children together in one grave as the lovers would have wished, but this was impossible. Maggie's suicide had rendered her unfit for Christian burial. Instead she was put into unconsecrated ground beyond the churchyard gate.

Several times in the weeks to come her apparition was seen to appear at the door of The Hawk and Scarecrow, the ill-fated wedding veil in her hands. This was witnessed by many of the villagers, including the vicar. Finally, hoping to put her wandering spirit to rest, he had her body dug up and reburied within the churchyard, where she seems to have lain in peace for the next three hundred years.

Unaccountably the sightings started up again in 1950. In July of that year a hiker claimed to have seen a woman "dressed in the clothes of King Charles's time" wandering near Smuggler's Cove at dusk. Believing she was only an actress performing in a local *tableau,* the hiker came toward her in order to ask about accommodations in the village. She disappeared from view not twenty feet away. There were several other such sightings the remainder of the decade, all believed to be the ghost of Maggie.

On the 320th anniversary of poor Maggie's death, a group of parapsychologists from U.C. Berkeley in California spent the night in the common room of The Hawk and Scarecrow. They saw nothing, but their tape machine recorded a low, sibilant murmur that was very much like the sound of a woman weeping. In the 1970s Maggie's ghost was glimpsed at least eight times, and always standing just outside the churchyard gate near the spot where she had initially been buried. In time this area just below the Hollow came to be known as "Maggie's Corner."

The church of St. Audric (mostly seventeenth century with minor Georgian and Victorian revisions) and the graveyard sat a little apart from the village, below Alfred's Lane. The Hollow bordered it on the easternmost edge, the Friston Forest just beyond. The church could be reached on foot by way of the Downland path, or by car from New Clergy Road. There was a church school near the Hollow, close beside the vicarage. The vicarage itself was a relatively new building, the newest in St. Audric. The Reverend Thomas Pryce had ordered it built when he married in 1954, the old vicarage being too small a place to lodge a family.

Beyond the Hollow, east on a narrow path called Leper's Way (used in the Middle Ages by the sick and dying who went into the forest for sanctuary) was the only remaining Saxon structure in the area. It was the manor house known as Goat's Rue, which for many years belonged to the lords of Alfriston. Since it was common for Saxon dwellings to be made of wood, or mud/wattle, it was believed that Goat's Rue had once been a pagan temple in pre-Christian times. Since the death of Simon de Falaise in the great Plague of 1349, it had been used alternately as an inn, almshouse, hospital, coach house, and finally, since the 1860s, as a private residence.

Above Alfred's Lane was an old flax mill, abandoned and ruined since the Great War. The miller's house nearby, aptly named The Sheaves, was built about the time Queen Anne was pinning victory medals on the duke of Marlborough, and though it bore no fleeting resemblance to Blenheim, The Sheaves had a quite distinguished history all its own. Many a French nobleman and his lady had sheltered there for the night before traveling on to London during the bloody Days of Terror in France. Later during Napoleonic times, The Sheaves became a smuggler's booty house, its cellar loaded with contraband French wines and other dainties to satisfy the discriminating palates of local gentlefolk. It had been an inn or bed and breakfast establishment since 1914.

Little Gospels was the original vicarage thought to be too small by Reverend Pryce. Indeed it had something of the look of a Victorian confectionary box, with its neat white boards and sugar-pink latticework design and shutters. Little Gospels lay at the east edge of Alfred's Lane in a straight line from The Sheaves at the opposite end. There were rumors it had its own ghost: the spirit of a vicar's wife who had died in an unfortunate bathing incident in 1936.

Taken by itself, architecturally and otherwise, the village of St. Audric seemed something more than merely a collection of structures from various periods. It was more like a patchwork of English history, complete with all those things and more than a visitor from the outside might expect of such a place.

Over it all, on the slope beyond, brooded the Long Man, a figure so old no one knew his origins. Celts may have carved him into the hill chalk as a god to worship; Romans to mark the conquest of this strange new place; Saxons to frighten away the invading Danes. In a very real way the history of the valley and the history of St. Audric village was the Long Man's history, too.

Whatever came, he would be there to witness it, mutely holding
up his twin staves and gazing eyeless toward the sky.

* * *

Joanna took the A27 to Wilmington. Twice she overshot the ill-
marked highway that led five miles into St. Audric, so that it was
after three o'clock by the time she turned onto the narrow road
that gave entrance to the village High Street.

She had seen a good many picturesque villages during her
time in England, villages that rated the inevitable American epi-
thet *charming*. But she had never seen one quite like this. It had
a changeless look, as if time did not exist here. There was no evidence of modern additions, no council house tackiness, only a
marvelous array of Jacobean-style shops and beautiful Georgian
houses beyond. It all looked so serene and undisturbed she
thought of Brigadoon, waking from its supernatural slumber
every hundred years.

There didn't seem to be anyone about, no open shops where
she could ask directions. Still, in a place this size one building
should be easy to find. In Wilmington they had told her it was the
only bed-and-breakfast place in town. At the bottom of the High
Street she braked the car and peered both ways down Alfred's
Lane. Then she saw a gravel drive and a gaunt black brick house
just beyond.

There was a small car-park adjacent and she pulled the Ford in
a few spaces away from a red Volvo, the only other vehicle in
sight. Even though there didn't seem to be anyone around she
took her luggage out of the trunk and hauled it up to the front
entrance in two trips. She knocked at the big oak door and
waited. No answer.

Forty-five minutes later she was still waiting. Irritated, she
leaned against the wall wondering where everyone had gone.
Once again she pounded on the door, this time using the
wrought-iron knocker; she called. Nothing. No one.

There was a high fence enclosing the back grounds of the
house and the gate was locked, so even if a window had been left
open (it *was* summer, after all) there was no way she could get

in. This was ridiculous. Joanna felt as if she had wandered to the very rim of the world. In three-quarters of an hour she had not seen one person, one cat or dog, not even one car. Maybe it really *was* Brigadoon!

As always her imagination began to spin an absurd scenario. *She had been deliberately lured away from London to this bizarre village on the Sussex Downs where no one walked by day. But when the moon was at its full . . .*

She laughed out loud at her own silliness. Jayson had said more than once that she had a Twilight Zone mentality. Still, if he were here even he would have to admit the situation was a curious one. Okay, so England pretty much closed up shop on Sundays. But this was unreal!

Trying to dispel her frustration (and that little bit of fear that still sat somewhere in a corner of her mind) Joanna began to tick off the various reasons why working here in St. Audric might be interesting and fun. It was pretty. It was charming. It was secluded—hell, it was practically off the map! And if this was any indication of how the people here kept to themselves, she should have lots of privacy as well.

She was glad to be here. Sussex had always exercised a particular fascination for Joanna. So much of England's history had been played out on its landscape. Because of that it was never difficult for her to conjure up a story here, to feel as if she'd stood on this spot or that before. She looked to the grove of trees beyond the wall, and from nowhere an idea whispered in her ear: *Two sisters, exiles from France, begging bread at the abbey gates.* Joanna knew nothing of Alicia and Adelina, of their terrible struggles and unhappy end. Yet at that moment the essence of their tragedy was very close to her. Later, when she would incorporate the similar (though fictional) account of Delores and Desirée into *The Scourge,* she would not remember where the inspiration to use a pair of sisters had come to her, but it happened at that moment as she stared at the trees and dreamed.

A car door slammed, rousing Joanna. She looked up to see a short, heavy-breasted, middle-aged woman in a dark blue dress coming up the walk. Just behind her was another woman, younger, taller, obviously her daughter.

"Are you Mrs. Munro?" Joanna asked the unsmiling older woman.

"I might be," she answered snappishly, fishing for keys in her handbag. She frowned, looked up. "You wouldn't be that American woman come for the room a day early, would you?"

"Yes," she answered, smiling tightly and holding out her hand, "I'm Joanna . . ."

Mrs. Munro stood in the doorway, hand on her hips, and scowling. "Tomorrow," she said. "You weren't supposed to come until tomorrow."

Joanna drew her hand back self-consciously. "I didn't think one day would make a difference."

"You'd be surprised," the woman answered, pushing the door open, making way for Joanna to pass. "Well, now you're here you might as well come in."

The young woman was her daughter, and her name was Caroline. She was only a little friendlier than Mrs. Munro and offered to take the luggage up while Joanna registered at reception.

Joanna counted out three fifty-pound notes and pushed them across the counter to Mrs. Munro, waiting as the woman filled out a receipt and stamped it.

Joanna's gaze carried around the room and she thought dismally that The Sheaves was far better looking on the outside or at the very least that Mrs. Munro was no decorator. Nothing showed any taste or value. Worn carpet, cheap furniture, tatty drapes, and everywhere collector plates depicting the high points of recent British history: the Coronation, the wedding of Prince Charles and Lady Diana, the wedding of Prince Andrew and Sarah Ferguson. Mrs. Munro seemed like the type who actually believed such things enlivened the décor.

"Up here, miss," Caroline called, and Joanna followed the voice.

She was happier with her room, a bed-sitter with a nice view of the trees across the road and the church beyond. The decoration wasn't exactly something out of Laura Ashley, but it would suit her well enough. The walls were a pale yellow (*not* her favorite color; blue would have done better). The furniture was all Period Copy, but very nice all the same: mahogany-stained bed and matching pediment bureau, a cheval mirror in the corner, writing desk and chair near the window, nightstand with lamp beside the bed. Curtains and coverlet matched and they were ugly: huge white roses on a background of dull harvest gold.

The bathroom was just across the hall, very country-modern with pink tile and vanity dust ruffle ("Pathetic" she could imagine Jayson saying) and there was a big bathtub with makeshift shower attachments and a stiff pink plastic shower curtain to cover it all up.

When she had finished peering about the place she turned, nearly colliding with Mrs. Munro, who stood directly behind her, the receipt clutched in her hand. "You forgot this," she said, handing it to Joanna. "And I've added another day at the regular rate."

"Fine," she said, stuffing it into the bustier of her sundress, "I'm just glad you could arrange for the extra night."

Mrs. Munro, her thinning, baby-fine gray hair lit up like a halo from the late-afternoon light coming through the octagonal window on the landing, nodded and said, "I should have told you there's no dinner on Sunday, and supper's not till seven."

"That's okay, I ate on the way down," Joanna answered. "But I did want to talk to you about breakfast. I keep really funny hours and the last thing I want is to be awakened at seven when I haven't gone to bed till five."

Mrs. Munro's marblelike blue eyes grew round at the idea of anyone staying up till 5 A.M. "Breakfast is seven till eight," she answered stiffly, "no exceptions." She hurried on, "You can see my point, surely. Why, I'd be running upstairs and down all day with trays and things."

"I'm not asking to be waited on," Joanna explained. "I'd just like to have use of the kitchen whenever I like, that's all, since I won't be having my breakfast brought to me. Less work for you I'd think. . . ."

"Very well," she said at last, as if the matter were a great decision requiring considerable sacrifice on her part. "So long as it's neat. I keep my kitchen neat."

"Don't worry, I'll be neat." Joanna turned toward her room then, remembering, turned back. "There's no television," she said, "in my room, I mean."

"There's one in the lounge," Mrs. Munro said. "You'll have to content yourself with that."

"If that's the best you can do," Joanna answered pertly, "I guess I'll have to."

She went back into her room, surprised to find Caroline calmly unpacking her things. Big, ungainly Caroline with her crooked smile and mop of red hair could be pretty in the right clothes, Joanna thought. She looked a little like the Duchess of York.

"I'll put everything away in the drawers," Joanna called out to her, and then coming closer, realized it had already been done.

Caroline zipped the last case shut and stowed it with its mate beneath the bed. "Mum says you write books," she said.

"Yes," Joanna answered, "I do."

"Funny thing for a woman," Caroline said. Then she laughed, showing all her teeth.

Early that evening Oliver North came into Joanna's room and explained that she had just been drafted into the U.S. Army. She tried to tell him that as a Marine he had no authority over Army personnel, but he only smiled and passed a note to her. She unfolded the square of paper and found it blank, but Ollie told her it had been written with invisible ink and could only be deciphered in a glass of Pepsi-Cola. When she told him there was none he winked and said he already knew that, and wasn't it a shame that Ronald Reagan had died in childbirth? Yes, it was very sad, she replied, but could he please tell her the time? He reached into his pocket for a watch but instead brought out a flashlight that he held against her face and chanted, "Sup her, Joanna, sup her . . ."

"Supper!" The word sounded in her ear. A woman's voice. *Ollie North had turned into a woman.* Joanna, squinting into the flashlight, sat up on the bed. Above her bent Caroline and over her shoulder blazed Ollie's flashlight. But now it was only a lamp.

"I was dreaming," she mumbled, still only half awake. "I was . . ."

"Mum said to call you when it was on the table," Caroline announced. "Funny thing to be taking a nap at this hour . . ."

Joanna's hand felt along the bedspread for her robe, then pulled it tight around her shoulders. Caroline still had not moved. "I'll be downstairs in just a minute," Joanna told her, "just as soon as I put on some clothes."

"Supper," Caroline muttered. After a momentary pause she turned and walked away.

"Supper" was fatty gammon steak with jacket potatoes and wilted Brussels sprouts on the side. Joanna picked at the meal, thinking she was going to have to find another place to eat. If she was going to load her body with cholesterol she wanted it to be from food of her own choosing, and this was definitely not it.

She felt slightly uncomfortable too, sitting alone in the tacky dining room with all the other empty chairs (eleven) and place settings (the same) vacant. Was she the only one in residence here? She didn't relish being the lone guest in this big place, though she'd probably get used to it before too long.

Mrs. Munro came to collect the dishes, grumbling when Joanna pushed her half-finished plate aside. "I guess I'm just not very hungry after all," she offered lamely. "I think I'll have a walk instead."

"You'll be wanting your coffee and sweet?"

"I don't think so," Joanna said, sliding cigarettes and a lighter into her hip pocket, "I'm really not hungry, and I never ever drink coffee."

"Fussy," she heard Mrs. Munro mutter as she left the room.

Although The Sheaves was only set a little back from the road, it had a look of complete isolation, hemmed in by lime and elm trees. Joanna crossed the lane and started off down a narrow blacktop marked NEW CLERGY ROAD. Hedgerow lined either side. To her right, beyond a stile, the downland path curved to a terminus at the cliffs.

As she drew nearer, bits of the church became visible, like dislocated pieces of a jigsaw puzzle. She could see its crenellated tower, and the stone facing of the north wall through a veil of hawthorn and yew branches. A low iron gate, waist-high to

Joanna, enclosed the churchyard. She pushed the gate open and entered.

The old part of the cemetery was here, behind the church. An annex, newer by the look of its straight white stones, lay across the road. Here the monuments were either very large or very humble, many worn thin by the wind and rain of many centuries. Near the edge of the grass a few wooden crosses tilted, thin as sticks.

There was still a rosy light hanging in the sky although the moon was up, full and perfect as a pearl. Joanna slipped out of her thongs and walked barefoot on the grass, wandering happily among the stones. Joanna liked cemeteries, especially the kind found at the back of nearly all old English country churches like this one. There was always such a feeling of peace—so many generations resting side by side together. Tomorrow when it was light she'd have to come back with her notebook and copy out a few names for use in *The Scourge*. Of course none of these graves dated back nearly so far as that, but she might find something to use, some name or inscription, just to lend an air of authenticity to her fictional narrative.

She was sitting on the ground, her back to one of the larger stones, when she heard a door inside the church open and close. A few seconds later footsteps sounded on the path outside. When she saw it was the vicar, still robed in surplice and cassock, she nearly called out to him. Then, feeling like a trespasser, she ducked down behind the stone.

He stopped in the middle of the cemetery, almost where she was, and stood for a moment looking straight ahead. Then, fumbling with his clothes, he bent closer and began to urinate against a headstone. Unbelieving of what she saw, Joanna held her breath, afraid he might turn his head at any moment and see her spying on him, but he did not. When he had finished he shook off the last drops, stuffed himself back inside his clothes, and strolled back into the church.

It took Joanna a moment to catch her breath. Then she ran as if chased down New Clergy Road toward The Sheaves. Only when she was out of sight of the church did she slow to a walk. Her breath still came in little heaves and her face was hot. It was a few minutes before she could stop shaking.

Mrs. Munro and Caroline were in the kitchen when Joanna let herself into the house and hurried down the hallway to find them. The kitchen door grated open as she pulled it toward her. Both Caroline and her mother looked up, surprised.

"Who is the vicar here?" she demanded.

Mrs. Munro sat at the table drying silverware; Caroline was at the sink. She glanced over her shoulder at the distraught Joanna. "That would be the Reverend Peter Burroughs," she said.

"Well he's hardly *that*—I just saw him peeing on the gravestones!"

Mrs. Munro chuckled. "Why would you want to watch a thing like that? Odd way of spending time, I'd say."

"I wasn't *watching!*' Joanna fairly shouted, "I was in the churchyard looking at the graves when he just came out and did it!" She looked from one woman to the other. "Well, don't you think that's a weird thing for a vicar to do, especially when he's still in his robes?"

"A man's got to relieve himself robes or no," Mrs. Munro replied, sorting forks from spoons. "He's no different from any other."

Arms folded across her breasts, Joanna shot back, "Well, I'm sorry but where I come from ministers don't piss on their dead parishoners!"

Caroline stacked the last plate in the plastic drainboard tray and turned off the tap. "Look here, miss, how about something cool to drink? Sit yourself down and I'll get it for you." She bent to the refrigerator. "There's soft drinks if you'd care for one." She held up a can of Diet Pepsi.

Joanna plucked it out of her hand. "Thanks, I'll take it with me. I'm going to the lounge to watch TV."

"Mind how you go," Mrs. Munro said as Joanna pulled at the door handle. "That one sticks."

"Happy dreams," Caroline called after her, but pausing for a moment just outside the door Joanna heard her add, "the silly bitch," and both women laughed.

Furious, as much with herself for having told them about what she had seen as she was with them for having laughed about it, Joanna settled herself on the tatty sofa and watched television for the next several hours, changing channels repeatedly, too distracted to enjoy anything she saw. She read the *Sunday Times* and the *Express,* sipped her drink, and brooded over her first day in St. Audric. Finally when there was nothing left to watch but snooker matches she turned off the downstairs hall light and went to bed.

Her dreams were nightmares. The vicar, horn-hard and huge, was ravishing her from behind, smothering her face in the pillow. She sobbed; her insides felt on fire, as if he'd torn something in her. She woke, tangled in the bedclothes, and was just able to unwind herself from them in time to rush to the bathroom across the hall where she vomited the unsightly remains of her supper into the toilet.

After she had cleaned the tile and rinsed the soiled towels in the bathtub, Joanna stripped off her nightgown and replaced it with an oversize Sleepy-Tee. Over that she pulled her blue terrycloth robe. On shaky legs she walked to the window and pulled it open. There was no screen and she leaned far out to breathe the rich air gladly. A scent of roses, thick as honey, overlaid the air and made her feel momentarily breathless. In the distance she could see the church, its tower gilded by the moon's silver dust.

Later, propped up in the big squeaky bed and drinking a Dr. Pepper she'd brought with her, Joanna felt wakeful but much better. The pain in her stomach had gone and her skin felt cool, so at least it wasn't flu that had made her ill. Probably just nerves after that incident in the churchyard, and that horrid meal that had been too greasy for her stomach. Having seen it floating in gruesome bits around the toilet bowl had in no way endeared Mrs. Munro's cooking to her.

Yet now that her stomach was empty she felt hungry, wishing for something hot like good stock soup or clam chowder. Mrs. Munro kept a fair supply of such things in the larder; she'd seen them while making her own tea that afternoon. But then she thought of how the stairs squeaked, and that horrible sound of the kitchen door, the fussing with pots and bowls and lighting the gas ring—all these things discouraged her. So instead she finished her drink, forced a few burps from her antagonistic innards, and settled back into the bed, the covers thrown over her face like a corpse's.

She woke abruptly and disoriented, to the sound of a knock at her door. She sat up, blinking away flecks of dried mascara, and picked up her watch from the bedside table. Only ten. She had very pointedly asked to be left undisturbed till noon.

After last night's miseries she felt surprisingly good this morning, but she recoiled as Caroline, entering on the second knock, began to draw the curtains open.

"Please don't do that," Joanna protested. "I don't usually get up this early. I told your mother that. I told you that."

Caroline's bulk shut out some of the sun. "But it's gone ten and mum wants the room cleaned."

"I'm sorry about that," Joanna answered, reaching for her cigarettes, "but it doesn't need cleaning, not today. Perhaps every week or so. I'll be working, mostly at night, and I just can't be disturbed as early as this. Do you understand?"

"You won't be wanting any breakfast then?"

"No," she answered, stifling a yawn. "I'll get my own when I'm ready."

Caroline shuffled out the door without answering, leaving Joanna to smoke her cigarette in silence. An hour later, after a scalding shower, she felt better. It was mildly cool outside so she pulled on jeans and a sweater, then went downstairs to have a cup of tea before going out in search of Kate Callison and the St. Audric library.

Mrs. Munro had made brandy snaps; they were cooling on the windowsill when Joanna came down.

"Smells good," she said, sniffing at the sweetness in the air as she poked in the cupboard for tea. Then cheerily she added, "You really get started early, don't you?"

Mrs. Munro splashed vanilla into a mixing bowl and stirred it into the batter, saying nothing.

I'll give you something to be sour about, Joanna thought and said, "I'm afraid I was sick in the night. I stripped the bed and rolled the towels up in the sheets. I left everything out on the landing. Sorry about that."

"Sheets too?" Mrs. Munro looked up. "Couldn't you get to the loo in time?"

"I was afraid I might have something catching."

"You'll be in later for tea?" Mrs. Munro asked a moment later.

"No," Joanna said, splashing boiling water into a cup, "I don't think so."

* * *

The library, so Caroline told her, was at the other end of the village, off Trespass Lane. Joanna walked swiftly up the street, full of purpose, promising herself a better look at the village later in the day.

There was a CLOSED FOR LUNCH sign taped on the library door when she arrived so Joanna was obliged to sit on one of the stone benches just outside and wait. Like most every other building in the village, the library was Jacobean, but its stern façade had been reformed by ugly Victorian windows, ruining the effect. She could almost imagine some pompous Gladstonian edict about "Letting in the Sun Among Ideas . . ."

It was nearly two when a smart-looking woman in tailored slacks and neat white blouse stepped from her car and approached the library door, a stack of books in her arms.

"Excuse me," Joanna said, coming up to her almost shyly, "are you the librarian?"

She was struggling with the lock and didn't turn around. "Yes, I am."

"Kate Callison?"

"That's me." She pushed the door open and stepped inside. Hesitating a moment, Joanna followed.

"I'm Joanna," she said at last.

"Oh, yes?" Kate Callison put the books down on the desk and shuffled through some papers, finally picking one out from all the rest. She was medium height and very slim. In her youth she had no doubt sported a boyish figure, and even now there was something faintly unisex about her. Her pale hair showed a little silver and she wore it in a plain, blunt-cut style. She had only one truly beautiful feature: large brown eyes flecked with hints of green.

She looked quizzically up at Joanna. "Can I help you?"

"I'm Joanna," she said again.

"I'm sorry, but you're saying that as if I should know who you are."

Her embarrassment (could she have made a mistake?) was all at once superseded by fear (could she have come to the wrong village? Dreamed the whole incident, even the letter?). But she had the letter with her in her purse and she dug for it now, drawing it out. "You sent me this letter, you asked me to come here." She paused, then said more forcefully, "I'm Joanna Latimer."

"Of course, the novelist." The woman's face lit with a smile "You must forgive me, I should have recognized you. I've read all your books, I really have. And they're all here in the library as well."

Joanna waved the letter. "I got your letter about two weeks ago. I was . . ."

"Letter? What do you mean?"

Joanna offered it.

Kate scanned the letter, reading it quickly. After a moment she handed it back. "But I never sent this."

"It's your name," Joanna insisted.

"My name perhaps, but not my signature."

"I don't understand. Why would someone send me a letter with your name signed to it?"

Kate took back the letter and looked at it more closely this time. "I think I can tell you about this," she said. "Every once in a while we have volunteers come into the library to help me catch up on some of the clerical tasks: filing, cataloguing, letters—things of that sort. Obviously one of them used such an opportunity to send off that letter to you."

Joanna seemed doubtful. "But why? What's the point? I don't understand. . . ."

Kate's smile offered reassurance. "It was probably just a fan who wanted to meet you and used this method. Signing my name to it was no doubt meant to give it a bit more weight." She wrinkled her nose. "A little off-putting, I'll admit, but quite harmless all the same. Things get pretty dull in these little villages, you know. Meeting you was no doubt someone's idea of a wish-fulfillment. Call it a fantasy if you like. . . ."

"But I think that's horrible," Joanna said, dropping onto one of the chairs.

"It's not," Kate answered. "Just a rather elaborate hoax, that's all. St. Audric's not such a bad place for a holiday, and since you're already here you might as well take a day or so to look around. It's pretty. Have you ever been before?" Joanna shook her head. "Well, then, you see? You'd never have come round these parts if our little oddball, whoever she might be, hadn't played a trick on you."

"But that's the funny thing," Joanna said. "I would have come, not here perhaps, but around this area, because my new book is set here, in a village much like this, during the fourteenth century."

Now it was Kate's turn to look surprised. "Really? That is peculiar. Writing a book about this place are you? Well, there is a lot to tell. I suppose you've already done your research."

"Most of it, and as I say it's not about St. Audric, but a fictional village I've called Oatenham. I was going to drive to Lewes and look around for a fictional setting. I already had it in my head to do that; then your letter came. Well *that* letter anyway. I don't mind telling you it's very unsettling."

Kate seemed honestly amused that Joanna was taking it all so seriously. "Well, even if it is a hoax," she declared, "it was to a good purpose in the end, wasn't it? And now you're here, we'll have to make you welcome. We have some wonderful books in the library, rare ones. They'll be a help."

"I should have realized that damn letter was too good to be true," Joanna sulked. "Promising all those documents and diaries."

"Oh, there really are such things," Kate was quick to reassure her, "but they aren't here in the library. They belong to a private party, but he's out of the country now, I'm afraid, and won't return till mid-October."

"Great," Joanna muttered, "that's six weeks from now."

Slipping a pair of glasses on her nose Kate turned to a bookshelf behind her desk. "Yes, but they'll be worth the wait, I promise you. And in the time between we've got a few things here to interest you. Not just ordinary books either, but some papers, and a few monographs, privately printed. And of course there are the parish records." She stretched for a book on the top shelf and pulled it out.

"But wouldn't parish records be kept by the Council Records office?"

Kate turned around, a dark blue folder in her hands. "In most cases, yes. But St. Audric has its own rules about such things. The Reverend Thomas Pryce—he was vicar here before the present Reverend Peter Burroughs came—was a bit of a historian as well, a good one, too, so I've been told, and he had one or two books published. One was on the history of St. Audric, and then there was another one about Alfriston—he was from here, you see. We've got copies of both in the back, I'll have to dig for them— but all the same I'll see you get them."

Joanna had already slipped a notebook and pen from her bag and was scribbling swift notes in broken phrases. "What about the parish records?" she asked. "You were saying something about them."

"Well, our Reverend Pryce was very keen on research, and it seems he wanted the parish records kept close at hand. He was very insistent about it, even when Council wanted them gathered up. He even took it to court and got a favorable ruling in the end."

"He must have been a remarkable man," Joanna said, looking up from her pad. "Did you know him?"

Kate selected two medium-size books from the shelf. "Good Lord, no, that was back sometime after the war. Not that I'm not old enough to remember, but I'm not from here, you see. In fact I think I'm about the newest resident. I only came to live here a few years ago."

There was something honest and approachable about Kate, and Joanna liked her at once. "You seem to know so much," she said. "I'd have thought you'd lived here all your life."

Kate shrugged off the compliment with grace. "Well, my position promotes that sort of interest in the community." Then she laughed gaily. "Or perhaps I'm just one of those horrible village busybodies who turn up in all the Agatha Christie tales." She handed the two books and folder to Joanna. "These are very good, they'll help as a start. Legends about the Long Man and all that, and some stories about St. Audric, who the village is named for. I dare say you've already done some reading about him. The folder has a few very general facts in it, town-meeting stuff mostly, but you might be interested."

Joanna took them and slipped the items into her oversize

purse. "You've been really helpful," she said, getting to her feet. "I'm sure you know I'll take good care of these. By the way, I'm staying at The Sheaves."

"Yes, of course," Kate answered. "It's the only place around here, isn't it? All the same, a nice place." Her voice trailed off. "I do hope you decide to stay, at least till you can see those other records. They're a treat."

Joanna shrugged. "I probably will. My boyfriend's had to go to California for a couple of months so there's not much use in going back to London. Of course, if I do decide to leave, I'll bring these back to you." She tapped her bag with a fingernail. "And thanks a lot."

She was halfway to the door when Kate's voice turned her around. "Look, if you can, why don't you come to dinner one night this week? Wednesday would be good. I'm afraid I'm invited out tonight, and tomorrow I've got to go into Brighton for a few hours after the library closes. But I'd love to have you the day after if you'd like. There are a lot more stories I could tell you about this place if you're keen to hear them."

Pleased to have made a new friend so quickly, particularly in light of the two grudging women she was staying with, Joanna agreed at once. "But you'll have to draw me a map," she said immediately, "even if its only a little ways. I'm hopeless with directions."

Kate, laughing, bent to a tablet on her desk and began to draw the outline of a road. "So am I," she said.

*   *   *

Little Gospels was a lovely, tiny house nearly buried in climbing roses. Their pink and white shades sat nicely against boards of the same colors. As she came up the lane, Joanna thought how out of place it seemed with the dour, Jacobean look of most of the village. This charming little house had a character all its own.

Kate, wearing a bibbed pinafore over her slacks outfit, came quickly in answer to Joanna's tapping at the door. "Please make yourself at home," she said, leading her across a tiny vestibule to a front sitting room, "I'm afraid I have to man the galley for a while." She indicated a closed cherrywood cabinet. "If you'd like a drink there's everything you could possibly want in there. Just give a shout if you need anything else." Then she whisked out of the room, trailing efficiency like a cloud of dust behind her.

After finding a lime Perrier and pouring it into a glass, Joanna walked from wall to wall examining the room. Kate had done it up remarkably, with no cheap bric-a-brac to spoil the decoration. Above the white brick fireplace hung a pair of wooden bellows and a seventeenth-century copper warming pan. A second look told her it was an original, and nearly identical to the one Jayson had given a hundred pounds for last spring in the Portobello Road.

Bookshelves, tier upon tier and reaching almost to the ceiling, claimed two walls, meeting at the corner. A wickerback sofa covered in gay chintz mats flanked the opposite wall, a low coffee table in front of it was decorated with a huge bouquet of roses arranged in a green Lalique jar. The whole room had a cozy, countrified personality that endeared Kate to her all the more, especially after seeing the cruel way in which the Munros neglected the interior of their splendid home.

She was scanning the bookshelves, examining titles, when Kate came in, carrying a huge bowl of tortilla chips in one hand and a tray holding smaller bowls of salsa and guacamole in the other.

"Being from California I thought you must like this kind of food," she explained, setting out the dishes on the coffee table. "But just in case you don't, I've got steak and kidney pies in the freezer and it won't take but a few minutes to defrost them in the microwave."

"Not a chance," Joanna said, fingering one of the chips. "I haven't had Mexican food outside a restaurant since I came to England. It's my absolute favorite."

"Good. Then I trust you'll have no objection to chicken enchiladas with fried rice as the main course."

"None at all. Can I give you a hand in the kitchen?"

Kate declined the offer. "Why don't you go on looking at the books? There are a few of yours in there as well, and not just for show, I assure you. Perhaps you'll be good enough to sign them for me after the meal."

It turned out to be one of the best Mexican dinners Joanna had ever eaten and she told Kate so. "Have you ever lived in California?" she wondered. "You cook like a native."

Kate's cheeks flushed a little at the compliment. "No, I've never even been there. But cooking is one of my hobbies and I'm rather good at it, if I might say so myself. I don't often have the chance to try out my Mexican menus, though, people in this part of the world being altogether unadventurous."

"They don't realize what they're missing," Joanna replied, wondering if Kate, who seemed rather well off for a woman in her profession, was a widow who had been left a little money by her husband.

As though she had read Joanna's mind, Kate said, "I'm alone a great deal. I never married, and when the man I was living with died, that was five years ago in Hove, I left and came here to settle. The job at the library was open, a friend had put me on to it, and it was a change, which was what I needed most. Then when I settled here I found I had an awful lot of spare time on my hands, so I went on a cookery course. It had always been something I was interested in but never seemed to do anything about, so I decided to take it up properly. Now I cook a full meal nearly every night of the week, whether I'm eating alone or not. And then of course I *collect* things which have to do with cooking as well. It's a lot of old rubbish, but I like it."

Joanna looked around Kate's cheerful red-and-white kitchen. The walls were hung with various utensils and pans; a highboy choked with cookbooks sat in the corner. "I wouldn't say that, but I do know what you mean about collecting things: it does always seem to get out of hand."

Kate made coffee for herself and a pot of lemon tea for Joanna and the two went back into the sitting room. Kate kicked off her shoes, prompting Joanna to do the same. They both lit cigarettes and talked easily for a little while about this place and that (Kate had traveled extensively in Europe) but gradually the conversation came back to the subject of St. Audric.

Drawing her legs up under her, Kate reached for her cup. "I have to tell you, Joanna, that if you plan to stay here for any length of time you're going to find St. Audric—like any English village—is a very 'closed' environment. *I* say that and I've lived in such places before. But for you, well, coming from Los Angeles and living in London . . ."—she spread her hands palms up in a gesture of impending futility—"it might not be easy."

"You sound as if I should pack up and leave," Joanna said, stubbing out her cigarette and immediately lighting another. Being around another smoker always made her smoke more than usual.

"Oh, no. No, no." Kate reached and patted Joanna's knee. "What I really mean is that most of the people here tend to be instantly distrustful of outsiders. That's common to most villages of course. Something you're not used to, I'm sure."

"Oh, you get used to all sorts of things," Joanna answered vaguely. "You always find some unfriendly people no matter where you go. Mrs. Munro and her daughter aren't exactly the two hostesses I would have picked, but there you are. . . ."

"Those two!" Kate laughed. "They're a regular pair of loonies. Caroline never married, though she could have: she's got a bank balance big enough to buy out this entire village. Mrs. Munro— her name is Eleanore, but so far as I know no one calls her anything but *Mrs. Munro*—anyway, she had Caroline 'out of wedlock' as people used to say, and by a very well known member of the government, Conservative, don't you know. Of course, he was married, and it would have caused a huge scandal. Remember, this was right after the Profumo business and everyone was still a bit skittish about such things. So he simply settled a huge sum on her and the two old birds have lived on in comfort to this day. I say 'old' because Caroline is exactly like her mother. Mind you, she's not even thirty, but she acts like one of those left-on-the-shelf spinsters you read about in dreary Victorian novels."

The idea of the sour Mrs. Munro cavorting in black knickers and a push-up bra to arouse the ardor of a kinky cabinet minister taxed even Joanna's vivid imagination. "How do you know about that stuff?" she asked Kate. "Surely Mrs. Munro doesn't go around telling people."

"Not *actually,* no. But she sees it gets whispered about. That's how I first heard it. I suppose in a way she's rather proud of her little sin. You really can't blame her. Who'd think to look at her now she was ever anybody's bit of fluff?"

"She's such a grouch," Joanna said. "I don't think she likes me at all."

"She doesn't like anyone! And for God's sake be careful what you say to her or around her, because she's the biggest gossip around for miles. About two years ago there were a couple of businessmen who used to stay at The Sheaves whenever they came round this way, and they always took adjoining rooms. Well, Mrs. Munro started finding these strange stains on the bedcovers. She blabbed it all round the village so the poor fellows couldn't step a foot into one of the pubs without being stared down like criminals. Needless to say they stay in Alfriston now. Now I don't hold much with men fooling with men myself, but to be fair, it is their own business, isn't it?"

Later while Kate searched the refrigerator for a bottle of wine she'd tucked away to cool before dinner ("a good California red, they told me at the shop in Lewes . . .") Joanna told her the story of the vicar in the churchyard.

"It doesn't really surprise me, though bad luck on your first evening here!" Kate said. "He is quite a character, and I'm sure he has more than one woman on the side. His wife died a few years ago, and every woman in the parish seems to see it as her spiritual duty to comfort him." She hurried to add, "No, I'm not one of them. . . ."

Joanna was beginning to see St. Audric in a different light. Its quiet façade hid a lot of secrets, if Kate's tales were to be believed. "Who else should I be warned about?" she asked playfully. "You know, I think I'm going to have to put some of these characters in my book—in fictional disguise, of course."

"There's Roland Jaspar," Kate said immediately, and Joanna thought, somewhat uncharitably, that Mrs. Munro was not the only gossip in town. "You'll see him before very long; he's hard to miss. Lost his left eye in a freak accident. Some say his wife did it while they were making love. He wears a black eye patch."

"Is that what makes him odd?"

"No, more than that. He's also the local medium, holds regular séances, two a month. I've never gone, but many do. He's reputed to be quite a ladies' man too, and for the present he's having it off with Sally Bradshaw. She and her husband run The Hawk and Scarecrow. You probably saw it on your way to the library the other day, it's a pub in the High Street. In a way it's a funny situation because Sally's husband Colin is very good-looking and Jaspar, besides being at least twenty years older, is nothing to write home about. But you can't always tell by looking, can you?"

Joanna shrugged. "I guess not."

"Did you think such things didn't happen here?"

"No, not really," Joanna admitted. "Still . . ."

"Keep in mind this is a very isolated village, Joanna. People may be a bit different on the surface, but down deep they're the same. There are bound to be adulterers, embezzlers, sinners of all kind no matter where you go."

"St. Audric is hardly isolated," Joanna argued. "I mean, there are a dozen other little villages around it, to say nothing of Brighton, Eastbourne, Lewes. Alfriston itself is only two miles away."

"That's true," Kate answered, leaning to refill their wine glasses, "but it is isolated in a way. The geography rather cuts us off from everything else. We're not on the main road, remember. And we're sandwiched in between the river—tiny thing that it is—the Downs, the forest, and the Long Man. Those are the kind of natural boundaries which separated people in centuries past. But, of course, as a writer of history, you'd know all about that."

Joanna nodded, almost grateful that Kate had finally turned from gossip to something more enlightening. Not that the other wasn't interesting, but it gave Joanna the feeling of reading someone's diary. Perhaps later, when she had gotten to know some of these people, hearing about their habits and secrets wouldn't seem so much of an intrusion.

"There's a house here," she said to Kate, "a very famous house called Goat's Rue. Does anyone live there now? I'd love to be able to see it on the inside. I've been looking at pictures of it in books for years."

"I shouldn't think there'd be a problem with you seeing it," Kate answered. "Old Granny Love lives there on her own. Mind you, it is an awfully big place, but she seems to do quite well by it all the same. I don't know how she manages to keep it so clean, with only a girl twice a week. But each year she opens it to the village for the Bal Masque." She nudged Joanna's arm. "If you're still in these parts at All Hallows' you must come. It's quite something."

"Granny *who?*" Joanna asked, wrinkling her nose.

"Granny Love. Well, that's what everyone calls her, but her

name is actually Nora Lovelace. She's the oldest woman in the village, probably in all of Sussex. I don't think anybody knows her true age. She's very spry though, and when the weather's fine you'll see her outside at six every morning working in her front garden."

"Do you think she'd let me look around her house?" Joanna asked hopefully. "I've always wanted to see that place."

"I'm sure she wouldn't mind. She's an interesting woman. Knows a lot about herbal cures, brews, things like that. So far as I know she never even went to school, but she's very clever in her way. And don't let this surprise you, but some people even say she's a white witch. Oh, I know how it sounds, medieval and superstitious and all that. But I've seen her work some near-miraculous cures, things the doctor had given up on. I suppose it's really all quite natural—herbal medicine and homeopathy, that sort of thing. But I wouldn't completely rule out the possibility of some occult agency in what she does. I think it's quite amazing."

"I'd like to meet her."

"Would you? Yes, of course you would, being a writer. A writer's curiosity is very keen, isn't it? Well, in a village this size you can't help but meet everyone before long."

"Is she really a witch?" Joanna asked, twisting the empty cigarette pack into a slender golden horn. "I mean, does she admit to it? Because I'd be interested in using something like that in my book, done from the medieval perspective, of course."

For the first time that evening Kate went dead silent and Joanna sensed that she had said or done something very wrong. "I don't think you should *question* Granny Love," she finally said, trying to make the words sound light. "She is old, after all, and you know how cranky old people can be. And of course she's bound to be forgetful, too. I really doubt if she'd be much help to you."

The words were Kate's but there was something behind them that seemed completely alien. Even in the brief time Joanna had known her she was able to sense that this was a deliberate ploy to get her off the subject of Granny Love, although Kate herself had brought the matter up. Joanna almost said this, but she didn't; couldn't somehow. So instead she remarked, "I can probably get all I want from books anyway."

Kate brushed a few imaginary crumbs from her lap and got to her feet. "As usual, I've said too much, but that's the curse of living alone. When you have the chance to talk someone's ear off, you do it. Now I'm afraid I've prejudiced you in some way, and I didn't mean to."

"No." Joanna smiled. "You didn't."

Kate smiled back, but it was a false smile. "Good," she said. "Now: would you like to have a spot of brandy before you go?"

Joanna helped with the dishes and stayed on a little afterward, but there was no more talk of St. Audric or its people that evening. Kate deftly turned the conversation to talk of books and spent a good deal of time discussing Joanna's novels with knowledge and extravagant praise. Flattered but not fooled, Joanna asked no further questions. All the same she was made more curious than before.

At the door Kate said, "You must come to supper again very soon, I mean that. And be sure to come by the library tomorrow and I might be able to show you those books I promised. You won't want to miss those."

Joanna said yes, she would come and thanked her for the meal and conversation, but all the while she wondered why Kate had suddenly changed, and why she was pretending that she hadn't. She was a pleasant, helpful woman, yet there was something not quite right about her attitude. Given her own talent for making mysteries out of things, Joanna thought she could have imagined the intrigue. But hadn't Kate gone out of her way to impress upon her how odd the townspeople were? And then, when asked too many questions about Granny Love, hadn't she purposely changed the subject?

Of course it could be just what Kate herself had said: someone talking her head off when given the chance. That was the logical answer, the probable one. But Joanna wasn't sure she believed it. There was something else.

By the time she reached The Sheaves all the lights were out, so Joanna fumbled in her purse for the key Caroline had given her and quietly let herself in. She thought about going into the lounge for some television and did—only snooker again—then went upstairs to bed.

Joanna made a late start the following day and so when she finally got to the library she found that Kate was occupied with a committee of women from Alfriston.

"Sorry about this," Kate said, leading Joanna to a table near the back of the library's main room. "It's about the charity book sale we're having next month. I'd forgotten all about this business when we talked last night, but it is terribly important—the proceeds go to Oxfam and we only hold it once a year—so I really can't call the meeting off." She put her hand on a stack of books piled high in the center of the table. "But I've put out some things you might find useful. Just let me know if you need anything else."

Joanna spent the better part of the remaining afternoon hours going through the books Kate had selected. There were a few obvious choices, while others were hard-to-find items. She leafed carefully through each volume, making frequent notebook notations in her tiny script. *Curious Sussex* by Mary Delorme, *Early Anglo-Saxon Sussex* by Martin G. Welch, and *The Sussex Landscape* by Peter Brandon offered general facts, most of them already known to her, yet she dutifully turned the pages, looking for anything interesting she might have missed.

At the bottom of the pile were several out-of-print books, slim prewar treatises published by obscure houses; and a few pamphlets, all their titles suggestive of an association with Sussex during the Black Death period. They looked interesting, but surely these weren't the "fascinating papers" that Kate had spoken of in her letter. Then remembering she had denied having written it, Joanna thought that the promised papers probably weren't so fascinating after all.

She fingered *The History of the Village of St. Audric* and its companion volume, *The History of the Village of Alfriston*. Both had been written by Reverend Thomas V. Pryce and published privately in 1957. If he had been as good a historian as Kate had implied, these might prove to be very helpful. She looked inside, saw that Kate had already initialed them out to her, then tucked them into her bulky purse.

It was nearly six when Joanna finished her perusal of the remaining books. She stacked them neatly to one side, capped her felt-tipped pen and put it away in her purse with the steno pad. Kate was still back of her desk with the women from Alfriston, all of them talking and making lists, so Joanna merely threw a wave in their direction as she passed.

"See you tomorrow," she called out to Kate, who looked up briefly and smiled.

*   *   *

By Friday Joanna had ceased to make up reasons why she would not be "in" for supper; in any case Mrs. Munro seemed not to care. Several out-of-season tourists had come to stay, including two businessmen traveling together. (Joanna guessed they were not the same offenders banished earlier.) Mrs. Munro could therefore inflict her gastronomic tortures on them and not feel bad that Joanna was not among those held captive at her table.

On Tuesday and Thursday evening she had driven over to Eastbourne for Kentucky Fried Chicken and frozen yogurt; now it was time she sampled local fare. So on Friday night she walked briskly up the High Street to The Plague Maiden. It was a large place, noisy, smoky, full of people, but considerably cheerier than its name implied.

She paused at the bar to give her order: steak, chips, and peas. Hearing her American accent, the owner stepped forward, his hand extended.

"I'm Stephen Halliwell," he told her with a grin. "And you must be the young literary lady who's come here to immortalize us in yet another steamy epic." His blue eyes shone with mischief.

Joanna was forced to giggle. "You make me sound terrible! Actually it's not really about St. Audric, just a village like it, back during the time of the Black Death."

"Only joking, miss. We're really very pleased to have you here." He motioned to a tall, bosomy redhead standing a few feet away. "My wife will certainly want to meet you."

Joanna recognized her at once as Sarah Jeffers, a former actress who had decorated many Hammer horror films back in the early seventies. Sarah knew Joanna's books equally well; the two women chatted amiably for several minutes. It was quite remarkable how little Sarah had changed from her screen incarnation as the beautiful prey of some caped or masked man: she even dressed the same, her off-the-shoulder, cut-nearly-to-the-navel blouse a masterpiece that revealed far more than it concealed. In the pub's dim light she didn't look her age (forty plus) though Joanna thought her hair was overteased and that she wore far too much makeup. She also sported a fabulous tan, no doubt the result of a recent Mediterranean vacation.

When Joanna mentioned she was staying in St. Audric for a month or more, Sarah registered surprise. "Good Lord, you must be stopping at The Sheaves," she exclaimed. "How are you liking it?"

"It's okay," Joanna answered, not certain what response Sarah had expected. "Well, the house is nice . . ."

Sarah laughed. "If those two get to be too much for you, Stephen and I can let you have the room above. It's small, but it could do in a pinch."

Feeling immediately ashamed for her silent critical opinion, Joanna answered, "Thanks, but I can manage well enough at The Sheaves."

Sarah patted Joanna's hand. "Just let us know if anything changes. We'll see you right, won't we, Stephen?"

Their niece, a pretty blond teenager named Chloe, brought the dinner, fussing over the smallest details of the table setting, hovering awkwardly as she poured Joanna's tea.

"She's a nice girl," Stephen said when she had gone, "but slow as slow. Give a shout if she's forgotten anything."

The main meal was only fair, but dessert was a luscious lemon gâteau. She had nearly finished it when Stephen came by the table once again, pushing away the credit card she offered. "The least we can do for a new arrival is give you a meal on the house your first time in here," he said. Finally after several attempts at a refusal, Joanna agreed and thanked him. She thought of how in an identical situation Jayson would still have complained about the dinner, saying that the steak was undercooked, the peas cold as little stones. She almost wished she had the nerve to do the same. But Joanna had never learned the trick of being firm, and behaving as if she were in the right. Whenever she complained she merely whined; it was better to keep still, saying nothing.

"What does his lordship think about your new book?" Stephen asked.

Joanna looked up from her dessert. "I'm sorry, I don't know who you mean."

"Sir Geoffrey." He seemed surprised she didn't know. "I assumed you were family."

"I don't know a Sir Geoffrey *anybody*," she said.

"But I thought, a Latimer . . ."

She still didn't understand.

"Latimer, miss. I'm talking about Sir Geoffrey Latimer. He lives all on his own now up at the ruined abbey, Blackmantle they call it. His people were the lords of Alfriston centuries ago. I thought you might have come here to St. Audric to see him."

"Geoffrey Latimer: imagine that." She was talking to herself, not him. "Kate never mentioned it."

"Perhaps he is family, after all, and you knew nothing of it," Stephen offered. "Wouldn't that be a coincidence?"

"Yes," Joanna answered slowly, drawing out the word. "Wouldn't it though?"

The library was closed all day on Saturday and since she didn't wish to make an uninvited call at Little Gospels, Joanna had no chance to quiz Kate about Geoffrey Latimer, and inquire why she had neglected to mention him, of all people.

On Sunday morning she was asleep when Caroline came to call her with a heavy rap at the door and a single shouted word.

"Telephone!"

Rousing herself unwillingly, Joanna pulled a T-shirt over her head and ducked out to the upper hall landing where an extension phone sat on a graceless Victorian end table. Yawning, she lifted the receiver.

"Hello?"

"Joanna, it's Kate. Are you awake?"

"Just barely."

"Sorry to get you up then, but I thought you might like to come to church with me this morning. It would give you a chance to meet some of the people here. Afterward we can have tea at The Trelawnay."

"What's that?" Joanna asked, rubbing her eyes.

"You'll see," Kate answered and rang off.

Inside, the church was a handsome place, with all the relics common to an English house of worship, particularly those found in country parishes. Sir Gerald Latymere was represented on a marble bier alongside the north wall where he had reposed since 1604. High on the opposite wall hung two narrow wooden plaques inscripted with the Ten Commandments. Joanna could almost envision the grim-faced vicar who had posted them: *Duty-full in the name of Our Lord Protector Oliver Cromwell, and to the most gloryous edyfication of Chryste* . . .

Near the back of the church on the same wall was a marble memorial tablet recording the names of parish members who had made the Supreme Sacrifice in the Great War. Beneath it was a less attractive brass recounting the names of fallen heroes of World War II.

Joanna saw these things at a glance and then found her attention drawn to the windows. North and south walls showed only plain glass in mullioned patterns. The altar and west windows were a pair of beautiful stained-glass designs. After only a few moments of scrutiny she recognized the familiar Rossetti motif in both. The altar window depicted the Annunciation in a composition much like his 1850 painting *Ecce Ancilla Domini:* Mary on her narrow couch, the archangel proferring a stemmed lily. The west window displayed Mary kneeling before the same angel. Consummation was hinted by the radiant halo now visible behind her bowed head.

The processional hymn was being played and Kate motioned Joanna to the fourth pew. Two other people already sitting in the box, doubtless a man and wife, moved to admit them. The woman's felt hat obscured her pretty face for an instant as she bent eagerly to whisper in Kate's ear.

Kate nodded, speaking excitedly. "Yes, this is Joanna Latimer, the girl I was telling you about." She turned to Joanna. "This is Sally Bradshaw. She and her husband—that's Colin there—run

The Hawk and Scarecrow in the High Street." Then she gave Joanna a discreet wink to remind her this was the selfsame Colin who was being cuckolded by the one-eyed tobacconist some twenty years his senior.

Sally beamed and the unknowing Colin extended his hand; Joanna nearly dropped her revised hymnal as she reached to take it. "Glad to know you, Miss Latimer," he said. And Sally added, "How wonderful to meet you! I've read all your books, I *really* have. Are you staying in the village?"

"Yes," Joanna whispered back, "for a month or so. I'm researching a new book."

"Thrilling!" Sally answered, and the feather on her hat quavered with excitement.

"You'll have to come round and see us at the pub," Colin leaned in to say, one arm draped across the shoulder of his faithless wife. "Sally puts on a marvelous spread, and much better than anything you'll find at The Maid, if I might be permitted to say so myself."

"I will come by," Joanna promised, skimming the pages of her *Book of Common Prayer* for the order of service. Glancing up she felt instantly conspicuous. Everyone in the church was staring at her.

Kate tapped her arm. "That's Cynthia Marrow over there." She indicated a pale young woman holding two small children by the hand in the pew just opposite. "Her husband died two years ago in a car accident, poor thing." Another nudge. "And that is old Tim Rackstraw." She leaned closer to whisper the rest into Joanna's ear. "He runs the Cash & Carry and lives with a woman young enough to be his daughter."

"So where's she?" Joanna asked, momentarily curious.

"She doesn't come here." Kate's voice dropped lower. "She's *Catholic . . .*"

The sleeve of Reverend Burroughs's surplice fluttered over Joanna's hand as he came swiftly up the aisle and she watched as he took his place in the pulpit. The other night it had been too dark to see him clearly, but now she saw that he was just as she had envisioned him: heavy-featured, sly-eyed. *A vicar with a face like Nero.* There was no humility in his bearing, no reverence whatever. She thought of her own father, so gentle and pious, how she had always loved watching him perform Sunday service. She'd never really enjoyed church since his death.

After recitation of the Litany and Collect, Reverend Burroughs announced the singing of Hymn 349. Joanna flipped to the appointed page. It was a hymn that she loved in its Lutheran context, but the plodding, unmelodic English tune spoiled it for her. Jayson had tried many times to convert her to the Anglican church, and her greatest objection was always that she *hated* the music. So now she mouthed the words, saying more than singing them.

> *Just as I am without one plea*
> *But that Thy blood was shed for me,*
> *And that Thou bidst me come to Thee,*
> *O Lamb of God, I come . . .*

Following the reading of the Gospel and the singing of yet another hymn, Reverend Burroughs launched into his sermon theme: *No Man can serve two masters: for either he will hate the one, and love the other; or else he will hold to the one, and despise the other.* He had a thin, piping voice which carried easily in the small enclosure. Joanna found it difficult to look at him because when she did she thought not of the sermon but of that first night in the graveyard and the terrible dream that had followed her experience. So instead she concentrated on the altar window, pondering the reason Rossetti had designed them for this particular church. In her study of the PRB she couldn't recall reading of any tie between him and the village of St. Audric.

All at once a chord of inspiration thrummed in her mind; she could almost feel a new novel being born within her. Her thoughts pranced ahead, charting an outline. *Grieving over the death of his wife, the tragic Lizzie Siddal, Rossetti has become involved with an anonymous model, a beautiful Downland girl. When their brief but tender affair is ended, he commemorates her likeness in sketches he has planned for a series of stained-glass windows . . .*

Common sense interjected. The "Virgin" windows, like the painting that had inspired them, had been modeled on his sister

Christina. The thought spun in her mind for a few seconds before speeding off in another direction. Not the subject itself, but the place. A memory. A *day*.

Rossetti and his Lizzie in the days before her illness and his obsession made life impossible for either of them. A quiet place out from London for the weekend, a fashionably bohemian picnic on the Downs. Climbing the grassy slope to investigate the Long Man. Wandering through the village streets, passing the church, Lizzie ducking inside for a prayer: "She knelt to the altar, her face transfixed with eyes closed as if staring inward. It was a look he would remember all his life and after she was dead. The same look he would give her to wear forever in Beata Beatrix . . . *"*

Kate's hand was on her arm and Joanna jumped a little, starting from her daydream. The recessional filled the church with rousing strains. Quickly she leapt up and pushed out the door.

"You've certainly had your mind on something other than church," Sally Bradshaw said with a touch of intimacy that Joanna didn't appreciate. She walked swiftly down the aisle ahead of Kate. Stopping at the rear of the church, she stood for a long while examining "Consummation."

Kate joined her. "Come meet the vicar," she said. Joanna gave her a look that said she didn't want to and why, but Kate said, "It'll be all right, I promise."

He made a great show of being friendly, but it didn't alter her opinion of him. It was obvious he had never heard of her, and Kate explained who she was and why she had come to St. Audric, ending with, "Joanna's even been profiled in *Woman's Week* and *Best.*"

"I'm sure you are a very famous woman," he said to Joanna "but I'm afraid I don't read novels or pay any attention to those who write them. Very old fashioned of me I'm sure, but there it is. However we are glad to have you here among us, and look forward to having you attend services while you are."

"I'm Lutheran," she stammered without knowing why she had said it.

"You won't find any Lutheran churches here, I'm afraid." He chuckled as if she had said something incredibly stupid.

Diplomatic Kate stepped in. "I told Joanna you would let her have a look at those early parish records, the ones our Reverend Pryce was so devoted to."

There was the slightest sign of hesitation on his part, but he covered it well. "Of course, come by my office any time you like, Miss Latimer."

Kate beamed a smile of thanks and jostled Joanna's arm. "We should be off."

The vicar clasped Joanna's hand for just a moment. His palm was cool and moist; the sensation communicated something disturbing and sexual. Trying not to seem too abrupt, Joanna pulled her hand away and followed Kate outside.

A whole contingent waited at the gate to get a view of the new visitor to St. Audric. Surprised and a little ill at ease (the encounter with the vicar had shaken her nerves) Joanna slid her sunglasses into place. ("Who does she think she is, a film star?" she heard one female voice mutter unkindly as she walked past.)

Kate doled out introductions as though she had been doing it all her life. Joanna tried to remember the names as she heard them but they came at her too quickly to be mated with a face and easily recalled. Of course she recognized Roland Jaspar at once. Hadn't Kate said something about his wife having put his eye out while they were making love? The dull woman at his side, undersized and slightly dowdy, didn't look the type to do anything so forceful, but who could say?

Kate pulled a pretty teenage girl out from the crowd and pushed her gently in Joanna's path. "This is Chloe Bibble," she said, sounding proud as a mother, "and she's a very great fan of yours. She's had every one of your books out of the library, most of them more than once."

Joanna recognized her as the young girl from The Plague Maiden—Stephen and Sarah Halliwell's pretty niece. "Yes, I know Chloe," she replied and got a pleased smile in return. It was difficult to tell how old she was. She was tall and fine-boned, all legs and elbows like a colt. Her print dress had a matronly look as though it had been sized-down from someone much older. Certainly not her aunt: Sarah Jeffers would never wear anything like it. Long, light hair pulled back by a tortoiseshell clip gave her something of an Alice in Wonderland look, utterly naïve and charming.

"You'll be seeing a lot more of Chloe," Kate said. "She's my right hand at the library. Comes in twice a week after school to help with putting books away and filing. Ever since the Council cut our budget we've had to make do with fewer staff, but Chloe has more than made up for that. And she's a wonderful typist too: does all the letters . . ."

Her flowing speech came to a verbal precipice on the last word and hung there for a moment like someone who waves her arms above a cliff to keep from falling over. She recovered and went on, but Joanna heard nothing else. She had caught the momentary lapse. It was enough to tell her something that she didn't wish to know.

*   *   *

Chloe had sent the letter.
Joanna sat at a window table of The Trelawnay Coffee House in King George's Row, her mind distracted and confused. She nibbled a bit of cherry cake, sipped Keemun from a dainty Royal Albert cup decorated by a pattern of Moonlight Roses; she pretended to hear Kate's bubbling chatter, but she was somewhere else entirely.

Chloe had sent the letter and Kate knew that she had done it. No wonder she had been so blasé about it, her explanation so smooth and plausible. For some reason, and probably a silly one, Chloe had wanted to meet Joanna Latimer, and Kate had helped her to achieve that goal by promising Joanna the kind of research material no writer could resist.

A quick spate of anger flashed in her. Kate and Chloe had played a dishonest little game, with her visit as the prize: they had plotted, they had schemed. However innocent it might appear on the surface, there was something vaguely sinister at its heart.

The question was not so much why they had done it (Chloe was obviously a dreamy girl searching for a role model) but why Joanna was incapable of asking Kate about it. Of course there was always the possibility she was wrong, although she doubted it, but more to the point was a feebleness of purpose that had always plagued Joanna at times when she had to look someone in the face and ask a dangerous question.

Kate's voice came back to her like an echo. "Joanna, is there something wrong?"

She wanted to shout *Why did you lie to me? Why did you pretend to be my friend?* Instead she took a breath and felt her tiny resolution fade and fall away. She stirred her tea vigorously and dropped a slice of lemon into the cup; after a while she thought of a milder grievance and asked, "Why didn't you tell me about Geoffrey Latimer?"

Peering over the rim of her glasses, Kate looked genuinely surprised. "But I did, on that first day you came into the library, remember? I told you he had a lot of documents you might be interested in seeing."

Joanna's voice was hopelessly shrill and quarrelsome. "But you never mentioned his name, Kate."

There were a few raised eyebrows at the table opposite. Kate kept her own voice low. "I thought I had, Joanna, I really did. What is this all about? Why are you so upset?"

Why was she? Joanna felt her hand begin to tremble and she quickly set the cup and saucer down. Lately her nerves had been terrible, a common problem for her: too little sleep and too much imagination. She had been alone too much recently; she needed more rational opinions than her own. Perhaps Kate *had* only forgotten to mention Geoffrey Latimer's name; perhaps there *was* a reasonable explanation for the letter. She had a manic tendency to allow her mind wide latitudes of exaggeration.

Deliberately she made her voice sound light and casual. "Well, it is a bit of a coincidence, you must admit it."

Kate shrugged, indifferent. "My dear Joanna, I would imagine there are a lot of Latimers in England. A lot of Latimers. That sounds funny doesn't it? In any case I don't suppose it's too odd, your having the same last name as his."

"But that's the funny thing," Joanna admitted. "My last name isn't Latimer, not really. It was actually my mother's maiden name. My real last name was Lynne: Joanna Latimer Lynne. But when I got older I didn't like the way it sounded, so I switched the names around and became Joanna Lynne Latimer."

"Does your mother have any English relatives?"

"I don't know: I don't know very much about her, hardly anything really. She died when I was born. My father married Sylvia about the time I started school, so she's always seemed more like my mother than the woman I never knew."

"What a shame—I was orphaned early myself," Kate said. She buttered a pastry and sliced it down the center. "Well, I suppose it would be a bit too profound for us to expect you are somehow related to *our* Latimers."

"Geoffrey's not the only one?"

"Actually he is. I only meant . . . you see, it was Sir Gerald Latymere, one of Geoffrey's ancestors, who really *began* St. Audric, and the family have been represented here in one form or another since that time. Geoffrey's the last, I'm afraid. He has no children."

"He has a wife?"

Kate's face was turned to the window showing a girlish profile, prettier than the rest of her face. Finally she said, "That's quite an unhappy story actually. Geoffrey did marry a few years ago, a beautiful young girl named Geraldine. She was many years younger than he, young enough to be his daughter I believe. Then suddenly last spring she disappeared . . ."

"Disappeared?" Joanna emphasized the word as if she weren't sure she had heard it correctly. "What do you mean? Did she leave him or what?"

"I don't think anyone knows for certain. The sad thing is they seemed so happy together, but then that's usually the case isn't it? Poor Geoffrey, he's been at loose ends ever since. He spends most of his time traveling in France these days. It must be terribly embarrassing for a man when his wife runs out on him that way . . ."

"Perhaps she died," Joanna said without thinking. She saw Kate's look of surprise. "I meant to say, she might have been kidnapped, something like that. It happens."

Kate shook her head and managed an indulgent little smile. "This isn't Los Angeles, Joanna. Things like that don't happen every day in places like St. Audric. No, the girl doubtless found some younger man more suited to her fancy . . ." She seemed genuinely affected by the story.

"Stephen Halliwell called him 'Sir' Geoffrey. Is he that?"

"No, but the Latimers were lords of Alfriston for so many centuries you can't help thinking of Geoffrey as one of them. Actually his father was created a life peer; unfortunately he died young."

"So what does he do?" Joanna asked.

"*Do?* How do you mean?"

"Do. Work. Make a living."

Kate's calm brown eyes lit with amusement. "My dearest Joanna, men like Geoffrey don't *do* anything, not for a living, that is. He inherited the family fortune and estate at Blackmantle; there are farm rents, chattel . . ."

"Jesus, he's a landlord," Joanna muttered.

"Something like that." The door opened and Kate strained to get a look at the arrival, a tall brunette woman in a cherry-colored suit. Disappointed, Kate relaxed back into her chair once more. "That's Gemma Slade from Wilmington," she said. "I thought it might be Meg St. Denis. Meg runs the craft store in the High Street. She and Gemma look amazingly alike. You must meet Meg, she's awfully nice . . ."

But Joanna's attention was centered outside where a young man and woman stood arguing on the opposite side of the street. She recognized the woman as the widow Kate had pointed out in church that morning and so the man was not her husband. Lover? St. Audric appeared to have no end of trysts. The man was tall and fair-headed, good-looking in a typically English way.

"The widow seems to have a love interest," Joanna said, tapping lightly at the glass to indicate the pair. Just then the woman raised her hand as if to slap his face and he grabbed her arm, holding it aloft. "Or perhaps not . . ."

"Cynthia's a bit dramatic," Kate explained, launching into one of her thumbnail sketches eagerly. "Everyone believes that she's in love with him. Perhaps that's what they're arguing about. Of course, she's hopelessly empty-headed and doesn't deserve anyone half so good . . ."

"I didn't know there were any young men in this town," Joanna said archly, "or at least he's the first I've seen. Who is he?"

Kate slipped one of Joanna's cigarettes from the pack and lit it; her words came out amid the smoke. "That's Simon," she said.

Simon Cherrystone was St. Audric's resident poet. The fact that his fame was limited mostly to the Sussex area was sufficient to make him a celebrity in the tiny village. He was young, just two years down from Cambridge, and he was rich, the result of a trust fund and inheritance settled on him by parents who'd had the misfortune of dying young. He didn't need to make a living from his poetry, yet he could have, a circumstance that caused him no small amount of pride.

He had lived most of his twenty-six years in East Sussex, and it was of Sussex he wrote to the exclusion of all else. Upon publication of a new series of his poems collected under one cover as *Memories of Vanished Summer—and Other Sussex Ballads,* an admiring female journalist from Eastbourne had christened him "the new Charles Dalmon."

Kate Callison spoke of him simply as "our poet."

It could be argued that Simon's celebrity was linked in some measure to his youth, good looks, and a certain secrecy that he was able to maintain about his life and habits—an unusual accomplishment in any village, particularly one as small as St. Audric. He lived alone at Rosemary Cottage, one of the modernized Pre-Raphaelite workshops near Fiddler's Green, and he kept very much to himself.

Nor was he often seen in the company of women, unless it was to accompany Kate Callison to the Berkshire Music Festival each year or the opera in Brighton—or to take Cynthia Marrow (who didn't drive) into Lewes once a week to get her shopping. Many of the more curious residents of the village had hoped this association would flower into a romance—and in view of what Joanna had witnessed from her window at the Trelawnay that one Sunday afternoon it was possible such a thing had happened. But Simon kept that part of his life in secret, too. It was only because of his celebrity status in the village he was able to maintain a deliberate air of mystery without managing to offend his friends and neighbors who doubtless would have been happy to "know all."

There was a constant, unspoken plot afoot by the concerned women of St. Audric (most of whom entertained no end of romantic fantasies about the good-looking young poet) to find him a wife or at the very least a live-in girlfriend. Predictably there were already those who thought Joanna Latimer would be perfect. A few of the village men dismissed Simon as a "nancy boy" but there were no proven facts to back that up. More likely than not they were only jealous.

Joanna stayed in at The Sheaves for the next week and a half, hardly even stepping foot outside her room. The skies had turned sodden all at once—her favorite kind of weather—and each day she sat at the desk looking out at a dripping world as she worked.

In the afternoons when Mrs. Munro and Caroline were out at the shops Joanna would go down into the kitchen and make tea for herself and a light meal. Then it was back upstairs to her typewriter once more. She had settled into a pattern of noninterrupted work. She saw no one; no one called.

She had finally broken through to the heart of her story and nothing else signified now. Her protagonists, snatched from the airy reaches of her imagination, became living entities in her mind and on the page. *Delores and Desirée, French sisters seeking refuge in rural England during the height of the Black Death.*

In her other novels women characters had played important roles but men had been the main protagonists, with the exception of *Tabitha's Claw*. Mercurial, alchemical Tabitha: a sixth-century "cunning woman" who cured sickness in others by means of her own deformity, a clawlike rudimentary sixth finger on her left hand. She had been a fictional creation, but Joanna had come to regard her as more real than any of the kings or archbishops of history she had written about in the past.

Now in *The Scourge* women would once again be at the heart of her narrative—two sisters with powers to repel the plague while all those about them died in wretchedness. Out of her own quickly sketched historical shorthand grew Oatenham, a tiny village at the foot of the Long Man, where the sisters came, begging for bread . . .

Simon Cherrystone and Joanna Latimer met quite by accident at the Cash & Carry one rainy afternoon in mid-September. At least once a week she came into the store to stock up on Pepsi, bread, cheese, and produce—her typical working diet. Joanna had always preferred makeshift meals when she was really busy. Nibbling was so much easier than cooking or going out to eat.

She pushed a five-pound note across the counter to old Tim Rackstraw, took her thirty-eight pence in change, and was just turning to go when she spotted him. She immediately recognized Simon as the man she had seen with Cynthia Marrow outside the Trelawnay.

"I know you," she said as he turned from the counter with a bag of groceries in his arm.

"Do you?" he asked, smiling down at her. "How very lucky for me . . ." He had an easy sort of elegance associated with an earlier generation, and a kind of pompous dignity that marked him as an Englishman even more surely than his accent.

"I'm Joanna Latimer," she said, putting out her hand.

They talked for a while just outside the door; then Joanna suggested that they go for coffee next door at The Hawk and Scarecrow.

"Not a chance." Simon laughed. "You know what these little villages are like: put a beautiful young girl and a reasonably good-looking young man together in a public place and they're reading out the banns of marriage next Sunday at the church."

Joanna nodded. "I see what you mean."

"Listen," he offered, "I do want a chance to talk to you. I knew you were in town and Kate told me you spent a lot of time up at the library but I kept missing you. If you aren't terribly busy now, why don't we pop over to Alfriston for lunch? I could run you back to The Sheaves in my car to drop off your groceries and we could go on from there? How about it?"

She looked down at her UCLA T-shirt and tatty jeans. "If you've anything fancier than McDonald's in mind you might want to give me a few extra minutes to change."

"Right," he said. "Let's make a start . . ."

A half hour later they were sitting in the dim oak-beamed restaurant of The Star Inn, one of the oldest buildings in the Cuckmere valley. It reminded Joanna of the type of place she and Jayson always sought out on their weekends in the country. The decoration was in keeping with the building's fifteenth-century history, and there was a lovely view of the Downs.

"So . . . what do you think of our little inbred circle?" Simon asked Joanna as they sampled their cheese salad and sausage brioche. "That is to say: have you been suitably snubbed by everyone, treated as an outsider amid all of us who have been here since the Domesday survey . . ."

"You haven't been here that long," Joanna said, remembering Kate had told her he was the only person in the village who was a more recent arrival than she.

"No, but I'm from Pevensey, which is close enough."

"Everyone's been pretty nice to me," she said. "Well, Kate has been more than that, she's been extremely helpful."

"Yes, she's a very fine person," Simon mused, putting down his fork. "We've gotten to be quite good friends. I suppose if there weren't so much difference in our ages people would assume that we were lovers, or something equally romantic and ridiculous . . ."

"I imagine there's a lot of gossip about you and Cynthia Marrow," Joanna ventured carefully.

"You've heard?"

"I've seen. Well, I was in The Trelawnay one Sunday when the two of you were having something of an argument just outside."

"Cynthia was just a bit overwrought, that's all. We're just friends—hardly that even—acquaintances. But there are times she treats our relationship like one of those dreadful afternoon dramas on the telly. I'm not saying there's never been anything between us, but, good Lord, that doesn't bind two people together for eternity, does it? Unfortunately, women . . ."—he paused a bit to measure out his words more carefully—"that is to say, *some* women see every coupling as an act of everlasting romance. Poor thing, she's been lonely ever since her husband died, and I've just helped her out with a bit of solace."

"Actually it's none of my business," Joanna admitted, her cheeks having gone a little pink. "I wasn't trying to find out anything, honestly. I only meant . . ."

"It's all right. It's only natural for people to be curious. The truth is I'm not all that interested in women. That's not to say that there aren't times I enjoy waking up next to one, or that I'm gay or anything. I just don't see the point of all this useless involvement and emotion unless it's really love." He pushed the last of the salad onto his fork and finished it. "I suppose the day will come when some witchwoman gets me in her grasp. But till that time I'm more than content to write my poems and spend my leisure time learning watercolors and to read *Beowulf* in Anglo Saxon." He grinned at her. "I daresay that sounds slightly lunatic to you."

"Not at all," she admitted. "Only truthful . . ."

Over white wine and a dessert of raspberry suédoise Joanna told him the plot of *The Scourge*. "As long as I can remember I've wanted to write a book about the Black Death," she told him at the end. "Oddly enough, I'm using a book written by my boyfriend as one of the primary historical sources."

"Jayson Gardiner, yes," he said. "I read something about the two of you in the *Mirror* once." He smiled nicely at her. "Do you know I've never met a novelist before? Mind you, it was hard enough getting to meet you. Kate has been trying to get us together for the past week or more, but I understand that you've been rather busy."

"Busy *and* reclusive," Joanna admitted. "I know it's awful, but it's always like that when I'm working on the first draft. It's just so much easier concentrating when you don't have to worry about seeing people or being polite to them."

Simon laughed and raised his glass to her. "My thoughts exactly! I could really learn to like you, Joanna."

"Good," she responded. "Because I already like you."

They passed the next hour talking about her books and his poetry. Although Joanna had seen some of his poems in copies of the *Sussex Journal*, she was not well acquainted with the main body of his work. "I wouldn't be too offended if I were you," she consoled him as they left the restaurant. "I'm really a terrible ignoramus when it comes to poetry. Jayson's always saying so . . ."

Over a pot of cinnamon tea in the tiny kitchen of Rosemary Cottage, Simon explained the background for a series of poems he was working on. "I call it the *November Cycle*," he said. "It's based upon fragments of early Saxon literature and legend." It had turned chilly and begun to rain again, so he made up the fire and brought Joanna a wool throw to put around her shoulders. Settling into the chair across from her, he asked, "Do you know the ceremony of the Oats Goat Moon?"

She thought for a moment. "I know that the Oats Goat is a field or grain spirit venerated in rural Eastern Europe. Frazer wrote about it in *The Golden Bough.*"

"Yes, but this is something different. The Ceremony of the Oats Goat Moon is (or was) confined to rural England, more specifically, to the Cuckmere valley. It dates from early Saxon times as a kind of magic rite to appease the sleeping grain in winter. A girl, virgin of course, was given to the tribe's most potent male for a single night—the night of the Oats Goat Moon in November. If, after this one night, the girl became pregnant, it was a sign that the earth would yield up great bounty in the following year. If she did not, there would be want and famine." A waggish grin spread across his face. "I grant you it's all fairly conventional stuff, but some of the incantations or the prayers used in the ritual are still extant, in their Anglicized form. Such rich, marvelous images! I'm using fragments as a basis for the *November Cycle.* I think it'll prove to be quite an effective device . . ."

It was nearly ten o'clock that night when Simon dropped Joanna off at the gate outside The Sheaves. "I'm sorry I took up so much of your day," he told her as she stepped from the car. "But I can't remember the last time I enjoyed talking to anyone so much."

She leaned to the open door to shake his hand. "Me, too, Simon. I really mean that. Do you think we'll be the subjects of gossip by tomorrow morning?"

"Probably," he said. "Sod them all. Let's keep them guessing, shall we?"

Upstairs in her room, Joanna changed into a Sleepy-Tee and tried to make a start on the new chapter, but after a while she gave it up as a poor job. Promising herself to make a good and faithful start early the following day, she clapped a tape into her Walkman and climbed into the squeaky bed.

She had enjoyed the hours spent with Simon. He was interesting, quirky. There were a few things she didn't like about him— that business about Cynthia for one thing. Imagine calling the woman an acquaintance after admitting he was sleeping with her! Still, that was a personal thing and had no bearing on her own relationship with Simon, and it was nice to have made another new friend. All the same, she made a mental note to be really nice to Cynthia Marrow when they finally met face to face.

After a few minutes Joanna had drifted away to sleep on the bubbles of Rachmaninoff's *Etudes-Tableaux*.

* * *

The last week in September the sun came out warm as summer. Weary of being cloistered in her upstairs room, Joanna began taking one long walk each day. Sometimes she wandered up the grassy slope to the Long Man, sometimes southward to the cliffs. Often she brought along a lunch and steno pad and wrote sitting on a flat rock or an overturned log.

The first draft of *The Scourge* was progressing toward its finish. There were some gaps in the material; scenes written from a faulty point of view; a note of artifice here and there. But the overall effect was exactly what she had been struggling to achieve. Her characters were no longer bits of a polemical puzzle, they were her own voice, alternately veiled and magnified.

On Monday morning September 30, Joanna called the flat in London and left a message on the answering service so Jayson would know where to find her when he rang up to break their "pact of silence" on the following morning. They had now been separated for thirty-eight days and she missed him more than ever, but even Joanna had to admit the time had passed more quickly than she had thought possible.

Downstairs in the kitchen Joanna fixed herself a thermos of lemon tea and some tuna-salad sandwiches that she wrapped in waxed paper and tucked into her purse for lunch.

"I'll be out all afternoon," she called to Caroline, who was mopping the laundry-room floor wearing high-heeled shoes and a rose-colored silk kimono. Joanna had been at The Sheaves long enough to expect the unexpected from Caroline, who had a penchant for peculiar behavior.

Joanna had planned to spend the afternoon writing down by the cliffs, but first she turned her steps toward St. Audric church. She had been meaning to collect the parish records from Rev-

erend Burroughs for the past two weeks but had never gotten up
the nerve to meet with him in private. It was a foolish prejudice
and Joanna felt stupid hanging on to it. Besides, she needed the
records. Of course they wouldn't date back as far as the fourteenth century, but the historical atmosphere would be a help,
and she might be able to pluck some interesting names from the
documents as well.

Joanna turned off New Clergy Road, cut across the grass, and
pulled open the squeaking gate. The church was unlocked but
empty, and immediately she felt a coolness settle over her. She
walked swiftly up the side aisle and cut across the nave to the
vestry. The door stood partially open.

"Reverend Burroughs?"

She pushed against the door, disclosing a room empty but for
a desk, a chair, and a file cabinet. She was about to turn when a
speck of movement caught her eye. The room's only window
looked out upon the old churchyard cemetery. Near the end of
the grass amid the faded, tilted stones a man dressed in a vicar's
robes was kneeling at one of the graves. It was not Reverend Burroughs. This man was slim, almost a boy. Joanna watched, half
hypnotized, feeling as though she were spying on some
intensely private act of love or penitence.

Jayson came to mind for no reason except that this man had
something of Jayson's single-mindedness as he prayed. He
raised his face; a pale profile delicately made stared out toward
something Joanna could not see from where she stood. At last he
rose, and, fearing that he might see her, Joanna drew back against
the door and collided with a fleshy bulwark.

Joanna screamed like someone stabbed.

Reverend Burroughs put a comforting arm across her shoulder. "Miss Latimer, are you all right?"

"You scared me!" she snapped at him, feeling her knees go
weak. She fell back against the door, leaning on it for support. "I
came in here to look for you . . ." she stuttered.

He smiled, his pink face shining. "And here I am. What happened to frighten you?"

Carefully shrugging off his arm, she answered, "You just startled me, that's all. I was watching someone outside in the grave-

yard." She turned back to the window. "He's gone now," she said.

He seemed amused. "Who are you talking about?"

"There was a priest out there. He was praying at one of the graves. I was watching him."

"I imagine you only thought you saw someone."

"I know what I saw!"

He held up a clenched and ruddy fist from which a few roses bloomed. "You probably saw me. I've just been out back gathering a few flowers for my desk."

Or out back pissing on a few gravestones. "It wasn't you," she said, her face flushed with anger. "It was someone who looked quite different."

He chuckled, obviously enjoying his ability to make her feel uncomfortable. "That's impossible, Miss Latimer. I would have seen him."

"It's pointless to stand here arguing about it," Joanna snapped. "I know what I saw." She brushed past him and went quickly down the center aisle.

"What did you want to see me about?" the vicar called after her.

"Never mind!" she shouted back and swung the door open.

Outside she looked for the stranger; he had gone, but she found the grave where he had been praying. It was marked by a thin, weathered stone half sunk into the ground. The ruined glyphs were unreadable, but at its base rested an offering of white camellias and a card, its ink inscription mottled by moisture and reading simply *Maggie.*

Half reaching, Joanna's trembling hand drew back.

She knew the poignant story of Maggie Glynne. Kate had told it to her, and she'd heard it repeated by several other sources, including Chloe Bibble, who had recounted it to Joanna one afternoon when they were both at the library (". . . the most romantic story I ever heard . . .").

Without a doubt this worn stone marked Maggie's grave. The identity of her mourner was a puzzle. Why had he cried? From what she had heard about it in the village, Maggie's sad tale drew many people each year in a romantic pilgrimage; she supposed a vicar could be romantic, too. Joanna could still remember her own father shedding tears over the film version of *Wuthering Heights.*

She was about to rise when suddenly her gaze fell on a stone in the next row, a glistening pink marble slab. Joanna scrambled to her feet and rushed to see it closer. She read the inscription aloud.

PRYCE

Pauline Cassandra Latimer
1936–1964

Wife of Rev. Thoms. Pryce
Vicar of this Parish

SUCCISA VIRESCIT

As if shot from her mind by a swift arrow, Joanna's consciousness spun effortlessly back many years to a time when she was no more than seven. A relative from the Lynne side of the family had died. Even now she could see her father carefully penning the name and date inside the family Bible. Above it, written in another hand, the words *Pauline Latimer Pryce: died November 15, 1964,* stood out. She had reacted to to the inscription because it was the very date and day of her own birth.

"Who is that lady?" the little girl Joanna had asked her father, and now across the distance of two decades the grown Joanna whispered his answer to the empty air. "She was your mother's sister . . ."

Another coincidence, Kate?

Joanna nearly bolted for the library, then she remembered there was a poetry reading group meeting there this afternoon: at least a dozen people. Kate had invited her to Little Gospels for a chop suey supper that evening, but Joanna couldn't wait that long to talk to someone about what she had just discovered. She had a hundred questions to ask about Pauline.

All at once she came back to herself. What could Kate possibly know about a woman who had died nearly thirty years ago? She was a newcomer to St. Audric. It was equally unlikely that Simon would know anything about her since he was an even more recent arrival. She thought about going up to The Plague Maiden to solicit information from Stephen Halliwell; he had lived in the village all his life. But Joanna preferred a more private means of collecting her information.

There was someone: someone old enough to remember the last several vicars and their wives. Joanna had been meaning to go to Goat's Rue for many weeks but had not; this was her chance. Kate had warned her against "questioning" Granny Love, but what harm could there be in asking for information about a woman dead for thirty years?

Goat's Rue sat at the very edge of Alfred's Lane on the other side of the Hollow. A little path from the churchyard led into it, a deep bower sheltered on either side by tall beeches whose leaves were just beginning to burn with color at the tips. There was an almost preternatural quietness in the Hollow; the sound of Joanna's footfalls hardly seemed to echo as she walked the path. Behind her something crackled and she spun around to look, but there was nothing. Unnerved all the same, she ran the remainder of the way to Goat's Rue.

As Kate had said she might do when the weather was good, as it was today, Granny Love was busily working in her garden. Joanna approached slowly, trying to formulate a casual introduction in her mind. In all her time in St. Audric she had never seen Granny Love, not once. The old woman obviously kept very much to herself.

She wore a gay yellow gardening dress and pinafore and was bent over a small windowbox, weeding a bed of herbs. "Hello," Joanna called out, pausing at the iron gate that fronted the garden, "my name's Joanna Latimer. Can I talk to you for just a minute?"

She didn't look like the oldest woman in Sussex. Granny Love was tiny; she probably didn't weigh a hundred pounds. Her head was covered by a yellow scarf and straw hat, but a few pale curls spilled out around her face. She had bright eyes of such a pale dimple appeared at either side of her mouth. There was no doubt Granny Love had been a "stunner" in her youth.

"I know who you are," she said, coming up to the gate, "and I know why you are here. Do you want to come inside my house? It's a very famous place, you know . . ."

"How do you know me?" Joanna asked, half frightened, half pleased.

"Did they tell you I was a witch who could work magic?" she asked, looking up at Joanna, a doll-like hand to eyes, shutting out the sun, "Do you think I need magic to identify the only stranger biding in the village?"

"I suppose not." Joanna's words came a little breathless. "I would like to see your house. I've admired pictures of it in books for many years."

Granny Love swung the gate inward. "It's old," she said.

Inside, the house was curiously bare with only a sofa and a few chairs scattered about the huge common room. High above their heads a Jacobean boxwood gallery decorated three walls. The bare north wall opened upon a giant fireplace where today no fire burned.

Joanna declined the old woman's offer of hot tea and biscuits. "I can't stay for very long," she said. "I only wanted to ask you a few questions."

"Very well," Granny Love replied, showing Joanna to a lone wing chair in the center of the room. She took a place on the sofa and soon a ginger cat came to sit beside her, purring.

Joanna's hands felt cold and she warmed them beneath her sweater as she talked. "I need to ask you about a woman who used to live here in the village, a woman that you might have known . . ."

Stroking the cat, she said, "You want to know about Pauline Pryce, don't you, girl?"

Startled, Joanna asked, "How do you know that?"

"Because she was a Latimer by birth, like you. And a relation too, I've no doubt."

Annoyed by her inability to take charge of the interview, Joanna denied what she herself already believed to be true. "That's most unlikely. Latimer is not an uncommon name."

"Is that so?" The old woman's glittering eyes seemed fixated

"Is that so?" The old woman's glittering eyes seemed fixated on Joanna's face. "It gave me quite a turn when I saw you today, you look so much like her. It were as if Pauline had got up from her grave and came walking down the lane to say hello . . ."

"She looked like me? Pauline Pryce *looked like me?*"

"She did. Oh, you might be a bit prettier—girls are today—aren't they? It's all this hair they wear. Hers was cut short, but except for that, she was your double."

Events and information were piling up faster than Joanna could analyze and catalogue them. *It was not coincidence. Pauline Latimer Pryce was the aunt whose name was recorded in the family Bible.* But there was still so much she didn't know. "She died young," Joanna muttered.

"She did."

"According to the stone she was only twenty-eight. What killed her? How did she die?"

Granny Love looked tiny as a doll propped up on the big sofa. "Ah, that were a sad thing. She was drowned one evening in her bath. She must have gone to sleep and choked herself, poor thing . . ."

"That's a strange way to die," Joanna said, as if challenging the story. "Didn't anyone think it might have been murder?"

"That were most unlikely with her husband the vicar in the next room. And there was no one would have wished to kill her anyway. Pauline were a sweet lady, even if she were a trifle odd . . ."

"Odd? How do you mean *odd?*" Joanna leaned forward, her body tense.

The smile came back, but it shone more from her eyes than from her lips. "There were some folks said she could foretell the future. Now that's an *odd* thing for a vicar's wife. And there were others called her crazy."

Joanna felt the breath leave her body as though it had been squeezed out. "What do you mean crazy?"

All at once the cat squawked and jumped down, running across the floor after some unseen prey. "She were always strange, nervous. She prophesied her own death. Now who but a crazy woman would do that?"

For a long while Joanna sat staring into the empty fireplace try-

ing to put her thoughts in order. *Suicide?* Had Pauline deliberately drowned herself after first predicting she was going to die?
My God, if that was true she really had been crazy . . .

In view of what the old woman had said regarding her resemblance to Pauline, it was virtually unnecessary to ask the final
question, but she asked it anyway. "Do you remember if she died
on the fifteenth of November?"

"She did. I remember because it were the night of the Oats
Goat moon . . ."

"Then Pauline was my mother's sister after all," Joanna said,
more to herself than to be heard. To Granny Love she explained,
"My mother, Cassie Latimer Lynne, died on that same date in San
Francisco, California. That's a very strange coincidence, don't
you think?"

"Aye, but the world is full of strange happenings near and far,
and that's the truth."

Joanna got up to go. "There's one more thing: I was at the
church this morning where I saw a man, dressed as a vicar, praying at the grave of Maggie Glynne. I had the feeling he is a frequent visitor. Who is he, do you know?"

"You saw that?" The old woman leaned forward, taut with
interest. "Then perhaps you have the power to look into the past
the way your aunt could look into the future." She nodded,
knowing. "It were *him.*"

Joanna felt her scalp prickle. "Who? Who do you mean?"

"The man she were pledged to wed, of course. Her lover."

Remembering the story as Kate had told it to her, Joanna protested, "But he was one of Cromwell's men—a soldier."

"No," Granny Love answered, her eyes shining. "He were
Cromwell's vicar. . . ."

"But don't you see how *weird* this whole thing is, Kate?"

Half listening, Kate bustled about the kitchen preparing supper. She drained sprouts in the sink, then turned them out into a
patterned serving bowl, glancing every few seconds to her sink-
side telly for a quick look at "Coronation Street." She hated missing it and Joanna *would* talk on and on.

". . . as if I was supposed to see Pauline's grave: I mean, if I
hadn't seen that man—or *ghost,* I should say—I'd never have

looked at Maggie's grave, never seen Pauline's name at all." She paused a moment, waiting for Kate to comment, then she asked, "Well, why didn't you tell me about her?"

"What? Did you say something?"

"Why didn't you tell me about Pauline!"

"Should I have? There wasn't any reason."

"Another *Latimer,* you didn't make the connection between the names?" Joanna's voice had begun to go shrill.

"Should I have?" Kate asked again, moving to the refrigerator, opening it, stooping to look for something. She took out a pink plastic tub of spreadable margarine and carried it back to the counter. "Really, Joanna, I don't know why you've got this sudden paranoia about everyone named Latimer." She whirled to set the sprouts on the table beside a platter of baked chicken breasts. "Sorry about postponing the chop suey," she told Joanna, "but I just felt like making something simple tonight. I hope you've no objection." She touched a match to candles in the center of the table. "I'm afraid at heart all we English are dull cooks."

"It doesn't matter, I'm not really hungry . . ."

Joanna stayed to help Kate clear away the dishes and then together they watched "Panorama" to its close. "I've got to get back," Joanna said, getting reluctantly to her feet, "I was up till all hours last night and early today; I can barely keep my eyes open."

Kate looked up from the chair where she had been half dozing. "I should run you back in the car."

"That's okay, it's just a little after ten, and besides you're too sleepy."

"So are you. Why don't you just stay here? I'll get you a spare pillow and a blanket and you can bunk here on the sofa." Without waiting for Joanna's answer she got up and went at once to the airing cupboard. A few seconds later she was back with a folded yellow blanket, sheet, and a plump pillow atop them. "I would give you my bed, but my old bones aren't comfortable anywhere else."

By the time Joanna, assisting with the chores, had put the cat out, locked up, seen the gas fire and lights turned out, and undressed to the exclusion of bikini briefs, she no longer felt sleepy. She got into her makeshift bed anyway, hoping to be carried off to sleep by warmth and comfort, but three-quarters of an hour later she was still awake, twisting this way and that on the rigid sofa, restless and annoyed. Inevitably her thoughts drifted to the day's events.

She hadn't said as much to Kate about it as she would have liked because she refused to understand how curious the whole thing was. *Crazy.* Granny Love had said some people in St. Audric had thought Pauline was crazy. And even now, so many years removed from the experience, Joanna could see her father's strange and hooded look when she asked, "Who is that lady?" and he answered, "She was your mother's sister." He had said the words simply enough, but even then she had sensed the heaviness behind him, the *other* voice that seemed to warn, *Don't ask about her because I can never tell you the truth.* . . .

Pauline.

And Cassie.

For as long as Joanna could remember, the subject of her mother had been a tacitly forbidden subject in the house. When she was only four, her father, Reverend Paul Lynne, had married Sylvia Charles. The last vestige of her own mother's dormant personality had been quietly driven from the house on Seaside Drive with the arrival of Sylvia's Danish Modern furniture and bright embroidered cushions.

It had never mattered much to Joanna that her real mother was dead. She'd never known her, never known any mother but Sylvia, who was a more than adequate substitute for any of the girl Joanna's fantasies of what a mother should be. For years the three of them were a happy family. Each summer they took a two-week vacation to some all-American scenic point of interest like Carlsbad or the Grand Canyon or Washington, D.C. Joanna was given piano lessons and braces and a membership at the San Mateo Figure Skating Club, which was later superseded in her affections only by a membership in the Young Republicans. And sometimes at Christmas or Thanksgiving there were visits to or from Aunt Pru (whose name, misspoken by Joanna as a child, had endured a corruption to 'Aunt Rue') in Royal Oak, Michigan.

It was all so wholesome, so secure.

Then came Joanna's two years at Berkeley; everything was changed. She embraced Eastern mysticism and her psychic arts professor. There were endless shouting matches at home about priorities and late nights and too many weekend absences, till at last she moved out altogether. Shortly after that she discovered medievalism, became a Catholic, began work on an unpublishable novel, moved in with yet another professor, and dropped out of school for a semester. It was then the breach widened to a crevasse and she'd stopped coming home at all, or wanting to. Reverend Lynne, who could forgive all talk of astral bodies and karma and the Akashic Record, was horrified to learn his daughter was sharing her life with Rome and a married man.

Following a trip to England, the aborted love affair with David, and her meeting with Jayson, she had moved to southern California, determined to make a new life there away from all the criticisms of her parents. In the middle of reading galleys for *The Beggarman King,* she took a week off to spend her annual reunion with Jayson in an Anaheim motel, and when she got back to Costa Mesa, Sylvia's telegram was six days old. Joanna's father had been ailing for some months, but she never guessed that he would die before she had the chance to see him one more time.

Suddenly she was an orphan, a twenty-four-year-old orphan. There was Sylvia, of course, but no direct biological link to her own past. Until today, when a simple inscription on a gravestone had illuminated things best left forgotten—or never learned at all.

Pauline and Cassie had died on the same day half a world apart. Coincidence? Possible. Not likely. Sometimes things of that nature happened to twins, but so far as Joanna knew (and she really knew very little) the two women had not been twins. What then? Why the lifelong secrecy about the two of them (*she was your mother's sister*), the rumors about Pauline here in St. Audric; the covenant of silence surrounding Cassie?

Cover her face; mine eyes dazzle; she died young.

Both sisters had died young, and tragically, and there was some secret connected with it that she had never been allowed to know, and she resented it. If there was madness or suicide or some other unspeakable Latimer secret, then Joanna had the right to know. It was her history; her birthright.

She closed her eyes and saw the stone, but the picture in her mind was incomplete. Something was missing, something half-seen, half-remembered. An inscription, some meaning that she could not place; now she could never sleep.

As quietly as she could manage Joanna got up and began pulling on her clothes. She found a flashlight in the kitchen drawer and borrowed a scarf from the coat stand in the hallway. Outside the wind was blowing hard and the moon was a thin thing, sleek and polished as a scimitar. She went noiselessly down the lane, hesitating only when she reached the Hollow. The flashlight made a feeble path for her to follow, a pale stretch of whiteness moving just beyond her feet.

The Hollow, not an inviting place in daylight, was terrifying in the dark. Tonight it was full of creaks and hisses like a strange and forbidding cave. Breathless, she followed the trembling ball of light, half certain that something would dart across her path at any moment. The tunnel stretched on in an unending corridor until at last she saw a faint glimmer of stone—the pale, crenellated wall of St. Audric's church.

She didn't let herself think of what would happen if she turned this corner onto the path leading to the graveyard and saw the ghostly vicar kneeling at Maggie's grave. But when she reached the gate Joanna looked ahead and saw only gravestones standing upright like raised hands, and dry leaves scooting across the grass pushed by the wind.

It was difficult to find her way with nothing more than a ball of light bouncing off the stones, palely illuminating unfamiliar names; till at last she found it. PRYCE the surname stood out boldly at the top with its attendant names riding meekly beneath it: *Pauline Cassandra Latimer,* telling Joanna all that she needed to know.

She stared at it, the light wavering in her hand.

They had lied to her; all of them had lied.

There had never been an "Aunt Pauline" who died on her mother's death day. Pauline Cassandra Latimer Pryce and Cassie Latimer Lynne had died on the same day—not as a mysterious coincidence as she had first thought—but out of necessity. Because Pauline and Cassie were one person and the same.

It explained so much; everything. Her own mother's nonexistent grave ("cremated, her ashes scattered" had been the official explanation); the absence of her mother's name from it's rightful place alongside Pauline's in the family Bible. And the mystery: never any talk of Cassie, all memories preserved in secret. Her father had lied, not once, but always: systemically manipulating her own perceptions, and taking the secrets with him to his grave.

But why did a woman who died giving birth in San Francisco end up buried six thousand miles away? And how did the "fictitious other woman" have a past and legend all her own? She could hear Granny Love saying *It give me quite a turn . . . you look so much like her . . . it were as if she had got up from her grave and come walking down the lane . . .*

One woman, two separate lives. How was it possible?

Engrossed with questions, she had nearly forgotten to be afraid. Now as she crouched by the grave she was aware of a noise beyond the gate, the staccato sound of footsteps coming up the road. A figure, swathed in dark and secrets, advancing toward her . . .

The flashlight fell from her hands and she stood up, ready to run. The figure came to the gate and stopped, and then she heard the gate creak open. She screamed, tripped over a stone, and fell, her face pressed to the cold ground. She heard quick running steps and then hands reached out to pull her up.

"Joanna?"

"Simon!" she fell against his chest, her tears of relief bubbling into laughter. "My God, what are you doing here at this time of night?"

He stooped for the flashlight and thrust it into her hand. "I was about to ask you the same thing!" His coat made a warm wrap for her shoulders as he led her toward the gate. "Jesus, Joanna—I'm taking you back to The Sheaves."

"I was spending the night at Kate's," she explained as he helped her out onto the road. "but I can't go back there now, it would be too hard to explain, too embarrassing. Let me come back with you, Simon. I've got to talk to somebody. . . ."

He built up the fire and brewed a pot of lemon tea while Joanna shivered on the couch, a blanket across her shoulders. As he set out the cups and a plate of cookies she told him the story and her suspicions. By the time she had finished he had brought the tea in and put it down before her on the coffee table.

"I don't understand why you are so certain that Pauline was your mother," he said, settling into a chair. "Naturally, I never knew her, but there are plenty of people in the village who did. How can that be if she was who you think she was? It just doesn't make sense."

"Who said it did? But you have to admit it all makes sense in a crazy kind of way. My mother always called herself 'Cassie,' it was even on my birth certificate. And Pauline's middle name just *happened* to be Cassandra . . ."

Simon tasted his tea and set the cup back neatly on the saucer. "So what? It's not odd for parents to give one child a name and then use it as a middle name for another. A case in point: my brother's name is Matthew and that's *my* middle name. It was probably the same with Pauline and Cassie."

She had been through too much to let him yank her suspicions away and claim them void. "I don't think so. Besides, I look like her. What about that?"

"Who said you looked like her?" he asked, sounding skeptical.

"Granny Love told me that this afternoon when I went to her house. She said that when she saw me she thought it was Pauline alive again."

"Joanna,"—and his voice was lightly scolding—"she's an old woman, probably senile. Are you going to take her word for this against every edict of common sense?"

"She isn't senile!" Joanna argued vehemently. "In fact she is remarkably clear-headed. She told me all about Pauline, how people thought she was strange, how she could see into the future, how she died by drowning . . ."

"So she drowned! So what? What does any of that prove?" He sounded almost angry. "Joanna, I really think you're making far too much of this." He took the cup of half-finished tea from her hands. "Get some sleep. I'll call Kate in the morning and explain why you ended up here. She can bring your things over before she goes to work."

"No, don't call her. I didn't leave anything there. She'll just think I left early in the morning before she got up. Besides, this whole thing is too complicated to explain over the phone." She reached across for his hand and held it tightly for a moment, her fingernails sharp on his skin. "Just promise me one thing—please don't tell anyone about the stuff I told you tonight."

"Why not?" he asked, mildly puzzled.

Joanna threw her head back against the cushion in mock exasperation. "I don't really know. I just want it that way. Promise me, Simon . . ."

"Of course—but I do think your rather marvelous imagination is working overtime. Just try to forget this business, baby. And get some sleep, for heaven's sake."

She nodded weakly, snuggling under the covers he'd put out for her. He would never believe that it was not coincidence, that she had been brought here to find what she had found tonight.

"Shall I leave you a night light?" Simon asked. "Or is the fire enough for you?"

"It's fine," she mumbled.

"Are you sure?" He stood for a moment with his hand on the light switch.

"Turn it off, I'll be okay." Then, remembering, "Simon, how did you happen to be out there tonight?"

He turned around, standing still in the doorway for a moment as though he hadn't heard her.

"Simon?"

"I just felt like a walk," he said. "Good night."

She waited for the sound of his door closing then sat up, feeling along the edge of the coffee table for the cigarettes he'd left there. Smoking, she replayed the day's events. Reason and imagination struggled for preeminence in her mind as she tried to make sense of what few facts she had.

Near morning she stood by the open door and watched night's deep colors fade slowly from the sky. Then she crept back to the couch and covered herself; soon she was asleep.

When Simon rose a few hours later, she didn't even stir.

*   *   *

By three that afternoon she was back at The Sheaves and eating an enormous breakfast when the call from Jayson came through.

Mercifully she was the only one at home, Caroline and her mother having disappeared as they so often did.

She wanted to tell him about all that she had learned in the past twenty-four hours; it was on the tip of her tongue to do so. But at the last, like Cranmer, she recanted her beliefs and spoke only pleasant heresies instead.

"There are some weird people here," she said, giving a twist to the word, hoping to convey some of her meaning through it, but she could only manage to sound belligerent.

"Here as well," his voice came back. "Last evening I saw a naked man driving a pink convertible . . ."

She laughed, tears bubbling in her throat, "Only in L.A."

"Are you all right?" His voice came close against her ear, its sweetness distorted by distance, and so achingly familiar.

She closed her eyes as tears rolled down her face. "I just miss you, Jayson. I wish you were here with me right now."

He could tell by the quivering pauses in between her words that she was crying. "I miss you too, my love. But here's some happy news. It looks as though I'll be free by November twentieth. That's a full ten days sooner than we had expected . . ."

"Any pretty girls over there?"

"Not a one." She could tell that he was smiling. "None named Joanna, with beautiful breasts and soft, soft hair . . ."

He could always make her blush, even from a distance. "I suppose it really isn't *so* long, is it? Not even eight full weeks."

"It isn't long if we both keep busy. Is the book going well for you?"

She told him about the plot developments that had taken place since his departure, of the many hours each day she spent working on the book (that would please him), even about some of the people she'd met since coming to St. Audric, and the experience in the churchyard that first evening.

"You're obviously having a more interesting time than I am," he said. "I'm glad you've made some friends."

"I'm still lonesome," she said. "Why couldn't you come over for a visit some weekend? You can't possibly be busy every day, every weekend. It would make it so much easier if we could at least see each other once . . ."

"Actually, I am busy every day," he told her, "researching the new book. And I do have four lectures a week, pet. It would be silly to come over for just a day or two. And you *know* how much I hate flying."

In the end she agreed as she almost always did, and Jayson rang off promising to call her on November 1.

Joanna cried for several minutes after she put down the phone, certain with some dreadful prescience she would never hear his voice again. His plane would crash, Los Angeles would be swallowed by an earthquake, the local Tesco would be firebombed by terrorists while she was in it. But after a while she realized that none of this was likely to occur; she would see Jayson again; she had a book to write and nothing was so terrible after all.

She had planned to research Pauline Latimer's past among the older residents of St. Audric this afternoon; at the very least talk with Stephen Halliwell about her. But now Joanna was feeling gloomy and it had begun to rain, so she went upstairs to bed and dragged the covers over her. Anything she wished to learn about Pauline could wait until another day.

INTERVAL

She Who Weds the Sky

Los Angeles, California
November 1964

The woman in the mirror resembled Jacqueline Kennedy.
Blond hair turbaned with a scarf, face made unrecognizable behind a pair of huge black sunglasses—the kind the former first lady wore out to dinner with the Averell Harrimans or to walk the streets of Georgetown unmolested by curious sightseers—she might have been any young American woman with a sense of style.

But she was only Cassie Latimer after all.

English. And lost.

She was at the airport now with two days and nights of driving behind her and one hundred eighty-seven dollars in her purse. That would buy her an airline ticket somewhere and keep her in an inexpensive motel until the baby came. There was no Department of Health and Social Security in America to fund medical care for the poor, but Pru had told her about "county hospitals," and Cassie would find one of those in which to have her child. After that she could go home again; she could simply pick up the telephone and call him, without any fear of what would happen to herself or to her sister, because by that time it would be too late.

Out of nervous habit she checked her money once again, then stuffed it down deep inside the wallet Pauline had given her for Christmas. One hundred eighty-seven dollars and change, and she would have to make it last.

Of course she couldn't stay too long in Los Angeles, they might be looking for her here. She had parked Paul's new white Mustang on an affluent-looking sidestreet in Culver City, and then hired a taxi to the airport. She was sorry for having taken his car

141

in the first place (it was only six weeks old) but Pru's Chevy was in the shop and so there was no other way. Her first plan had been to lose herself amid the great maze of American highways, but that was impractical with the baby due at almost any time, so she'd driven straight to Los Angeles instead.

At the United window she was helped by a pretty, perky girl with too much eyeliner and teased hair. But she was patient and friendly while Cassie asked about several destinations and their prices.

A ticket to Seattle cost her a good many of her precious dollars, but it was worth it because no one would be looking for her in the north. Her trail would stop in Los Angeles, and from that point she would disappear till it was safe to let friends and family know where she had gone. The ticket, bought under a fake name that popped suddenly into her head, found a place in her purse; then she moved on.

The lounge was small and dark; a pink neon airplane hung above the door. She ordered hot tea with lemon (it was lukewarm, ghastly) and sat drinking it while looking nervously out at the carpeted concourse, expecting to see him suddenly rise up before her eyes—however unreasonable that fear might be.

Paul and Pru, the police; they wouldn't find her easily, but he *might*. All the way down the coast she'd had the feeling she was being followed, no matter how many wrong turns she made or side roads she took. It might have only been imagination after all, but she could never quite relax, never feel completely safe till she had got where she was going.

She was troubled by the things she had been forced to do in order to escape him: forty-two dollars taken in secret from Pru's purse, another eighty-seven from the wallet of Paul's lawyer friend from Sunnyvale. She had stolen Paul's new car; she had disappeared from the house on Seaside Drive without a word or a good-bye. Paul and Pru deserved better than that; she would have to make it up to them somehow.

After November.

At a table just across the way a girl with puffed pink hair was drinking Metrecal from a can and flipping pages of a *Modern Screen* ("Debbie Tells: 'Why I Don't Want Eddie Back'"). She wore the placid, faintly bored expression of a housewife; her eyes—heavily made-up and virtually obscured behind false eyelashes—were blank as little stones. Cassie felt a wave of sympathy for her. *She looks as though she needs a friend as much as I.*

By the time she'd finished with the tea there was still a two-hour wait till boarding time. Cassie wandered from gift shop to gift shop and back to the lounge again, and this time she spent five quarters and a nickel for chicken salad and a plate of french fries. It was the first food she had eaten since two o'clock yesterday afternoon when, hidden in the parking lot of a Safeway store in Monterey, she'd devoured a pack of Oreos and a bag of buttered popcorn. Just two weeks short of her delivery date she was plagued with gas pains no matter what she ate—she might just as well indulge her snack-food habit.

The pink-haired girl had gone, probably to meet her husband. Cassie wondered if she had any secrets and if so did they pursue her? She carried her own beneath her breasts, a terrible secret she had never wanted, did not want now. Still, however it had come to be, it was a life, and she owed it some measure of safety.

Poor thing, what a strange history you have.

She would never understand the stupidity that had caused her to refuse Paul's offer of marriage. Although he and his sister only knew the peripheral matters in her situation (they wouldn't have believed the truth anyway; no one would), he understood she was in trouble and he wished to help. She was no doubt an idiot to have turned him down, but it would be wrong to draw him into this circle of corruption.

Paul, Pru—one day you'll understand.

One hour twenty minutes to boarding time.

Cassie went into the ladies' room again; locked in the stall she checked her money one last time. Afterward she stood before the full-length mirror and smiled with some approval. At the very least, pregnancy had grown her meager breasts to melon size. If not for the swollen mass below, she might look very nice in a bikini . . .

She crossed the wide concourse to a waiting area beyond where high windows looked out upon a smoggy afternoon. Cassie took a seat next to the exit, determined to be the first one on the plane. There was a discarded copy of the *Herald Examiner* at her elbow (TIME RUNNING OUT FOR GOP) but she had just begun to read when someone called her name in a familiar voice.

She looked up, startled and yet not surprised.

She had always believed that he would catch her out and now he had. She could have called for someone to help her, could have seemed to faint or tried to run. Instead she only stared, the newspaper sagging like a ruined kite to her knees as he came toward her. Relief had caught her by the throat.

"Geoffrey . . ." she said.

BOOK THREE

Bloodmonth

St. Audric, East Sussex
Today

A dead man with an arrow in his eye.

Poor Harold.

The rites of Hastings Day were celebrated each October 14 throughout Sussex to commemorate William of Normandy's victory over King Harold in the year 1066. In most villages it was treated as a country fair. Stalls were set up to sell crafts and wares, the local town hall decorated for a festive gathering and communal meal. Parades and outdoor activities took place if the weather was fine, and a pageant, too: the village children mimicked Saxons and their fierce Norman opponents with spears and swords of cardboard.

Joanna's only experience with the holiday dated from 1986 when she and David Lair had made an afternoon run down from London to Hastings for the celebration, ending their day with a good dinner at the most trendy eatery in Hastings, The Poor Harold, where clever, colorful wall murals depicted scenes from the Bayeaux Tapestry. One panel showed Poor Harold with an arrow through his eye.

Hastings Day in St. Audric, where Saxon history was still venerated, was celebrated differently than in any other part of Sussex. Each year at noon on October 14 a procession began in the churchyard, winding its way slowly up New Clergy Road and the High Street to Fiddler's Green. The procession included fourteen girls walking in two rows of seven each, and carrying baskets filled to the brim with twigs and apples—items that were sacred to the Saxons. At Fiddler's Green the "maidens" turned out their baskets; then the vicar came forth to light a giant bon-

147

fire. As flames consumed their offerings the girls danced round the fire chanting remnants of an ancient Saxon charm:

Burn higher
Mother fire,
Fly nigh
Father Sky.
Bring birth
Mother Earth,
Seed daughter
Father Water . . .

Afterward there was always a huge supper and cider drinking on the Green, the first toast given over to "Our good King the late Harold of England, may God in Heaven preserve his good Memory . . ." By three o'clock the crowd dispersed, only to reunite once more over at The Plague Maiden for the annual jumble sale (proceeds going to the local Women's Institute), followed by another annual event: the Hastings Day Community Cream Tea and Supper.

Despite her commitment to *The Scourge,* Joanna had managed to get involved in plans for Hastings Day. Twice she had been over to Lewes to pick up bags of discarded clothes and shoes collected by the Council, and she had likewise scoured the houses of St. Audric's Malting Road for additional cast-offs. She had even agreed to man one of the tables at the jumble sale. Meg St. Denis, chairman of the event this year, had recruited Joanna one day when she came into the High Street Craft Centre to buy a packet of pens.

Meg was a cheery, somewhat officious woman, middle-aged and meddlesome in a friendly way. Her greatest aim in life seemed to be getting other people organized, and it was one of the things Joanna liked about her because it was a characteristic shared by her Aunt Rue. Widowed for several years, Meg had no children, yet she was a virtual encyclopedia of information on how to bring them up properly, information that she shared willingly (and often) with the young mothers of the village. Strangers, too. The first time they talked, Meg had confided to Joanna that Cynthia Marrow's little Blanche cried all the time because

Cynthia always gave the child cold milk with her supper, thus inflicting her with a chronic case of stomach ache. (*Stupid woman! She ought to spend more time with her children than running after Simon Cherrystone. He doesn't care* THAT *for her!* Sound of fingers snapping under Joanna's nose.)
Life in the village.
She was beginning to feel very much at home.

* * *

Early in October Kate invited Joanna to tea at Little Gospels to meet Geoffrey Latimer, who had just returned from France.

He and Kate were sitting together on the wickerback settee when Joanna came hurriedly into the room. She had promised to be at Little Gospels no later than four thirty, but time had gotten away from her, lost within the walls of her narrative. So she let herself in and came directly to the sitting room where she paused for a moment, hearing voices pitched low, almost breathless, though the door was open.

Immediately they stood up.

She hadn't known quite what to expect, but at first glance he didn't seem to be the lordly figure of mystery she had heard Kate and others in the village describe. He was rather unprepossessing, and somewhat older than Joanna had imagined he would be. He had the bland attractiveness of so many English men, the type who cut a good figure from a distance but whose features are forgettable seen close-to.

"Sorry I'm late . . ." she began.

He had gray eyes and a pale face set with neat, composed features. He was sixty, perhaps a few years older, though his hair had more dark than gray in it. When he took hold of Joanna's hand and kissed it as a greeting she nearly giggled but was saved by Kate, bent over the tea things, her hand poised.

"Shall I pour?"

Later Kate looked ill at ease as Joanna launched into a query about Pauline Latimer Pryce ("I'm almost certain that she was my aunt . . ."), and wondering aloud if Geoffrey and Joanna herself were somehow related.

Bad move.

Geoffrey began to fidget, the cup and saucer tinkling between his hands. At first Joanna didn't notice the silence, preoccupied with stirring sugar into her tea. When she looked up she saw Geoffrey staring at her and Kate's eyes averted to the window.

"What's the matter?" she asked archly, "did I say something wrong?"

"No." Geoffrey's answer was decisive, convincing. "It's quite a charming thought actually. Though you must realize that Latimer is quite a common name in these parts."

She looked across at Kate; no answer there.

"So I've been told."

Geoffrey held the cup to his lips. "Have you come to St. Audric looking for your family?"

The question was so deliberately polite and at the same time accusing, Joanna answered with a snappish, "No, I've come here to research a book. I'd have thought Kate would have told you all about it by this time."

He nodded. "She has, a little."

"I didn't even know there were any Latimers in this town till I saw Pauline Pryce's gravestone in the cemetery." She waited for him to make a comment. "Pauline *Latimer* Pryce?"

"Oh, yes?"

Was he being purposely evasive? "I assume Pauline was a relative of yours . . ."

He shook his head. "I wouldn't know."

"But surely . . . you both came from the same village, it's a small place, and you have the same last name. It stands to reason you must have known her, and if you did you must have been able to say if the two of you were related or not . . ."

Kate looked up, startled, as though Joanna had commited some unpardonable social sin, but Geoffrey only smiled.

"So far as I know, Pauline and I were not blood relations. As I say, it's a common name. Also it may interest you to know that although I was born in St. Audric I passed my youth and adolescence in the United States and Canada." He smiled at her puzzled expression. "My parents, as so many well-to-do people of their time did, evacuated me to family friends there before the war began, and I didn't return to St. Audric until 1950. Since then I've spent more time away from Blackmantle than in it. That is, until my marriage in 1986, when I settled here in the village for good, or so I hoped . . ."

Joanna colored with embarrassment at having led him into the admission. Of course that only showed her all the more to be aware of his unfortunate situation, so she merely said, "I see," and sounded like an idiot for saying it.

For the next hour the three of them made polite if somewhat stilted conversation, most of the exchanges taking place between Geoffrey and Joanna. Kate said little. Geoffrey seemed genuinely interested in Joanna's plans for *The Scourge,* commenting admiringly on her knowledge of the period.

They chatted amiably about other things, small things: "Are you staying over for Hastings Day?" "Yes of course, I wouldn't miss it . . ." "Last year it rained the whole week; what a pity . . ."

It was genial and ordinary and polite but there was something false in it. Kate seemed nervous whenever Joanna asked a too-personal question (she no doubt feared a direct assault along the lines of "Who did your wife run off with?"). But when Geoffrey turned the conversation to the topic of Blackmantle she seemed to relax.

"I'd be happy to show it to you anytime," Geoffrey offered after Joanna had evidenced an interest. "Perhaps living there on my own I don't keep it up the way I should. The decoration, for the most part" (Joanna could tell he was thinking of his wife), "is pretty much the way my mother did it up many years ago, but there are some arresting architectural features, including one wall dating from the original eighth-century structure. . . ."

Joanna had seen Blackmantle from the outside many times during her hikes to the Long Man. More impressive than beautiful, the Elizabethan and Jacobean renovations had done a lot to alter the original medieval character of the place. "Monk's Ghost" she had christened it in her mind, because it looked as though no one but ghosts walked there.

"I'd like to see it," she admitted. "It's one of those places I've read about in books for years and wasn't sure I'd ever see for myself."

He smiled nicely at her. "And now you shall."

"Just let me know when you're free to give a tour."

Geoffrey looked at Kate, then back to Joanna. "I will," he said.

Because of her talents as an organizer ("the bossiest woman in the village," Sarah Halliwell said) Meg St. Denis had given herself the job of plotting Kate Callison's birthday party. It was to be a surprise, and in this matter Joanna was her willing accomplice.

One afternoon shortly before Hastings Day, Meg and Joanna drove into Brighton to shop for Kate's gifts. Chloe Bibble was with them, thrilled at the chance to choose her own gift for Kate, and happy at the opportunity to spend additional time with Joanna, who enjoyed it, too.

She had never wished for a little sister but if she had, Chloe, dreamy and sweet, would have fit the fantasy. From the beginning Joanna had felt sorry for the wistful little waif who hovered around The Plague Maiden trying her best to serve the patrons well, only to be told repeatedly by her aunt or uncle that she had done this or that thing wrong. Except to criticize, they didn't seem to pay her any attention at all. It was no wonder the child was so devoted to Kate. Now some of that affection had spilled over in her attitude toward Joanna, whom she shadowed at every opportunity.

"You spoil that child," Meg observed as she and Joanna walked along the Prom. Both women were bundled in scarves and sweaters; the sea was rough today. "You and Kate both . . ."

Chloe lagged well behind them, all her interest centered on the charm bracelet she'd gotten earlier that morning at the jewelry counter in Boots. It was only a cheap metal thing with gold paint covering it, but Chloe had spent fifteen minutes in fingering the treasure. Joanna, who still remembered what it was to be a teenager with little money, had slipped Chloe the three pound coins to buy it.

"Spoiling people does no harm," Joanna answered, turning her collar up against the wind. "It's better than ignoring them. I think both Sarah and Stephen ignore her."

"She's a regular little miser," Meg sniffed, looking back over her shoulder at the loitering girl. "I've seen her—with my own eyes, mind—change the pound coin Stephen gives her for church each week into five twenty-p. coins at the Cash & Carry so she can put only one twenty p. in and keep the rest for herself. You don't get to be that wily without practice."

"Enterprising, I'd say . . ."

"Yes, very clever little thing in her way, though Mrs. Fitzstephens at the school says she can hardly do her sums. Imagine that, at her age! I really don't know why Stephen and Sarah aren't more strict with her." She shook her head, no doubt thinking that the pair could do with a good chat on the subject. "You have to be strict when a girl gets to be *that* age. God only knows what she'll be up to next . . ."

"How old is Chloe?" Joanna wondered. "When I first saw her I thought she was a very tall twelve-year-old. But she must be older than that. I've seen the work she does for Kate at the library and she's really quite accomplished."

"She's fifteen." Meg pronounced it like an accusation.

"She seems young for her age."

Meg sniffed again. "Old enough. My sister's got a girl that age. Lord, nothing but problems! Emma's terrified she's going to come home pregnant or infected by one of these sex diseases. They're only babies at that age, yet doing things we never would have thought to do till we were women. And even then . . ."

"I hardly think that's true of Chloe. She's about the most innocent child I ever met."

"I remember when I was that age," Meg went on, seeming not to have heard, "there wasn't any time for foolishness or ill-considered behavior then. Things were still very bad here in Britain, you know. The war was over, but there were shortages, poverty, bad times. In some ways things were actually worse than they had been before . . ."

Joanna had heard enough *you-have-it-easy-compared-to-me-at-your-age* stories from her own parents to be thoroughly bored with them. "It's never easy growing up," she said to Meg. "And I don't think it would kill Sarah to buy Chloe a new dress now and then instead of forcing her to wear those ghastly made-over things. There isn't another girl in the world her age who has to dress the way she does."

"Kate buys her things at term time." Meg stopped for a moment, poking in her handbag for a second glove. "Of course Kate's very taken with her. But then I've always thought poor Kate was a lonely sort of woman. No family, you know. It's a shame she never married."

It was only then Joanna understood what she was *really* saying. In Meg's well-meaning, all-too-curious judgment, Kate was a spinster, one of those pathetic, drab little women who have no man in their life and thus no life. *I wonder what you would say if I told you I thought Kate and Geoffrey Latimer were having an affair and that nobody in St. Audric has guessed but me?*

It was tempting, but she only said, "I rather think Kate likes living alone. That doesn't necessarily mean she's lonely." It was only a vague attempt to take Kate's part, but Joanna felt better for having said it. Both Kate and Meg took too much interest in other people's business, but there was a difference. Kate was curious, interested, the consequence of her life-style as librarian in a tiny village. Meg was simply nosy. And her comments about people and events were rarely flattering.

Joanna pointed ahead and they turned onto the King's Road, peering down the street for La Petite Chartreuse, an exclusive Brighton antiques store. Joanna saw the scrolled sign halfway down the street and continued on her way with Meg at her side, stopping every few paces along the way to frown at a display in a shop window and complain about how outlandish the prices were.

"I hear you've been to tea with Geoffrey Latimer," Meg said close to Joanna's ear.

Gossip.

The village thrived on it, everyone content to live vicariously off the sins or harmless tidbits of other people's lives. But then Joanna was forced to smile as she realized it was not so very different from what novelists did, constantly living through someone else's skin, experiencing their joy or sorrow as deeply as their own. . . .

"Have you?" Meg's voice had risen in anticipation of an answer.

"Been to tea with him? Yes. At Little Gospels."

Meg nodded, seemingly well pleased at the news, a dark curl dancing on her forehead in celebration of the event. "And what did you think of him?"

"He's nice," she said, deliberately choosing the blandest words she knew. They would be echoed and reechoed (she felt sure) throughout St. Audric in the days to come. Well, let the curious of the village read something into *that*.

Just then Chloe came running up behind them, her fine blond hair flying beneath the captive edges of her knitted cap. "Can we have lunch at McDonald's?" she asked hopefully, looking at Joanna.

"We'll see," Joanna answered, touching the girl's shoulder lightly. "But let's get the presents first, okay?"

La Petite Chartreuse was a Regency-style shop dealing in French and English antiques. Joanna had never been inside but she had heard Jayson speak well of it, and that was recommendation enough. Meg was scandalized by the prices, finding them far too steep and the shop itself too posh ("Kate would never forgive us if we bought something too extravagant!") and she hustled Chloe out the door and down the street to Debenhams, where Meg selected a good set of knives with their own cherrywood rack ("always remember, Chloe, that a well-stocked kitchen needs *good* knives . . .") and the girl picked out a pair of opalescent hanging earrings "to match Kate's new blouse."

Meanwhile Joanna went delightedly up and down the crowded, crooked aisles of the antiques store. She looked at clocks, at silver chains and brooches, at candlesticks. Then she spied something wonderful that would look lovely in Kate's cheery sitting room: a pair of matched pewter goblets, hammered and decorated with vine leaves at their stems. Another candidate was a gold-flecked gesso saint, unsigned but clearly showing a late Pre-Raphaelite influence, done sometime in the mid 1890s, Joanna guessed. After a brief deliberation she bought the twin goblets for Kate (eighty-nine pounds) and the saint for Jayson (one hundred fifteen pounds). It would be her homecoming present to him. That and a few other things . . .

Packages in hand, she crossed to W. H. Smith, where she signed two dozen copies of *Tabitha's Claw* and bought two for herself, along with a decorative clothbound version of *Victorian Love Poesy* for Chloe, who cooed over it happily when Joanna caught up with them at The Violet Tea Room, a glass-walled restaurant on the sea-front.

Shocked at the evidence of Joanna's extravagance, Meg

insisted on treating them to lunch. Afterward Chloe went across the street to watch kittens in the pet-shop window, while Meg and Joanna lingered over steaming cups of Darjeeling and bowls of hot plum cozy.

"What does Geoffrey Latimer think about your book?" Meg asked, her clever dark eyes searching Joanna's face for a clue. "I'd have thought he'd have something to say about it, that's for sure."

"Why does everybody say that?" Joanna asked, mildly irritated by Meg's interest. "People act like I'm stepping on his toes by writing it. It's not as if the book is really about St. Audric, anyway. And even if it was, why should he mind more than anyone else in the village?"

"Not stepping on his toes," Meg said. "Not that exactly. But it has occurred to some people in the village that the two of you might be related."

"I doubt it," Joanna said, trying to deflect Meg's curiosity. "And we didn't really go into that. I don't want him to think I'm presuming on the family fortune."

Meg laughed out loud, a rich and quite lovely music that belied the droning sound of her voice. "I doubt if there's that much, not in cash money anyway. You know what they say about the English gentry: all silver sconces and no brass."

"I've never heard that."

Meg nibbled happily at her pudding, content at having made her point. "Now, *my* dear husband, he was in computers, and when he died he left me quite well off. Not rich, you understand, but comfortable. I'm not afraid to wager I have more on account than old Latimer has." She nudged Joanna and gave a knowing wink. "And after seeing all you spent today I wouldn't be at all surprised if you have more than both of us put together."

Hardly a scrap of privacy left.

Joanna only smiled.

In the car going back to St. Audric, Meg and Joanna reviewed the plans for Kate's party. "If her birthday's the nineteenth, why are we having the party Friday night?" Meg wondered.

"The séance," Joanna reminded her. "I've been invited to attend. I've been bugging Roland Jaspar about it the past few weeks. As it turns out I only get to go because one of his own 'regulars' dropped out for the evening. I never knew there had to be a set number of people at a séance, did you? I just always thought it was 'the more the merrier.'"

"Yes, you would, wouldn't you?" Meg squinted at the tiny transparent beads that had begun to dance on the windows, and reached to flick on the wipers.

"Have you ever been to one?" Joanna asked. At her elbow the autumnal landscape rushed by, dun-colored, dying.

"To a séance? Good God, yes. My mother was a spiritualist. She had quite a following back during the war. I never saw much point to it myself, but many do." She gave a quick sideways look at Joanna. "You do, I suppose, or you wouldn't be going."

"I guess I do. I'm not really sure. A parapsychologist I knew at Berkeley said they were all faked, but he turned out to be an asshole, so what did he know?" She leaned back against the headrest, her eyelids fluttering. "Who are Jaspar's regulars? Do you know?"

"My Aunt Sarah," Chloe piped from the backseat. "She goes to talk to a boyfriend she had back in California who died of a motorcycle crash."

"And there's Dr. Wallin from Alfriston," Meg said. She took a turn too sharply and skidded just a bit. "Oh, and of course there's Cynthia Marrow."

"And she goes to talk to the spirit of her husband," Joanna said. "It's kind of depressing to think about talking to a dead man twice a month."

"There'll be eight in all, counting Jaspar," Meg said. "I know that much. My mum always had a circle of eight, too. Or as she put it: four plus four."

"What the hell does that mean?"

"Four was the holy number of the ancients, rather like seven is regarded today, or three, to represent the Trinity."

"But why four?"

"To symbolize the elements: air, earth, water, fire. It sounds frightfully conventional today of course, but they seem to have believed in it."

"They?" Joanna frowned.

"The ancient Saxon folk. You must have realized by now how

strong those influences are. They still exist, in small ways. Things like the holy numbers."

"Well, yeah," Joanna conceded, "but it's just myth . . ."

"Maybe," Meg replied. "But if a people believe something for enough centuries, perhaps that makes it true, in a way."

Joanna shook her head, disbelieving. "People don't swallow that kind of stuff today."

Meg smiled back at herself from the overhead mirror.

"They do in this part of the world," she said.

*   *   *

The morning of Hastings Day it threatened rain, but by noon the clouds began to fall away and patches of pale amber sunlight showed in the sky.

Following the procession and pageant there was the customary cider-drinking on the Green. Sweets, too, contributed by several female members of the parish. Meg had brought trays of sand tarts and homemade crullers. Sally Bradshaw had made a batch of spirit bread. Granny Love's contribution was an old Saxon recipe for phallic cakes, honoring a dead hero. Joanna took one look at them and gladly passed them up. The idea of nibbling on Poor Harold's testicles made her feel rather sick.

Chloe, delighted at having been chosen to lead the procession of maidens from churchyard to the Green, was equally excited about the work she'd done to decorate The Plague Maiden's common room for the Supper and Cream Tea. Sarah had let her do most of it this year.

The pub's back room, used as a storage space and larder most days, had been emptied to accommodate tables for the jumble sale. Kate and Meg had done most of the setting-up the previous evening. Every table was piled high with discarded clothes and oddments of many descriptions. Joanna's assigned table was of "Ladies' skirts and jumpers for forty p. and up."

Chloe, who had never had the chance to wear a costume before today, kept her white tunic on all the afternoon, though Joanna was quick to spot that her tammy shams had been replaced by Reeboks.

She hovered close to Joanna, who was straightening out her wares, having managed to root out a very nice blue cashmere that she put aside for herself. "Did you see how I laid out the plate and silver on the serving table?" Chloe asked hopefully. "Aunt Sarah says I did it regular."

"It's nice," Joanna answered. "And you were very good in the procession, too. The best one, I'd say."

"I nearly tripped on my hem," she admitted, looking momentarily woeful, "but all the same I love this dress. I wish I'd lived in them days when girls wore dresses that was long. I think things were better then."

"Not everything." Joanna laughed. "Not for women. I don't think you would have liked having a husband picked out for you, things like that . . ."

"I guess." Chloe wrinkled her nose. Then her pale profile disappeared as she turned toward the big double doors that had been propped open to admit people for the sale. "I have to help Kate take the tickets," she said, and slipped from the room quietly as a ghost.

There were nearly five hundred people in the village of St. Audric, and it seemed all of them had crowded into the common room of The Maiden for today's sale. Joanna minded her table diligently for two hours, but by that time most of the items had been sold and the crowd in the back room had thinned, most everyone having gone to scan the huge potluck table for the supper of his or her choice.

Joanna watched all the activity with a sense of nostalgic fondness. It had been years since she had been involved in any sort of community project, not since an afternoon ten years ago when her senior class had sold Tofutti bars in the parking lot of the Seaview Theater to help pay the school band's passage to the Rose Bowl. How insular she had become since that time, especially this past year. It startled her to realize suddenly that since moving in with Jayson she'd had little personal contact with anyone else. Perhaps he had been right in thinking that this separation would benefit them both. He'd no doubt sensed her growing dependence on him as an unhealthy symptom.

"You look as though you've done your bit," Sarah Halliwell said, coming up behind her. "I've just put out the tea and sweets, supper, too, if you're ready."

Joanna indicated her nearly empty table. "I hope my till balances out. I haven't had to make change since I had a garage sale my second year in college, and that was American money!"

"Don't worry about it. I think you sold more than anybody else." Sarah bent close. "By the way, remember those awful shirts of Stephen's I told you about, the ones he bought two years ago in Manitoba?" She gave a conspiratorial wink. "I managed to unload a few of those. Marvelous, isn't it? And for *charity*. I feel absolutely saintly."

"Men hate when you do things like that."

"I know." Sarah laughed. "But I've found ways to get around it in the end."

Joanna finished counting up her till (seventeen pounds, thirty-five pence) and turned it in to Meg, then joined Kate and Simon at one of the tables. Simon was sporting a cheeky pink blazer he'd bought at the sale for fifty pence. Joanna complimented him on it, hoping secretly that it wasn't one of Stephen Halliwell's unbidden discards.

"Kate brought Chinese food as her contribution," he told Joanna as she squeezed into a chair beside him, "and I brought Swedish meatballs." He whipped the aluminum foil neatly off a Pyrex baking dish.

"I didn't know you could cook," Joanna said, pretending to sniff at the meatballs with disdain. "Forgive me, but I'm more in the mood for Chinese, or maybe some of that lasagna Sarah made." She started to get up.

"Don't bother, ladies," Simon announced with mock chivalry, "I'll get plates for you both. Chinese for Joanna . . ." He looked to Kate. "And for you?"

She didn't have to think. "Spaghetti bolognese, if there's still some left. Betty Wallin brought it, and she's one of the best cooks I know."

Simon made an insufferably silly face, gave a little bow, then went off to get the food.

"What do you think of our little village do?" Kate asked as Joanna busied herself lighting a cigarette. "I suppose it seems rather dull to you, but believe it or not, it's things like this that are the highlights of the social year in tiny villages like St. Audric."

Joanna tapped her cigarette ash on the floor. "I do believe it, and I don't think it's dull. Come to that, I guess this is the first social event I've been to in a long time." She found herself scanning the tables, looking for what? She didn't know until the words were on her lips. "Funny, I don't see either Caroline or Mrs. Munro here today."

"They don't mix much with the rest of us," Kate observed. "I suppose they feel themselves above the crowd . . ." Joanna was mercifully spared hearing a rerun account of Mrs. Munro's affair with the cabinet minister because just then Simon came up to the table with their plates.

"Looks delicious," Joanna said, looking at the two plates. "Aren't you going to join us?"

"Ladies first," he said, "then I'm off to get mine." He nipped her nose lightly with his fingers. "I suppose I should put my meatballs out there for the world to see, though after admiring all the goodies up there at the table I've rather lost my taste for them." He scooped up the baking dish.

"Bring some fortune cookies for Joanna," Kate called after him. To Joanna she said, "You can't possibly eat Chinese food without fortune cookies. Isn't it funny how often the messages ring true? I remember once in Scarborough . . ."

Her words seemed to fade away into the most distant part of Joanna's ear. Two tables away sat Cynthia Marrow, staring at Joanna, looking pale and martyred and miserable. It wasn't the first time Joanna had spied her looking on when she and Simon were together. She felt mildly sorry for the young widow, but she didn't own Simon, did she? If she was jealous, well, there wasn't anything Joanna could do about that either. But all the same it gave her an eerie feeling to look up suddenly and see Cynthia looking at her with such—was it actually an expression of despair? Self-conscious, unnecessarily guilty, Joanna looked away.

Simon returned, carrying a plate heaped high with food, and sat down across from Kate and next to Joanna. He dropped a fortune cookie into her hand. "There weren't any left on the buffet table, but Chloe remembered Sarah kept some in the back, so here you are."

Kate pointed her fork at Simon's plate.

"Lasagna, whipped potatoes, spaghetti? It's obvious you aren't watching your waistline, Simon."

"But someone is watching Simon," Joanna said quietly, nudging his arm.

He looked up briefly from his food, saw that she meant Cynthia, and went back to eating. "Ignore her," he muttered.

"I'm not the one she's looking at."

"She's only looking at me because I'm sitting here with you. Ignore her."

He had a right to be annoyed with Cynthia she supposed, but there was something insensitive and careless about the way he tossed off the remark.

Sarah appeared at the edge of the table just then, a small blue teapot in her hand. She set it down in front of Joanna. "Chloe told me you were eating Chinese so I thought you might want some Formosa oolong to go with it." She spent the next several minutes chatting with Kate about how much money the sale had brought in ("Almost ninety pounds—we've never made that much before!" and Kate's charitable reply, "Joanna must be a good-luck charm!"). Watching her, Joanna thought that even in a plain skirt and blouse covered by a white pinny Sarah managed to look like her sexy self, and she was reminded of afternoons spent in Pacifica's Seaview Theater, stuffing herself with popcorn and Pepsi while up on the screen Sarah Jeffers swooned under the spell of Ralph Bates or Christopher Lee. Horror films had been a staple of Joanna's preteen and teenage years, and many of the images culled from that past included Sarah.

At her elbow Simon made a comment about the food. Turning to answer him, Joanna reached for her cookie and cracked it open, extracting the curled paper fortune without much interest. She glanced at the words without really reading them, then looked again and nearly dropped the cup she was holding in her other hand.

YOU HAVE NOT LONG TO LIVE

It was printed in pencil, all capital letters, and there was a reddish smudge, almost a fingerprint, at the corner. A bloodstain? Strawberry jam?

She didn't remember very much after that, only that her head had gone light as a balloon though all the rest of her body had suddenly become too heavy to move and she began to rise slowly from the table, poised to take a step. Then the cup she still held began to waver in her hand and slipped from her grasp to the floor. And then Joanna followed it, hitting her head on the table as she went down. The last thing that she remembered was a shrill female voice pitched high in excitement crying out, "My God, she's dead!"

It was hours later when she woke up.

Jayson?

Joanna was in an unfamiliar bed with all her clothes off and a hundred people in the room. No, not so many; her skewed vision was unpredictable, told lies. Squinting up at a stranger, she felt herself come more fully awake and she tried to rise, only to fade back against the pillow with a horrible pain in her head.

"Don't move, young lady. You've had a bad fall."

It was a man's voice, gruff, not Jayson's. Of course not Jayson's, he was in California. This man's face was unfamiliar, a mystery.

"What happened?" she asked.

"You fainted and hit your head as you went down. Don't you remember?" It sounded like an accusation.

She could see him now. Middle-aged, a sunburned face, blue eyes. He tested the bump on her forehead with his finger and she pushed his hand away. "Who are you?" she demanded. "I don't know you . . ."

"I'm Dr. Wallin from Wilmington. Just be glad that I was here today. Saved you a trip into Lewes by ambulance."

Kate leaned into her frame of vision. "Whatever made you faint like that, Joanna, dear? It's a good thing you don't need any stitches on that pretty face of yours."

"Where am I?"

"Upstairs at The Maiden." Kate again. "Stephen and Dr. Wallin carried you up here after you fainted."

Joanna pushed herself up, realizing that she wasn't naked after all. She'd mistaken the feel of a silk robe, probably Sarah's, for her own skin. "I'm fine," she declared, "and I *didn't* faint." Then she remembered. "The fortune cookie! What happened to the message in the fortune cookie?"

"Fortune cookie, what fortune cookie?" Dr. Wallin asked, bending close, examining her eyes with a pinpoint beam of light. She could smell beef stroganoff on his breath. Then he straightened up, shaking his head. "No evidence of a concussion, for which you are extremely lucky." Then to Kate he said, "What is this cookie she keeps asking about?"

"Nothing," Joanna said forcefully, "nothing at all." She touched her forehead gingerly. It hurt. "I guess I was just dreaming."

Sarah came in with tea on a tray and looked questioningly at the doctor. "Can she drink something hot? It won't hurt her, will it?"

Why was everyone talking as if she weren't in the room?

"Tea's fine, but no alcohol. And *no* smoking for at least twenty-four hours." He frowned darkly at Joanna. "I mean that."

"Okay," she answered meekly. "Maybe I should just try to sleep."

It was difficult to hide the sense of urgency she felt. If only he would go, if only they would all go and leave her alone to think. She had purposely broken off her account of the sinister fortune cookie (great title for a story!) because they wouldn't believe it anyway. No one else had seen it, not even Simon, who had been sitting next to her.

"Where's Simon?" she asked suddenly.

Dr. Wallin and Kate looked at one another as if the information she sought was a matter of national security. Sarah answered. "He's gone home. He waited a while for you to wake up, but I'm afraid he wasn't feeling very well himself." She smiled. "Too much lasagna, I suppose."

"Has everybody gone?"

Sarah again. "Nearly. It's almost eight."

So late. No one had seen the little scrap of paper, and when she had fallen it had flown out of her hand and gone God only knew where. Hours had passed, it had probably been swept up with all the other table litter and thrown away.

Or carefully retrieved and disposed of by its author.
The words appeared, just like that, in italics across the gray window shade of her mind. Dr. Wallin charged her to stay in bed for the next twelve hours and deputized someone to look after her. Kate volunteered but Sarah Halliwell prevailed, since the spare room where Joanna had been put was quite small with no space for another bed, however temporary, to be brought in. Sarah or Chloe would spend the night "popping in to check" on their patient at regular intervals. It was nearly nine before Kate went, promising to come by the following morning on her way to work, though Joanna assured her a visit was unnecessary, as she would no doubt be back at The Sheaves by that time.

Sarah interrupted to say no, she would not, because Joanna was going to be spoiled royally with a late lie-in and a full breakfast in bed. It was the least they could do for her.

So much for liberty.

Sarah dispensed the aspirin Dr. Wallin had left and went away and finally, after nodding off a few times in the chair, Chloe did, too. At last Joanna was left alone, all alone, to puzzle out what had happened to put her in a bed in this tiny room and wearing the borrowed robe of a former movie star. But by that time she was too tired and dizzy to think and her eyes felt heavy and unfamiliar as if she were wearing false eyelashes the way she had that very first time she'd gone into Goethe's and seen David, handsome and lordly as a medieval knight, piping melodies on an ancient recorder, pausing to read a stanza of his own design . . .

Sarah and Chloe came to check on her several times during the night. Sarah even brought an extra quilt to toss on the bed when it grew very cold around 2 A.M. By morning all the shrubs and streets and back gardens had been magically dusted over with a thin layer of white powder, fine as talc.

First frost. Joanna stirred to wakefulness and the wonderful aroma of country cooking and cold air.

"Mrs. Munro said you don't like English breakfasts much, so I thought I'd treat you to something I learned to make in California once while I was there making a film."

Sarah hoisted the rattan-weave bed tray and slid it into place over Joanna's knees. There were two plates, one large, the other small, both covered with tin domes. A pot of steaming tea (Twinings English Breakfast; Joanna knew the bouquet) and a rack of toast with a jar of quince and raspberry preserves beside it. Sarah swept the domes away to disclose huevos rancheros on one plate and cottage-style fried potatoes with a thick slab of Canadian bacon atop it on the other.

"My God, this is a feast!" Joanna declared. Having been denied the greater part of her dinner the day before, she realized now she was absolutely starved. Sarah had even troubled to include a bud vase with lilac spider mums on the tray. "You really are thoughtful," Joanna said, looking up.

"It's nothing. Enjoy." Sarah took up the tin domes and carried them to the door.

"Don't you want to stay and keep me company while I put away this luscious meal?" Joanna asked, bending eagerly to the food.

"Sorry"—she already had her hand on the doorknob—"but Stephen is a bear if he doesn't get his oats before eight." She winked at Joanna. "By the way, Dr. Wallin rang this morning to see if we'd done right by you during the night. I told him I'd been in to see you around five and you'd no fever and were sleeping well. He said I was to call him when you woke with news of how you felt."

"I'm really fine," Joanna began to say, touching her forehead, "just a little soreness . . ."

". . . But that no matter what, you were to spend the day in bed and that I should see to it you do. You might as well stay here the day. Stephen will run you back in the car before supper."

Joanna was about to resist, but it was pointless, so she only said, "Thanks," though the door closed heavily on the word.

She ate, slept a while, woke to use the second-floor loo, then crept back into bed once more to hide beneath the covers. When she woke again it was nearly noon.

The pain in her head had gone and she could think more clearly now. All her dreams had been confused reprisals of yesterday's events so that it was hard to sort the images into proper order: truth, and what had been imagined.

You have not long to live.

Those words, that memory, were real enough. She had seen

the words, held them in her hand. Who could have written the note? It seemed less important at this point to ask why.

How could it have been managed if it had been managed?

Simon had brought the cookie to her, but Kate had suggested that he bring it, and so far as Joanna could remember it had been either Chloe or Sarah who had made the cookie available to him. Four people: none with any motive to threaten, scare, or even tease her. Of course it was just possible that the cookie message had been a cruel prank aimed at no one in particular and that she had only happened to get it by mere chance.

Joanna pondered that for a moment, wondering why the logic didn't fit. And then she knew. There was something, a single fact that determined it was no random prank but a deliberate menace (real or pretended) aimed at her.

Someone had put something in her tea.

It might have seemed to everyone else that she had fainted, but Joanna knew better. The message had startled her to be sure, but she had already begun to feel dizzy after tasting the tea, and when she'd tried to stand up she'd simply toppled over. Whoever had written the note had put the knockout pill in her tea, so the message *had* been meant for her after all. What had been the purpose/intention of causing her to faint? To draw attention to the matter? Perhaps whoever it was had wanted the message to be found and read by others. She filed that possibility with a dozen others, though she could think of no motive for it all. *Unless . . .*

Unless it was linked to the letter that had brought her to St. Audric in the first place. Yet even that line of thinking seemed oddly suspect. The letter had been an invitation, almost an entreaty. Surely the fortune cookie and the bogus "fainting spell" might be seen to have the opposite effect. Logical assumption: Two separate people or groups of people were at work in this.

Team A versus Team B.

Facts: Team A wanted Joanna in St. Audric. To this end a player on Team A had scripted the letter, using Kate Callison's name as a logical and realistic-sounding cover. Why? Unknown. Team B on the other hand had a decided interest in keeping her away and had adopted scare tactics as their game plan. Why? Once again: Unknown.

Team A suspects: Many possibles, no probables. Simon, Sarah, Chloe, Kate. No, times four. They were all her friends and equally incapable of perpetrating such acts of deception. (Joanna had long ago discarded the theory that Chloe had written the original letter.) Team A score: 0

Team B suspects: Cynthia Marrow, certainly. She'd been hard to miss yesterday, her great sad eyes fixed on Simon and accusingly on Joanna. She was obviously very much in love with him and jealous of the time (however innocent) he spent with Joanna. It was very possible, if not wholly probable, that the fortune cookie and the tea owed themselves to Cynthia Marrow's tampering hand. Joanna honestly could not think of anyone else who had a motive for doing such things, though in all truth she had to admit that Cynthia didn't seem the type either. Team B score: 1, with an asterisk.

So after all her figuring Joanna was left with very little evidence, but going over the possibilities had helped her to see the matter from a more analytical perspective. After Stephen dropped her off at The Sheaves that evening she pampered herself with a scalding shower and a lemon facial; later, back in her room, she nursed a cup of herbal tea and scribbled notes on a pad. She thought over her peculiar circumstances, which were beginning to interest her every bit as much as her work on *The Scourge*.

In the silent confines of her rented room (oddly familiar now) Joanna promised herself two things. She would never again second-guess herself regarding any future "coincidences" (should they occur) and if they did she would be very careful what she said about them and to whom. She couldn't be certain what game she was playing, but she knew the ground rules all the same.

Joanna filled four full steno-pad sheets with her list of questions and comments, suspicions and notes. It was intriguing, almost like outlining a mystery novel (which these events might lend themselves to after *The Scourge* was finished).

Then, on a separate sheet she wrote, underlining the words:

Team A knows about Pauline/Cassandra, wants Joanna to know.
Team B afraid Joanna will learn the truth.

Team A is working against Team B.
Can't tell teams without a scorecard.

The pen twitched restlessly between her fingers, darting to sketch a quick Cleopatra eye, a bird, a pretty flower. Joanna drew an oblong around it like a cartouche. Then back went the pen, tapping restlessly against the word *scorecard.* Beneath it, indenting neatly, she penned another sentence.

How to find scorecard?

*   *   *

At two thirty the following afternoon Geoffrey Latimer rang up and invited Joanna to tea, offering a tour of Blackmantle afterward. Though she was in the midst of describing Father Julien's first meeting with Delores and Desirée, Joanna agreed readily enough. From what Kate had said, Geoffrey was something of a hermit and she might not get this opportunity again. So she touched up her face with a little makeup (she hadn't worn mascara since the trip to Brighton), pulled on a lilac skirt and sweater, fluffed out her hair. Just before ducking out the door she dabbed a little Jontue at her throat and wrists, wondering secretly if maybe that wasn't going a bit too far (just how *did* one dress and behave when having tea with the gentry?) and went on her way.

Geoffrey was waiting at the side car-park entrance that skirted Abbot's Way. "Welcome to Blackmantle," he said, his smile taking some of the formality from his words. He offered his hand as she alighted from the car. "We'll have tea first; then I'll take you exploring."

An ambitious if somewhat misguided Georgian planner had put in a set of Palladian marble steps leading up the low rise from the road to Blackmantle's entrance. The stairs in no way matched or complemented the building that they fronted.

Blackmantle was something of an architectural oddity in southern England; indeed, Joanna had never seen anything to rival its diversity anywhere in the country. At first view (and from a southern vantage point) its medieval origins were most obvious. The monks' refectory and adjacent dormitory had since been joined and reformed by an Elizabethan "shadow" roof, but the effect was still monastic and medieval. Joanna could also see a trace of Lombardic influence in the stonework of the windows. The cloister and chapter house had also long ago been linked by an open corridor to the chapel beyond, which, save for the rounded belly of its apse, was now in ruins.

Gray stones of differing ages, dyed by time.

Joanna passed beneath them and held her breath in awe.

Incredibly, the interior of Blackmantle was almost cozy, if a place of such history and dimensions could be so described. Geoffrey led her to a sitting room gay with flowers and pictures and pastel walls. It was a chilly day and a new-made fire danced on the grate.

Geoffrey wheeled in tea and cakes. As he passed a plate across to her he explained, "If I were truly the English gentleman you had no doubt imagined me to be, I should have servants bringing the tea things and fresh baked sweets at the ready in silver trays and salvers. Instead you must content yourself with Tetley—which I brewed myself—and pastries from the local bakery at Lewes. I hope you aren't disappointed."

She wondered if perhaps he really was short on cash, the way Meg St. Denis had intimated. "Do you have trouble keeping staff?" she asked politely.

He laughed, as if envisioning her thoughts. "Oh my, no! Did you think I was a pauper? Not rich, I'm afraid, not by your American definition of the word, but I do well enough. It's very hard to keep money in one's pocket here in England. So much of it must go to taxes, though I refuse to join that disloyal brotherhood of men who keep their money in Switzerland or some such place. No, Miss Latimer, I've money enough to pay servants, and at one time I kept quite a few. But I am so rarely in St. Audric these days that the necessity of employing staff seems rather purposeless to me."

His lengthy explanation had embarrassed Joanna more than a little. She responded quickly. "It certainly doesn't look neglected. Actually I was thinking it seems almost homey."

That seemed to please him. "Despite its history and its size, Blackmantle is just a home after all. And so far as it looks lived-in, well, I drop in from time to time. The place was empty for many years following my parents' deaths; then I returned to inherit it, but I did very little to improve upon its comforts. My wife contributed somewhat to the décor . . ."

Aware that the conversation had turned a very private corner, Joanna began immediately to talk about something else. "Kate mentioned that you are a collector of antiquities, things like that. I'm sorry, but I'm afraid I don't know very much about what you do."

Geoffrey cleared his throat and sat forward, hands in his lap. As he spoke she found herself studying his hands. They were beautiful, expressive, sensitive. It was something she always noticed in people, particularly in men, since so few men had such artistic-looking hands. It was one of the first things she had noticed about Jayson. She was suddenly aware of his voice.

"I'm a scholar. Oh, a very minor one, but most of my life has been devoted to the study of medieval history through documents and artifacts. I've even written a few books on these subjects, privately printed, I might add. And I've been fortunate enough to collect some exceedingly fascinating documents. My own private archives . . ."

"Kate said you had a lot of stuff, diaries and journals and things, from the time of the Black Death. She also said you'd probably let me have a look at them . . ." A question mark hung timidly over the end of the sentence.

He had a nice smile; it sweetened the gaunt lines of his face when he showed it to her. "Yes, of course. I would be very happy to let you work with the papers I have. Kate no doubt told you the diaries of Geoffrey Fitzstephen make up a sizable part of my collection. I'm sure if you are writing about his time, particularly in this place, you know something of him."

Everyone seemed fixated on the idea that her novel was actually set in the real St. Audric, but she didn't go into an explanation of that now. "I'd love to see Fitzstephen's papers, anything you're willing to show me."

"There's a great deal of material," he said, leaning to refill her cup, then jumping back a little as she brought her hand down quickly over the rim to discourage milk. "Perhaps you know something of Sir Gerald Latymere."

"Just a little," she admitted. "Reverend Pryce talks about him in his books. He was the one who first inherited this place, right? As a home, I mean."

"Yes," Geoffrey said and went into a brief account replete with textbook accuracy. He ended by saying, "Sir Gerald was very interested in Geoffrey Fitzstephen's history, in his work. Particularly the translations he made of the books written by Audric himself. But by Sir Gerald's time few people cared about such things. He did, and that's the reason he wanted to make Blackmantle his home."

"The translations you spoke of, do you have those as well? Copies of them? *The Allfather,* the Saxon book on magic . . ."

He seemed pleased that she should know of them. "Yes, I do. I'm afraid I've had them with me in France, so at the present time they are all still boxed up. But once I've settled in again and put everything to rights, I'd be most gratified to have you come to work and study here whenever you like. I do hope you will be staying here a while yet . . ." She nodded. Again the shy smile came over his face. "I'd be equally glad of the company. As you might guess, it gets very lonely here."

All at once Joanna felt a great surge of pity for him. He was such a sweet, mild man, so obviously damaged by pain and sadness. Why would any woman leave a man as good as this? And why did good men always fall in love with the kinds of women who could leave them so easily? She looked up and saw the flash of disappointment in his gray eyes as if he'd read the pity in her face. Flushed, she turned her eyes away.

Later he took her through the main body of the house. Owing to its original structure and the vast reforms it had known over eleven centuries of history, Blackmantle was of necessity eclectic, each room a distinct, solitary bit of the whole. With a quiet air of pride, Geoffrey led her to the original north wall of the cloister. Its pitted, ugly stones dated to the time of Audric himself.

A heavy velvet drape, Burne-Jones blue, covered the wall, and Geoffrey held the cloth aside for her to see. "It's only a portion of the original wall, you understand. But it serves as a link and a reminder to the foundations of this place and the man who brought it all about. You know his history, I feel sure."

"Yes, I do," Joanna answered, unaware that she was speaking in a whisper as she scanned the stones. Far from being worn, they were crooked, irregular, virile. They looked as if they had been scattered, then taken up and put together once again.

The "Audric Wall" was located in the northernmost section of the house. It was part of a large room that had been decorated with rich blue hangings and mahogany furniture; a bedroom. A rice-poster stood in the center of the room, hung with a lovely reembroidered damask coverlet, its Byzantine designs depicting peacocks and exotic indigo-colored flowers. A dressing table, the flat surface covered with a runner of the same design, held a superfluity of perfume bottles and flacons, all made of the same blue Bristol glass.

At the door Joanna paused to look back at the room.

"This is the most beautiful bedroom I've ever seen," she commented. "I bet whenever you have guests they all want to sleep here because of the Audric wall."

His placid expression grew somber, almost grim. "No one sleeps here," he answered, closing the door heavily at his back. "This room belonged to Geraldine."

Joanna was surprised to hear him speak her name. She'd been careful to avoid any mention of the subject but now he had brought it up she boldly asked, "Geraldine left you, didn't she? At least that's what everybody says."

His answer was a wan smile. "Yes, she did. I suppose Kate told you."

Joanna nodded. "It sounds terrible, you saying it that way. As if we were sitting around gossiping about you."

"It's something to gossip about," he conceded. "In a place like St. Audric you get used to that. There's not much else to do here."

"I'm sorry," Joanna said lamely, wishing she'd said nothing at all. "It's so personal. So sad."

He put his hand gently on Joanna's arm to steer her forward. "It doesn't matter," he said. "I accepted that misfortune long ago. Now come, let me show you something very beautiful."

A passageway off the bedroom led to a door that led outside. The original medieval courtyard, many times reformed to reflect a current style, now had the look of a Victorian Gothic Folly and dated from that time. It had been cleverly concealed as an open passageway between the east and west portion of the house. A black basalt fountain, choked with leaves, sat in the middle. Beyond lay the crumbling remains of the chapel.

"How long has it been like this?" Joanna asked, wondering why one Latimer or another hadn't cared enough to have the ruined stones rebuilt.

"Not so long as you might think. The chapel was grazed by a bomb during the 1914–1918 war. Happily the west window was left undamaged."

Following his steps, Joanna turned onto the gravel pathway leading to the rear of the church. The entire middle section of the building was gone, but at either end the chapel had survived. The apse was nearly untouched. Beyond its dark façade the west window bloomed in the setting sun.

In blue and mauve and sea-green glass backgrounded by shades of white and lemon it depicted the scene of Mary Magdalen washing the feet of Jesus. Joanna recognized a likeness to the windows of St. Audric's parish church. Like those, this one was the work of Rossetti.

"It's beautiful," she gasped, too affected to say more. After a while she asked, "How did it come to be here?"

"It dates to the time of the parish church windows, 1857 or '58. There was another. . . ." He pointed toward the crumbled eastern façade, where an altar had once stood. "Unfortunately it was lost in the bombing. We have photographs of it though, if you would care to see them. The lost window showed Mary Magdalen at the tomb of Christ. It was a very beautiful thing according to the photos. Of course they are in black and white so we have only an idea of the colors he used. Likely as not they were a match to these."

"He must have loved this place very much to leave such beauty here." She sighed. "I don't think I ever read anything about his connection to St. Audric."

"So far as I know the story, it was a short-lived thing. He had planned to do a similar series of windows for a church in Kent, but the vicar there didn't think that Mary Magdalen was a fit subject. About a year later he came here to design the parish church windows. Again the Magdalen motif was considered to be inappropriate, so he used a theme of one of his own earlier paintings. But he saw Blackmantle during that time, and became friends with Edward Latimer, who was master here then. Rossetti planned the Magdalen windows at that time and they were fitted about two years later."

She couldn't take her eyes away, drawn almost inside the window by its flawless beauty. "May I come back and see it again some other time?"

Her question, gently asked, touched upon the reverence that he, too, felt for the window and its gifted artist. Some chord had been struck between them; any words that followed could only be banal. "Of course," he answered, "anytime you wish."

The sun was going, the window's image fading with it. In a moment there would be only gray, faceless space to see. The loss of it made Joanna want to cry, to beat her breast and cover herself in black like a widow. As they turned to go a flock of nesting birds above rustled, and flew away as one. . . .

Blackmantle's only living room, situated in the old monastic chapter house, was rather informal and countrified, even to an impressive set of stag horns high on the fireplace wall. In the far corner Joanna spied a treasure, an Elizabethan-style court cupboard. Wrought from heavy black oak and sinuously carved with scenes of hunting hounds and horses, it bore the scripted legend *Gerald Latymere Anno 1604.*

The rest of the furniture was Victorian: rosewoody and scrolled and over-stuffed but comfortable all the same. It didn't seem as if the absent (yet strangely omnipresent) Geraldine had left her decorating touch here. The room was decidedly male, and stuffy. A heavy-legged spinet wearing a yellow sunburst runner held up a superfluity of framed photographs. She studied them discreetly as Geoffrey poured peach brandy into snifters, hoping to find a likeness of the enigmatic Geraldine among them, but all the pictures looked many years too old. He had probably removed all traces of her from the house.

Yet there was something of her here; not in this room, but somewhere in the house, drifting through the passageways like perfume. Her bedroom didn't seem empty of her at all, only waiting her return.

Geoffrey must have seen her looking at the photos but said

nothing as he turned to put the glass into her hand. Joanna sipped the brandy enjoyably—it was delicious and certainly French—as Geoffrey made up the fire. They talked casually for a while; Geoffrey promised to call her about the research materials in no longer than a week's time. "I'll put everything to rights as best I can, and soon. Of course I don't know how long you plan on staying in St. Audric. Kate didn't say. . . ."

Joanna tipped back the glass and swallowed the last of her brandy too quickly. A sticky drop rolled down her chin and fell onto her sweater. She dabbed at it with a moist fingertip. "I really haven't decided. Several people, including Kate, have urged me to stay for the All Hallows' celebration, and since that's only a little more than two weeks away I suppose I will. There's really no reason why I can't. My boyfriend is in Los Angeles till the middle of November."

"Ah, yes," Geoffrey said. "Kate mentioned that you had a chap. A writer fellow, isn't he? Or perhaps I should say, a fellow writer
. . ."

Kate certainly didn't waste any time getting out the facts to all who'd listen. For that reason, if none other, Joanna was determined to say as little as possible to Kate about her new suspicions. Kate's perspective might turn out to be a very helpful one, but it would be expecting too much that she could keep it to herself. And then what good would any of Joanna's theories be, with everyone knowing what she was looking for, and why?

"Perhaps you'd like to come to dinner on Saturday night," Geoffrey said as she was getting ready to leave. "I'll have installed a cook by that time, if that's an incentive to you."

She would have liked to come and told him so, but Roland Jaspar's séance was the same night.

"You aren't going there, surely!" he said, sounding incredulous, slightly annoyed. "Talking to the dead! What a lot of rubbish. . . ."

"I've got an open mind."

"I'm afraid I haven't." They walked together toward the front entrance hall. "But we all have our prejudices and our follies. In any case, perhaps you'd like to come for a meal some other time."

"I'd like that very much," she answered, meaning it.

As she trotted down the stairs and across the gravel to the car-park she was aware of him watching her. Then just before she ducked into the car, Joanna turned and waved good-bye to him. He waved back, looking rather thin and pathetic leaning against the stones. The image lit a memory; it flared and faded before she could see it clearly.

When she turned back a moment later, he had gone.

* * *

None of the "regulars" had arrived when Joanna showed up at seven fifteen in front of The Briar Pipe. The shop was closed, its shade pulled down, but after a few sharp raps she could hear footsteps on the other side.

Pamela Jaspar, tiny and drab in dull gray wool, led Joanna through the darkened shop to the back where a narrow staircase waited. "Up here," she called, going on ahead, leaving Joanna to flounder for a handrail in the near dark. Upstairs a long hallway led to a series of small, lighted rooms. Somewhere beyond, Joanna could hear water slapping against a sink.

"We weren't expecting anyone for another quarter of an hour," Pamela grumbled, pointing Joanna to a chair. "I still have the washing-up to do from supper."

Good for you.

Joanna pulled off her stadium coat and tossed it down. "I didn't mean to put you out by being early, but I thought I might have a word alone with your husband before the meeting starts."

Pamela turned abruptly and shot Joanna a scowling look of dis-approval. "You can't see him before! He's in the Spiritual Room, preparing." She made a mocking, chuckling sound. "His power is a gift. He can't be expected to sit and chatter with you lot as if it were Saturday night swilling at the pub!"

Rebuffed and a little angry, Joanna retreated to a wing chair near the window while Pamela hustled back to the kitchen, pre-sumably to finish with her washing-up chores. Idly she scanned the room. It was unremarkable except for two unlighted Rigaud candles sitting atop a carved dower chest like an altar offering. Were they props for the coming ceremony?

Despite a longtime interest in the supernatural, Joanna had

never attended a séance and she wasn't completely certain what to expect or even why she had been so eager to come in the first place. She actually felt a little queer about hoping to call up the mysterious Pauline Pryce, but wasn't that what this was really about? If Pauline Cassandra Latimer Pryce and Cassie Lynne *had* been the same woman, this might be her only chance to find it out, and in front of witnesses.

The "regulars" arrived, all five together, punctually at seven thirty. Joanna recognized three: Sarah Halliwell, Cynthia Marrow, and Dr. Wallin. The other two were introduced to her as Toby and Tamara Bigelow. They were a middle-aged, avant-garde couple who owned one of the Georgian houses in the Row. Antiques dealers, they spent a good deal of time shuttling between London and their Alfriston shop.

Tamara had finished reading *Tabitha's Claw* the previous weekend and raved about it at some length, which made Joanna quite self-conscious since she had experienced an almost immediate antipathy to the pair. They took such obvious pride in not acting or dressing according to their ages, the sort of people who would have said "caun't" and "shaun't" if they'd been born in Kansas City. They dressed in the manner of the Sloane Square "trendies" and their talk was just as effusive and meaningless.

Joanna knew their history from Meg St. Denis. They were originally from Hove, had studied art in London during the sixties, gone retro with antiques in the seventies, and become New Age believers in the eighties after their only child, a daughter Justine, had died in a swimming accident on the eve of her eleventh birthday. She was presumably the reason for their presence here tonight.

By seven forty-five Roland Jaspar still had not appeared. Pamela served ginger biscuits and coffee and everyone sat around the living room looking at one another and saying nothing. Joanna was beginning to feel distinctly out of place. All of these people knew each other well. She was the outsider.

"Whose place am I taking tonight?" she whispered to Sarah.

Sarah leaned close, smelling of deep musk and wood notes. "Reverend Burroughs. He had to go over to Brighton to his sister's birthday dinner. She's a spinster and he's unusually devoted to her. Don't ask me why. I've met her and she's an absolute *dragon*."

"The vicar? At a séance? You're joking."

"I'm not."

"But surely . . ."

Sarah cut her off quickly. Gathering up the emptied cups and saucers from the coffee table she said, "I'll take these in to the kitchen, Pam." She gave Joanna a look that said to follow.

Pamela was drawing the curtains. "Hurry along," she said. "He'll be ready in a moment, and you know we always start at eight."

In the kitchen Sarah lowered the dishes to the sink.

"Were you serious about the vicar?" Joanna asked.

"Of course. Why should that surprise you?"

"It just seems weird. A vicar at a séance. It's not what you expect."

"Because he's a vicar? There's nothing wrong in it. You see yourself as a good Christian, don't you?"

"Yes, of course," Joanna said, sounding affronted.

"Well then, there you are. I mean to say, you've got to be a believer to come to one of these dos, right? Not much sport for the atheist or casual unbeliever. How could you expect to contact someone from the Other Side unless you were certain such a place existed?" A faint smile lurked just behind her placid expression, as though she were amused by Joanna's middle-class prejudice. "Come on," she said, taking up Joanna's hand. "Let's join the others."

The sitting room, where they had been congregated only a few minutes before, was empty now, everyone having gone into the Spiritual Room, which was just beyond it. Pamela led Joanna and Sarah in. There was a large Queen Anne table in the center of the room, a flaming candelabra atop it, and eight matching chairs. The room itself was plain and unadorned except for a few framed pictures on the walls, but it was too dark to make them out.

Roland Jaspar sat at one end of the table and Pamela took her place at the other. On the far side sat the Bigelows with Dr. Wallin between them. Sarah slid gracefully into a place between Pamela and Cynthia Marrow, so Joanna took the only remaining seat, between Cynthia and Roland Jaspar.

There was nothing on the table except for the candelabra, not even a cloth, and the wood gleamed like dark honey in the tremulous light. There seemed to be a definite and instinctive rhythm to the proceedings. Everyone sat with arms limply at their sides, eyes staring straight ahead. Joanna tried entering into the spirit of it.

At last Roland spoke. Although he did not look at Joanna, his words were addressed to her. "Because we have a newcomer to our circle tonight it may be best to say a few words. I am not a physical medium. I am a mental medium. You will witness no show of ectoplasm, no acts of levitation—no outward signs of any kind. The voices of our friends who have passed over to the Other Side will speak through me. Now, please take hands. We are ready to begin. . . ."

Joanna slipped her left hand into Jaspar's right hand and from the other side she felt Cynthia's dainty fingers clutching hers. The candle flames, no longer flickering, stood tall and still like painted golden light, illuminating each face. The room became quiet as a cave.

Then Jaspar began to speak.

They wait for us.

They cannot reach us without our help.

Joanna was aware of a sudden chill in the air, hovering around the level of her chin. She shivered involuntarily and wondered if the cold were only her imagination, then tensed as Jaspar's arm began to twitch. His voice came again.

Guide them to us.

Project their memory into the air.

Joanna squeezed her eyes shut again, trying to concentrate, though the very act seemed to distract her all the more. She was acutely aware of a dozen tiny disturbances. The wall clock ticking madly in the other room. Somebody's stomach growling. Cynthia's hand gone curiously cold in hers. She tried to focus inward, to picture Pauline's headstone in the cemetery a mile away, with the moon's chilly light shining full upon her name.

All at once Jaspar jerked forward and slumped with his face against the table. Joanna peered cautiously through one half-open eye. No one else was peeking. He lay motionless for what seemed a long time, then all at once he rose up again. The light focused on his face, the black patch cutting an assymetrical scar across it. His expression was curious; he seemed somehow changed. And when he spoke his voice was changed too.

"Mum? Dad?" The sound of the voice was so girlish, the accent so uppercrust, Joanna heard her own gasp follow on the heels of it.

The voice of the entity came again.

"I've met a friend of yours. Her name is Pippa and she's new here . . ." A few excited whispered words passed on the other side of the table. "She's too nervous to come forward on her own, but she wants me to ask if you remember what happened on November tenth, 1967." More whispers. "Mum, she wants you to know it only happened because Dad was drunk, and that she is very glad the two of you are still together. . . ."

"Justine" chatted on for a while longer before slipping away with a few sentimental words of good-bye. Then almost as if he had been waiting patiently in line behind Justine, Robin Marrow came forth in words from Roland Jaspar's mouth. He seemed a Milquetoast entity by the sound of him, warning Cynthia about trying to find true love with a man who was unworthy of her. He also brought up several quite personal memories, including one about a time he and Cynthia had made love on the four twenty from Victoria.

Cynthia sobbed throughout the message.

Sylvia, Dr. Wallin's departed wife, refused to answer her summons ("They don't always come," a woman's voice whispered, and another whispered back, "Sometimes they're busy . . .") while Jack, Sarah's American motorcycle boyfriend, talked on and on when his time came, using a profusion of four-letter adjectives and verbs to describe their past experiences together.

Joanna, grown suddenly restless, felt her own senses lapsing into boredom. What a performance, what theater! True, if Roland Jaspar was a fake, he was by far the best damned actor Joanna had ever met face to face. But there was still something queer about the whole setup. None of the visitors from the Other Side seemed to have anything important or worthwhile to say. What right or reason did they have for crossing over when it was only to rehash all the same pathetic rubbish from their mortal existences. Nothing very elevated in that! What was the point, the purpose of it all? No more than a party line for spooks. . . .

She tried to tell herself that her own purpose was different, important. She had come to learn the truth about Pauline and Cassie; about her mother.

She whispered the word aloud.

Jaspar answered her in a series of light groans, his head moving back and forth as though a string were pulling it. The minutes passed. Joanna fidgeted, unnerved by the sound of his deep breathing. Now all the other little annoyances had been dispelled and the room was insufferably quiet but for him.

"Mother," Joanna crooned the word again, feeling tiny beads of sweat crawl down her neck to nestle in her clothes. "Mother . . ."

Suddenly Jaspar whispered "No!" and slumped forward to the table once again. For the next few moments no one spoke, and Jaspar lay unmoving as if dead. Then slowly he rose up, his eye open, his face pinched and pale. He signaled his wife from across the table and she jumped up to switch on the overhead light. Eight pairs of hands automatically unclasped and fell away. The séance was over.

Joanna turned abruptly to Jaspar.

"What happened?" she asked.

Pamela clapped her hands together. "The meeting's over," she announced. "Roland's exhausted."

"You'd better come along," Sarah said, touching Joanna's shoulder lightly. "You won't get any more from him tonight."

Joanna pulled away, ignoring her, leaning toward Jaspar. "What happened?" she asked again. "What did you see? Did you see my mother? Why didn't she speak to me?"

He waited till the room had cleared and Pamela was seeing everyone to the door. Then he grabbed hold of Joanna's hand and held it in a clawlike grip. His one eye, pale blue and bulbous, fixed steadily on her face, his lips twitching in anger. "Who are you, who are you really? And why did you come here?"

Joanna stared back at him.

"What do you mean? You know who I am, you know why I came. I told you last week I wanted to contact my mother. . . ." She drew her hand away.

He eyed her closely, suspiciously. "Are you trying to expose me as some sort of fraud? If that's what you had in mind, you picked the wrong man! I'm no fake, girl! I'm no fraud!"

She felt as helpless as someone caught up in the whirlwind of a nightmare. "I don't know what you're talking about! I never called you a fraud. I only wanted to talk to my mother."

He stared at her for a moment without speaking, trying to determine if she were lying, trying to fool him, or if she really didn't understand what he was saying.

"You knew there was no reason for you to come here."

"No reason?"

"You knew I couldn't raise her no matter what I did."

"How could I know that?"

"Because your mother isn't dead!" he shouted into her face. "You knew that, you must have known that. . . ."

"What?" The single word escaped her lips like a faint hiss of steam.

". . . So you can stop pretending. . . ."

Tears of frustration rolled down her cheeks. "I'm *not* pretending! My mother *is* dead, she died when I was born! I *never* knew her!" She hit the tabletop with the flat of her hand. *"I swear to God, it's true!"*

He looked at her, his blue eye pale and glistening as a marble. "Look," he said, his voice gone hoarse, "I don't know what's wrong with you—if you're really off your nut, or just one of those women who go round the bend each month—I don't really care. But what I know I'll say. And I know that your mother is not dead."

Searching through her purse Joanna came up with a scrap of Kleenex. She sniffed into it a few times and dried her eyes. "But how do you know, how can you be sure?" she asked.

Pamela had come to the doorway and paused, silent.

Jaspar's voice was softer now, more believing. "Because I *know.* I cannot force a spirit forward that does not wish to come. But I can feel it all the same, dwelling in the darkness beyond my reach, but *there* all the same. Like a blind man feeling out of sight, I sense its will, its purpose." He gave a meaningful pause. "Your mother is not among the Others."

Trying to wring some logic from her untenable position, Joanna cried out, "Perhaps . . . perhaps she's been reincarnated!" The words had a victorious flourish. "That would explain why you couldn't contact her, why she . . ."

"No," he answered, certain. "The young woman who bore the child Joanna Lynne is alive and as she was on the day of your own birth. But she is hiding . . ." His voice dropped and he began to

wring his hands fretfully before him. "And there is danger. I saw
. . ."

"What? What did you see?" Joanna leaned close; their faces
were almost touching.

"A man, the figure of a man dressed as God's servant."

The breath left her body as if it had been squeezed out.

"Danger from him?" She thought instantly of Burroughs and
she pulled at Jaspar's sleeve. "Tell me!"

The words came with difficulty. "No, a warning *from* such a
man. He says . . ." Then Jaspar began to shake, hands vibrating
against his chest, palsied. His eye closed and he choked the
words out between his teeth. "He says *Go, Joanna, do not stay,
Joanna, there is only danger for you here, Joanna . . .*"

The frenzied motion of his hands sent the heavy table suddenly plunging forward and Joanna jumped up, spilling her chair
over on its side. For a moment she stood, horrified and yet transfixed by the spectacle, unable to move.

Then Pamela reacted. Pushing Joanna away, she rushed to her
husband, kneeling at his side, her hands busy over his quivering
flesh.

"A doctor," Joanna stammered. "Does he need a doctor?"

"Go away!" Pamela screwed her head around and glared at
Joanna. "You've done enough damage here. . . ."

Joanna grabbed up her purse and whirled around for the door,
stopping just long enough in the other room to claw her way into
her coat. A lamp tipped as her purse twirled out in a long arc; she
didn't even stop to pick it up. The stairs was a sloping, treacher-
ous corridor whose end she would never reach, and then her foot
touched down on the floor and she blundered her way through
the darkness to the meager light glowing like a promise of salvation at the end.

*Go Joanna, do not stay, Joanna, there is only danger here,
Jo—*

She slammed the door against the sound of her own name.

Outside, trembling on the empty street, Joanna managed to
get control of her emotions, though her breath still came with
difficulty in excited little heaves. She moved quickly down the
street, her footsteps resounding ominously across the way.
Where the pavement ended, cut off by Alfred's Lane, she stood

for a moment, undecided, staring into the trees that hid the path to Kate's house. It would be a relief to tell the story, to have the willing ear of a friend.

And if not Kate, who?

Then she thought dismally of all the questions that would follow, and of the answers she was unready to give. So she took the narrow turn-off to The Sheaves, the gravel crunching beneath her feet as she went. She could hear her own heart beating in the darkness, it sounded far away, outside herself. The air had a strange, ashen smell of autumn and played a little in the trees above.

She shivered.

Now there was a scorecard.

*   *   *

Not dead.

Joanna said it to herself over and over and still it made no sense. Her mother. Not dead, but hiding.

Who was she?

During the past few weeks Joanna had come to believe so completely in the theory of Pauline and Cassie as the same woman it was nearly impossible for her to separate their identities now. But if Roland Jaspar was right, she had been misleading herself—"Cassandra" didn't mean "Cassie" after all, and the woman she had been taught to mourn since birth still lived.

The implications, curious at first, came clear.

They had never married.

Reverend Lynne had fallen in love with Cassie, who, for some reason, could never be his wife. Probably she had lingered only long enough to bear her child by him before going off to lose herself somewhere strange and distant.

Not dead, but hiding.

Why hiding? Why, after all these years? Had she cared so little for young Reverend Lynne and her own infant daughter? It was hard for Joanna to believe that all the stories of a martyred wife and mother had been nothing more than lies to hide the consequences of a commonplace affair. She was filled with sadness and anger at having been deceived so completely and for so long, for having been denied a truth that she deserved to know.

But she was filled with curiosity, too. Where was Cassie now? Did her disappearance have anything to do with Joanna's letter of invitation to St. Audric? Someone—though preferably not Cassie—wanted Joanna to discover something about her own past. The question was who, and to what purpose?

And now some unknown agency was trying to keep her away at the same time. So it was back to making rosters for Teams A and B. The problem was she really had not a single gut feeling of who might have brought her here, who might be trying to keep her away. After a while it was all so confusing she wished the whole silly business away, but that wasn't possible now.

Her stay in St. Audric was limited. Jayson would be back in London by mid-November, and she wanted to be at the flat to greet him. But in the time that still remained to her here, Joanna intended to find out all she could about the enigmatic Cassie and the circle of mystery that surrounded her original disappearance.

It would not be easy. She didn't dare ask too many questions for fear of giving herself away, and she had a novel to finish writing as well. But the matter was never far from her mind, and like the lover of detective stories that she was, Joanna began to analyze the actions of everyone she came into contact with. (Recently Reverend Burroughs had turned over the complete set of church records to her so easily she had accorded him a place on Team A.)

For the dozenth time she scribbled the familiar names on paper, dividing it with a line drawn down the center.

Team A	*Team B*
Chloe Bibble	*Mrs. Munro*
Simon Cherrystone	*Caroline Munro*
Sarah Jeffers Halliwell	*Roland Jaspar*
Rev. Burroughs	*Pamela Jaspar*
??? Kate Callison ???	
??? Geoffrey Latimer ???	

Kate Callison and Geoffrey Latimer were the hardest to classify for several reasons. She liked them both, and she had come to trust Kate. At the start she had denied having penned the letter and Joanna had no reason to doubt her. And Kate, even if she *had* a secret, could surely never keep it! Joanna had learned nearly everything she knew about St. Audric and its people from her.

Geoffrey Latimer's name had been veiled by hints of intrigue and mystery since Joanna's arrival in the village, but there was nothing very unusual or mysterious about the man himself. Indeed, he seemed mild almost to the point of blandness. He claimed no knowledge of Pauline Latimer Pryce, and Joanna believed him about that; she had yet to question him concerning Cassie. But she had no doubt he would respond truthfully, for he seemed very much a man of his word.

So once again Joanna ripped the list in half and then into a hundred tiny pieces too small to be deciphered, and burned them in the ashtray on the desk, amused at her own compulsive attempts at secrecy. Names. They might mean everything, or nothing at all. She hardly knew anymore. Yet it was every bit as fascinating as her research on *The Scourge*. There were times she felt as if she was writing one book, living another.

She resumed her walks to the Long Man, to the cliffs.

Dressed in her "bum suit"—Bruin sweater, tatty jeans, ancient Reeboks; a Walkman flooding her ears with sounds of Delibes and Puccini—she hiked the countryside. Although the sun shone, it was cold most days now and there was color all around her. Only now did she realize that summer had ended and that seemed strange, because it never really did in California, a land where autumn never came at all. Not a true, fever-bright, blue-skied, leaf-trembling, smoke-smelling autumn.

Joanna had enjoyed watching the beech trees grow gold from her window, but it was a near-spiritual experience to walk beneath them, to fill up her lungs with rich, sweet outdoor air that tasted of the sea. The walks reminded her of the ones she and David Lair had taken daily on Hampstead Heath during the brief weeks of their affair—he, always anxious to show off some bit of greenery to her as if it had been a thing of his own making.

David had been very keen on nature. In perfect contrast Jayson never walked anywhere there was a road wide enough to accommodate a car.

She felt curiously cut off from Jayson even though she knew exactly where he was and even what he would be doing at such and such a time—for Jayson kept to his own schedule no matter where he might be. He had promised to telephone her on November 1, and he would; he was dependable above all else. That was not so very far away, yet all the same it seemed too many days to count, to wait. Her current sense of isolation was made all the more uncomfortable with Kate and Simon gone for the week—Kate, in Brighton on a visit to "an old school chum"; Simon, who knew where?

One afternoon she walked to Little Gospels and pushed a chatty handwritten letter through the mail slot, and on her way back across the lane she passed Goat's Rue on the garden edge. She waved to Granny Love who stood atop a tall ladder pruning dead branches from a fruit tree. Odd little woman, doing such chores at her age. Joanna doubled back and paused at the gate.

"Hi," she called, squinting up into the sun. "Do you have a few minutes? I'd like to ask you another question about Pauline."

The tiny woman on the ladder tossed her pruning hook to the ground and immediately began climbing down. She was amazingly agile for someone so old, though Joanna had never been able to discover her exact age. "Ancient" was all anybody ever said when she asked.

Joanna hadn't been on a ladder for ten years and it impressed her to see how easily the old woman scampered down. "I always seem to be interrupting you," she said, apologetic.

The little woman came to the bottom rung where she was just Joanna's height. "I was about to take a rest," she said. "You can pass the time with me if you like."

At the side of the house was a set of iron lace furniture ("My late brother brought it back from the city of New Orleans many years ago . . .") and they settled themselves there, Granny Love having declared the house off limits.

"My nephew's son is inside setting up for the *masque* next week and we'd only be in the way." She had a plastic bottle filled with water on a cord around her waist; she offered a drink to

Joanna who shook her head, declining. Taking it back, Granny Love bent her head for a swig. "Gardening's thirsty business, even when it's not so warm a day," she said.

Joanna, shivering under a coat and sweater, marveled at Granny Love's thin print dress and tatty sweater pulled over it, sagging at the shoulders. Hardly enough to keep a rag doll warm.

"Your yard—garden—is very pretty," Joanna offered.

"It's my pride and joy. The only thing I've got, save for this house." She squinted her odd, silver eyes at Joanna. "You said you had another question about Pauline. . . ."

"I look like her; you said I look like her."

"And so you do, the very image."

"That's why I thought she might have been my mother, but now I know she couldn't have been." Joanna paused. "What I mean is, I have reason to believe Cassie's still alive."

"There was no Cassie in the family, none I ever heard of."

It was so frustrating to ask these kinds of questions over and over again and never receive the sort of answers that told her anything at all. Joanna tried once more. "But if I look so much like Pauline, it makes sense to think she must have been related to my mother."

The old woman nodded. "It does."

Joanna had the feeling of being pulled against her will toward something she couldn't understand. "*Were* Cassie and Pauline sisters?"

"They may have been for all I know."

Joanna leaned forward, elbows on the table, attempting to stare the old woman down. "What *do* you know?"

Granny Love drank from the water bottle, then capped it and wiped a hand across her lips. "Just this: there were two daughters in the Latimer family. Pauline was one, the other was just a baby when the children were sent abroad. She could have been the Cassie you speak of. I never knew her name."

A sigh of profound relief—something learned! Joanna took a second to recover her composure. "What else do you know about the family?" she asked. "You said they went abroad to live."

Unbidden, the memory came back. "Their parents sent them away to live with friends they had in America early in 'thirty-eight. Rich folks, those in the government like Sir Giles was, knew a war was coming. They wanted their children safe and they'd the money to see it through. The rest of us . . ." Her hand, milky white and threaded with veins like an opal, did a strange little dance in midair. "Well, we had children too, but weren't so lucky."

"How many were there in the family? How many children?"

"Three," she answered without pausing to think. "The baby. Pauline, two years or so older. And Geoffrey."

Joanna's head jerked up. "Geoffrey? Geoffrey Latimer?"

"Yes."

"The one who lives at Blackmantle, *that* Geoffrey Latimer?"

"Is that so surprising to you?"

The words were out before she could stop them. "Geoffrey denied knowing if Pauline was even related to him."

"Did he?" The old woman's colorless eyes held steadily to Joanna's. "Did he so?"

It was a tangle, some sort of perverse joke. Geoffrey Latimer must have spotted her resemblance to Pauline immediately and yet he had deliberately lied. There might be more here than she had originally suspected. How had she thought of him? As a man of his *word?*

"What do you remember about the Latimers?" she asked, finding her voice at last.

The old lady grinned elfishly, a stain of pink showing in her cheeks. "A high-and-mighty bunch they were in those days before the war. Lady Latimer—an actress—was a great beauty, and she spent much of her time up in London with the fine folk. Mind you, I didn't know the family. But I remember how handsome they were sitting in the front pew box at church every Sunday. Then in the spring of 'thirty-eight (I remember because it was the same spring I nursed my sister who was ailing fit to die) they sent their children away to friends in America, as I told you. Then they closed Blackmantle and moved up to London."

"And?" Joanna prompted.

"Sir Giles and his lady never returned. They drowned in a boating mishap the following summer. Many years later Geoffrey came back to Blackmantle, a young man. A few years later Pauline married the vicar, Reverend Pryce. She died in a drowning accident too, some years later ..." Her voice rippled into silence, the story told.

"And Cassie?" Joanna asked.

"I never knew Cassie Latimer."

"But the baby, the one who was sent away with the others, she had to have been Cassie, right?"

"Perhaps, but I never knew her. So far as I know she never came back to St. Audric, or if she did I knew nothing of it. Mind you, there's no reason I should. The gentry don't give reasons for what they do."

"So she *could* be alive. . . ."

"Perhaps, but there's no one to tell you where she is."

Joanna said, "He can."

The stalwart, gray-haired matron at the door showed no sign of moving to admit her.

"Mr. Latimer is at his supper," she repeated.

"I have to see him," Joanna said, brushing rudely past her on the way to the hall. "Tell him I'm here."

The older woman made a huffing, exasperated sound. "Very well," she said, leading on. "Follow me."

He was in the little dining room just off the kitchen, his attention riveted to a cut of meat before him. Joanna recognized the sound of a Locatelli concerto playing somewhere in the background. Geoffrey in a dark brocade smoking jacket completed the image of an English gentleman at leisure.

"Joanna, how nice to see you, won't you join me?" he asked, looking up to see her standing in the doorway. "Nina, bring another plate for Miss Latimer."

"No thanks, I'm not staying." Joanna stepped forward, feeling conspicuously untidy in these surroundings; the look Nina gave her was further affirmation.

"All right," Geoffrey answered, waving Nina from the room, "but at least sit down and join me in an after-dinner coffee."

"No," she said again, not moving.

Nina, lingering for a moment at the door, caught Geoffrey's sharp look and slipped quietly out, closing the door behind her.

"You lied!" Joanna blurted the words.

"I beg your pardon?" He drew a napkin across his lips. "Would you care to tell me what this is all about?"

"I want you to tell me the truth for a change! Why did you say you'd no idea if Pauline was related to you?"

"Oh, God . . ." One hand went to his face. "All right, what have you heard?"

She came to the edge of the table but did not sit. "She was your *sister,* Geoffrey, not just any relative. Why did you lie about it? Why didn't you want me to know the truth?"

He shook his head. "I'm sorry. I'm really very sorry."

"You had another sister, name of Cassie—she was my mother. I told you all about her that first day at Little Gospels, and you still said not one word to give me any hint she might be a relative of yours. Why, Geoffrey?"

He met her gaze reluctantly, as if looking at her caused him pain. "Yes," he answered simply, "Cassie . . ."

She waited for more. "Well, is that *all* you're going to say?"

"Joanna, please sit down and give me the opportunity to explain."

Grudgingly she slid into the chair directly opposite him. "What's there to explain? You're my uncle, and you must have known it from the start, but you lied to keep me from finding out about it. Why? Were you afraid I'd demand my share of the Latimer estate? I've got money of my own, you know."

"I'm certain of it."

"Then why?" she shot back at him. "And where's my mother?"

It took a long time for him to say his next words. "I don't know."

"That's a lie."

"Unhappily it isn't. I simply cannot tell you where she is because I've no idea myself. Sorry I can't tell you more."

"More? You've told me nothing!"

He looked defeated, weary. "Give me the chance."

Striking a resentful pose with arms folded across her chest, she snapped, "Okay, go ahead."

"We were evacuated to America as children . . ."

"I've heard that part."

"If you'll kindly allow me to finish?" His voice, pitched like a schoolmaster's, rendered her silent. "Cassie was only a baby then, Pauline a bit older. I was the eldest. We would have been brought back when the war was over but unfortunately our parents were killed in the summer of 'thirty-nine. I didn't return here till 1950. Pauline came with me, but Cassie stayed behind. She had friends, was enrolled in a good school, that sort of thing. Some years later I heard that she had become involved with a young man, your father I suppose. I'm not at all sure what kept them from marrying, but there were certain problems, so I urged Cassie to return at long last here to Blackmantle. I even went over to California to bring her back myself. But she refused to come. And that is the last I ever saw of her."

"I'm sorry," Joanna said, trying to keep her voice calm, "but I don't believe you."

"I've no reason to lie about it."

"You lied before," she reminded him.

He wore the expression of someone longing to be understood. "Joanna, there are things in my past which are altogether too painful to remember. If I seem reluctant to discuss them you will simply have to make allowances."

She couldn't help but feel a little sorry for him, this was so obviously unpleasant. "Do you have any reason to suppose she's dead?" she asked.

He seemed surprised she had interpreted his words in that way. "Dead? Why should I think that? She'd be quite a young woman yet."

"Because I was told she died when I was born. My father told me."

"Well then, it must be so."

"No," she answered, shaking her head, "I don't think so, not anymore."

His gray eyes narrowed; he leaned closer, as though she had him on a string. "Why do you say this? What has changed your mind?"

"Because . . ."—here she faltered—". . . someone told me, quite recently, assured me that she is still alive."

"Someone who knows her told you that?"

"Not her, not really. Just *knows*."

"Then he must know where she is."

"It wasn't like that," Joanna insisted. "It was all very vague, very unusual."

He read her face. "It was Roland Jaspar who told you that, wasn't it? At the séance . . ."

Her mouth literally fell open in surprise. "How did you know that?"

"I guessed. As I remember you were anxious to go to the séance. Why would you have wanted to go unless it was to find out something about your mother? I suppose Jaspar failed to 'contact' her, so you assumed she must still be alive and of course Jaspar, in order to save face, did not refute you. . . ."

She gave him a false, sarcastic smile in return. "You must have read my diary." But all the while she felt the weight of her own inefficiency and doubt pressing down on her. "I want her to be alive, Geoffrey," she said. "I want it to be true. Is that so terrible?"

Now the kindness she had seen in his face the first time they met returned. "No," he answered quietly. "So do I."

She warmed to him again, suddenly embarrassed at having burst in upon his supper, Wild West–style, demanding information. They had coffee together and talked about things that had nothing to do with Cassie. Later Geoffrey showed her the library, where she spent several hours admiring his collection of documents, diaries, and letters, many of them related in significance to the Latimer family. Also included were the Fitzstephen diaries, his translations of Audric's three books and collected writings. Geoffrey promised her that the photocopies would be ready for her the following week. Nina brought in a pitcher of hot cocoa and served it to them as they talked. Finally, after refusing a ride home, Joanna ran most of the way back down the hill in the rain, sheltering under the cover of the umbrella he had lent her.

She lay in bed that night unable to sleep, feeling odd and somehow incomplete. She knew even less about her situation now than she had this morning—was it only this morning?—before talking to Granny Love and Geoffrey. Nothing had come clear except for one thing: Geoffrey Latimer hadn't seen Cassie for at least as many years as Joanna had been alive.

What did it mean?

One thing. It proved her original assessment of him had been correct. He really was truthful, sensitive, kind. It made her happy to know he was her uncle; more likely than not it was as close to Cassie as she would ever get. Hypnotized by the lure of sleep, her eyelids fluttered. The scent of rain was stronger now, filling the whole room. . . .

In the morning, squinting at the autumnal golden light coming through the rose-printed drapes, Joanna had a lingering sense of recognition, a dream symbol danced through her mind just beyond reach. Unable to catch it, she sagged back beneath the covers; the memory faded back into the secret hollow of her pillow and was lost.

* * *

Joanna was coming out of the bank early the following afternoon when a voice she recognized called out to her.

"I hear you're packing up at The Sheaves. Not leaving us yet, are you?" Simon Cherrystone, standing in the open doorway of the post office, raised a hand and waved to her.

She came quickly up the street to meet him. "Not quite yet," she said. "I'm not leaving for London till the middle of the month, so Kate's letting me use her spare room till then."

"Saving yourself a piddling two weeks' rent?" He grinned.

"Among other things. I'm sure Mrs. Munro will be crushed."

The smile disappeared and he regarded her seriously. "I will be. After all Joanna, *I hardly knew ye.* Will you be back?"

"I expect I will, many times. This place has become sort of my second home now. We'll probably come down for weekends every so often."

"You and Jayson." He managed to make the name sound unpleasant.

"Yes," she answered carefully. "But you'll like him, I know you will."

"I've read his books; he's a brilliant man—so I suppose I will," Simon admitted. "But I like you better."

There was something missing from his usually breezy attitude today; she couldn't place it. "I'll be sure to look you up before I go," she said and turned toward the street again.

"Hey," Simon reached out and pulled at her coat sleeve, "you can't just go off like that. The last time I saw you, you were passed out on the floor at the Hastings Day supper. What was that all about? I was quite sick myself the next few days, too sick to phone you, and then by the time I was feeling well again I had to go out of town."

An idea flashed in her mind and for an instant she nearly told him everything: the letter, the note, the stuff given her to make her faint, all of it. Then she wavered, asking a question instead. "Simon, you were sick that same day, weren't you? Right after the dinner I mean. . . ."

He nodded. "I left just a little after they carried you upstairs. And none too soon: I was up half the night with what my old nanny used to call 'tummy-trouble.'"

She paused, tapping the toe of her boot (£115 from Midas) on the sidewalk. "You're better now, I hope," she said, still distracted, uncertain of how much she could confide to him.

"Much," he answered. "In fact, I was hoping you'd agree to come to supper at Rosemary Cottage tonight. We can get caught up." He added a wheedling smile.

Joanna pictured him as a small boy, able to charm any number of between-meal sweets from his mother. "Okay," she agreed. "There are a few things I need to talk to you about. But you'll have to promise to cook up something I really like."

"As for instance?"

She'd already started off down the street. "Sloppy joes," she called back across her shoulder.

Simon watched her as she went, toe-dancing neatly out of the way of a squawking Volvo as she crossed the street.

"Soppy *what?*' he asked himself, and looked off down the street where she had gone.

It wasn't exactly the recipe she'd fed him over the telephone an hour earlier—he'd used Italian bread rolls instead of hamburger buns and substituted Worcestershire for Tabasco sauce— but on the whole it was a fairly decent meal. For the dessert he'd stirred up a typically English concoction of sponge cake layered with raspberries and vanilla pudding. He had made enough for six small servings but together the two of them were able to finish it all, capturing even the tiniest crumbs and leavings with their fingers.

It was at least twenty minutes before Joanna could rouse herself to washing-up chores ("It's only fair; you cooked . . .") and while she busied herself Simon searched his record collection for a rare album of *f* trumpet solos he wanted her to hear. She listened from the kitchen to music that sounded very much like Haydn, but could have been Mozart on a bad day. As a veteran of four years playing flute in the Oceanside High School marching band, Joanna had developed an antipathy to brass (as nearly all ex-band members do, having spent untold hours and miles marching with the sound of trumpets in their ears). But afterward, when Simon launched into a lengthy explanation regarding the music's antecedents and composer (Haydn on a *good* day) with such eagerness and enthusiasm, she held her tongue.

He was a little pompous (well, slightly more than that!) but Joanna liked him all the same. Like her, he talked easily, and she had learned a great deal about him from their conversations, including certain things that had earned her sympathy. As a seven-year-old boy he had been sent away to school by his *indifferent parents* (Joanna's italics, not his) who died ten years later. They might just as well have died earlier and had it done with for all the worth they'd been to him. The tales Simon had told her of his life at school—the harsh discipline, purposeful humiliations, and general indifference meted out to him there—had brought Joanna close to tears. Her own childhood, commonplace and pampered, filled with all the love and material comforts her middle-class parents could give, stood in violent contrast to what Simon had known. There were many other things she liked about him, but the stories from his childhood would have been enough.

He encouraged Joanna to select musical choices of her own. She paged through hundreds of slip-cases, drawing some out for examination, or in recognition as ones she had owned. He had an amazing collection of both classical and jazz. Many of the albums were older than he was.

She finally selected Graffman and the Boston Symphony with

Chopin's Piano Concerto Number One and settled it on the turn-table, remarking with surprise at the absense of a CD player, or even a cassette tape player in the record cabinet.

Simon shook his head. "I hate those things. These are real arti-facts, the way music was meant to be listened to. . . ."

The music bloomed in the background as they talked.

Joanna, cross-legged on the floor and leaning forward with her arms propped on the coffee table, asked, "Simon, do you see anything curious or unusual about what happened at the Hastings Day supper?"

He had settled into his place on the sofa, feet propped on a damask-covered footstool in front of him. "You fainted," he said. "That was unusual. Curious, too, I suppose."

"That's what it looked like, sure," she agreed. "What it was obviously *meant* to look like. But I've never fainted in my life. Now, that's unusual. . . ."

Simon arched an eyebrow. "What's the curious part?"

"You getting sick, just a few minutes afterward." She paused, letting the idea sink in. "Doesn't that seem curious to you?"

"A bit. I don't really see what you're getting at, though."

"Think back," she prompted him. "What made you sick? Do you know?"

"I suppose I ate too much." He paused, thinking too. "I had a great deal on my plate, in any case. But as I remember I'd only eaten a little when I began to feel sick at my stomach so I guess I really didn't eat that much after all." He looked closely at her. "What's this all about, Joanna?"

"This might sound crazy," she said. "But hear me out before you disagree. I think whatever it was that made me faint or seem to faint is the same thing that made you sick. . . ."

"Something in the food?"

"Not just the food, *my* food. At first I thought it must have been the tea, somebody had put a sleeping pill or two in it or some-thing. But I've been thinking a lot about it these past few days and I put a few things together."

"Such as?"

Joanna took a deep breath and began counting them off on her fingers. "I'm sitting at the table, right?—feeling fine, right? And then the next second I faint, or seem to faint. You're sitting next to me, you're feeling just perfect, and then all at once, right after they take me upstairs, you start to feel sick and have to leave." She seemed disappointed that he didn't seize upon the information. "Don't you see?"

"Not really."

She sighed. "You didn't really get sick, Simon—I mean, you did, but not for the reason you thought." She looked at him. "The stuff that made you sick was in the food."

He considered that for a moment. "But you said *your food*," he reminded her.

"But don't you remember, you took some of the sweet-and-sour pork off my plate. I don't think you thought I saw you, but I did. And then you ate it. And then you got sick."

"All right, suppose that's true. Why would anybody put anything into your food?"

She told him about the fortune cookie.

"A joke?"

Joanna shook her head doubtfully. "Not likely."

"But who?"

"I don't know," she repeated. "Kate made the Chinese food, but of course she'd never do anything like that. Or Sarah; I think you got the fortune cookie from her."

"I don't remember. But look, Joanna, couldn't this all be just coincidence?"

"The message in the cookie?"

"No," he answered, "not that. But the rest. I mean to say, who would want to do that to you, and why? It all seems so pointless."

It was time to tell him everything.

He listened carefully and with obvious interest as Joanna narrated the story beginning with the letter she'd received in London signed by Kate and ending with the séance and her subsequent additions to Teams A and B.

"You put my name on Team A?" he asked, sounding mildly insulted.

"It's not an accusation," she assured him, "I just wanted to separate the people who seemed to want me to stay here in St. Audric with those who seemed bent on getting me to leave."

"Cynthia's a logical suspect, I suppose," he said. "But I can't picture her going to such lengths, she's not clever enough, and of course why would she concoct some ruse to bring you here then do things to chase you out?"

"That's the point of A and B," she reminded him. "Somebody brought me here; somebody's trying to get me out of town."

He thought for a moment. "You know," he said, "I think you might be right."

In the kitchen they nursed cups of orange cappucino and tried to make sense of Joanna's "clues."

"I can't believe you haven't said anything before this," Simon commented. "Not even to Kate?" She shook her head. "But you can't believe she's anything to do with it."

"Of course not, but she does *talk,* and that wouldn't help much, would it? I mean, how could I keep my suspicions secret if Kate was gossiping them around?"

"There's something I don't quite understand. Why didn't you leave once you found out you'd been tricked into coming here?"

She gathered up their empty cups and carried them to the sink. Running warm water over them, she said, "Well, my book is set in a place very much like this. I might have even searched out St. Audric for myself eventually. Then once I was here I had research to do. . . ."

"But surely there wasn't any need to stay so long. What's kept you here all this time?"

She couldn't find an easy answer. Turning from the sink, she said, "Kate told me about the records and things Geoffrey Latimer had—I thought they might be useful—and then I had to wait till he came back from France. There wasn't any reason I shouldn't stay. I told you Jayson's in Los Angeles till the middle of next month; St. Audric's as good a place as any to work while I'm alone."

"But if you feel in danger . . ."

"Not danger, not really."

"I don't think I'd take the chance if I were you. What do you think it's all about, Joanna?"

Snuff, Simon's ginger-colored tabby cat, meowed piteously at Joanna's feet and she bent to scoop him up into her arms. Holding the purring feline close against her shoulder she answered, "I'm not sure. I think it has something to do with my mother. Somebody wants me to find out about her, but there are others who don't. And then," she paused, tweaking at the cat's ear, "I keep thinking of that Oats Goat stuff you told me about, all that pagan earth-worship business. Do you think there's a possibility . . ."—she rolled her eyes theatrically—". . . God, I know how dumb this sounds—but do you think there's a connection somewhere? I mean, is all this weird stuff I've been telling you about in some way related to"—she flinched at the word—"*witchcraft?*"

She had expected him to laugh, but he didn't. Instead he regarded her seriously, chin propped thoughtfully on his fist. "If you mean is the answer to your mother's whereabouts tied up with some secret cult—no, I can't see what or where such a connection would lead. I wouldn't rule out there is such a thing, though, or that it might be behind the plot to bring you here. . . ."

"Plot?" she repeated the word and her face went a little pale as she said it. "You make it sound so serious."

"You must think it is or you wouldn't have given so much thought to it," Simon replied. "But what gave you the idea there might be such a connection?"

"My birthday. It's November fifteenth, the same as the celebration of the Oats Goat Moon. . . ."

They both jumped as Snuff, tired of being cosseted, suddenly squawked and leapt from Joanna's arms, leaving a trail of brutal red marks across her forearm. With shouts of "bad cat!" Simon chased Snuff in and out of four rooms, finally cornering him behind the library door. After the unrepentant animal was tossed without ceremony into the back garden, Simon washed and salved Joanna's arm, then bandaged it tightly.

"Do you have any theories about Geoffrey Latimer's place in all this?" Simon asked as he secured the bandage with tape at the edge.

"Geoffrey? Well, I'll admit he lied to me at first, not admitting the truth about Pauline and Cassie, but apart from that—and I understand it now—there's no reason to think he has any part in all this. Why would he connive to bring me to St. Audric, then deny knowing either my mother or Pauline?" She looked down at her neatly wrapped arm. "It really didn't need all this, it wasn't that bad. . . ."

They walked together back into the living room. "I'm not so

eager to dismiss Geoffrey Latimer from suspicion," Simon told her as he settled himself with grace into a chair opposite her. "He's an odd sort, all those rumors about his wife gone off with someone else last spring. But you know something, I never saw a trace of her, not once in two whole years. Now that's *odd,* wouldn't you say?"

"Hmmm," Joanna mused, "and he must have married her somewhere else, because I've been through the parish records and there's no mention of any marriage between Geoffrey Latimer and anyone."

"By the way, if he denied being related to you that first time you visited Blackmantle, how did he ever explain the picture?" Simon wondered.

"What picture's that?"

"The one on the piano. Well, you must have seen it." When she looked blankly back at him he explained. "There's an eight-by-ten of you in a lovely pearl-edged frame on the piano. I saw it myself last April when he allowed our Alfriston poetry circle to hold a reading there. Don't tell me you didn't notice it."

"I didn't see anything like that," Joanna answered, her forehead creasing in a frown, "and I couldn't have missed it. In fact I did look at on the photos on the piano, but there wasn't one of me." She gave a soft whistle. "Last April; so he *did* know about me before. That's very strange."

"I think he's got a crush on you."

"Simon!"

"I do. So what if he's your uncle? It's been known. . . ."

She laughed. "He's not the type. He's very proper, very Old World. And besides, he's a scholar."

"If that makes a difference then someone forgot to tell me about it."

She giggled. "I wish you wouldn't make jokes about him, Simon. I really like him; I think he's nice."

"And?"

"*And* I don't think he's got any incestuous designs on me."

"Well, maybe not. Can't say I'd blame him if he did. It was a very lovely picture, though I like your hair better the way you have it now."

"How do you mean?" she asked. "I haven't changed my hair in years."

"The color. Is it natural?"

"Of course it is, silly! Nobody dyes her hair *brown*. If you've got it, you were born with it."

"So you changed it back," he said.

"Back how?" Joanna asked, puzzled. "It's always been this color."

"But the photo. You were blond then."

She turned to look at him. "Simon," she said, her voice so odd, remote that it was hardly hers, "I've never been blond."

It troubled her for a few days, but when Geoffrey Latimer called her up, asking her to be his own guest at the Bal Masque, she promptly lost her nerve and said nothing of it to him. It was possible after all that Simon was wrong, that the photo had been of someone else.

And there was little enough time to consider such things; the next week was extremely busy for Joanna. Kate's birthday party, twice postponed when Kate had to be away on matters relating to the library, was finally fixed and held on the twenty-eighth, and now there was the Bal Masque to get ready for as well. It was all anyone seemed to talk about.

Joanna had imagined it would be a costume party: everyone coming dressed as their favorite character. She had imagined Chloe breaking out of her childlike image to dress as Madonna; Caroline Munro fluffing out her lank red hair and going as the Duchess of York; Roland Jaspar impersonating a pirate, and so on.

Kate soon put her right on that.

"It's nothing like your Halloween," she explained. "Everyone wears their best clothes, usually black or white (black for the men, white for the women) and a fancy mask to cover up the face. The fancier the better."

"I don't have a white dress," Joanna told her. "Black will have to do."

"That's good enough," Kate chuckled. "Just don't come

dressed in costume! I can imagine how everyone would stare if you walked in tarted up as a Persian princess or some other such rot."

"Where do I get a mask?" Joanna wondered.

Sally Bradshaw had recently opened a boutique in Malting Road, but when Joanna could find nothing there to her liking she was urged by Sally herself to seek out the Bigelows' shop in Alfriston. "If you're looking for something *really* special," Sally told her, "you're certain to find it there."

The Priest Hole, a typically gaunt Jacobean structure, was located in the middle of Alfriston's busy High Street. Tamara, peering from the window, recognized Joanna at once and came out onto the street to greet her.

"I suppose they've sent you here looking for a mask," she said, anticipating Joanna's request. "Well, come inside and you'll see we've masks of all kinds." A ripple of Indian bells sounded as she pulled the door open.

Tamara stood with arms planted on her full hips as Joanna sorted through a plethora of masks, hiding her face behind them, posing. Starched silk. Ceramic. Beaded. Lace-covered. Velvet-trimmed. Sequined. Feathered. Finally she chose a half mask of black and purple sequins depicting elongated eyes in "Cleopatra" style; it was exquisite and expensive at nearly fifty pounds. A bit of a luxury considering she'd probably never have cause to wear the thing in public again, but Jayson had been known to favor masks while they were making love; this one (historically related) would thrill and surprise him. She had a diaphanous purple baby doll nightie back at the flat that would complement it perfectly.

Tamara snatched it from her and carried it to the counter, gauze skirt trailing like fog at her feet as she went. There was something so decidedly "California-ish" about the Bigelows, Tamara especially. She reminded Joanna of the middle-aged hippies of Marin County who frequented the Renaissance Pleasure Faire each year, or their more chic "cousins" who ran antiques or art galleries in Carmel and Santa Monica. So it hadn't surprised her to learn from Kate that the Bigelows had not only traveled widely in the U.S. but had once owned a fashionable shop in San Francisco's Union Square.

The Indian bells tinkled above the door.

Sarah Halliwell, stunning in a red jumpsuit, came inside with Cynthia Marrow trailing languidly behind, looking down-at-heel and frumpish by comparison, though she was at least fifteen years younger than Sarah.

"I've brought Cynthia in for a look at your stock," she said, waving gaily to Tamara, bending to peck a kiss on Joanna's cheek. "What do you have for the masque that might suit her?"

Tamara led Sarah toward the display of decorative bounty in the center of the shop that Joanna had so recently plundered. Cynthia made no move to follow, standing meekly in the space between door and counter, her fine blond hair hanging limply, her narrow shoulders stooped under the baggy blue sweater she wore. Everything about Cynthia seemed thin to the point of tautness; her eyes overlarge in the nervous pallor of her face.

Pausing on her way out the door, Joanna turned to Cynthia and smiled nicely. "I'm sure you'll be able to find something you like here," she said. "There's so much great stuff."

Cynthia's placid expression turned suddenly vivid as she snapped, "I don't know how you even have the nerve to speak to me."

Joanna stared back, unbelieving. "I don't know what you mean."

"It's humiliating the way you've gone after Simon, knowing he belongs to me!" she shouted, and when Joanna tried to deny it Cynthia screamed her down. "Every time I turn around I see the two of you together! You, parading around like Lady Muck, the famous novelist from California—well, why don't you go back to California where you belong and leave Simon to me!"

Joanna felt as though she had stepped into the midst of a 1940s three-hankie movie ("He's mine, I can't live without him!" "But it's me he loves . . .") At the edge of the shop, Sarah and Tamara watched, wordless.

"Simon and I are friends," Joanna said, trying to keep her voice calm and unoffending.

"Well, I was his friend once, more than a friend, till you came here. . . ."

Sarah suddenly found her tongue and came to Joanna's aid.

"I've found the perfect mask," she called out to Cynthia, and swept up to the counter with it, holding the pink-and-gray blocked satin mask aloft. "Isn't it pretty?"

Cynthia took it, then looked up at Tamara. "How much?" she asked.

"Twenty-seven-ninety-five."

"Too much!"

Tamara rallied. "Only ten pounds to rent it."

Cynthia undid the snap on a cheap red plastic wallet and slowly extracted a wrinkled ten-pound note, which she pushed grudgingly across the counter. Tamara, her bracelets tinkling like fairy bells, rang up the purchase, wrapped the mask in tissue, and put it into Cynthia's hands together with the scribbled rental receipt.

"It's due back no later than November second at four o'clock," she said.

Cynthia, this time with Sarah following, was halfway out the door, Sarah turning to throw Joanna an apologetic smile as they went.

When the door swung shut, Tamara, leaning against the register, rolled her eyes at Joanna in an expression of complete disbelief. "I'm really sorry about that," she said.

A thin stain of pink had come into Joanna's face. "I don't know why I didn't just walk out. I guess I was just so surprised anyone would act that way in a public place," she explained.

"She'll never hold that young man," Tamara prophesied, "not making a fool of herself like that. . . ."

Joanna, sensing questions about Simon from Tamara, turned to go. "Thanks," she called over her shoulder, hearing the bells obscure her reply.

Out on the street Joanna held the tissue-wrapped package and her purse close against her chest, trembling, her face gone hot. In her mind she saw herself as a sixth-grader fighting with Donna Elmore in the middle of the volleyball court, the whole student body watching. It had been the same then: Donna, spiteful and furious after having spied Joanna and—what was his name? She couldn't remember now—together at lunch in the cafeteria. It had been the most innocent of encounters: something about a science project they'd been assigned together. Joanna had tried to convince Donna that she and Mike—yes, Mike Ackerman, she remembered now—were only working on a school project, that she was not trying to steal away Donna's boyfriend. But Donna had refused to believe it and for a long time Joanna's girlfriends had not spoken to her. "Boy-stealer" and "thief" were just two of the more unfortunate sobriquets she had to deal with for the next few months.

It was a trivial memory, no longer painful, yet it illustrated something Joanna had learned a long time ago, perhaps from that very experience. There was nothing quite so unsettling as two women battling over one man, for whatever reason. It showed up some basic incongruity in the female character best left undetected, unrecognized.

Joanna stood in the street and shivered.

Nothing had changed.

* * *

The night of the Bal Masque was Joanna's last as a guest at The Sheaves, and Mrs. Munro surprised her with a decorative "fare-well" cake, prettily iced. Considering that the woman had rarely said more than good morning to her in all the time she'd been there, Joanna was amazed and a little guilty for all the unpleasant thoughts she'd entertained about both Mrs. Munro and her daughter.

Geoffrey rang at six and asked if she minded coming round to Blackmantle and they would take his Bentley to the masque. Joanna agreed readily since the little Escort was packed to the brim with all her things in preparation for her move to Kate's. He had the photocopies for her, too; Joanna was delighted at finally being able to lay claim to them.

"Come up for a brandy before we leave if you like, and if you don't mind walking," he told her. "I'm afraid I got rather caught up in my books today and I'm only going in for a bathe just now."

Joanna, who had already dressed even to her makeup, prom-ised to slip into a pair of walking shoes and make the trek up High Street and Abbot's Lane to Blackmantle. So she thanked Mrs. Munro once more for the cake, grabbed a second pair of shoes and a black shawl from her car, and started on her way.

The moon, thin as a dime's edge, offered little light, and she

almost wished she'd brought along a flashlight as she picked her
way carefully along Abbot's Lane. When she had gone about two-
thirds of the way the road she knew so well in daylight but had
never trod in dark suddenly dipped, revealing the pale lamps of
Blackmantle's vast front garden. She shivered under her light
wrap; no wind, but a wet chill hung in the air like basement
damp. By the time Joanna reached the gravel drive she was happily anticipating the chance of a few minutes beside the fireplace
in Geoffrey's sitting room.

Nina, gray and scowling, came to the door wiping her hands
on a tea towel. "He's dressing," she said, "but he'll be down
soon. He said to wait in there." She gestured toward the customary sitting room. "He's set things out. . . ."

There was a fire, as she had hoped, also brandy and sweets on
the sideboard; and three big envelopes banded by a string were
propped against the leg of Geoffrey's chair. For me! Joanna
thought happily, eager to seize upon the envelopes and plunder
their contents, but she forced herself to wait till Geoffrey showed
up to hand them over, which was a good twenty-five minutes
later.

"I apologize for being so long," he said in his slightly formal,
gentlemanly way. He hesitated, then bent to kiss her lightly on
the cheek. "As a relative I presume I'm allowed that privilege,"
he said, smiling. And then, "You look exceptionally beautiful
tonight."

She held up the mask for him to see.

"Very nice. Did you get that over in Alfriston?"

Joanna nodded. "At The Priest Hole."

"The Bigelows." He made it sound like a curse. "Tacky, tire-
some people . . ."

Because it was so near the way she would describe them,
Joanna, in a flash of guilt, added, ". . . But very nice."

"It was an unkind remark," he admitted, settling in his chair.

He didn't look well tonight; there were shadows underneath
his eyes as if he'd been sleeping poorly. And his thinness was
accentuated by the smart black suit he wore.

"Are you sure you feel okay to go?" Joanna asked somewhat
artlessly, then retreated to the safety of understatement, "You
look a little tired."

He seemed to be trying to decide whether to answer her; at last he said, "You might as well know that I'm not too long for this world, Joanna." He saw the quick flicker of concern come into her eyes and immediately held up his hand to silence her. "Don't get upset—I've never been any good at handling hysterical women. In any case it's not going to be tomorrow or the next day, or even next month. . . ."

She tried to swallow, her throat gone suddenly dry.

"What's wrong with you?"

"I've suffered for much of my adult life from a rare kind of scrofula, which is particular to the male line in my family. My father didn't have it; his brother did. It acts very much as a pernicious anemia does, attacking the blood and lymph glands. I've been to nearly every spa known to man to help arrest it somewhat; I've only just come back from Cauterets in France." He gave her a wise, indulgent smile, divining her all-American, middle-class allegiance to doctors and miracle-medicine. "You see, there's nothing can be done, not medically, so it only seems the best alternative is to visit spa after spa and see if Nature can repair its handiwork. . . ." His voice fell. "And its mistakes."

She felt tears coming into her eyes, melting her mascara, burning. "I don't know what to say," she mumbled. "It's so terrible!"

He laughed. "At your age it would be. But when you've lived for sixty years you grow somewhat more accustomed to the idea of dying. I could have several good years left; and it's not really debilitating, this disease—only at the end when lumps and boils form on the body in the groin and armpits." He shook his head. "But that doesn't bear discussion. I suppose all forms of death have their discomforts. . . ."

"Why did you tell me?" Joanna asked.

"I probably shouldn't have. I only thought that since we've become rather fond of one another—at least I speak from my own point of view—it wouldn't be fair to keep it a secret. I hope I haven't made a mistake."

"Oh no," she answered quickly. "I'm glad you told me. . . ." Then thinking how it must sound she explained, "That is, I'm glad you trusted me enough to tell me."

"I do," he said. "So please stop looking at me with those quite beautiful but tragic eyes—I'm not about to drop down dead in front of you. In any case, I've been anticipating my mortality for many years now. You can't study history for as long as I have and not be aware of it." That seemed to remind him of the envelopes and he bent to pick them up. "I've got the copies here," he said, "all the things you asked for. . . ."

Her excitement vanished, Joanna could only smile wanly as he slipped the bulging envelopes into a canvas bag and held it out to her. A thought came from out of nowhere—*He can enjoy the evening now, having spoiled it*—and fell away just as quickly. "Thanks," she said, taking the bag, "shouldn't we be on our way?"

He flourished his mask; Thespis's tragic pose.

She bit her lip and looked away.

The interior of Goat's Rue didn't look much different than it had to her the one time she'd been inside, though wreathes of holly adorned the gallery above, and new tapestries could be seen decorating the walls. Candles—slender and white, many hundreds of them—spread their tremulous golden light to every corner of the room. It only now occurred to Joanna that they served a practical as well as aesthetic purpose; that there was no electricity at Goat's Rue.

She had expected a party. Cocktails, finger food, dancing. But it was all very different, she could see that after only a few minutes inside. Geoffrey patiently explained that it was in keeping with tradition and the occasion they were celebrating.

"As you know, All Hallows' was originally a Druid holiday," he told her, "but the Saxons celebrated it too, though in a different way, with simple feasting and a procession of many candles. They believed this to be the one night of the year when Man had the ability to influence his fate, and so everyone masked himself, hoping to give the Fate Weaver some clue as to how they wished their lives to be in the coming year."

Joanna wrinkled her nose. "The *who?*'

He steered her to the edge of the room near the great fireplace and pointed to a hanging tapestry. Its soft beige, blue, and lilac hues were woven in a curious pattern that depicted a dark-haired woman who plaited the edge of an identical tapestry, which portrayed a woman doing the same, and so on, till the repeated image became too small to see. Joanna stared up at it, awed by its timeless message.

"The Fate Weaver," Geoffrey said, indicating the tapestry with a wave of his hand. "She's myth of course, like most of the things Man believed in—or *believes*. Lady of Legends."

"What legends? Whose?"

"Saxons, Frisians. They believed that she held their Fate in her hands, that she could be charmed, cajoled, even fooled, but never ignored."

"Fate is a woman," Joanna quoted, thinking of the phrase Audric had used.

"Yes, that's how they saw it: a beautiful woman as the arbiter in the affairs of men."

"Women, too?"

"Oh, yes, the Fate Weaver wove the special pattern of all lives."

"Like God?" Joanna wondered.

"No. Woden was God. He would be perceived as guiding all events, large and small. The Fate Weaver had a hand in the special circumstances of life, the highlights. Birth and Death, Love and Loss. . . ."

"Why do you suppose they saw her as a woman?"

"Women have always been mysterious, the unknowable. . . ."

She saw how intently he studied the silent figure on the wall. A legend? She seemed more, somehow.

"Do you believe in her?" Joanna asked.

Music, played on antique instruments and in the style of many centuries ago, drifted toward them, soft as incense. He gave Joanna a curious look. "I don't know what I believe," he said.

She was at the bread and cider table searching for a Pepsi when someone came up behind her and said, "Boo!"

A handful of cream crackers slipped from her grasp and scattered neatly over the damask cloth. "Simon," she said with a quick look over her shoulder, "you scared me!"

He wore a cocky Robin Hood hat and a green half mask above his usual boyish grin. "How did you know it was me?" he asked.

"Because you're the only one silly enough to wear that hat." She turned back to the food, fingering a wedge of cheese.

"You don't sound very glad to see me."

Her voice had a clipped, unfriendly sound. "I'm not sure I should be. I saw Cynthia in the Bigelows' shop the other day and she really let me have it. In front of people, too. It was really embarrassing."

"What did she say?"

"That I had better keep my hands off you or else; words to that effect, at least. She's probably watching us right now."

"She can't," Simon declared. "She isn't here."

Joanna thought of her sitting at home with a mask she'd paid ten pounds to rent and couldn't wear. That was probably a lot of money to her. "Why didn't she come?" she asked. "She was looking forward to it."

"Was she?"

His tone was utterly callous, and she was suddenly furious with him. "If she couldn't get a baby-sitter you might have stayed home and kept her company."

He seemed really puzzled that the situation had riled her. "Cynthia decided that she didn't want to come. It had nothing to do with getting a sitter for the children. And what are you so worked up about? Why should you care?"

"I care," she snapped at him. "I *care.* You should, too. In case you haven't noticed, Cynthia's in love with you! Doesn't that mean anything to you at all?"

"Yes," he answered quietly. "It means she's out of luck, because I'm in love with you."

Joanna stared at him, unsure for a moment of what she'd heard. "You can't be serious!"

"I'm serious."

She felt herself blushing beneath the mask. "I don't know what to say."

"It's all right, I know you aren't in love with me. I'm not trying to make you feel guilty or myself foolish—I just want you to know there's no reason to bring Cynthia into it, because we've split up—if indeed we ever were a couple."

"Because of me?" Joanna wanted to know.

"Not entirely. She never really got over Robin's death. I've just been a substitute. So while it might seem like I've been using her, it's really the other way around."

Her fingers tapped nervously against the cider costrel. "Why are you telling me all this stuff?"

He took hold of her arm, maneuvering her toward a hidden alcove near the stairs. "Look," he said, "I want you to know the truth because I think that might make it easier for you to trust me. . . ."

A clammy, anxious feeling came over her. "Trust you? About what?"

"About your uncle, Geoffrey. Stay away from him, Joanna. There's something weird about him; he's still lying to you. Did you know he has a daughter?"

She remembered Kate remarking he was childless. "How do you know that?" she asked.

His voice dropped almost to a whisper. "I was up to London a few days ago visiting an artist friend of mine. I hadn't seen him in at least five years and he was surprised to learn I was living in St. Audric now. Seems he painted Geoffrey Latimer's daughter Geraldine last autumn; all the sittings took place at the studio in London. By the time the work was finished Geoffrey Latimer didn't want it; his daughter had run off with some man, and I guess he didn't approve. But he definitely referred to Geraldine as his daughter." He took a breath. "Well, I snapped a few Polaroids of his preliminary sketches and brought them back here with me. I showed them to Kate, the Halliwells, a few others. They all said the same thing. That it was Geraldine, Latimer's *wife*."

"Whatever happened to the painting?" Joanna asked, not wanting to think about what the whole thing might mean.

"It was sold, to someone else. Maybe the guy she ran off with bought it, I don't know."

"Maybe he was just embarrassed to admit to the artist he had married such a young girl," Joanna said without much conviction.

"Embarrassed by what a total stranger might think, not embarrassed by what his friends and neighbors think? That doesn't make much sense, does it?"

"I guess not." Joanna shifted from one foot to the other. "All right, I'll ask him about it. . . ."

Before she could say any more, Geoffrey was at her elbow.

"I'm afraid I'm not feeling very well," he said. "Do you mind very much if we leave early?"

She turned around, surprised, Simon forgotten. "Are you okay?" She put a protective arm around his shoulder.

"Just very tired suddenly. I hate to ruin the evening for you, but I feel as though I should see you home."

"Don't be silly. I'll get back all right; it isn't far. But let me help you outside to the car." She caught the stern look Simon gave her and elaborated, "I have to get my research stuff out of the car anyway."

"I'll walk Joanna home," Simon told Geoffrey.

"Very well," the older man said. "Then I shall say good night."

Joanna brushed past Simon without a word.

A few minutes later when he came outside, Geoffrey's venerable Bentley was just pulling away. Its mellow lights silhouetted Joanna for a moment, then left her in darkness as the car glided slowly down the drive.

The sweet essence of her perfume stirred in the air as she turned toward him. "Don't say anything else about him," she declared. "I don't want to hear it."

"Joanna . . ."

Her voice quavered. "He's going to die, Simon. Just that: he's going to die. . . ."

When Jayson called her at The Sheaves the following morning Joanna told him everything: That she was related to the Latimers of St. Audric, that Geoffrey Latimer was her uncle, that although her mother (his sister, Cassie) had been estranged from him since the time of Joanna's birth, she was nonetheless believed to be alive.

Jayson sounded perplexed at all her news. "Was it your uncle Geoffrey who sent the letter to you?"

"I'm not sure," she answered, realizing she had never asked him and probably would never be able to. "He hasn't admitted to it, of course, but it's possible. Anyhow, he's given me copies of some wonderful documents, Jayson. You should see them. . . ."

"Don't get too occupied with work," he said, and it surprised her; she'd never heard him voice anything like that before. He must be feeling as lonely for her as she was for him. "I'll be back in London on the eighteenth."

"You'll miss my birthday!" she groaned, sounding as disappointed as a child.

"It can't be helped. We'll just celebrate it a few days late."

"Okay." She giggled. "Bring me something nice. . . .''

That afternoon she moved all her things from the car into Little Gospels and the room Kate had made ready for her. It was smaller than the one she'd had at The Sheaves for the past two months. Kate had been using it as a storage room but had thoughtfully removed all packing crates and boxes, moving in a chair, desk, and folding bed. Even with all the nonmatching pieces it was a pleasant, cheery room.

The following Tuesday was Guy Fawkes day; when it began to get dark Joanna could see the cliffside bonfires from her bedroom window. Kate and Simon had walked down to watch, but Joanna, under threat of a cold since Halloween, stayed indoors drinking hot honey-tea and, swathed in blankets, was forced to watch the ritual fires from a distance.

That night when the embers had blown away into the sea—the ashes scattered to anonymity on the beach—and a pale half moon looked on, a tall thin man came out of Friston Forest and walked to the very edge of the cliffs beyond. He stood there for a long time, swaying just a little forward as if daring himself to jump as he stared off toward the land where all this madness had begun, and cursed it.

Let it end. Sweet Jesus, please let it end at last.

* * *

Kate and Joanna sat cross-legged on the floor, eating.

"I'm really sorry this came up so soon," Kate said, serving up glazed chicken and deli-style coleslaw, "but among the many perks of being a 'documents adviser' to the National Trust there are certain drawbacks—namely, being made to come running whenever they crook their little finger." Demonstrating, she held out a sticky pinky, then sucked it arduously to prove her point, sending Joanna into giggles.

"You'll be back before I leave for London, won't you?"

"Oh yes," Kate assured her, "I shouldn't be more than a few days. Thursday at the latest, I should think."

Joanna chomped on a giant dill pickle. "I won't be going till Sunday morning."

That pleased Kate. "It gives us time to plan a proper send-off for you. Maybe a fancy-dress dinner or so; invite the Halliwells—you like them—Chloe, and Geoffrey of course."

"Don't go to any trouble," Joanna said obligingly, though she meant it.

"No trouble. Perhaps we could go to services the following morning before you're off. The parish would like a chance to get one last look at you, I'm sure. And it's Sacrament Sunday as well."

Joanna made a face. "Do you know I haven't gone to Communion in all the time I've been here? It sounds silly, but it makes me feel sick to think of taking it from that vicar."

"You didn't like him from the first, did you? Not too unusual I suppose, given your experience in the graveyard."

"More than that. The first week or so I had the most . . ." she shook her head, ". . . I don't know, *gross* sex dreams about him! It made me feel quite ashamed, and dreams haven't been able to do that to me since I was thirteen. He was always about a mile long . . ." She felt her face go suddenly red. "Anyhow, I know I'd be thinking of that up at the communion rail. Just too embarrassing . . ."

"How extraordinary to have such dreams about the vicar!" Kate said, licking her fingers. "I must say he is quite a *man,* if you know what I mean. Of course he can't compare, size-wise, to our friend Simon."

Joanna wasn't sure if she had heard correctly. "But how could you possibly know that?" she asked.

Kate tore a chicken breast in two between her fingers and nibbled on it before answering. "It's not how you think. Each year on Maypole Day the men of St. Audric doff their clothes and take the ritual Washing in the Cuckmere. It's an old Saxon thing."

"All the men?" Joanna wondered.

"Young and old alike." She saw Joanna's look of surprise. "It's innocent, you know."

"Reverend Burroughs? He's one of them?"

"Of course."

Joanna thought of Roland Jaspar, Dr. Wallin, Toby Bigelow, and all the other middle-aged-and-over men showing off their pendulous parts—the younger men, Colin Bradshaw, Stephen Bradshaw, Simon cock-proud beside them. . . .

"Not Geoffrey Latimer," she said hopefully.

"Geoffrey is the hereditary lord of this place," Kate reminded her. "He doesn't have to abide by rules."

"The women watch?"

"Yes," Kate answered, a note of irritation in her voice. "For heaven's sake, Joanna, there's nothing wrong in it; that's to say there's no sex involved. It's just a custom."

They didn't speak of it again, but it bothered Joanna all that evening while she and Kate watched television and later attempted several hands of gin rummy. She didn't know exactly what about the story had disturbed her, till halfway through the night when she woke suddenly with the very words on her lips. *The Oats Goat.*

Someone, who was it?—Simon!—had first told her the story. The pagan Saxon ritual where the most virile man of the village took a virgin to his bed on the night of the Oats Goat Moon. Simon was writing a cycle of poems about it. In her tossed and dizzy thoughts the only probable virgin she could think of was Chloe. Chloe, who was Cynthia Marrow's baby-sitter, and in that she followed a logical connection to Simon. Simon the Large. Simon the *Virile*.

But none of it made any sense. It was all idiotic, unreasoning, unthinkable. All the same it kept her wakeful the remainder of the night as her thoughts swirled like water spinning down a drain. Simon had warned her about Geoffrey Latimer, but was it Simon instead she should be warned against? The thought distressed Joanna to the point of sending her running to the wash-bowl, where she wretched with dry heaves and then went trembling back to bed.

In the morning, still feeling the ill effects of her night fears, she rang Rosemary Cottage only a little after dawn.

Simon came to the phone at once.

"I was just on my way out," he explained. "I have to go up to London for a few days; something's come up. I should be back by Friday. Will you still be here?" He sounded anxious.

"Till the seventeenth," she said, wondering what was taking him away so urgently on such short notice. He'd said nothing about it at lunch the other day.

"What did you want to talk to me about?" he asked.

She hesitated. "Nothing. Nothing at all."

"Call you when I get back," he promised, and rang off.

But she kept thinking about the Oats Goat business and wondering if she were losing her mind or really seeing things clearly for the first time. She borrowed a few of Kate's books on legends and customs from Saxon times, paging madly through them, trying to find answers to questions she barely knew. At last on Monday, the day of Kate's departure, Joanna decided it must all be nonsense and vowed to think no more of it. There were still the envelopes Geoffrey had given her the night of the Bal Masque to get through. And Simon was no Oats Goat.

She was well into the second draft of *The Scourge,* but that was put aside now as she gave herself over to the study of St. Audric's writings. Drawn inexorably into his world, she spent all the afternoon and evening bent over the desk, reading and scratching out notes on her steno pad, analyzing, till she lost all sense of time.

She had worked with many historical documents in the past five or six years: speeches, diaries, notebooks, and letters; church records too, some from as early as the thirteenth century. At college, a minor in modern American history had brought her into contact with presidential papers and the letters of Civil War generals. It was her experience that most events, most people, spoke to their own time, and were part of it, shaped by it.

But not Audric.

He stood apart somehow, ancient in knowledge, yet his ideas were revelatory, stunningly modern. Most shocking of all was that despite his stature as a saint, he had obviously rejected the basic tenets of Christianity early in his career. His writings showed more than just a simple empathy for the pagan Saxon

folk of Sussex. They had converted him to their ways. The opening phrases of his own *Allfather* confirmed the contradiction.

Each stone upon the earth is as much God as God.
He lives equally in the harvest and the sleeping corn of
winter. What need of Bleeding Christ; of dying and reborn
Christ? Simple men have no need of such things. Only the
learned, who are strangers to all things in Nature. And for
themselves they fashion a God of sophists' cloth; it is all they
know.
Dead stones and vines that grow are God enough.

And in a section on "blood forgiveness":

A man's heart may be as flint, yet should he open a single
vein and let the blood flow in droplets to the ground, in this
way shall he make his penitence with Nature.

And still later:

What matter if a man seed his wife or some other woman to
his choice? Nature goes as it will; it is no sin.

Nature. Audric's God.
He had, it seemed, rewritten the Bible and the Ten Commandments too. No wonder the Council at Whitby had declared *The
Allfather* a work of heresy. How could Audric have thought it
would ever be accepted by the churchmen of his own time? The
answer came in an open letter to the Council wherein Audric
declared (somewhat feebly, Joanna thought) that all foregoing
sentiments represented his attempt to write a true history of the
pagan Saxons. His words were obvious lies. Anyone who read
The Allfather (in any century!) could see that Audric's fascination
with pagan rites and religion had succeeded in turning him
against the people of his own class and culture.
Audric, pagan saint . . .
Compendium Magico was a virtual recipe book and bible of
spells and incantations, and filled with interesting bits of lore.

Despite the remove of thirteen hundred years and three translations, Joanna felt Audric's personality bleeding from each written word.

The Wyrd ("Fate Is a Woman") was the last of Audric's three great books. An astonishing document, it was virtually a feminist tract from start to finish—all 186 photocopied pages of it. How extraordinary that *any* man could have thought in such a way so many centuries ago!

Nothing she had read or been told about Audric could have prepared Joanna for his astonishing opinions, though they were decidedly more than that; it was as if he had a strange understanding of women—more than just their sex or flesh—as if he saw the mysteries of life through their eyes. Fascinated, Joanna read, underlining the words with a blue felt-tipped pen.

> *Men bring war into the world; they fight each other over a strip of land and make ghosts of themselves and their brothers because of it. Where is the meaning in such a life? For men know nothing of the creative powers of Nature, and these fires burn only in the souls of Womankind. She guides Man where he knows not. It is Woman who spins Man's fortune, rules his Fate . . .*

Joanna looked up and stared across at the bleared lamp atop the desk. The light hardly showed itself against a window shade grown pink with morning. She'd read all night, hardly marking the passing of the hours. In her mind she could see the abbot, Geoffrey Fitzstephen, bent low over a sputtering candle, studying the same words she had just read. Centuries strung together like a rope of pearls. Reluctantly she stood up and stretched, yawning.

Kate hadn't gotten to the shopping before going away, but there was still half a ham and some cold potatoes in the fridge. Joanna scrounged further, found bread and butter and raspberry preserves, then made up a hearty breakfast for herself. She ate it swiftly, suddenly consumed by hunger; later she took time to muse over a pot of steaming Irish Breakfast tea.

The house was suffused with quiet, a preternatural quiet that made Joanna feel slightly tense and ill at ease. When she had drunk her tea to the dregs she went to stand a while in the back garden, just inside the gate where the lawn ran halfway down to the cliffs. The sun, fully up now, gave off a bilious, sulfurous glow that looked like smog but was only autumn haze and fog wafted up the slopes from the sea below. She sniffed at the air. Mild, and so few clouds. But there would be rain by evening.

Inside again she locked the doors, checked every window. Force of habit; who needed such precautions in a place like this? Then she pulled off her clothes and slid contentedly between the warmth of flannel sheets. When she woke, hours later, the light was already fading and it had begun to rain.

Joanna filled the early evening hours with a myriad of little chores. Kate's tidy kitchen was put back in order, the dishes washed and set out to dry, all crumbs from her breakfast whisked away to the bottom of the red plastic dustbin below the sink. Joanna did a load of her own laundry, then tossed in some towels Kate had left in the hamper.

By nine she had showered, shampooed her hair, thrown on a colorful silk caftan. Outside the rain washed down against the windows, trees bent to the wind. It was her favorite kind of weather, the kind that Californians knew only for a few short weeks each year.

Kate's room had a fireplace, so Joanna moved her work in there, built up a fire, and settled herself on the floor in front of it, research material scattered at her feet. She took up the big envelope marked FITZSTEPHEN DIARIES and slid out a thick wad of pages.

She read for about an hour, making notes in the margins, underlining whole paragraphs. At the point where the plague came into Sussex, Fitzstephen's entries grew lengthy; strange. Joanna switched to the bed and lay on her stomach, reading Geoffrey Fitzstephen's confession of lost faith. The early entries were prayers shot through with pessimism; they soon changed to one long soliloquy of despair and doubt. Joanna trembled as she read them.

Tonight it rains.
I think of Ranaulf of Athens who was once my good friend

*when he came to study at the University in Paris many
years ago. We met on a night like this in a dirty street off the
Chasée St. Lazare where we had come to find the women of
that place. We ended in speaking to each other instead and
became friends, discovering we were fellow students.*

*I think of him now for it is Michaelmas and in his land St.
Michael is special patron of the sick. How well could we use
his help within these walls.*

My brothers ail; they die. And God cares nothing.

* * *

Black sluiced with silver.

Joanna stared at the window; shivering, queerly cold. So much
that she had assimilated into the character of Father Julien in *The
Scourge* was here in these pages. The same doubts and dilem-
mas, the same portents whispering evil in the ear. She read on,
excerpts from an ominous October . . .

*Each day I pray at the Long Man's feet and wait for him
to answer. I tell no one of this. Matthew, though he keeps
close his silence, watches me with wary eyes. He knows, but
does not wish to know. In his heart he likely feels as I.*

* * *

*We know not the God we worship. We have built his
image from the myths and legends of a thousand years of
history. He lives, but not as we would have him: father to a
family of nations, omnipotent instrument to guide and
shape our way with love. For he is not these things.*

*He is the god of stone and wood that Clovis bowed to,
before St. Rémi drowned his wits in water. He is the battle
master TIW. He is THUNOR, god of thunder. He is WODEN,
chief of all the gods. He is the ALLFATHER of Audric's
visions.*

A god of blood will be appeased by blood alone.

* * *

Two more die.
I despair.

* * *

A dream.
I am in darkness on a road which is familiar though I
cannot see my way. In the distance I hear waves breaking
on the shore. A voice, of sweet yet indeterminate accents,
sounds against my ear.
Two faces, the voice says. She has two faces.
I know a sudden sense of awe and wake to find sweat
running on my face.

* * *

It is Jour des Morts.
We eat privately now and take the Eucharist from sepa-
rate cups. Four more fall ill. Their poor wretched bodies
prove the lumps of Plague.
In the absence of all miracles, we are lost.

* * *

La Toussaint.
And first frost.

* * *

I have seen them at last.
They are named Daumier, Alicia and Adelina, but they
have been sent to me as the incarnations of the goddess.
They have healing blood in their sweet bodies, and despite
all horrors which they have seen and passed through, no
mark of Plague has touched them.

* * *

The diary ended here.

A margin note provided by the translator explained at this point that the running commentary either ceased or had been lost. Geoffrey Fitzstephen was believed to have survived the plague and fled to Rennes late the following year when the abbey was closed down; a vague mention of "a former Abbot of St. Audric's in Sussex" appeared as debtor to the duke of Brittany in the Pipe Rolls of 1350–53, after which time there was no further word.

So far as the Daumier sisters were concerned, the account told of a woman answering to that name and alternately calling herself the Lady Mimir, who was believed to have retired into obscurity with her infant daughter at Lewes under the protection of the abbot there, though there were few facts to document the story. . . .

The papers sagged in her hands.

The story was eerily familiar.

In *The Scourge* Father Julien had lost his faith, placing all trust in metaphysical miracles instead. He sheltered the fleeing Delores and Desirée La Vallier, whose nursing skills saved so many members of the Oatenham Priory. How closely the relationship between Fitzstephen and the Daumier sisters mirrored her fictional account she could only guess, but the many proven "coincidences" were enough to give her gooseflesh.

Long ago Joanna had accepted the reality of her own psychic awareness; the fact that it extended to her writing could only add credibility to her academic knowledge of history. But there were times—like now, shivering down to the skin at two in the morning and not from cold alone—when she feared her abilities trespassed on the boundaries between sensitivity and just plain spookiness.

She was feeling spooky now. There was too much of Geoffrey Fitzstephen here in the stillness of this room. His religious doubts, his fears, even his absorption in dreams and fantasies, were too close to what she had already imagined him to be. History was whispering in her ear again, and she was afraid.

Trying to shake the mood, Joanna went into the kitchen for a ham sandwich and some of Kate's delicious potato salad, which she found tucked away in a Tupperware container on the top shelf. Then she curled up on the big living-room sofa with a cashmere throw over her and fed the VCR a steady dose of movie comedies till midmorning.

At noon she dressed in warm clothes and walked down to the cliffs. It was still raining—splashes of silver out of an amethyst sky—the wind gusting rudely in her face. It was invigorating to be outdoors after having closeted herself in the house these past two days. Joanna smoked a cigarette and stared out across the water at some distant, invisible point of land that had held sway over the lives and fortunes of so many English. The Daumiers, like her own La Vallier sisters, had crossed this ruffled bit of water seeking safety; in the same pursuit Geoffrey Fitzstephen, like Father Julien, had fled back across it hoping to find obscurity and peace.

Joanna squinted as the wind spat rain into her face, and after a while she tossed her unfinished cigarette over the edge, down onto the narrow strip of sand where waves washed it away into oblivion.

Kate called that evening to say she'd been delayed and would not be back till Friday noon. As they talked, Joanna moved easily around the kitchen fixing herself a salad; later she went off to Kate's bedroom once more, the heavy envelopes tucked beneath her arm.

INFORMATION RELATING TO THE LIFE OF SIR GERALD LATYMERE AND HIS SON read the top envelope; she dumped its contents into her lap. The history of the Latymere family. It was still hard for Joanna to think of these people as her own ancestors: Sir Gerald, his son Thomas, who had been a well-known playwright of the Jacobean era. Maggie Glynne, his niece, was part of the family too. Having glimpsed her long-dead lover, Joanna had returned to the cemetery many times in hope of seeing Maggie's ghost, but she never had.

Sir Gerald Latymere interested Joanna. Scion of the family, he had turned the crumbled, ruined Benedictine abbey into Blackmantle; his edicts had caused the first buildings of St. Audric village to be raised. For so much of her time here Joanna had been preoccupied with finding out about Pauline and Cassie that she had neglected (till recently) to investigate her own personal

(however distant) ties to the early Latymeres of St. Audric. Now
she skimmed the pages, noting facts and studying details, trying
to put together a picture of the men and women who had pre-
ceded her as addressees of that name.

They were her family. And Sir Gerald had been the first.

*Born at Pevensey in the same month and year Anne Bol-
eyn presented her royal husband with a girlchild instead of
the son he coveted, Gerald Latymere was the son of a wine
importer. Well schooled, he spent his young manhood in
constant, if undistinguished service to Sir William Cecil. As
Cecil's star rose so did Gerald's, till at last he found himself
secretary to the Council in the middle years of Queen Elizabeth's reign. He married Frances Latymere (a first cousin) in 1564 and had seven children by her before she died
in childbirth with number eight. In later years he took as
wife the widow of a close friend, and the couple lived out
their lives together.*

*From 1584 till the time of her execution three years later,
he was set to spy upon Mary Stuart, a royal prisoner at dis-
mal Fotheringay. During his tenure he managed to
uncover one of Mary's clever plots to have Elizabeth mur-
dered, and for his wit and good service was rewarded with
the promise of any Sussex manor as his choice of living.*

*To this point in his life Gerald Latymere had seemed very
much the typical Tudor gentleman: a sly achiever risen out
of the great merchant class of his time. But in truth there
was nothing typical about Gerald Latymere. He was crafty
and pragmatic, but he had secret knowledge. By choosing
St. Audric's long-abandoned abbey (which he named
"Blackmantle" in recognition of the black habits worn by
Benedictine monks) he accomplished something he had
been scheming to do since his youth.*

*Thomas Latymere, Sir Gerald's firstborn son, inherited
Blackmantle at his father's death in 1604. (Ironically, the
elder Latymere's life had spanned approximately the same
period as that of his sovereign Elizabeth, who had died the
year before.) Unlike his younger brothers, who sought positions in the government under two Stuart kings, and his sis-*

ters, who married landed lords for titles and vast fortunes, Thomas pursued a career as a playwright and actor, and married an actress out of love for her. As a very young man he performed alongside Will Shakespeare at the Globe; later he became quite a worthy playwright himself.

Upon the tragic deaths of his wife and his best friend and fellow dramatist Christopher Marlowe (both in 1593) Thomas retired from the active stage and went into a self-imposed exile at Blackmantle where, to the scorn of his aging father, he wrote plays and drank himself into melancholy. No one believed he would outlive his spartan father—a man who rose every day before dawn and could still hunt for sport all day in his seventieth year—but he did.

It was during this period, from 1604–1611, that Thomas Latymere wrote his greatest plays: The Dark Veil; Truth-teller; And Death Shall Cover Her; *and his most controversial work of all,* The Plague Maiden. *Performed only once and for a royal audience at Whitehall in 1610, the play had the typically Jacobean stock-in-trade: madness, incest, cruelty, revenge, and a few other blasphemies. But its plot, even judged by the violence-ridden standards of the day, was deemed too terrible for future audiences to see. King James's sour consort Anne of Denmark labeled it "as great a piece of filth as ever saw the light of day. . . ."*

Worse yet were the rumors (widely circulated in his time) that Thomas had based his play on facts relating to his own father. Because Sir Gerald's memory was still very much respected, the allegations leveled in Thomas's play caused such an uproar there was talk of a prison sentence, even death. But before anything could be decided, Thomas Latymere obliged his critics by dying at Blackmantle of a ruptured bowel. More than a few people had reason to believe he had been "done to death."

The Plague Maiden, *never performed again, became the province of dramatic scholars and historians whose interest ran to the study of such things. The original manuscript, with inclusive annotations by J. Middleton Murray, resided in the British Museum Reading Room, but there was a pri-*

*vately printed copy kept in the archives room of the library
in Lewes.*

*   *   *

By the time Joanna had finished with the Latymere papers, her
single, compelling thought was to get to the library at Lewes and
read Thomas Latymere's play. She found herself at the door,
jeans and a sloppy sweater covered by an unbuttoned coat, car
keys tinkling in her hands—only to realize quite suddenly with
a sense of mild embarrassment that it was five in the morning.

She went anyway, waiting in her car outside the library, drinking sugared lemon tea from a thermos, watching the sun come
up upon a bed of raspberry-colored clouds. At 9:02 when a middle-aged man wearing a trench coat and carrying an armload of
books came ambling up the walk, Joanna leapt from the car and
hurried past him inside the building just as soon as he had
unlocked the door.

From the same startled man she learned that all "special collection" materials and documents were kept upstairs, then
waited with ill-concealed anxiety as he systematically sought the
key among a dozen look-alikes from his top desk drawer. At last,
displaying a lethargy that seemed to be his trademark, he led her
to an undecorated loft above that resembled any grade-school
classroom: low chairs and tables in the center, bookshelves on
each wall with locked cabinets below.

More jingling of keys, more maddening efficiency as the librarian bent to the shelves, searching while Joanna stood by, curling
and uncurling her fists deep in the pockets of her coat.

"Yes, here it is: *The Plague Maiden,*" the librarian said, cluck-
ing his tongue in satisfaction as he straightened up. "I shouldn't
think we've had anyone call for this for a very long time." He
smiled, his cheeks flaming like red roses as he led her to a table
at the edge of the room, beside a window. "It's a privately
printed copy, and so far as we know the only one extant. It was
done for Henry J. Latymere by William Morris and the Kelmscott
Press in 1893. As you can see, it's a very beautiful edition." When
Joanna sat down, pulling pen and a steno pad from her shoulder
bag in one movement, the librarian looked instantly alarmed.

"No marking on the manuscript, miss!" he said, seeing the felt-tip twitching nervously in her left hand. "And *no* smoking . . ."

She hadn't really been listening, but the frown on his pliant, hairless face told her of his worry. "Of course," she said at last. "I just need to take some notes."

"So long as you're careful . . ."

Joanna wanted him to go but he paused for a moment at the door, frowning with wonder at the pretty American girl who wore her sweater inside-out and had traces of a faint mustard stain on her chin. Curious. He closed the door behind him.

Joanna sat staring at the book for a long time, wanting to open it yet unable to take her eyes from the artwork on the cover. Its faded linen bore an insert drawing, obviously in the hand of William Morris. A woman in the throes of agony or passion, her head in profile and thrown back, while stylized sweeps of hair curled like pale ribbons down her back. Opposite her, also in profile and an attitude of extremity, was her twin, identical but for the color of her hair, which was very dark, almost black.

The Goddess Frig with her two faces, one fair as morning and the other shaded dark as night. Audric's words came to her like atavistic memory and her hand shook a little as she reached out to stroke the cover drawing, and still more as the vellum pages fell under her touch. The drama's plot emerged from beneath the heavily ornate phrases that seemed to decorate its violence with even greater horror; velvet cosseting a bleeding harlot.

Lord Lethe has gone to live in a ruined country abbey with his twin nieces Alice and Adele, who have become his willing whores. But Lethe is motivated by something stronger than a mere incestuous lust. He has learned that his family line originally sprang from the unholy union of an abbot and his French paramours during the dreaded time of Plague in the fourteenth century. Having surrendered himself to the ways and rites of pagans, the abbot had sought to appease the ancient gods by means of a strange sacrificial ritual. One woman bore him a child and on that same night the woman's sister was sacrificed on the altar of Woden. This banished Plague from the abbot's house.

Now, centuries later, Lord Lethe seeks the same method

*to insure good fortune for his line and to save his own life,
which has been threatened by a disease common to his family. Not aware of their impending fate, Alice and Adele
cooperate with his plan. Alice becomes pregnant and bears
her uncle's child, while her sister Adele is poisoned. When
Alice finds what Lethe has done, she goes mad, murders her
child, and then throws herself into the river. Lethe, given up
to his book of spells and magic ritual incantations, pro-
claims his own madness in a powerful concluding
soliloquy.*

Joanna's throat had gone thick as paste.

It was all there in front of her, everything she had ever feared
or wondered about since coming to St. Audric barely ten weeks
ago, and all of it too fantastic to be anything but true. *The Plague
Maiden,* with its wicked echoes of Ford and Webster, nonetheless told a story Joanna could recognize, and it all pointed back
to Sir Gerald. He had taken Blackmantle, schemed to have it
because he knew its vacant libraries were full of secrets, all the
pagan rituals set down by Audric and Geoffrey Fitzstephen.

The things Sir Gerald had been so curious to learn.

The same things Geoffrey Latimer wished her to know.

Not daring to think further, Joanna stuffed the precious book
into her purse along with pen and pad, grabbed up her car keys,
and fled down the stairs past the librarian. He turned to look,
surprised.

"I'll put the book away, shall I?" he called after her. When he
went upstairs a few minutes later he found that it had gone.

Outside Joanna fumbled for her keys, dropped them, and had
to scramble about a bit in the gravel to retrieve them. At last she
clawed her way inside, slamming the door on her coat and driving off without looking to left or right.

A few miles away she braked the car in the parking lot of a Cash
& Carry and sat for a long time staring down at her hands, white-
knuckled, clinging to the steering wheel as though it were a life-
preserver. In a way it was. She was in danger, terrible danger. Her
stomach convulsed. She had to think, to analyze, but her mind
was numb and her thoughts going round and round like circus

horses. Only one thing stood out with any clarity and it was almost too horrible to contemplate.

Tomorrow was November the fifteenth.

Friday, Frig's Day. The anniversary of the Oats Goat Moon. First day of winter according to the ancient calendar of the Saxons. And Joanna's birthday.

A day of sacrifice.

How could she have been so impervious to all that was going on around her? All the hints, the intimations had been there since the beginning, and she'd only played with them, making up a silly game of Team A and Team B, never grasping what was at stake here. Curious, and fascinated with the little things, she had never once realized that all the single threads were being taken together by an unseen hand, the Fate Weaver spinning her will. And as Joanna huddled in the car, chilled to the scalp with fear while sweat coursed down her face, she knew one thing more clearly than she had ever known anything in her life.

Geoffrey Latimer was going to kill her.

Simon had been right about him from the start. He was dangerous, probably insane—no doubt seeking to restore his failing health by using the pagan ritual of human sacrifice, which his own ancestor had borrowed from Geoffrey Fitzstephen. And Joanna was needed to play a part in the bizarre obscenity.

A god of blood will be appeased by blood alone.

Geoffrey Latimer had sent her the original letter invitation to St. Audric. He had arranged the bogus fortune cookie message. (Irony? A joke?) He had lied about Pauline and Cassie; when Joanna had faced him with the truth he had made up a feeble story about wanting to forget the past. Eager to secure her trust, he had pretended friendliness, had even given her the research material to read, as if challenging her to learn the truth.

After a little while Joanna stopped shaking long enough to drive to a *Pizzaland* a few blocks away where she nibbled on a salad, trying to reconcile her new knowledge with her newer fears. It was terrible to know what she knew, but it was not inevitable. She had only to return quietly to St. Audric, pack the remainder of her things in the Escort, and drive off toward London. Even if Geoffrey Latimer was insane, he was not all-powerful. She had only to put herself beyond his reach in order to be safe.

The food and a pot of tea gave her a sense of calm; emboldened, she left the restaurant an hour later. It was only three o'clock, but the curdled silver sky already showed faint tints of deep gray and navy blue far to the east, prophesying rain.

She passed The Star Inn on her way through Alfriston and immediately slowed the car, wondering if it might not be better to stop the night here and continue on her way to London in the morning, after pausing to collect her things. Anything seemed safer than passing a night alone at Little Gospels, where Geoffrey might come looking for her. Tomorrow Kate would be there so it would be safe to go back. Certainly Kate would wonder if she left without saying a good-bye, to say nothing of leaving behind her clothes, typewriter, and manuscript.

She swerved her car into the adjacent car-park.

Exhausted, she slept for several hours. By eight she was downstairs in the bar, nursing a cup of too-sweet hot chocolate and wondering what she was going to do with herself the rest of the evening and night that lay ahead. Fearing it was all too likely she might be spotted by someone from St. Audric, she finished the drink quickly and retraced her way upstairs, lifting an issue of the *Times* from the reception desk as she went.

But the paper was full of bad news and television offered only gabby public affairs shows and tacky American reruns. Stripped down to her bra and bikini underpants, Joanna paced the room, distracted by her own thoughts and blowing cigarette smoke at the ceiling.

Sisters.

Two of them had come to Blackmantle that dark winter of the plague. And in Thomas Latymere's play there had been two. Pauline and Cassie had been sisters; it was the *leitmotif* of this incredible affair. Twenty-eight years ago tomorrow one sister had died mysteriously while the other had borne a child then run away to lose herself forever. Pauline and Cassie had been the victim of their brother's madness all those years ago, and now he wanted—needed?—Joanna.

But there was something missing, something not quite right.

The match flared in her hand and she tossed it neatly into the ashtray. If Geoffrey meant to reprise the ceremony the way it had been set down by Fitzstephen and Sir Gerald, he would need a compliment to Joanna, an opposite—a "sister." A woman who was about to bear his child.

He's got an eight-by-ten of you in a frame; you were blond then.

It had seemed only a coincidence, but she understood it now.

The girl in the photo. The blonde who was not Joanna yet looked enough like her to be mistaken by someone who knew Joanna well. The girl whose likeness had been hidden away whenever Joanna visited Blackmantle. The girl whose empty room had been so curiously alive with personality, an essence that Joanna felt to her very soul. Not Geoffrey's wife. His daughter. And Joanna's sister.

Geraldine.

How it had been worked she couldn't even guess. But one thing was clear. There had been two of them. Geraldine had been taken away at birth by Cassie or Geoffrey or both; Joanna had been allowed to grow up under the guidance of her rightful father.

Or was he?

Something cold and hideous moved inside her like a snake.

Geoffrey and Cassie.

Brother and sister.

Her parents.

No wonder Cassie had run away, kept herself hidden, never wished to show her face again. Joanna wanted to run, too, but instead she crept beneath the covers and pulled them up close about her chin, silently absolving Reverend Lynne of all blame for the lies she'd *thought* he had told her, ever since that day she had seen Pauline Pryce's headstone in the cemetery. She remembered Roland Jaspar's words about "a man dressed as a servant of God . . ." and felt the tears roll sideways on her face into her hair.

She was better in the morning; capable, composed. She drove the few miles to Kate's house and let herself in via the back door, then went from room to room turning off all the lights she'd left burning in her haste to get away the previous morning. The blaze of electricity must have been visible even through the thick covering of trees surrounding Kate's house, and Joanna wondered what all the curious inhabitants of St. Audric had made of that.

She put out travel clothes, tidied the kitchen, made tea. This she set out to cool while she showered, wishing all the while that Kate would hurry back. Joanna was itching to be off to London now, eager to be away from this place. She was not so frightened as she had been last night, only edgy, wondering what she would tell Kate about her premature departure. She couldn't possibly reveal her suspicions about Geoffrey Latimer. Joanna had long ago ceased to believe the two were lovers, but they were certainly good friends. In light of that, Kate could hardly be expected to believe anything so unsavory about him. So she would merely say that Jayson was returning early from California and she wished to be back in London to greet him when he arrived. Close within the white-tiled cubicle of Kate's shower Joanna let the scalding water wash her anxieties away.

Back in the silent kitchen she downed two quick cups of cooling tea and studied the ornate copy of *The Plague Maiden.* It only struck her now that she had actually stolen it; once she'd settled into the flat she meant to put the book into an envelope and send it back to Lewes. That poor, ponderous man at the library, what a state he'd be in! For a moment she even considered backtracking to Lewes on her way to London so she could return the book in person; no, he could wait the few extra days and get it in the post, *insured,* of course. . . .

The sound of letters being pushed through the mail slot startled her just a bit. Barefoot, Joanna padded into the living room and bent to scoop them up. Three letters and a copy of *Country Living;* she tossed them onto the kitchen table and was about to turn away when a half-glance, oblique, disinterested, caught something in its path that drew her back again. Slowly, feeling all warmth run from her hand, Joanna reached out for the top envelope and brought it closer, though she knew well enough already what it said and what that meant.

She was in the sixth grade at Vallemar Elementary School, Miss Powers's homeroom; the year of the Bicentennial. Every student had been assigned a twelve-page report dealing with some aspect of American society related to precepts set down in the Declaration of Independence. Joanna chose the subject of women in media, thinking that the emergence of women in the field of television news and talk shows and stand-up comedy on TV fulfilled the "pursuit of happiness" clause quite nicely.

For a week she diligently researched addresses and sent off a precocious and polite letter to each, stating her purpose and requesting information regarding their careers. During the next few weeks it was a thrill to get off the school bus each afternoon and run across the street to the house on Seaside Drive just as the mailman was coming up the walk, pulling envelopes from out of his clumsy pouch.

Only four of her two dozen subjects replied, Joanna's first lesson in rejection. Marlene Sanders sent a terse but courteous letter with a thumbnail sketch attached. Joan Rivers sent virtually no information, but her funny, chatty letter wished Joanna well. Barbara Walters answered with a ten-page press kit and cordial cover letter that was as polished and elegant as the lady herself.

Then there was Catherine Mackin.

She was Joanna's favorite because she was beautiful, a cool, aristocratic Jacqueline Kennedy look-alike with blond hair. Joanna treasured her letter and the photo she enclosed. And many months later after the report had been finished and presented in class, she even typed out a duplicate of it to send off to Ms. Mackin in a sudden frenzy of hero-worship akin to unrequited love. The reply, when it came, was friendly and full of compliments; Joanna earned extra credit showing it to the class. For the remainder of the school year and most of the summer Catherine Mackin was Joanna's idol. Then Dorothy Hamill came to skate in exhibition at the Cow Palace that November, and Joanna's loyalties shifted and fell away.

She hadn't thought of Catherine Mackin in a dozen years, not since she'd clipped an article from the *San Francisco Examiner* back in the early eighties: FORMER HEARST REPORTER DIES. But she remembered that at some point the obit had mentioned Catherine Mackin's nickname was Cassie. It had impressed Joanna at the time because of the coincidence of her own mother's name. "Cassie" could be a diminutive of Catherine as well as Cassandra. That had never occurred to her before. When she had asked her father what her mother's whole name had been he'd gotten angry.

"Cassie is name enough," he'd answered cryptically.

And for good reason.

Now, as she stared down at the envelope, Joanna understood.

Miss Katherine Callison the letter read, and the proper address was beneath it, though it could have been directed to one of the nine moons of Saturn for all she cared. Incredibly she had never made the connection—not once, not ever.

Cassie was the same name as *Catherine.*

Catherine was the same name as *Katherine.*

Katherine was the same name as *Kate.*

She looked up, sensing someone there, and saw the last person on earth she expected to see, and then he was walking toward her, slowly, almost seeming to float, Joanna thought stupidly. *This time I really am going to faint.* And then she remembered how the teapot had stood unguarded on the table while she showered, and knowing it was too late Joanna moved instinctively forward until she felt the table's cold, sharp edge slide beneath her fingers as she fell.

When she woke a short time later (or a long time later or who knew *how* long) she was in a well-remembered room, a perfect stretch of blue wafting high above her head. *Geraldine's room.* And she knew it before even opening her eyes. The sound of the sea was in her ears, too; someone had moved Geraldine's room into the sea. Then she realized it was something very different. Water running in a sink across the hall.

Then the blue disappeared for a moment as a face leaned above her, leaned and came closer, making her afraid. A kiss or a touch stroked her cheek, then she was falling . . . falling far down into a dim cavern of unnatural sleep and she was helpless; she was his.

"Jayson," she whispered before her eyes closed, "*why?*"

*   *   *

If I have been wrong, then I am sorry.
So ran Simon Cherrystone's thoughts.

He had come up to London one week ago to do some checking on Geoffrey Latimer and his background, for it seemed to him there was something more than a little curious about the man, especially his attentions to Joanna (which Simon resented: fairly or unfairly—he couldn't be sure). So he had come to search out Geoffrey's past, eager for secrets. Yet the information yielded up by signed record and computer printout all gave evidence to a circumspect life given over to travel and the study of antiquities. The only really interesting bit of news to emerge from a week of research was the fact that Geoffrey had spent a good part of his youth in California. Did Joanna know that? Even if she did not it hardly qualified as "gossip." Perhaps Geoffrey Latimer was exactly what he seemed to be after all, a thoroughly decent man.

By late Thursday he was ready to leave London.

Stopping for lunch at a Clerkenwell pub just around the corner from his Charterhouse flat, Simon met Ian Blackstone, an old friend. They had been up at school together, though these days saw each other only rarely. Ian, an artist, had painted the portrait of Geoffrey Latimer's "daughter" Geraldine.

"Funny you should bring that business up again," Ian said over coffee as Simon told him something of what he had been up to in the past week. "The portrait—the one old Latimer refused to pay for when his daughter ran off—did I tell you I managed to sell it the following week?"

Simon remembered. "To her lover, wasn't it?"

"I suppose he was, now that you come to mention it. But that wasn't the queer thing about it." Ian sloshed a bit of milk into the coffee and stirred it furiously, adding several lumps of sugar as he went. "But look: though I didn't know it at the time, it was Jayson Gardiner who bought the portrait. . . ." He interpreted Simon's look of surprise for puzzlement. "You know, the writer. I didn't recognize him and since he paid cash I didn't get his name. Then a few weeks ago I opened up one of those toffy-nosed Sunday supplements—the kind which feature film stars and the like—and there it was! It was a piece about Jayson Gardiner. There were photos of his flat and in the background of one of them, Geraldine's portrait." He drained his cup and pushed it to the side. "Queer, isn't it? I remembered your interest in the whole business and thought you'd like to know. . . ."

There was more talk about other things, and then Simon went back to his flat and sat there all the afternoon, deeply puzzled by what Ian had told him. Jayson Gardiner, Joanna's lover, had bought the portrait of a woman who looked enough like her to be her twin? *Why?* It was possible he'd noticed the likeness and purchased it for that reason alone, and yet wouldn't it have been more sensible, more realistic, to have the same artist do a portrait of Joanna rather than pay good money for one that resembled her but was actually another woman?

He knew the answer and what the answer meant.

Something is wrong.

Suddenly, surely, he knew it; knew that Joanna was (in danger?) alone; that she needed him. He went to the phone and called Little Gospels. She should be there; she was staying in St. Audric till the seventeenth. Ten rings sounded; twelve. Annoyed, he put the receiver back into place. He was just reaching for his coat when the front doorbell went.

He didn't recognize her at first; she hardly looked herself. She was dressed oddly, a limp felt hat pulled low shadowed her face. Then she stepped forward and the fading afternoon light showed up her red eyes and drawn features.

"Kate!" He drew her in, felt her hand tremble against his. "What are you doing here?"

She shook off his hold and went to the sofa, fumbling in her purse. "It's taken me all week to get up the nerve to come here" she said, a cigarette trembling at the corner of her mouth. "Now you *have* to listen. . . ."

"What's wrong?" he asked, almost too afraid to hear her reply.

Her words came out in smoke. "Geoffrey's had a collapse. He should really be in hospital but he won't go." Then she started to cry. "I don't know what to do, Simon. I can't make him listen. . . ."

He was surprised at her intensity. So far as Simon knew, Kate and Geoffrey were friends and nothing more. "I don't understand what—" he began to say.

"Just listen," she told him sharply. "I've got a lot to tell you and I need your help. There's not much time left. . . ."

The time had come to tell it all.

In the beginning they were only three.

Geoffrey, Pauline, and baby Katherine, dubbed "Cassie" by the family nursemaid. They were children well appointed by fortune to a family of great wealth and many talents.

After the *Anschluss,* when many English began to think that war with Hitler was inevitable in time, Sir Giles Latimer and his wife Lady Margaret arranged to send their children abroad, where, if England was invaded, they would be safe. They had friends in America, John and Eleanore Lynne of Berkeley, California, who agreed to take the children. The two couples had met several years earlier at an archaeological dig near Vézelay in France. The Lynnes, both painters, had two small children of their own, Paul and Prudence, who were very near the ages of the Latimers' two little daughters.

In May 1938 the Latimers waved good-bye to their children at Southampton and returned to St. Audric on that same day to close up the house. Margaret, an actress, had a film to complete in London for Alexander Korda, and Giles had business with the Foreign Office. It was only a few months later that Margaret found she was pregnant once again. The child, a boy whom they named Jayson, was born the following April in Chelsea, where the family had taken a flat.

Jayson was only three months old when Giles and Margaret were killed in a boating accident during a weekend outing. The Logans, a Scottish couple who ran the guest house where the Latimers had been staying, took the child when no relatives could be found and raised him as their own. When Jayson was twenty-one and an honors student at Cambridge, he accidentally found out the truth about his background while searching through some family papers.

He had always been unusual: precocious, quiet, living very much within himself, and with a genius for history that allowed him to immerse himself so deeply in the past that it often seemed more real to him than his own life. Having found himself to be a member of the well-connected Latimer family, Jayson had managed to strike a connection between the two.

After Giles's and Margaret's death the Lynnes kept the children and brought them up. In 1950 Geoffrey Latimer inherited Blackmantle and the considerable sum of his parents' estate, and he returned to England. Pauline and Cassie, now his wards, were brought back to England and put immediately into French boarding schools. A few years later when she was only eighteen, Pauline married her brother's close friend, the Reverend Thomas Pryce, vicar of St. Audric's church. Cassie, intent on her education, attended the University at Geneva and later the American University at St. Germain outside of Paris. In the spring of 1961, armed with two master's degrees and no idea of what she wished to do with them, Cassie came to Blackmantle for a visit with her brother Geoffrey.

It was then that Jayson first came into their lives.

They may have doubted his story at the beginning—at least Geoffrey did—but Jayson was soon able to produce the necessary documents to convince them. As a scholar himself, Geoffrey was glad enough to accept the brilliant young Jayson into the family. Pauline, busy with her own life, kept a respectful if not entirely disinterested distance from the manse. For Cassie it was a different story.

She fell in love with him at their very first meeting. Geoffrey, when she confided it to him, was furious and alarmed. It was true she and Jayson had not been raised as siblings and had met as two attractive strangers with similar interests, drawn together by mutual attraction. But they were brother and sister all the same. And if that was not enough, Geoffrey had begun to wonder at Jayson's real motives in associating himself with the family. Jayson talked constantly of their ancestors, particularly Sir Gerald Latymere and the play his son had written about him which proved the respected Elizabethan courtier had revived a cult of pagan Earth Magic. Jayson's obsession with the subject was unnerving.

Geoffrey had already begun to believe Cassie was sleeping with him but it was not something he could bring himself to ask her. Jayson made no pretense that it was otherwise. He boldly admitted he and Cassie were in love and that although they could never marry they would live together no matter how Geoffrey felt about it. He even went so far as to say he and Cassie were determined to have a child.

Disowned by Geoffrey, the two profligate lovers ran away to

France where they lived for several months. When Cassie found herself pregnant in March 1964, Jayson told her why he had wanted them to have a child, that he intended to renew the ancient rite performed by Abbot Geoffrey Fitzstephen during the time of the plague, the same ceremony venerated two hundred fifty years later by Sir Gerald Latymere, who understood the power of pagan rituals. It had cured Sir Gerald of his scrofula and brought him long life. All the great families of the Middle Ages had disappeared into the urns of history, Jayson explained to her. But the Rite of the Two Sisters would assure the vibrant continuance of their line.

She had never guessed till then how unbalanced he really was, how rooted in myth and legend to the sacrifice of all reality. Now she saw that their love was only a means to an unspeakable end, which decreed that if she gave birth to his child, Pauline would have to die. . . .

Cassie, nearly penniless, ran away.

She couldn't go to Geoffrey: he had disowned her. So she went as far away as she could and still find friends: to Paul and Prudence Lynne and the place where she'd spent her childhood. They lived now in a little town just south of San Francisco where Paul, newly ordained, worked as a Lutheran minister. He and his sister Pru had recently bought a house together and when the hapless Cassie came to them they took her in. She couldn't tell them very much, only that she was pregnant and had to be kept hidden from everyone, including members of her own family.

But she knew from the start that one of them—Jayson or Geoffrey—would find her. The only question was who, and if she could have the baby first. It was Geoffrey who found her that day at the airport, and made arrangements to take her back to St. Audric immediately.

But it was too late. Cassie went into premature labor and before she could deliver the child Geoffrey received word from England that Pauline had died in a mysterious drowning accident. He left for St. Audric at once, putting Cassie in the care of Paul and Pru. After hearing the news about her sister, Cassie told the story to Paul, who needed a great deal of coaxing to believe it. That same night when Cassie was delivered of twin daughters, Paul claimed them as his own, hoping it would convince Cassie to marry him, though she refused.

Nothing was proven to tie Jayson to the death of Pauline, but Cassie knew he had done it. She also feared that he would stop at nothing to get control of their child. But since he had no way of knowing there were twins, she left baby Joanna in Paul's care and took Geraldine back to England with her.

After only a few months sheltering under Geoffrey's protection at Blackmantle, the bizarre events of the previous year and a half drove Cassie into a series of expensive sanitariums. Geraldine, after spending a few years in her uncle's care, was put into an exclusive school while her mother moved from one sanitarium to another and toward a complete mental breakdown. Her eventual "cure" took nearly twelve years and over one million pounds of her brother's money.

Jayson, who enjoyed an irony as much as any man alive, took for himself the surname of Gardiner and retreated to the solitude of academia, seemingly out of their lives forever.

Cassie reentered the world in 1978 as Kate Callison, having changed her name at the suggestion of her latest therapist. Craving a life of privacy and peace, she took a librarian job in the seaside resort town of Hove. There she met and lived with a man, but life was still difficult for her. Cut off from her past, still guilt-ridden and vulnerable, she lived determinedly on the surface of things. She and Geoffrey corresponded but in cursory terms, mostly over matters dealing with Geraldine, who had come to stay with her uncle briefly after she finished at university. Because of his refusal to make explanation for the beautiful young woman living in his house, talk soon began to make the rounds in St. Audric that Geoffrey had taken a young bride for himself.

For many years there had been no word from Jayson. But one day Geoffrey and Kate received separate yet identical telegrams that brought the nightmare of their past back into focus. *There are two* the message said. And Kate knew he had succeeded in finding out about Joanna at last and what that meant.

Geoffrey was afraid, too. There was talk of going to the police, but absolutely nothing could be proved. Also, Geoffrey had fallen ill of the Latimer scrofula by this time and Kate, who was always fearful of relapsing into a breakdown, moved to St. Audric to be near him. Not wishing to dredge up the past or be put to bother by endless questions, they told no one of their relationship as brother and sister. The former Cassie Latimer was merely Kate Callison now, the new librarian of St. Audric.

Then a day came when she opened the *Express* and saw a photo of author Jayson Gardiner and his live-in love, Joanna Latimer. The resemblance to Geraldine, except for the color of hair, was uncanny. So he had found her; and Kate was afraid for Joanna, but more for Geraldine. Joanna was her daughter, too, yet they had never known each other. And Kate knew of no way to warn her.

Shortly after Christmas Geraldine announced her intention to get a flat of her own in London. She was tired of staying with girlfriends whenever she went up for a weekend visit and a new career as the Genesse Cosmetics Girl model would keep her busy in the city now. She had never liked St. Audric, was tired of the grim masquerade her mother and uncle kept up, not quite certain what had brought it about in the first place. So she got herself a flat in Battersea and spent her days smiling into the camera. One day during a break on a photoshoot in front of St. Paul's, she met Jayson Gardiner.

He had a live-in girlfriend, he told her, but she was "difficult" and didn't want to give him the child he wanted so badly. Geraldine, easily captivated by his looks and charm, began spending afternoons with Jayson in her cluttered flat. After a few weeks she was so in love with him she decided to quit modeling and have a baby; anything to make Jayson happy and give her rootless life a sense of purpose.

And then at the end of summer Joanna came to St. Audric.

Kate knew at once, and Geoffrey too, what had brought her there, but neither knew what to do about it. No one could be expected to believe their outlandish story, least of all Joanna herself. A healthy Geoffrey would have found some way to stop it; he was too ill to interfere now. Kate, who was so frightened for

Geraldine, was almost willing to sacrifice Joanna to Jayson's madness so long as it meant Geraldine would be safe. At least that was how she felt in the beginning.

But in the past two months she had come to know Joanna, to feel affection for her. There had been so many times she had almost blurted out the story. Finding that impossible, she had done what little things she could to frighten her away, including doping her food with sleeping pills to make Joanna believe she had been poisoned, and arranging the fortune cookie message. Unhappily none of it had worked. She had never wanted Joanna to come to St. Audric in the first place. The letter, so very skillful at luring her to the village, had been Jayson's invention from first to last.

Kate had never really believed that it would happen.

Then one week ago the news had come from London. Geraldine's child, a son, was born. And Joanna's life was forfeit.

*   *   *

Kate leaned back against the sofa, out of the tiny circle of light that shone on her like a pin spot illuminating a performer. "He's going to kill her," she said evenly, all her emotion spent during the litany that had come before, "and I don't know how to stop him. I'm afraid Geoffrey might try, and if he does Jayson will kill him, too. . . ."

Simon checked his watch. "We can't get down to St. Audric much before ten, and even so, how can we be sure to find them? If he's gotten hold of her he might have taken her anywhere and of course she'd go willingly, never guessing what he's really up to." His voice shook. "Christ, she might be dead already."

"No," Kate said. "They'll be at Blackmantle, and he won't do anything tonight. Jayson's wedded to astrology, always has been. From what I know of this ritual there are certain astrological and symbolic timetables to be met: for one thing, the moon has to be in the sign of Scorpio and that won't happen till two o'clock tomorrow afternoon. I know. I checked."

"For God's sake," Simon shouted into her face, "he's insane! Do you think he's going to wait for some hypothetical go-ahead from the stars?"

"Oh yes," Kate answered, head thrown back, eyes closed, her fine profile pale against the burgundy drapes, "he *is* insane. And he will wait."

There was nothing could be done that night; Kate had convinced him. Having relived her story, she was exhausted and fell asleep soon after, while Simon passed the night restlessly on the sofa. Half the time he was condemning himself for not having picked up the hints of danger earlier than he had, the rest was given over to pondering the certain knowledge that Kate was mad and he equally so to have believed her.

By morning his sense of urgency for Joanna's safety had returned. Phone calls to Little Gospels and Blackmantle went unanswered; there was nothing else to do but put the matter in official hands. Kate suggested calling in the Yard but Simon thought they would have an easier time convincing the local force at Lewes, where Blackmantle and the Latimer name were well known.

He had only to tell the story to see how wrong that was.

Inspector Walker listened with a show of professional courtesy and considerable skepticism. Like everyone else in the district, he knew the Latimer name well, knew that Sir Geoffrey (the family's sole surviving member) was a life peer, or that his father had been, or some such thing. The name of Jayson Gardiner was only vaguely familiar to him as a respected author and one-time professor. Cambridge, wasn't it? Fine candidates for the kinky series of events this young man was asking him to believe! Not that fancy folk didn't get up to some queer things now and again, but that was the way of things and to be expected. But this rot? *Incredible.*

"Look here, young man," he said. "I've heard a great many things in my time, but this really is absurd. Moons in Scorpio, ancient rituals, pagan sacrifices! Do you honestly expect me to believe such nonsense?"

Kate sent Simon a fleeting *I told you so* expression but he ignored her. "Look," he said to Inspector Walker, "this is hardly the kind of thing one jokes about." He gave a quick look at his watch. "The longer we sit here arguing about it, the more dangerous it becomes for Joanna. . . ."

Walker rolled a pencil between his fingers. He was not gen-
erally an uncharitable man and had indeed heard many curious
stories in his time. But today he was suffering from a toothache
and last night his wife had turned him out of their bed for snor-
ing, so his humor was bad and this young man was trying his
patience all the more. Most likely he was or had been involved
romantically with the American lady writer he had mentioned
and she'd rewarded him by going off with a local nob (Latimer?
Gardiner?) and *that's* what this was all about.

In a tone that only vaguely masked an accusation, Walker
asked, "Got a grudge against this Latimer fellow, have you?"

Exasperated, Simon shouted back, "Haven't you heard anything I said? This isn't about Geoffrey Latimer—he's in danger,
too! Jayson Gardiner has this American girl at Blackmantle and
he's holding her there until . . . till he can. . . ." He rolled his eyes
in helpless frustration. "Christ, what difference does it make if
we don't get there before two o'clock?"

Walker shot a glance to the wall; it was twelve forty. He was
about to reply with something conciliatory and entirely rational
when the door to his office opened and young Sgt. Alan Rugger
came strolling in, an expression of quiet amusement on his face.

"May I have a word, sir?"

Briefly distracted from his business, the inspector looked up.
"Of course."

"In private, sir."

Irritated, Walker got to his feet and beckoned Rugger to the
file cabinet beside the window. "You know better than to interrupt me," he grumbled. "What is it?"

Rugger, a small man with a pink, nearly hairless face, tried his
best to restrain a grin. "Sorry, sir, but Thompson insisted I inform
you. We've just had a call from a chap out St. Audric way says a
woman's being held against her will at his house by a madman
set to kill her in some pagan sacrificial rite. . . ."

Walker's eyebrows met. "In what way is that funny, Sergeant
Rugger?"

"It's only that he claims to be from Blackmantle—Sir Geoffrey
Latimer, if you please. Thompson said he thought the place had
been closed up a good few months and Sir Geoffrey off to France

as always." He gave his chief a conspiratorial wink. "Almost better than that Paki bloke last week who thought the devil had taken up residence in the bed-sitting room next door." He shook his head. "A small bit of mischief left over from All Hallows', I suspect. November brings out the crazies; but shall we send a man out there all the same?"

"Jesus bloody Christ!" Walker muttered. His pale eyes riveted to Simon, then shifted back to Rugger. "Get your coat," he said. "You're coming with us."

They didn't believe him.

Geoffrey fell back against the bed, the phone still in his hand. Had he really expected anything different? Twentieth-century police didn't believe in thirteenth-century curses, or pagan sacrifices, or Earth Magic. Even to Geoffrey, who knew the truth for what it was, the whole thing seemed incredible. Jayson knew that, must have always known; it was his shield, his safety.

If the police did not come there was no one else to stand against him; Geoffrey was alone. Nina had gone for her holidays and he had not seen her since the previous day when she brought him his cup of hot milk laced with brandy, his nightly sedative. For one week he had been in this bed and felt no better for it; he needed more nursing than hot milk could give. Kate had tried her best to make him go to hospital but he had refused, knowing Jayson would come.

He was here now. Geoffrey had heard him come in the night and of course *she* was with him, doubtless drugged to insensibility just as Pauline had been twenty-eight years ago this same night. Geoffrey had failed to save her, but somehow he would save Joanna. Never mind that these days it usually took two canes just to get him to the bedroom door, he would manage all the same.

Outside it was raining and the scent of it was strong, filling the whole room. There was little light; his walls had the gray texture of a dream, dim as twilight though it was not much after twelve. Time to do what must be done. Soundlessly he pushed the quilt aside and sat up in the big bed. Pain scurried like rats to a dozen places in his body as he forced himself to stand, teetering at the edge of a walking stick. Breathless, he rested on it for a moment. A week in bed had sapped his strength rather than restored it. But he must try. One step; two.

Two steps more. His legs, foolishly splayed to uphold him, made silly jolting steps toward the door. The crook of a finger pulled it open. Light, gray as a ragged flag, shone across the passage from the window at the far side of the landing. Carefully he made his way to the very edge of the stairs. One of his carpet slippers creaked so Geoffrey kicked it off together with its mate. Leaning heavily on his cane with one hand, holding to the banister with the other, he edged his way along, slow as a snail. It seemed to take a little less than forever till he reached the bottom step.

He could hear vague sounds coming from the back of the house. Barefoot and silent he made his way along the passage toward the living room, stopping for a moment just outside it. Nothing stirred there, not even light—heavy drapes drawn against the gloom of a rainy afternoon—a ghost room. Looking in, he halfway expected to see the spectre of his younger self in one of the overstuffed chairs. *Portrait of a Solitary Scholar in an Overstuffed Chair.* He'd spent his life doing little more. Yet all the while he'd been woefully ignorant. Worse, he'd been a coward.

Reputation. Expediency. Peace at any cost. He'd prized them more than truth. Even after the dreadful events of November 1964, he had hidden from it, too timid to expose Jayson, too timid even to try. Too fearful for the Latimer name, when the whole lot should have been exposed all the way back to Sir Gerald's time. It was true that Jayson was the first since then to act upon the family's heritage, yet others, like himself, had been custodians of that secret for generations. Were they any less guilty than Jayson? Was he? Why hadn't Geoffrey thrown away Audric's heresies, burned Fitzstephen's unholy ravings? *Because like others before him he had been overawed by his family's history.*

He stopped for a moment, leaning against the wall for support. From beyond he could hear tuneless whistling, though it was nearly obscured by the louder sound of running water.

Kate was the only one to recognize the black Daimler at the side of the house. *He's here,* she thought, and a terrible excitement passed over her.

Simon helped her from the car, thinking what an ordeal this was for her and how, muffled beneath layers of coat and scarf, she looked suddenly old.

She made a move toward the steps ahead of them, but Rugger placed a restraining hand on her sleeve. "You had better wait here, miss," he said.

She gave him a look of unspeakable coldness but said nothing.

"Let her go in," Simon told them. "She might be able to talk to him. It's worth a chance."

Walker, looking grave, nodded. "Yes, all right," he said and started up the marble stairs.

The passageway leading to the back of the house was long, and Geoffrey moved cautiously, without sound. A snag in the worn carpet nearly tripped him; he righted himself and held his breath in gratitude. What contempt Jayson must have for him: a sick old man stuck away in a room upstairs! Nothing to worry about, nothing to fear. He hadn't even bothered to turn the key on the outside of the bedroom door.

He stopped. On his right was the "Audric" room where Geraldine had always slept. It was vacant, dark. Across the way at the end of the passage was the only ground-floor bathroom. The door stood open, throwing a hard square of light against the opposite wall. Geoffrey stood very still and seemed to feel the air rush past him like a breeze.

One look told him all that needed telling. Joanna, naked, lolled in the bath as if asleep, her expression transfixed as it had been on that afternoon when he had shown her the Rossetti window and he had thought then *She has a lovely soul.* Her dark hair and cameo face called up images of Pauline, and he had wanted to tell her everything, warn her to go away and stay away forever but couldn't find the words. So he had gone on playing the game of Kate's-my-friend and Geraldine's-my-missing-wife (or daughter: the lie had evolved with the years) all the while hoping that Joanna would be clever enough to sort it out for herself, and she had, she had!

But it had brought her here. Jayson, tall and slender in a dark robe of some probable significance, stood above her for a moment, then leaned forward, hands at her shoulders, pulling her down into the water till it floated above her. In her lassitude she barely even struggled.

Geoffrey had no plan, no real weapon, but in that instant all his past guilt and anger propelled him suddenly forward and he raised his stick into the air and brought it down hard on Jayson's head, striking blow after blow. Jayson, staggered, tried to turn, his arms waving furiously. Blood, like stigmata, streaked his face and fell in drops to the white tile below. He teetered precariously for a moment, then plunged forward into the water between Joanna's legs.

Geoffrey fell to his knees in weakness and relief, reaching for Joanna all in the same motion, dragging her up to the surface, hearing her cough and splash and scream while the world began to go gray behind his eyes.

He was suddenly aware that the room was filled with people. Simon was there, holding Joanna as she struggled dumbly in his arms and there were two other men—strangers—who pulled Jayson from the water and laid him out on the floor, but Geoffrey knew he was already dead even if they did not. One of the men ran headlong into the passageway toward the living room looking for a telephone while the other, with Simon's help, took Joanna from the bathroom wrapped in towels.

Then he was being taken—lifted?—from the floor and there were even more people now, and hushed voices asking many questions. A face he didn't recognize peered closely into his; there was a moment of stinging pain in his arm, then peace. Just before his eyes closed he caught a wavering image of Kate. She stood by the sink, not moving. But something—a look he remembered—had come back into her eyes.

Afterward there were some matters to be settled with the police, though the history of the strange brother/sister/brother triangle, plus Joanna's obvious vulnerability at the hands of Jayson, was enough to keep Geoffrey from standing trial for murder. He even seemed to recover his health, although he left Blackmantle soon after for a spa in southern France.

Kate was not so fortunate. She died in her sleep a few months later at a Yorkshire retreat run by Anglican sisters where she had gone to live shortly after "the tragedy." The shock of Jayson's reappearance and death had been too much for her fragile nerves, so her own was effortless, even blessed. Geraldine, who had been hospitalized at a fashionable Paris *clinique* after learning the truth about Jayson's death and all that lay behind it, suffered a relapse at the news.

What Circumstance and the Law did not dispose, the Media did. No amount of silence on the part of those involved could keep reporters from the *Sun, Enquirer,* or "A Current Affair" away. To millions of people who had never heard of Joanna Latimer, or knew her name only in the context of her work, she was suddenly as famous as a movie star. There was a period of at least six months when it was almost impossible for her to dodge sensation-seeking reporters and their rude questions. In time, of course, their interest flagged, and both tabloid press and TV went back to such common concerns as PRINCESS DI FROLICS AT KENSINGTON BASH and FRIENDS REVEAL SECRET HEARTBREAK OF OPRAH'S "CAN'T-WIN" DIET.

Joanna was relieved to be forgotten.

It was odd to have figured in an event of which she had virtually no memory. Nearly everything she knew about her own near-death experience had been told to her after the fact. In a way it was harder *not* remembering, leaving her with a sense of unreality, deceiving her into the belief she had put it all behind her.

Joanna's "recovery" consisted of three months spent in the Mediterranean with Simon before returning to California (also with Simon) to resume her career. It was only many months later that the nightmares began. Sleeping pills helped a little and Simon helped a lot, but for the most part she managed to hide the strain and plunged headlong once more into her work.

She finished *The Scourge,* published it, then started research for a novel set in Constantinople at the time of the Fourth Crusade. She knew that eventually the day would come when she would have to write about the events of St. Audric. Yet for years they remained unexamined, unexhumed—rusting in her past like broken toys locked away in a child's forgotten playchest.

She blamed herself more than anyone could guess.

How could she have lived with Jayson, loved him, yet not felt the pull of a biological tie between them? How could she have never guessed at his insanity? She had suspected nearly everyone in St. Audric of some complicity in the silly "plot" she had concocted out of her own imagination and Simon's tales about the Oats Goat; she had even believed in Simon's guilt for a few days. Yet never once had Joanna seen anything in Jayson but what she had wished to see: his brilliance, his talent, his love for her.

She often thought of him.

And when she did she would remember a rainy October afternoon in the English Midlands, and a battlefield where they had met that first time, and not by chance. And when she thought of that day and all the other days and nights that followed, it was not disgust she felt but only sadness, and a profound reluctance to let go.

There was one piece of unfinished business, the catalyst she was looking for and was afraid to find. Yet hardly a day passed when she did not think of it, wondering if the time would ever come when she could return, if only briefly, to St. Audric, and look into the face of the twin sister she had never met.

Cut Down, It Blooms Again

St. Audric, East Sussex
Tomorrow

It was five full years before Joanna could complete her healing by going back to St. Audric, where it had all begun. She and Simon, married for the past three years and living in southern California, drove down to Sussex from London one hot summer afternoon on a day-out trip, just like any tourists.

They stopped briefly at The Plague Maiden, where Stephen and Sarah received them happily, and they passed more than an hour there catching up on all the latest news. Chloe, now an airline hostess, came home seldom these days; she was engaged to an American journalist and had a wedding planned for August. The Bradshaws had divorced and moved away, separately, and no one was quite sure where either of them had gone. Their house on Malting Road was still empty.

Cynthia Marrow, remarried to a Pakistani shopkeeper, had gone to live with him in Hastings. Toby and Tamara Bigelow had moved their antiques business to Bath; they had dropped in regularly till only a few months ago, when Roland Jaspar died, severing their last tie to their daughter Justine. Mrs. Munro had died too, after a short illness. Now Caroline lived alone at The Sheaves, though it was no longer open as a bed and breakfast inn.

Many people remained in place, their lives unchanged. Meg St. Denis, Reverend Burroughs, even old Tim Rackstraw, who was nearing eighty-five, still lived in St. Audric.

"Of course you probably know that Geraldine inherited Blackmantle when Geoffrey Latimer died last year," Sarah told them. "She had a man living there with her for a while, even had another child by him, a darling little girl. But now it's just her alone there, with the two kids. . . ."

Geraldine, casual in blue sweats, was waiting at the door for them. She was taller than Joanna by several inches and her figure showed Kate's slim, boylike lines. After only a moment of embarrassed silence she and Joanna exchanged hugs and kisses. She had been expecting their visit: Joanna had called from London the day before, and though neither sister had mentioned the urgent need of such a meeting, both understood that it was overdue by many years.

Geraldine served a light lunch in the dining room, "All California cuisine," she said, "or at least what I imagined California cuisine must be like." Joanna looked appreciatively at the dainty fruit salad topped with decorative melon balls, a thin sesame-seed dressing drizzled over it.

As they ate, there was easy talk of insignificant things, yet all the while a sense of expectation hung heavy in the air. Simon, sensing it, excused himself and strolled out into the garden. Watching him go, Joanna felt a pang of anxiousness rise in her stomach.

Geraldine seemed less reluctant to speak. "I'm very comfortable with my life as it is now," she explained, her white-blond hair framing a face so like Joanna's own it was unnerving to look into it. "Of course it was terrible at first. I mean to say, it must have been awful for you as well when you found out, but at least you never had a child with him." She saw the look that came suddenly into Joanna's eyes; a question. "I wouldn't give little Gerry up, not for anything, of course, but if I'd had the choice. . . ." She took a deep, measured breath. "For a while I simply couldn't deal with it. Not that and mother's death as well."

Joanna's fingers touched hers lightly, tentatively.

"I think the worst part was the fact that you and I never got together to talk this over," Geraldine went on. "I know we didn't have much chance: bang, there we were, each suddenly finding she had a twin, and me having to go straight into hospital after it happened, and then you going off to Greece or Spain or God knows where."

"I think we must have been a little afraid of one another, or we would have managed it," Joanna said at last. "At least, I know I was afraid of you."

Geraldine's eyes, hazel with the slightest tint of blue, locked on Joanna's face. "I never knew: I want you to understand that. Oh, I knew Jayson was involved in some pseudopagan religious business; just a lot of rubbish I thought. I didn't know that my having his baby was tantamount to causing someone else's death."

It was Joanna who had to look away. "I never thought you did."

"Didn't you? I thought that might be the reason you never got in touch with me all these years. Regardless of all the ugliness that's come before, we are sisters. I think that's rather gotten lost in all the mess."

Joanna nodded. "And there's so much about it I can't let myself think of or remember. Was I stupid not to have seen what he was really like? Christ, he was insane—I mean, he must have been—but I never saw it."

"No one did," Geraldine said. "Jayson was so brilliant it was all anyone could see of him—the only thing he let anybody see."

"He always used to say the study of history was his life," Joanna mused sadly. "It was like some kind of mask for him, a way of separating himself from the rest of the world. I think he must have been that way from the beginning."

Geraldine's hand found hers. "And that's reason enough for being good at hiding it."

"Someday I'll have to face all of it," Joanna said, "maybe even write about it. But it's so hard to do. And it *hurts.*"

Geraldine already felt a kind of bittersweet peace, and it was in her voice as she spoke. "Yes, it hurts. And it bleeds. But after bleeding comes—I don't know—healing? At least I have to believe that, and so do you. . . ."

There were tears and kisses and shared avowals never to be separated again, at least in spirit. They were truly sisters now; closure, once thought impossible, had been reached. Later Geraldine took both Simon and Joanna on a leisurely tour of the house. It was greatly changed since Geoffrey's death. All the Victorian furniture and what-nots had been replaced with sleek blond pieces and light-colored fabrics. There was a time when

Joanna would have hated it. Now it seemed entirely appropriate, even comforting, as if Blackmantle had finally ceased to be a ruined abbey and had become a home.

"The babies are in the tub together," Geraldine explained as she threw open the door to the bathroom. "It's good at that age to have a playmate."

Joanna stood in the doorway watching them. Gerry, his pretty-child features showing more than a trace of his father's image, swatted a colorful plastic ball against the water while a beautiful little girl—her white-blond hair done up in a charming top-knot—chortled with glee, her tiny fingers stirring ripples in an attempt to splash him back.

"They're so sweet at that age," Joanna admitted, feeling a mild and momentary regret that she had no children of her own. She watched as the giggling boy reached out to touch his sister's cheek, leaning to kiss her.

"They're so close," Geraldine said. "I hope they stay that way."

The water rose in an invisible line to the white rim of the bath-tub and lapped gently over onto the floor below.

ACKNOWLEDGMENTS

I would like to thank for their help during the research phase of this book Marie H. Lewis (Assistant in Charge, Reference), Eastbourne Central Library; John Lake (Head of Bibliographic Support), East Sussex County Council; Josephine Jenner, Alfriston; Mary Fyfield, East Dean; and Eric Millward, who supplied materials and good wishes.